Katherine Mansfield

The Garden Party and Other Stories

KATHERINE MANSFIELD STUDIES

Katherine Mansfield Studies is the peer-reviewed, annual publication of the Katherine Mansfield Society. It offers opportunities for collaborations among the significant numbers of researchers with interests in modernism in literature and the arts, as well as those in postcolonial studies. Because Mansfield is a writer who has inspired successors from Elizabeth Bowen to Ali Smith, as well as numerous artists in other media, Katherine Mansfield Studies encourages interdisciplinary scholarship and also allows for a proportion of creative submissions.

Katherine Mansfield and *The Garden Party and Other Stories*

Edited by
Gerri Kimber and Todd Martin

EDINBURGH
University Press

Edinburgh University Press is one of the leading university presses in the UK. We publish academic books and journals in our selected subject areas across the humanities and social sciences, combining cutting-edge scholarship with high editorial and production values to produce academic works of lasting importance. For more information visit our website: edinburghuniversitypress.com

Edinburgh University Press Ltd
The Tun – Holyrood Road
12(2f) Jackson's Entry
Edinburgh EH8 8PJ

Typeset in 10.5/12.5 New Baskerville by
IDSUK (DataConnection) Ltd, and
printed and bound in Great Britain

A CIP record for this book is available from the British Library

ISBN 978 1 3995 0994 7 (hardback)
ISBN 978 1 3995 0995 4 (paperback)
ISBN 978 1 3995 0997 8 (webready PDF)
ISBN 978 1 3995 0996 1 (epub)

Contents

Illustrations

Acknowledgements

The editors would like to extend particular thanks to the judging panel for this year's Katherine Mansfield Society Essay Prize: Professor Elleke Boehmer, FRSL, FRHISTS, Professor of World Literature in English, University of Oxford, UK, and Chair of the Judging Panel; Professor Jay M. Dickson, Professor of English and Humanities, Reed College, USA; and Dr Claire Drewery, Senior Lecturer in English Literature, Sheffield Hallam University, UK. The prize-winning essay, 'Redefining "Photographic Realism" in the Short Fiction of Katherine Mansfield', by Daisy Birch, a recent graduate of the University of Oxford, UK, is featured in this volume. We would like to extend our sincere thanks to the staff at the National Museum in Kielce, Poland, and especially Małgorzata Stępnik, for permission to reproduce the front cover image of Stanisław Wyspiański's *Portrait of Eliza Pareńska*. We would also like to thank J. Lawrence Mitchell, Emeritus Professor of English, Texas A&M University, and the Cushing Library, for kindly allowing us to publish both images from their copy of the first edition of *The Garden Party and Other Stories*.

As always, our thanks go to the entire team at Edinburgh University Press for facilitating the publication of the yearbook, especially Dr Jackie Jones, Fiona Conn, Ersev Ersoy, Susanna Butler, and our diligent copy-editor, Wendy Lee. Finally, special thanks to our indexer, Ralph Kimber, for his professionalism and scrupulous eye for detail.

Abbreviations

Unless otherwise indicated, all references to Katherine Mansfield's works are to the editions listed below and abbreviated as follows. Letters, diary and notebook entries are quoted verbatim without the use of editorial '[*sic*]'.

N.B. Mansfield frequently uses style ellipses in both her personal writing and her short stories. Where these occur the stops are double-spaced thus: . . . To avoid any confusion, all *omission* ellipses are therefore placed in square brackets [. . .].

CL1
The Edinburgh Edition of the Collected Letters of Katherine Mansfield: Vol. 1 – *Letters to Correspondents A–J*, eds Claire Davison and Gerri Kimber (Edinburgh: Edinburgh University Press, 2020).

CP
The Collected Poems of Katherine Mansfield, eds Gerri Kimber and Claire Davison (Edinburgh: Edinburgh University Press, 2016).

CW1 and CW2
The Edinburgh Edition of the Collected Works of Katherine Mansfield: Vols 1 and 2 – *The Collected Fiction*, eds Gerri Kimber and Vincent O'Sullivan (Edinburgh: Edinburgh University Press, 2012).

CW3
The Edinburgh Edition of the Collected Works of Katherine Mansfield: Vol. 3 – *The Poetry and Critical Writings*, eds Gerri Kimber and Angela Smith (Edinburgh: Edinburgh University Press, 2014).

CW4
The Edinburgh Edition of the Collected Works of Katherine Mansfield: Vol. 4 – *The Diaries of Katherine Mansfield, including Miscellaneous Works*, eds Gerri Kimber and Claire Davison (Edinburgh: Edinburgh University Press, 2016).

***Letters* 1–5**
The Collected Letters of Katherine Mansfield, 5 vols, eds Vincent O'Sullivan and Margaret Scott (Oxford: Clarendon Press, 1984–2008).

CONTENTS

Frontispiece. Contents page of Edward Garnett's copy of the first edition of *The Garden Party and Other Stories*, 1922. Notes and marginalia by Edward Garnett. Courtesy of the Cushing Memorial Library, J. Lawrence Mitchell Collection.

Introduction

Todd Martin

The last collection of short stories published in her lifetime, *The Garden Party and Other Stories* solidified Katherine Mansfield's place as the most prominent modernist short-story writer. Of course, Mansfield had her critics. As Jeffrey Meyers notes, some of the reviewers of *The Garden Party* commented on the similarities between it and *Bliss and Other Stories,* identifying similar themes and character types. In particular, he refers to Malcolm Cowley's review in the *Dial.*[1] But while contemporary reviewers provided mixed reactions to the collection, *The Garden Party* reveals a shifting understanding of the value of what Mansfield was doing in her fiction. While *Bliss and Other Stories* was often criticised by reviewers as cynical and plotless, similar characteristics were praised in *The Garden Party.* Rather than critiquing the lack of plot, for example, reviewers often praised the stories for providing a 'slice of life' which enhanced her characters. Emphasising the psychological power of the stories, readers praised how she was able to bring her characters to life in a way simple action could not.[2]

Mansfield, however, proved to be among her own worst critics after *Bliss* was published. According to Antony Alpers, Mansfield felt the contents of the newly published collection 'were mostly slight or even makeweight stuff' and 'she knew that she must either do better very soon or die with her purpose unattained, leaving "scraps" and "bits"'.[3] However, Mansfield's new drive led to the 'most productive period she had known since 1917'.[4] Not long after the publication of *Bliss,* Mansfield wrote 'The Young Girl', 'The Stranger', 'The Lady's Maid' and 'The Daughters of the Late Colonel'. She also wrote the often overlooked 'Poison', which was rejected by Murry for the *Athenaeum* and perhaps for this reason was not included in *The Garden Party.*

The Garden Party contains some of Mansfield's most sophisticated and well-loved stories, including 'At the Bay', 'The Garden Party' and 'The Daughters of the Late Colonel'. However, several of the stories in the collection, which initially appeared in the *Sphere,* have often been dismissed as inferior, like the 'make-weight' stories of *Bliss.* Alpers argues that the *Sphere* stories did lasting damage to Mansfield's reputation. Monetary necessity, according to Alpers, forced her to write stories like 'Mr and Mrs Dove', 'Marriage à la Mode' and 'An Ideal Family', a 'return to the vein of *Bliss* for some of those clever stories of "English" couples toying with love'.[5] While Mansfield herself felt some of these stories fell short of her desired effect, Jenny McDonnell has convincingly argued that these same pieces play a vital role in Mansfield's development as a writer.[6]

The essays in this volume elaborate on the work McDonnell began, expounding on the greater complexity of the stories in *The Garden Party*; many of the essays engage with some of the 'lesser' stories, demonstrating how even these reveal Mansfield as a significant modernist writer.

The themed section of the volume begins with Daisy Birch's essay, 'Redefining "Photographic Realism" in the Short Fiction of Katherine Mansfield', which won the Katherine Mansfield Society Essay Prize for 2021. Observing that much scholarship that considers Mansfield's relation to visual culture tends to emphasise either painting or cinema, Birch focuses her attention on photography and its influence on Mansfield's work. Noting the generally negative response of modernist writers to the realism of photography, Birch evokes Roland Barthes's *Camera Lucida* to re-evaluate 'photographic realism', arguing that seeing photography as a referent of life is, in fact, what modernism – especially Mansfield's fiction – aspires to. Birch addresses this notion in several stories from *The Garden Party*, particularly 'Bank Holiday', 'The Daughters of the Late Colonel' and 'Marriage à la Mode' (which gets quite a bit of attention in the volume as a whole).

Jay Dickson, in 'Knowing What We Feel about Katherine Mansfield: Sentimentality and Expression in "The Garden Party"', provides a nuanced discussion of sentimentality in Mansfield, but one which has wider implications to modernism in general. Noting that critics during Mansfield's lifetime often dismissed her work for its apparent sentimentality while more recent assessments have tried to distance her from these accusations by emphasising her experimentation and political tendencies, Dickson argues that Mansfield's sentimentality stems from the fact that her stories 'directly confront the problems of emotional expression in a modern age' (p. 29); however, her assessment by her contemporaries was the result of the difficulty of distinguishing between sentiment and sentimentality, for modernist fiction is not without feeling.

'Life of Ma Parker' is the focus of Martin Griffiths's essay, which explores Dickensian and theatrical influences on the story. In 'Dickens,

Death and Mary Ann: Katherine Mansfield's "Life of Ma Parker"', Griffiths traces some of the possible sources for the character of Ma Parker, which leads him to Israel Zangwill's short story and stage play, *Merely Mary Ann,* in which Zangwill draws on Dickens's character Mary Anne, who makes appearances in *Pickwick Papers, David Copperfield* and *Great Expectations.* Griffiths discusses potential influences of theatre on the story, then turns to Dickens directly, suggesting that both played a role in the experimental prose of the story.

Moving from theatre to dance, Richard Cappuccio, in '"Passion in Movement": Katherine Mansfield – Gesture, Motion and Dance', discusses Mansfield's use of movement and gesture as a trope to examine women's inner lives. Cappuccio traces in particular the influences of Maud Allan, Raquel Meller and Edgar Degas on Mansfield's integration of movement and rhythm, particularly in 'Her First Ball' and 'Marriage à la Mode', arguing that Leila's return to the dance floor represents a triumphant epiphany, empowered by her body in motion. Likewise, he interprets Isabel's body in motion at the end of 'Marriage à la Mode' as a triumph over the anxiety William's letter has caused, thus freeing her to be her true self.

Anna Kwiatkowska also engages with 'Marriage à la Mode', offering another sympathetic take on Isabel in 'Katherine Mansfield's "Marriage à la Mode": "far too facile"?'. Drawing on the dialogic nature that Mansfield shares with earlier artists, paying particular attention to the work of William Hogarth, whose series of paintings shares its title with Mansfield's story, Kwiatkowska 'reads' these paintings – as well as works by Johannes Vermeer and John Dryden – alongside Mansfield's story, arguing that, rather than being a 'facile satire' (p. 83) published for money in the popular magazine, the *Sphere,* 'Marriage à la Mode' is actually quite complex, addressing the intricacies of modern relationships for women.

With a similar emphasis on relationships, Calvin Goh works to reassess Mansfield's attitude towards gender in 'The Quest for Autonomy amid Shifting Gender Expectations and Relationships in Katherine Mansfield's Short Stories'. He emphasises 'women's search for selfhood and identity amid shifting gender expectations and relationships' (p. 88), but he also discusses the impact of these on the men in her stories. Arguing that the dichotomy of gender is overly simplistic when understanding Mansfield's feminism, Goh demonstrates that her women and men, rather than being on polarised ends, can be arranged along a wider spectrum, including men who do not fit traditional expectations of masculinity and women who are sometimes complicit in their own oppression. Especially for the latter, it is vital to recognise one's complicity to be able to achieve autonomous selfhood.

In '"Forgive my Hat": Clothing as a Condition of Narratability in *The Garden Party and Other Stories*', Samantha Dewally investigates how Mansfield 'recodes' hats and clothing by using them as a narrative device which signals cultural values. 'By using clothing figuratively', Dewally argues, 'Mansfield exploits the interaction between it and the wearer to reveal underlying behaviours or to signal changes to their state of mind or in their perception of the world (pp. 110–11). To this purpose, she focuses primarily on 'The Garden Party' and 'Bank Holiday'.

Sovay Hansen follows a similar tack, arguing that, lacking language to articulate their desires, Mansfield's women rely on metonyms – typically manifest in physical objects – to attempt to express their longings. This method, Hansen argues in 'Katherine Mansfield's Desperate Housewives and Metonymic Desire', allows her female characters to create a new vocabulary, imbuing specific objects with fresh, subversive meaning. She gives special attention to Miss Brill's fox stole and Linda Burnell's fascination with the aloe plant.

The themed section of the book concludes with Sharon Gordon's essay on the political language of flowers in Mansfield's stories. Drawing on 'language of flower' books, which were popular in the nineteenth and early twentieth centuries, Gordon argues that Mansfield 'subverts the sentimental metaphoric association of women and flowers in order to indicate something darker, more subversive, even transgressive' (p. 129). Gordon explores several stories, paying close attention to flowers as they reveal implications about female sexuality, class and gender.

The Creative Writing section of the volume includes three short stories and two poems. In the first story, 'How Loud the Birds', Ailsa Cox portrays a couple and their son who work to make a life together; however, utilising the inward turn, she reveals how, in many ways, they struggle alone. In 'The Marquee', Paula McGrath presents us with a wedding party, a marquee, an STD, and a roadside death, while Bronwyn Calder's main character in 'Endless Sea' reassesses her life with her husband after her daughter gets married, travelling to the Antarctic to escape the stale relationship. The two poems in this section are both by contemporaries of Mansfield, both memorials. The first, 'On the death of Katherine Mansfield' by Chinese poet Xu Zhimo, is translated by Stuart Lyons, who also provides a note on the poem and the 'twenty immortal minutes' Xu spent during an interview with Mansfield. Gerri Kimber translates and provides a note on '*KM* 1932, In Memory of Katherine Mansfield' by Philippe Chabaneix, a previously unknown poem that has only recently been rediscovered.

Sydney Janet Kaplan opens up the Critical Miscellany with a fascinating reflection on her meeting with Christopher Isherwood and his own response to Mansfield, particularly his use of her as a pattern for Elizabeth Rydel in his *The World in the Evening*. More than this, Kaplan elaborates on other images and phrases in Isherwood's novel that evoke Mansfield. The second piece of this section publishes a previously uncollected review that Mansfield wrote for the *Daily Herald* on Joseph Conrad's *The Rescue* (which she also reviewed in the *Athenaeum*). John G. Peters, who uncovered the review, provides the accompanying note.

The volume concludes with Elyse Blankley's Review Essay, which provides overviews and assessments of six books and a special issue of the *Journal of New Zealand Literature* which either focus on Mansfield or have a direct significance for scholarship on her work.

Notes

1. Jeffrey Meyers, *Katherine Mansfield: A Darker View* (New York: Cooper Square Press, 2002), p. 227.
2. See Todd Martin, 'Introduction: Expanding the Horizon of Katherine Mansfield Studies', in Todd Martin, ed., *The Bloomsbury Handbook to Katherine Mansfield* (London: Bloomsbury, 2020), pp. 1–18 (pp. 7–8).
3. Antony Alpers, *The Life of Katherine Mansfield* (New York: Viking Press, 1980), p. 326.
4. Alpers, p. 321.
5. Alpers, p. 338.
6. Jenny McDonnell, *Katherine Mansfield and the Modernist Market Place: At the Mercy of the Public* (Basingstoke: Palgrave, 2010), pp. 150–1.

CRITICISM

Redefining 'Photographic Realism' in the Short Fiction of Katherine Mansfield

Daisy Birch

'Ah, but in my art rhymes don't matter. Only truth and the sun.'

– Julia Margaret Cameron in Act III of *Freshwater: A Comedy*[1]

The word 'photographic' has two slightly different meanings. One simply means something related to photography, while the other is a distortion of this, referring to 'minutely accurate' renderings of a visual scene in life.[2] It is this latter sense which Virginia Woolf evokes disapprovingly in a letter to Vita Sackville-West, asking her to question 'what made [Tolstoy's] realism, which might have been photographic, not at all; but on the contrary moving and exciting and all the rest'.[3] To see this remark as evidence of modernist writers' – or even Woolf's – unanimous disavowal of a photographic way of seeing in literature is misleading, and so the aim of this essay is to recentre the more expansive definition of 'photographic' in order to uncover the myriad ways this burgeoning art form influenced the work of Katherine Mansfield.

In a short essay entitled 'Royals', Woolf demonstrates photography's dependency on life for its meaning by examining contemporary photojournalism of royalty. 'We must call up battles and banners and many ghosts and glories before we see whatever it is that we do see in the picture of a child feeding a bear with a bun.'[4] The spectator's knowledge of the photograph's referent determines whether or not they can 'see' the image – and what we see is a royal child worthy of reverence. Woolf's theoretical stance on photography's contingency is shared by Roland Barthes in *Camera Lucida* (1980). Barthes describes how 'a photograph cannot be transformed (spoken) philosophically, it is wholly ballasted by contingency of which it is the weightless, transparent envelope'.[5] For Barthes, the photograph comes as close as possible to a perfect simultaneity between the signifier and the referent because 'it is as if the Photograph always carries its referent with itself'.[6]

It should not be overlooked that Barthes describes the photograph using the image of a 'transparent envelope', lifted from Woolf's essay 'Modern Fiction' (1925), and while these lines may be oft quoted in Woolf criticism, they nonetheless reveal a fascinating intertextual relationship here. Woolf argues that it is the novelist's task to convey a human mind's experience of life as it truly is, 'a luminous halo, a semi-transparent envelope surrounding us from the beginning of consciousness to the end'.[7] Placing these remarks in relation to one another, it becomes clear that photography's relationship to its referent – life – is the condition which fiction should aspire to, and it no longer seems unlikely that Woolf would take inspiration from photography in order to achieve this. By re-evaluating the phrase 'photographic realism', we can begin to suggest ways in which a consideration of photography can bear suggestively on Woolf's work and, as we shall see, Mansfield's.

Although Mansfield wrote fewer theoretical works during her lifetime, her aspirations for her fiction, revealed in diaries and correspondence, align closely with Woolf's preoccupation with representing life as it truly is. In a letter to Richard Murry, she describes her art's reliance upon life as a collapse of distinction between the two:

> I do believe with my whole soul that one's outlook is the climate in which ones art either thrives or doesn't grow. I am dead certain that there is no separating Art & Life. And no artist can afford to leave out Life. If we mean to work we must go straight to Life for our nourishment.[8]

Her theory is expressed mimetically by her choice of words with literal and figurative meanings, which both come into play in this context. 'Outlook' could refer both to one's perspective and to the prospect the author literally looks out upon; one's figurative 'climate' and 'nourishment' are both vital, combined with their obvious literal importance. Indeed, in her review of Mansfield's posthumously published notebooks, entitled 'A Terribly Sensitive Mind', Woolf quotes Mansfield's desire for the good health that would enable her to write. By health, she elaborates all that this entails:

> The power to lead a full, adult, living, breathing life in close contact with what I love – the earth and the wonders thereof – the sea – the sun [. . .] I want a garden, a small house, grass, animals, books, pictures, music. And out of this, the expression of this, I want to be writing.[9]

It is clear that Mansfield sees her work as so intimately entwined with her life that it is a direct 'expression' of it. In this way, her work is contingent on life, in a similar way to the photograph.

In terms of aesthetic theories circulating within the Bloomsbury group at the time, the suggestive commonalities between photography and Mansfield's literary representation do not cease. When explaining his concept of Significant Form in *Art* (1914), Clive Bell describes it as the essential quality of a work of art, and the cause of aesthetic emotion. Significant Form is defined in opposition to photography because the latter seeks to represent a referent: 'I have noticed a consistency in those to whom the most beautiful thing in the world is a beautiful woman, and the next most beautiful thing a picture of one.'[10] The image is a shadow of the beautiful woman, but it is the existence of this referent which makes the photograph beautiful. For this reason, Bell denies most photography the ability to evoke aesthetic emotion: 'For, to appreciate a work of art we need bring with us nothing from life, no knowledge of its ideas and affairs, no familiarity with its emotions'.[11] Thus, it would seem that the *raison d'être* of Mansfield's fiction has more in common with photography than with the non-representational art which Bell advocates for. Mansfield asks us to bring life with us when we approach her work. It is clear from the reflections in her notebooks and letters that life is the motive force behind her fiction. Therefore, life must also be the criterion against which we measure her short stories, much like Woolf's royal child.

Maurizio Ascari finds further evidence of contemporary visual art's definition of itself against photography in an article entitled 'The Triumph of Photography', in which Post-Impressionism is defined as 'the new negative art – the art of avoiding the photograph'.[12] Ascari goes on to demonstrate that in spite of – or, perhaps, because of, as I would like to suggest – the Post-Impressionist denigration of cinema as 'the apex of photographic realism', Mansfield sees this form's potential to inform her fiction.[13] While Ascari's argument only rests on photography briefly before considering its development into film at greater length, it seems to me that its 'ontological relation with reality' shares greater commonalities with Mansfield's literary endeavours than the Post-Impressionist belief that 'in the painter's conception of nature nothing exists beyond the magic circle of his own vision'.[14]

Ultimately, Bell excludes photography and 'descriptive pictures' not because they are representational, but because they are representative – the quality which they share with Mansfield's fiction. In this context, the former refers to art 'that seeks to reproduce aspects of the physical world as they appear to the senses, especially the sight.[15] Opposed to abstract and non-representational'. The latter refers to something which 'stands for or denotes another; a sign, a symbol; an image, an embodiment'.[16]

The discordance between Mansfield's fiction and Bell's aesthetic theory is perhaps most apparent in her story 'Bank Holiday' (1920). It forgoes conventional plot development and instead consists of a number of fragmented vignettes of description. As a result of this, Mansfield evokes her reader's experience and associations to render this story meaningful. The reader is prompted to imbue the descriptive scenes with their own experiences of the hubbub of a bank holiday and the characters that one comes across in the festivities. But it is also an experimental piece, which perhaps comes closest to Bell's Significant Form with its fragmented vignettes – 'lines and colours combined in a particular way, certain forms and relations of forms'.[17] However, it is clear that Bell's 'aesthetic emotion' does not accord with Mansfield's aspiration to dissolve the distinction between art and life and the corresponding visual form which Bell identifies with photography. It is the ideas, affairs and emotions of life which Bell disavows that Mansfield seeks to capture. In keeping with Erich Auerbach's characterisation of the particular realism of this period, she turns to 'a disintegration and dissolution of external realities for a richer and more essential interpretation of them'.[18]

Having indicated why photography is a pertinent form to consider comparatively with Mansfield's theoretical concerns, it remains to be shown what a redefined photographic realism could look like in short fiction specifically. As has been suggested, I will draw upon Barthes's *Camera Lucida* in my analysis, specifically in terms of the kinship which he identifies between photography and death, as the photograph embalms the photographic referent in stasis. The attention which I want to draw to the static visual image distinguishes my approach from those such as Ascari's, which have considered Mansfield's work in relation to cinema. I will engage with Walter Benjamin's idea of the 'optical unconscious', meaning the phenomenon whereby features of a photograph, and therefore the past, can be understood or reinterpreted belatedly by the viewer, and thus 'the camera introduces us to unconscious optics as does psychoanalysis to unconscious impulses'.[19] For this reason, it is not just the contemporary comparisons between short fiction and photography which have suggested my enquiry (Woolf herself uses this analogy in her review of Elizabeth McCracken's collection *The Women of America*, describing it as 'fourteen snapshots'),[20] but also the revelatory potential which is identified by Benjamin in the momentary nature of the photographic. This closely relates to the conventional epiphanic moment of the short story, which Mansfield adapted to create her own moments of being, often discussed in criticism without due consideration of their potentially photographic nature.

Theoretical works on photography, including Benjamin's and Barthes's, tend to take a psychoanalytic approach to photography. This is unsurprising, given its indissoluble connection to 'life', which I have sought to emphasise. Alternatively, my essay will take an approach which is both cultural and formalist. This resonates with Laura Marcus's remarks in response to criticism of new modernist studies, in which a false dichotomy has emerged between those who 'stress the context of social and cultural modernity' and those who 'focus on the specifically aesthetic dimension of modernism'.[21] Therefore, my approach indicates my agreement with Marcus that 'we need to transcend the sharp opposition that is sometimes presented between a culturalist and a more formalist approach to modernism'.[22]

Explicit Mentions of Photography in Mansfield: Framed Stasis

By first turning our attention to the explicit mentions of photography in Mansfield's early short fiction, we will be better equipped to identify when and how a more implicit photographic realism appears in *The Garden Party and Other Stories.* In these situations, the photograph represents a framed moment preserved in stasis. The preservation of a moment from the past has the potential to create a jarring dissonance with the continuing existence of the image's subject in the present.

In her work on Vanessa Bell's painting and Woolf's writing, Diane Gillespie observes that portraits 'ultimately are divorced from the people who sit for them'.[23] While their subjects grow old and die, 'portraits outlive them as mirrors of their viewers or as painted forms and colours to which the eye responds'.[24] As we have seen, Clive Bell believed that photography was unlikely to possess 'forms and colours to which the eye responds' – Significant Form – because photography is usually valued as representation. 'The photograph, however, introduces something new and strange' to its non-mechanical predecessors, Benjamin writes; there is some aspect of the image's referent that is 'not completely absorbed, something that cannot be silenced, obstreperously demanding the name of she who has lived, who remains real here and will never consent to enter fully into "art"'.[25] The emotional dissonance created by the relationship between a photograph and its referent allows Mansfield to break from the conventional structure of the short story, which is characterised by an uncomplicated moment of revelation. Indeed, Dominic Head argues that Mansfield breaks from the conventional short story because her epiphanic moment is 'an opening out of possibilities rather than a narrowing down, or a particular revelation'.[26]

Seemingly contrary to photography's stasis, Mansfield often animates pictures in her fiction. Her photographs eternally re-enact the moment they capture. For example, in 'Ole Underwood' (1913), at the climactic moment the reader is left to assume that the eponymous murderer has been triggered to repeat his crime, by killing a man sleeping on a boat. The concluding lines describe a photograph which looks down upon this scene as it is about to unfold: 'And looking down upon him from the wall there shone her picture – his woman's picture – smiling and smiling at the big sleeping man.'[27] Despite the fact that the woman in this image is animated in the present tense, the repetition 'smiling and smiling' conveys how she is stuck, straining, in that position for eternity. Her reaction does not change to the scene in front of her, although the 'personified' image is most likely about to witness her loved one being murdered.

The potentially problematic nature of this stasis is nowhere more apparent than in Mansfield's 'A Birthday' (1911). The central character, Andreas, begins to meditate on an old photograph of his wife, who is currently in labour. Initially, he animates the photograph, seeing it as synonymous with its referent, his wife: 'She seemed to droop under the heavy braids of it, and yet she was smiling. Andreas caught his breath sharply. She was his wife – that girl' (p. 742). He goes so far as to kiss the photograph, 'Then rubbed the glass with the back of his hand. At that moment, fainter than he had heard in the passage, more terrifying, Andreas heard again that wailing cry' (p. 742). This seems to spark Andreas's revulsion at the photograph, as while the image of his wife smiles up at him, a dissonance is created as he hears her scream in pain during childbirth. While the moment of the photograph is locked in stasis, its subject and the rest of the world continue to move through time. The photograph begins to change before his eyes, until the dissonance renders his wife unrecognisable: '"She doesn't look like my wife – like the mother of my son"' (p. 742). The photograph defamiliarises Andreas so much from his wife that he thinks 'Anna looked like a stranger – abnormal, a freak – it might have been taken just before or after death' (p. 743).

In contrast to Benjamin's alignment of the photograph with life, Barthes associates this form of image-making with death because the subject has been embalmed in stasis. He looks upon the photo of himself and 'what I see is that I have become Total-Image, which is to say, Death in person'.[28] Therefore, 'Death is the eidos of that Photograph.'[29] There is a sense of dissonance as the photograph is not only a testament to the referent's life, but also holds the referent in a death-like state in comparison to their continued existence. Through this, it becomes apparent that, as stated by Mary Ann Gillies and Aurelea Mahood, 'the pivotal moment in a Mansfield story is the instant in which competing or contradictory impulses converge and conflict'.[30] This is seen when we are reminded that the photograph is only an image because of the humorous note punctuating Andreas's self-pity: he has to wipe the mark left by his kiss on the frame; he feels the desire to burn the picture because it displeases him so – if it were not for the expensive frame. This is the blithe irony which is so characteristic of Mansfield's work, and her own version of the moment of revelation. This dissonance escalates when the doctor enters, as Andreas believes that his wife must have passed away, but contrarily he is congratulated on the birth of his son. It seems that Andreas does not register this, still under the impression that Anna has died, seemingly as a result of his meditation on the photograph. He feels exultant in the face of her imagined death, as people will no longer be able to claim that he is being oversensitive. The story ends with Andreas declaring out loud, '"Well, by God! Nobody can accuse me of not knowing what suffering is"' (p. 743). We see here how the dissonance created by the photograph destabilises the conventional moment of revelation of the traditional short story: Andreas experiences a revelation; it is just the wrong one.

In his 'Small History of Photography' (1931), Benjamin quotes art historian Alfred Lichtwark's remarks on the form: 'There is in our period no artwork that is contemplated so attentively than the portrait photography of one's own self, one's closest relations and friends, one's beloved,' and therefore, according to Benjamin, Lichtwark 'shifted the analysis out of the realm of aesthetic distinctions and into that of social functions'.[31] It is clear, however, that photography is a form which partakes in both of these realms constantly, due to its entangled nature as aesthetic representation of the social. The photograph's tie to the social due to its contingency upon the living referent can create complicated emotions, especially if the photograph is taken as identical to the referent who continues to move through time, and not the embalmed aesthetic moment in stasis which it is; the image has a constant 'aliveness' in that it can be reinterpreted in light of the future, but it cannot be taken for the present.

Evidence of Mansfield's awareness of the fraught nature of photography can be found in her personal life. While she is separated from her husband in Menton, France, Mansfield is appalled to hear that Murry has sent a photograph she detests to the publisher of *Bliss and Other Stories* (1920), to be used for the book's cover and advertisement. 'The Detested 1913 Photograph' (as Antony Alpers christens it)[32] preserves the image of a very different woman from the one seeking reprieve from tuberculosis. 'I am not an ox. I am weak: I feel my hold on life is fainting-weak. But that is ME, the real real me. I can't help it. Didn't you know?' She continues, 'I have been ill for nearly four years – and Im changed changed – not the same.'[33] Although certainly not malicious on Murry's behalf, Mansfield does seem permitted to question her husband: 'Didn't you know?' She refers to her historic dislike of that particular photograph, but also to how significant it would be to her if it misrepresented through her appearance such an unfortunately fundamental part of who she had become: her illness. It becomes clear that it is the very contingency of the photograph upon life, and its inability to enter fully into the realm of art, which account for the form's fraught nature to Mansfield.

Photography's contingency on its referent is summarised aptly in another of Mansfield's stories, 'The Daughters of the Late Colonel' (1921): 'Why did the photographs of dead people always fade so? wondered Josephine. As soon as a person was dead their photograph died too' (p. 283). While the referent bears upon its image to the extent that a photograph is changed by the referent's death, this also means that there is less opportunity for the dissonance that we see in 'A Birthday', as both referent and image are now static. This thought occurs to Josephine in the story's final section, as 'a square of sunlight' moves around the room, highlighting various objects, including her deceased mother's photograph (p. 282). Michael Levenson describes how 'nothing was beyond the reach of technical concern' for modernist writers, including 'the frame of a picture'.[34] Similarly, in her examination of different versions of Woolf's story 'The Searchlight', Marcus emphasises that 'the question of the "frame"' was implicated in 'the issue of how to construct a narrative rationale as well as casing for a "scene"'.[35] Therefore, as a formally self-reflexive motif, we can see that the sunlight fulfils the same role as a frame around an image in 'The Daughters of the Late Colonel': it is illuminating in both senses of the word. The sun's movement and other inexplicable aspects of the moment bring the sisters to a kind of epiphany, but when they try to express this to one another, they trip over their words, each prompting the other to speak first, until the moment of revelation is allowed to slip from their memories. Their deflation is punctuated by Josephine's sight: 'she stared at a big cloud where the sun had been' (p. 285).

A Flash upon that Inward Eye

In her introduction to Benjamin's works on photography, Esther Leslie describes how he employs 'a photographic style of writing': 'that is to say, he conjures up the workings of the self and memory in photographic terms'.[36] Such terms are used to describe 'those privileged moments when something akin to a magnesium flare sears indelibly onto memory an image or circumstance [. . .] as if memory were a photographic plate. Sometime later, that image flashes into consciousness's view.'[37] This offers a starting point for thinking about how Mansfield could also be said to employ a 'photographic style of writing'. This idea of the flash speaks to her short stories formally, in line with contemporary descriptions of the short story as a literary 'snapshot'. This allows Mansfield to bring her fiction closer to reality.

In a letter to Woolf following an early meeting in 1917, Mansfield describes her departure: 'I had a last glimpse of you before it all disappeared & I waved: I hope you saw.' She thanks Woolf for letting her see their house, Asheham: 'It is very wonderful & I feel that it will flash upon one corner of my inward eye for ever.'[38] The flash upon the inward eye recalls a line from Wordsworth's 'I wandered lonely as a Cloud'. The significance of this is increased by a passage from a 1920 notebook, in which the author copies down a number of quotations from Coleridge, expressing her approval. The selected quotations argue that literature should aspire to represent reality, decrying that 'we judge of books by books, instead of referring what we read to our own experience'[39]:

> Imagination acts by so carrying on the eye of the reader as to make him almost lose the consciousness of words, – to make him see everything flashed, as Wordsworth has grandly and appropriately said, –
>
> *Flashed* upon that inward eye.
> Which is the bliss of solitude.[40]

Coleridge relocates Wordsworth's lines into a purely literary context, using them to express the idea that the reader should be unaware that the text is a contrived work of art, and should read without realising that they are reading. Mansfield suggests that Woolf is unable to achieve this in her novel *Night and Day* (1919), in her infamous review which almost spelled the end of their already fraught friendship. 'There is not a chapter', Mansfield writes, 'where one is unconscious of the writer, of her personality, her point of view, and her control of the situation.'[41] If it is life that you seek to represent, then it is counterproductive for the reader to be aware of the author crafting the work before them; it would seem artificed, not cut out from life. Furthermore, Mansfield disapproves of Woolf's minor characters, as they do not sustain lives that the reader can believe in: 'they are held within the circle of steady light in which the author bathes her world, and in their case the light seems to shine at them, but not through them'.[42] Once again, we see this idea of transparency return, with it being framed as a quality that the writer should aspire to.

Woolf recalls literary transparency in her final letter to Mansfield, which would remain unanswered. Woolf praises what she terms the 'transparent quality' of Mansfield's work.[43] She laments that 'my stuff gets muddy', whereas Mansfield seems 'to go so straight and directly, – all clear as glass – refined and spiritual'.[44] While seeming vague, it is important to note that the vocabulary used by Woolf to describe Mansfield's work has been adopted by critics to this day, no longer just as opinion but as a matter of fact. In Ronald Hayman's study, he describes how, while reading Mansfield, we forget her and see only her stories: 'her mind projects vivid colours onto them and itself remains perfectly transparent', whereas 'Virginia Woolf never allows us to see through her in this way.'[45] Indeed, in an unsigned review of *Night and Day*, which Alpers suggests could have been written by Mansfield, there features the back-handed compliment: 'we rejoice more in the accessibility of Mrs Woolf's mind than in her story'.[46] It becomes clear that transparency means not only an absence of the mind of the author, but an absence which serves to minimise the reader's awareness that the text is a contrived work of art, instead allowing it to flash visually on their inward eye unobstructed. Crucially, it is this very quality of self-effacement which Woolf strives for more explicitly in her later work. She describes how her aim in *The Waves* was 'to eliminate [. . .] myself', and related to Ethel Smyth that 'I believe unconsciousness, and complete anonymity to be the only conditions [. . .] in which I can write.'[47]

For the flash of the visual image to have the effect desired by Coleridge, the image must be imposed upon the passive reader almost involuntarily. This is even suggested by the original source in Wordsworth's footnote to the line, added to the 1815 edition of *Poems*, but not subsequently reprinted, which clarifies that these lines describe a 'simple impression [. . .] upon the imaginative faculty, than an exertion of it'.[48] This specification recalls Mansfield's remark about the Woolfs' Asheham, as well as her later description of the psychological impact of the celebrations of the end of the war: 'I keep seeing all these horrors, bathing in them again & again (God knows I don't want to) and then my mind fills with the wretched little picture I have of my brother's grave.'[49]

Mansfield creates images founded on techniques potentially inspired by her psychological experience of these unbidden images in 'Marriage à la Mode', by using the paratext of visual art – in this case, conventional titles – to render the action of the moment static. One of the artists in Isabel's circle, Dennis, comments upon what is taking place around him, such as 'The Lady in Love with a Pine-apple' and 'A Lady reading a Letter':

> 'I've found the sardines', said Moira, and she ran into the hall, holding a box high in the air.
> 'A Lady with a Box of Sardines', said Dennis gravely. (p. 317)

Dennis's remark freezes Moira's dynamic movement and imprints the moment as a static image upon the mind of the reader. The typography here, with its capitalisation, strengthens this association. Woolf likewise plays with this convention in her only play, *Freshwater: A Comedy*, which features Julia Margaret Cameron, her great-aunt and a renowned early photographer.

> Mrs. C.: Another picture! A better picture! Poetry in the person of Alfred Tennyson adoring the Muse.
> Ellen: But I'm Modesty, Mrs Cameron; Signor said so. I'm Modesty crouching at the feet of Mammon, at least I was ten minutes ago.[50]

Ellen Terry, who married artist George Frederic Watts when she was sixteen, had just been posing as Modesty in a painting for Watts, when Cameron catches her speaking to Tennyson and demands that they pose for a photograph. The fact that Terry can move from one art form to the other demonstrates the way in which they overlapped at this time; she symbolises a different allegorical figure in each image, but still features as part of a formulaic title for both. The widening gap between painting and photography, with the latter developing towards the snappable Kodak cameras of Woolf and Mansfield's age, is suggested by the fact that Terry had to pose for four hours for Watts, whereas Cameron demands her stasis only for fifteen minutes. Similarly, Mansfield's literary representation in Dennis's pronouncement can be seen to take inspiration from an aspect of photography. Once again, we see the ambivalent relationship between Mansfield's art and this visual form. On the one hand, it seems to imply that the bohemians' is a lazy art; they snap away at images in life thoughtlessly. On the other hand, Mansfield is using photography's techniques to construct her representation of reality. Unlike the bohemians, she is discriminating with what she chooses to capture, and ultimately her use of this photographic technique demonstrates that the bohemians play at creating art, while never actually producing anything. She pushes us to measure books by experience, as opposed to books by books, in Coleridge's terms.

The Mind's Photograph: Moments of Being and the Optical Unconscious

When considering photography's literary influence, there is a need to develop insightful but unelaborated remarks such as Gillespie's comment: 'Woolf's early stories, like "Kew Gardens," might be read as experiments in presenting a series of snapshots.'[51] Instead, the discussion should be grounded in the writers' theories of their literature, foregrounding the influence of photography. Stef Craps, for example, criticises those who have reduced 'Kew Gardens' to 'a retreat into empty formalism', warning that 'one should be wary of overemphasising form at the expense of content – a pitfall which, alas, few critics have managed to avoid'.[52] However, there is a danger of overcompensating with social analysis, neglecting form in what is a highly formalist story. As with my criticisms of Gillespie – which resonates with Marcus's concerns about this analytic dichotomy in new modernist criticism – an approach which unifies both would be ideal. This will allow us to identify further the implicit appearance of photography in Mansfield and Woolf's short fiction, and how the optical unconscious allows them to update the conventional short story's epiphanic moment.

'Kew Gardens' resonates with Benjamin's remarks about the optical unconscious in close-up photography of flowers. In a review of Karl Blossfeldt's book, *Urformen der Kunst: Photographische Pflanzenbilder* [*Primal Forms of Art: Photographic Images of Plants*], Benjamin describes how these photographs reveal 'a geyser of new image worlds', defamiliarising us from the flowers so that we see unexpected analogous forms within them, like a ballet dancer in a bud.[53] According to Benjamin, this revelatory potential is exclusive to photography, 'For it requires a powerful magnification before these forms are able to cast off the veil that our inertia throws over them'.[54] In 'Kew Gardens', the reader inhabits a world where light may settle anywhere and reveal 'the branching thread of fibre beneath the surface'.[55] The optical unconscious in this story resonates with Mansfield as well, as in her review she praises how 'for a moment the secret life is half-revealed'.[56] Tellingly, the analogy that Benjamin uses to explain the world revealed by magnification and photography is that of the beholders 'wander[ing] beneath these giant plants like Lilliputians'.[57]

The world revealed within our own by the camera's ability to cast off the veil of inertia bears a striking similarity to Woolf's 'moments of being'. In 'A Sketch of the Past', Woolf describes these moments as 'a revelation of some order; it is a token of some real thing behind appearances'. '[W]ithout a reason, without an effort, the sealing matter cracks, in floods reality', and a visual impression of a scene is made upon the mind as a result of this feeling, 'for they would not survive entire so many ruinous years unless they were made of something permanent; that is proof of their reality'.[58] Mansfield describes a similar concept in a letter to her husband, labelling them the 'deserts of vast eternity', which she would convey covertly in her renderings of the most ordinary moments, such as 'a boy eating strawberries or a woman combing her hair on a windy morning'.[59]

Mansfield describes the visual impression preserved by such a moment in her review of 'Kew Gardens':

> It happens so often – or so seldom – in life, [. . .] that something – for no reason that we discover – gives us pause. Why is it that, thinking back on that July afternoon, we see so distinctly that flower-bed? [. . .] But, though we weren't conscious of it at the time, something was happening – something . . .[60]

This resonates strongly with Benjamin's 'photographic style of writing', in which 'the undiscriminating eyes of memory and cameras absorb more than is consciously perceived', allowing understanding to develop belatedly, 'just as a photograph snatches an image from time and presents it to the world again only after a period of development'.[61]

It seems bizarre to compare Mansfield's short fiction to a form that Woolf satirises in *Freshwater* through the character of her great- aunt, Julia Margaret Cameron, but Cameron's long-exposure photography is very different from the snapshot cameras that Mansfield engaged with in adulthood. It becomes clear that features which are seen as emblematic of Mansfield's work – breaks from the conventional epiphanic moment, formal innovations, descriptions of moments of being – have been informed by photography, and furthermore are tied to Mansfield's desire to represent reality faithfully. Therefore, the epigraph quotation speaks suggestively to her fiction. Rhymes become transparent if they represent reality so that it flashes upon the reader's inward eye, as Coleridge said. Finally, reflecting on Mansfield's desire to represent life as it truly is, simultaneous with a dazzling, semi-transparent quality that is often attributed to her work, it would not be amiss to say that her art is made of the same truth and sun as the photograph.

Notes

1. Virginia Woolf, *Freshwater: A Comedy* (New York and London: Harcourt Brace Jovanovich, 1976) p. 37.
2. 'Photographic', adj. 1 & 2. *Oxford English Dictionary.*
3. Joanne Trautman Banks, ed., *Virginia Woolf, Selected Letters* (London: Vintage, 2008), p. 238.

4. Leonard Woolf, ed., *Collected Essays*, 4 vols (London: Hogarth, 1966–7), vol. IV, p. 212.
5. Roland Barthes, *Camera Lucida: Reflections on Photography*, trans. Richard Howard (London: Vintage, 2000), p. 5.
6. Barthes, p. 5.
7. Virginia Woolf, 'Modern Fiction', in *Virginia Woolf Selected Essays*, ed. David Bradshaw (Oxford: Oxford University Press, 2008), p. 9.
8. *Letters* 4, p. 148.
9. Qtd in Virginia Woolf, 'A Terribly Sensitive Mind', in *Women and Writing*, intr. Michèlle Barrett (London: Women's Press, 1979), pp. 186–7.
10. Clive Bell, *Art*, rev. edition (London: Chatto & Windus, 1949), p. 15.
11. Bell, p. 25.
12. R. H. W., 'The Triumph of Photography', *Athenaeum*, 4683 (30 January 1920), p. 147.
13. Maurizio Ascari, *Cinema and the Imagination in Katherine Mansfield's Writing* (Basingstoke: Palgrave Macmillan, 2014), p. 26.
14. O. R. Drey, 'Post-Impressionism', *Rhythm*, 2: 12 (January 1913), pp. 363–9 (p. 369).
15. 'Representational', adj. 3. *OED*.
16. 'Representative', adj. II. 4. *OED*.
17. Bell, p. 8.
18. Erich Auerbach, *Mimesis: The Representation of Reality in Western Literature*, trans. Willard R. Track (Princeton: Princeton University Press, 1968), p. 545.
19. Walter Benjamin, 'The Work of Art in the Age of Mechanical Reproduction', in *Illuminations*, trans. Harry Zorn (London: Bodley Head, 2015), p. 230.
20. Andrew McNeillie, ed., *The Essays of Virginia Woolf*, 6 vols (London: Hogarth, 1986), vol. I, p. 46.
21. Laura Marcus, *Dreams of Modernity: Psychoanalysis, Literature, Cinema* (Cambridge: Cambridge University Press, 2014), p. 2.
22. Marcus, p. 2.
23. Diane Filby Gillespie, *The Sisters' Arts: The Writing and Painting of Virginia Woolf and Vanessa Bell* (New York: Syracuse University Press, 1988), pp. 208–9.
24. Gillespie, p. 209.
25. Walter Benjamin, *On Photography*, ed. and trans. Esther Leslie (London: Reaktion, 2015), p. 66.
26. Dominic Head, *The Modernist Short Story: A Study in Theory and Practice* (Cambridge: Cambridge University Press, 1992), p. 137.
27. Katherine Mansfield, *The Collected Stories* (London: Penguin, 2004), p. 566. All subsequent citations will be from this edition and cited parenthetically in the main body of the essay.
28. Barthes, p. 14.
29. Barthes, p. 15.
30. Mary Ann Gillies and Aurelea Mahood, *Modernist Literature: An Introduction* (Edinburgh: Edinburgh University Press, 2007), p. 50.
31. Benjamin, *On Photography*, p. 88.
32. Antony Alpers, *The Life of Katherine Mansfield* (Oxford: Oxford University Press, 1982), insert 13.
33. *Letters* 4, p. 114.
34. Michael Levenson, ed., 'Introduction', in *The Cambridge Companion to Modernism* (Cambridge: Cambridge University Press, 2011), pp.1–9 (p. 3).
35. Marcus, p. 222.
36. Esther Leslie, ed., 'Introduction', in Benjamin, *On Photography*, pp. 7–53 (p. 32).
37. Leslie, p. 33.

38. *Letters* 1, p. 327.
39. Clare Hanson, ed., *The Critical Writings of Katherine Mansfield* (Basingstoke: Macmillan, 1987), p. 42.
40. Hanson, p. 42.
41. Hanson, p. 57.
42. Hanson, p. 58.
43. Banks, p. 128.
44. Banks, pp. 128–9.
45. Ronald Hayman, *Literature and Living: A Consideration of Katherine Mansfield & Virginia Woolf* (London: Covent Garden Press, 1972), p. 19.
46. Hanson, p. 61; Alpers, p. 44.
47. Qtd in Susan Sellers, 'Virginia Woolf's Diaries and Letters', in *The Cambridge Companion to Virginia Woolf*, eds Sue Roe and Susan Sellers (Cambridge: Cambridge University Press, 2002) pp. 109–26 (p. 119).
48. Nicholas Halmi, ed., *Wordsworth's Poetry and Prose* (New York and London: W. W. Norton & Company, 2014), p. 418.
49. *Letters* 2, p. 339.
50. Woolf, *Freshwater*, p. 11
51. Diane F. Gillespie, '"Her Kodak Pointed at His Head": Virginia Woolf and Photography', in *The Multiple Muses of Virginia Woolf*, ed. Diane F. Gillespie (Columbia: University of Missouri Press, 1993), p. 144.
52. Stef Craps, 'Virginia Woolf: "Kew Gardens" and "The Legacy"', in *A Companion to the British and Irish Short Story*, eds Cheryl Alexander Malcolm and David Malcolm (Oxford: Wiley-Blackwell, 2008), pp. 193–202 (p. 196).
53. Benjamin, 'New Things about Flowers', in *On Photography*, pp. 123–8 (p. 124).
54. Benjamin, 'New Things about Flowers', p. 124.
55. Virginia Woolf, *A Haunted House and Other Stories*, ed. Susan Dick (London: Vintage, 2003), p. 84.
56. Hanson, p. 54.
57. Benjamin, 'New Things about Flowers', p. 126.
58. Virginia Woolf, 'A Sketch of the Past', in *Moments of Being*, ed. Jeanne Schulkind, 2nd edition (London: Pimlico, 2002), pp. 78–161 (pp. 85, 145).
59. *Letters* 3, pp. 97–8.
60. Hanson, p. 54.
61. Leslie, p. 34.

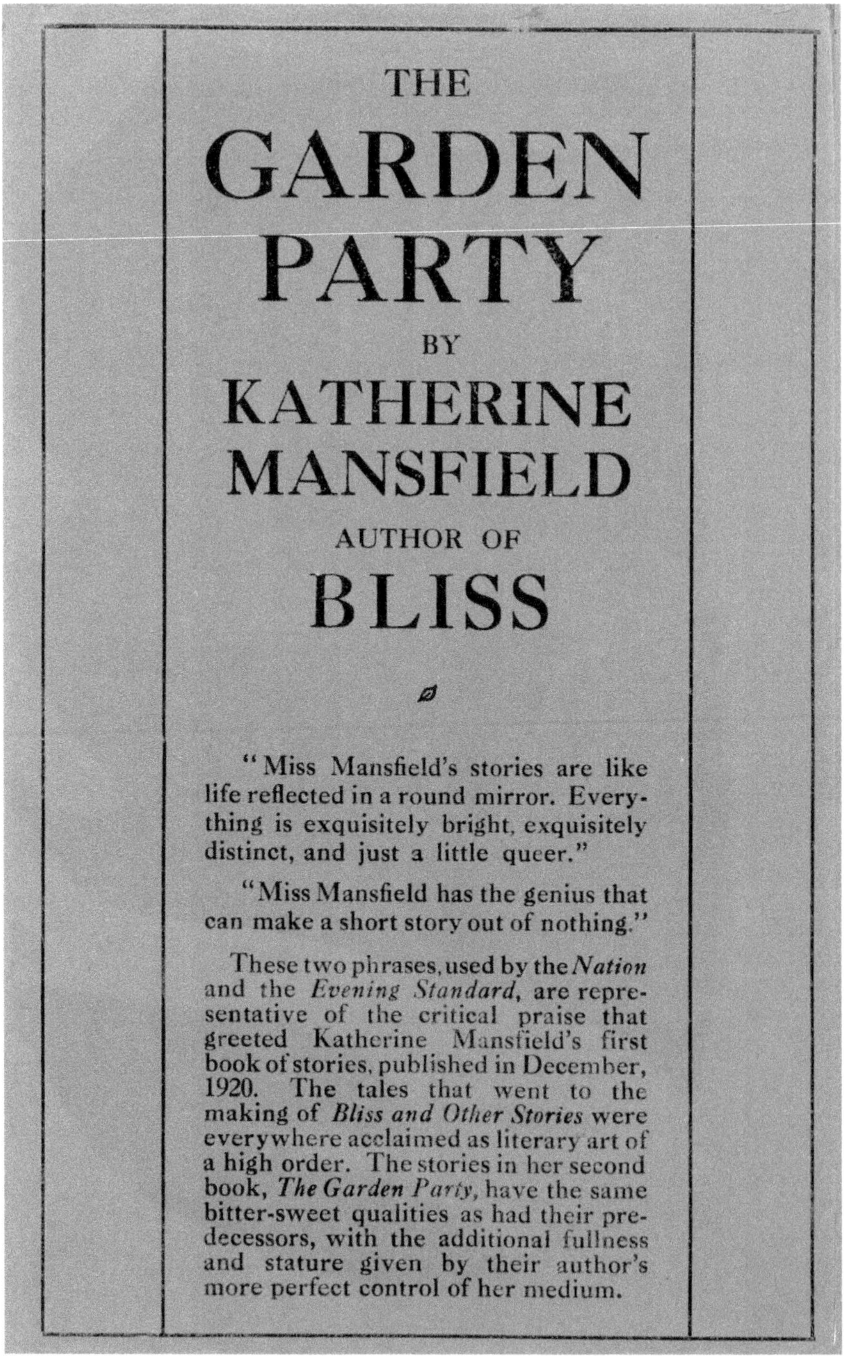

THE

GARDEN PARTY

BY

KATHERINE MANSFIELD

AUTHOR OF

BLISS

"Miss Mansfield's stories are like life reflected in a round mirror. Everything is exquisitely bright, exquisitely distinct, and just a little queer."

"Miss Mansfield has the genius that can make a short story out of nothing."

These two phrases, used by the *Nation* and the *Evening Standard*, are representative of the critical praise that greeted Katherine Mansfield's first book of stories, published in December, 1920. The tales that went to the making of *Bliss and Other Stories* were everywhere acclaimed as literary art of a high order. The stories in her second book, *The Garden Party*, have the same bitter-sweet qualities as had their predecessors, with the additional fullness and stature given by their author's more perfect control of her medium.

Figure 1 Pale rose dust jacket on Edward Garnett's copy of the first edition of *The Garden Party and Other Stories*, 1922. Courtesy of the Cushing Memorial Library, J. Lawrence Mitchell Collection.

Knowing What We Feel about Katherine Mansfield: Sentimentality and Expression in 'The Garden Party'

Jay Dickson

What we feel about Katherine Mansfield often depends on what we feel about her literary project – which, in large part, is itself about the expression of feelings. For Mansfield, the short-story form often serves as a vehicle for exploring intense if brief moments of emotion triggered by the conditions of modernity, but often from the subjectivities of those characters most often associated with popular Victorian fiction, such as the poor, or children, or *dames seules.* Critics both during her lifetime and after have often been distressed by this more sentimental side to Mansfield's fiction. While, for decades, Mansfield scholarship attended to the more avant-garde and overtly political tendencies within her fictions, it is true that though her writing often circulated in experimental modernist journals like *Rhythm* and *The New Age,* she also attracted a large audience within more popular and even middlebrow periodicals, such as the *London Mercury,* the *Westminster Gazette* and the *Sphere.* Mansfield's popular accessibility, coupled with her interest in exploring intense feeling, often made her an object of derision among many of her modernist cohort, both before and after her early death, such that Chris Mourant has noted, 'Mansfield's contemporaries often accused her of producing "sentimental" writing.'[1] T. S. Eliot, who famously decreed in his 1919 manifesto 'Tradition and the Individual Talent' against the 'turning loose' of emotion in poetry,[2] dismissed her in a letter to Ezra Pound not long before her death as 'a sentimental crank',[3] while Leonard Woolf also bemoaned in his memoir *Beginning Again* that he saw her unhappily enmeshed in 'cheap sentimentality'.[4] After Mansfield's death, Woolf's wife, Virginia, who considered her both a colleague and a rival, dismissed her stories to Vita Sackville-West thus:

> I gave up reading them [. . .] because of their cheap sharp sentimentality, which was all the worse, I thought, because she had, as you say, the zest and the resonance – I mean she could permeate one with her quality; and if one felt this cheap scent in it, it reeked in one's nostrils.[5]

Even the later modernist writers who greatly admired Mansfield would regretfully admit something similar. Elizabeth Bowen, who noted her awe over 'the stretching promise' of Mansfield's fiction, observed, 'Now and then the emotional level of her writing drops; a whimsical, petulant little-girlishness disfigures a few of the lesser stories. Some others show a transferred self-pity. She could not always keep up the guard.'[6] Katherine Anne Porter made an analogous argument, praising the stories for 'a certain grim, quiet ruthlessness of judgment, an unsparing and sometimes cruel eye, a natural malicious wit, an intelligent humor', while also deploring that '[there] are a few stories which she fails to bring, quite, and these because she falls dangerously near to triviality or a sentimental wistfulness, of which she had more than a streak in certain moments and which she feared and fought in herself'.[7] Christopher Isherwood even saw these two aspects of Mansfield (whom he and W. H. Auden had greatly admired, to the point of hero worship, as undergraduates) as at war with one another, with 'Writer A' the author of the more sentimental and cloying stories, while 'Writer B' served as the critical and witty writer of satire.[8]

Isherwood felt that Mansfield wrote her best stories when writers A and B worked together in tandem; even so, his sharp critical distinctions between her more popular domestic stories and her sharper satirical pieces reflect a trend in her critical estimation that continued for more than seventy-five years after her death.[9] In 1997, for example, Pamela Dunbar noted a division between critical estimation of what she called 'the tranquil pieces' such as 'Prelude' (1917), 'The Garden Party' (1921) and 'The Doll's House' (1921), which she says other critics have dismissed as 'mere "chocolate box" pieces', from the 'other, more patently disturbing pieces' such as 'the satirical *German Pension* sketches, the confessional monologues, and the early colonial tales'.[10] The modernist discrediting of Mansfield as a sentimentalist was rooted in considerations of her writing for decades, which seems to have been in part behind the difficulty, until the twenty-first century, of establishing her more firmly in the modernist canon. The writer disparaged by her peers for her emotional facility – which could occasion even Virginia Woolf to fling down her copy of the *London Review*, which published 'Bliss', exclaiming 'She's done for!', while complaining later to Janet Case that she found that Mansfield story 'so cold, and so hard, and so sentimental' – prompted a certain amount of defensiveness among Mansfield scholars.[11] What has yet to be undertaken, however, is an analysis of *why* Mansfield struck such an emotional reactive chord in her modernist peers through her own expression of emotions, and why this produced such marked distaste. This essay argues that Katherine Mansfield internalised this pressing modernist debate over sentimentality in her own fiction, and gave fullest expression to it in one of her most famous but also one of her most ambiguous stories, 'The Garden Party'.

What is at stake in an enquiry into Mansfield's addressing of this topic is the modernists' exceptionally vexed attitude towards sentiment and sentimentality, and their distinguishing of one from the other. The modernists dreaded what they saw as the Victorians' excesses towards sentimentality in their culture, which Aldous Huxley characterised (in his 1930 critical monograph of the same name) as 'Vulgarity in Literature'.[12] Simultaneously, however, they recognised the impossibility of escaping from feeling altogether. Even Eliot, that most strenuous detractor of what he called the 'dissociation of sensibility' that marked the Victorians,[13] admitted in 'Tradition and the Individual Talent' that, even though 'Poetry is not a turning loose of emotion but an escape from emotion; it is not the expression of personality, but an escape from personality', 'of course, only those who have personality or emotions know what it is to want to escape from them'.[14] The poet is thus not free of emotion, Eliot suggests, but rather is fully akin to what E. M. Forster famously termed 'the aristocracy of the sensitive',[15] in that only one with the requisite depth of feeling can produce great modern literature (and can recognise true feeling from falsely expressed feeling). But to substitute 'cheap' emotional expression for genuine deep feelings, as Eliot and the Woolfs believed Mansfield did, was of course to err on the side of vulgarity. Mansfield's colonial upbringing and her *louche* past in the European *demi-monde* (which so fascinated Virginia Woolf) only reinforced this suspicion about her more popular stories.

Moreover, the stigmatisation of sentimentality was something that bedevilled female modernists in particular, given how much women writers had been associated with sentimental literature during both the eighteenth and nineteenth centuries on both sides of the Atlantic. Suzanne Clark has noted of the modernist denunciation of sentimentality: 'The gendered character of this condemnation seemed natural: women writers were entangled in sensibility, were romantic and sentimental in nature, and so even the best might not escape altogether this romantic indulgence in emotion and sublimity.'[16] Mansfield's position as a woman writer was only exacerbated by the fact that she did not consistently write for the avant-garde journals, but frequently appeared in more popular magazines and newspapers, such that she seemed more vulnerable than even Woolf to charges of pandering to popular tastes through what her cohort saw as the facile expression of feelings.[17]

A central dynamic to this stigmatisation, of course, is the fact that sentimentality is by no means a fixed structure, but, as Eve Kosofsky Sedgwick has argued, is rather a relational one, such that its identification depends on external judgement as to the authenticity and justifiability under its circumstances of an emotional display.[18] This goes right to the problem of Eliot's proposed solution to the quandary of judiciously representing 'emotion in the form of art' in his proposal of analysing 'the objective correlative': 'in other words, a set of objects, a chain of events which shall be the formula of that *particular* emotion; such that when the external facts, which must terminate in sensory experience, are given, the emotion is immediately evoked'.[19] Yet, as Sedgwick points out, the judgement of the emotional display can never be fully 'objective', given the intense subjective experience of feelings and of subsequent external judgements of their authenticity, so that the term 'objective correlative' must always be a misnomer.[20]

Even Mansfield herself frequently decried easy or cheap sentimentality, especially in her own writings, as when she abandoned a fictional experiment in dialogue in her diaries, inserting after it the parenthetical self-critical comment, '(Oh, what sentimental toshery)'.[21] Similarly, she noted years earlier in a notebook that although she felt comfortable with the satirical bent in her writings, she recognised that she went in for facility when she tried for a softer aesthetic: 'If I try to find things lovely I turn pretty pretty.'[22] Mansfield was conflicted about both the success of her stories in mass-produced periodicals and the place of deep feeling in art. Like Eliot, she still believed strong feeling was crucial to a modern writer's success in her craft, and noted in a notebook while planning her story 'Susannah' (1921), for example, that 'All must be deeply felt.'[23] Virginia Woolf took great exception to these words when she read them in John Middleton Murry's posthumous collection of his dead wife's stories, *The Doves' Nest and Other Stories* (1923),[24] even though she would herself, like Mansfield before her, later be criticised for excessive sentimentality when she achieved greater popularity as a writer.[25] We should note, however, that Mansfield herself was not quite sure of what 'deep feeling' meant for an artist under a dominant aesthetic that devalued the easy expression of emotion. In a 1921 letter to Sydney Schiff on the subject of 'the Artist and his Time', which Mansfield termed 'the Question of Questions', she ended her summation of what art should entail by adding: 'But let me confess, Sydney. I feel something else as well – and that is *Love*. But that's so difficult to explain. It's not pity or rainbows or anything up in the air – Perhaps it's *feeling FEELING FEELING.*'[26] Here Mansfield rejects the easy reduction of Love (with a capital L) as the easy expression of pity or as signified by the conventional Romantic symbol of the rainbow. Instead, she describes it potentially as something that must be *felt*, and thus, as something *internal* to the writer; moreover, she qualifies her definition with a 'Perhaps' to signify her own uncertainty regarding her answer. What *is* love (or 'Love'), if not feeling? Yet how can it be described or named without relying on empty stock signifiers? How do we recognise the reality of the emotional creative subject while simultaneously recognising the pressures acting against them within the modern landscape that place a premium on hiding any feeling which may be easily mocked, or misunderstood, if publicly expressed?

These are the problems repeated time and again within Mansfield's own short stories. She has been repeatedly characterised as a sentimentalist, I would argue, because her stories directly confront the problems of emotional expression in a modern age. Mansfield's stoic protagonist in her story 'The Man Without a Temperament' (1920) is appalled when his seriously ill wife calls him by a childish nickname, 'Boogie': '"Good Lord!" he thinks to himself, "They haven't used that name for years."' He ambiguously whispers '"Rot!"' after listening to her simpering questions about his attachment to her, as if characterising them as decadently sentimental.[27] Yet his very need to express himself this way here (even if *sotto voce*), and his characteristic nervous playing with his signet ring around his finger throughout the narrative, point towards the ambiguous wells of deep feeling buried within him that belie the truth of the story's title. Often Mansfield's protagonists not only are decidedly *with* temperaments but stand in the position of recognising and even giving vent to the depth of their feelings prompted by their circumstances (particularly in the domestic sphere). Yet they also question what exactly these feelings are and how they can describe them or name them.

Such moments of aporia regarding the expression of feeling are perhaps the characteristic scene that most often recurs in all of Katherine Mansfield's fiction. We might think, for example, of the eponymous protagonist of her story 'Mr. Reginald Peacock's Day' (1917), a social-climbing music teacher who, as his name implies, betrays many affectations of dress and also of personal social habits, so as to promote his desirability among his wealthy and sometimes titled clients, whom he flirts with and flatters. Peacock also affects a special way of speaking decidedly at odds with that of his practical and more grounded wife, who stands apart from her husband's attempts to make entries into society. His repetition of his catchphrase 'I should only be too charmed' works wonders with his moneyed clients, but when he decides with his alienated wife 'to have one more try to treat her as a friend, to tell her everything, to win her' at the end of his day, he discovers '[f]or some fiendish reason, the only words he could get out were: "dear lady, I should be so charmed – so charmed!"'[28] Clearly, his pat phrase will not 'charm' her in this context, which is so different from where he usually employs it; his failure to tell his wife 'all the splendid things he had to say' points to the fact that he cannot speak of his feeling any more, except in the insincere register he uses to promote himself.

This becomes a repeated pattern among many of the characters in Mansfield's fiction, where the desire to express oneself transparently is always hampered by fears of the insincerity of emotional expression. We might think here of Beryl writing her letter to Nan Pym in 'Prelude', wondering what would happen if she were really to tell her friend how she felt: 'What rot – what nonsense,' she decides, reviewing her letter. 'It wasn't her nature at all. Good heavens, if she had ever been her real self with Nan Pym, Nannie would have jumped out of the window with surprise.'[29] Or, we might think of her sister, Linda Burnell, in the sequel to 'Prelude', 'At the Bay' (1921), who tries to be honest, even with herself, about what she feels towards her new male baby, as if anxieties about emotional authenticity were always being judged internally as well as otherwise: 'Linda was so astonished at the confidence of this little creature . . . . Ah no, be sincere. That was not what she felt; it was something far different, it was so new so . . . .'[30] Or, we might even think of Bertha Young, trying to find a name for her inner state in 'Bliss' (1918): 'Oh, is there no way you can express [a feeling of bliss] without being "drunk and disorderly"?'[31] Scholars in affect studies, such as Antonio Damasio, have distinguished between the experience of *feeling* an emotion and the cognitive *understanding* of that emotion.[32] Central to Mansfield's fictional project, I argue, is the exploration of the very gap between the two: the exploring of exactly what happens between the somatic experience of feeling, and the naming of that emotion and the judging of its applicability to its circumstances. Her writing reaches to understand not exactly how we know what we feel so much as the necessity and difficulty of trying to name it.

Complicating this, of course, is another key characteristic of Mansfield's characters: their frequent 'performing' of their selves, not only in public but even to themselves in private. Mansfield's critics and biographers have often commented upon this confusion between 'true' and 'false' selves among Mansfield's characters.[33] The experience of emotion (even somatically) does not clarify this frequent confusion, however, but rather almost entirely complicates it even further, for in Mansfield's stories her characters' emotions can be beautifully feigned for the benefit of others (as in the case of her title character in her unfinished 1921 story, 'Widowed') or even for themselves. Here we might think of Isabel in 'Marriage à la Mode' (1921). When her husband becomes demoralised by her factitious new behaviour among her Bloomsbury-like friends, Isabel and these same 'friends', in gales of laughter, critically dismantle William's love lines as if they were only half-heartedly mimetic of true feeling rather than directly expressive of it. Indeed, Isabel, who had been frustrated by their bourgeois life together, had previously dismissed the toys William had purchased for the children's nursery as 'sentimental', and the lines in his lengthy letter ('Pages and pages of it there were') do seem to partake of the sentimental fiction of the era, from his salutation to her as '*My darling, precious Isabel*' to his declaration to her, '*God forbid, darling, that I should be a drag on your happiness.*'[34] One of Isabel's friends, a novelist, even declares, '"You must let me have it just as it is, entire, for my new book [. . .] I shall give it a chapter,"' as if it were so stereotypical that it is ready to be published as fiction.[35] '"I always thought those letters in divorce cases were made up,"' one of them laughs. '"But they pale before this."'[36] Isabel's subsequent reaction against her friends' values, and of her new self as 'shallow, tinkling, vain', is only momentary. She postpones articulating this feeling to William in a letter she writes back to him and rejoins her friends, 'laughing in the new way', as if even her somatic emotive reactions were no longer certain of authenticity, and as if they will work now only so as to betray her own previous thoughts regarding her falsity.[37]

This crisis of determining when emotion is real and how it might best be expressed becomes most extendedly articulated, I would argue, in one of Mansfield's best-known short stories, the much-anthologised 'The Garden Party'. From its opening sentences, the narrator establishes a kind of affected voice that we will find common among the members of the wealthy suburban family whom Elizabeth Bowen dubbed 'the conversational Sheridans'.[38] Indeed, the narrator seems to begin the story in the middle of a kind of conversation with them: 'And after all the weather was ideal. They could not have had a more perfect day for a garden-party if they had asked for it.'[39] As Angela Smith notes, Mansfield often focalises the story's *style indirect libre* through the hyperbolic sociolect the Sheridan women use, particularly among themselves and their peers, while also alternately shifting it towards Laura Sheridan's point of view when she feels more critical towards her sister and her mothers.[40] The fondness of the Sheridans for using the former style of voice is something they indulge in as readily as they do the cream puffs bought for the party from Godber's. One of the more marked instances is when Laura's sister Jose interrupts a rehearsal of a particularly melancholic song about death, 'This Life is Weary', to beam '"Aren't I in good voice, mummy?"' while she signals her hypocrisy by flashing 'a brilliant, dreadfully unsympathetic smile'.[41]

For all that she is censorious of her mother's and sisters' behaviour, we discover Laura herself is not immune to copying their shared mode of speaking, even to the point where she derides herself for speaking to the outdoor workmen for the party in a voice copied from her mother 'that sounded so fearfully affected that she was ashamed'.[42] This voice, we find, is something that she has learned not simply to ape from her mother but to repeat with even further added affectation, so that when Mrs Sheridan tells Laura to relay to her friend Kitty on the phone '"to wear that sweet hat she had on last Sunday"', Laura embellishes the affectation further with added emphasis '"Mother says you're to wear that *sweet* hat you had on last Sunday."'[43] Laura borrows her familial voice not simply by applying such special tones of emphasis but also by employing gushing adjectives and adverbs ('"The passion-fruit ices really are rather special"'), and precious terms of address ('"Daddy darling"').[44] As a young woman, Laura clearly is in the process of learning how and when to use this voice to mark herself appropriately as belonging to the proper class, education and mindset. Even though she can criticise herself for speaking in this idiom, it is one to which she is willing to give herself over when she wishes to identify with her social position.

Only when the news of the accidental death of a workman living in the cottages below the Sheridans' great house makes its way into their kitchen does Laura's voice most decidedly begin to change – as does the voice of the narrator, which begins to echo Laura's own doubts and hesitations about the appropriateness of the party in the face of such catastrophe. The stakes of the ensuing argument among Laura and her sisters and mother are, of course, about the appropriateness of emotional display, as Jose emphasises when she tells her sister, '"I'm every bit as sorry about it as you. I feel just as sympathetic."' Jose then adds a claim which she belies by flashing her significantly 'hardened' eyes, saying, '"You won't bring a drunken workman back to life by being sentimental."'[45]

'Sentimental', of course, is the central operative word for the Sheridans' debate over the workman's death. While a reader might be appalled by their lack of feeling for the dead workman (despite Jose's obviously insincere words to the contrary), by the family's standards it is Laura's feelings that are out of place and excessive. Mrs Sheridan's expostulation that Laura is, indeed, being '"not very sympathetic to spoil everybody's enjoyment as you're doing now"' points to the question of how feeling must be directed in the Sheridans' upper middle-class New Zealand world, where public emotion must be channelled into the proper social pathways.[46] Her decision after the party to send Laura in her fashionable black hat with 'scraps' from the party for the workman's family in many ways could not be more appropriate to the standards of public displays of bereavement championed by her class in the later Victorian and the Edwardian periods. Even the arum lilies which she hopes to send along with Laura, to the latter's horror, would, of course, be the absolutely proper flower at the time for an expression of mourning. But Laura's confusion stems from not knowing what *is* appropriate for her feelings of sympathy with the dead man's family: 'if only it was another hat!'[47] Whatever should be appropriate for expressing solidarity of feeling with the workman's family, she believes, cannot be the sort of ostentatious display of sartorial and floral splendour upon which her mother stakes so much, an exhibition that would assert class difference rather than minimise it.

Laura's questioning of how to express what she feels comes to a head after viewing the dead man's corpse, which seems to suggest an emotional world far from her own:

> He was given up to his dream. What did garden-parties and baskets and lace frocks matter to him? He was far from all those things. He was wonderful, beautiful. While they were laughing and while the band was playing, this marvel had come to the lane. Happy . . . happy . . . . All is well, said that sleeping face. This is just as it should be. I am content.[48]

The narratorial language here significantly changes, eschewing all trace of the Sheridans' love of affected adverbs and intensifiers in favour of an aggregation of simple verbs of being that suggests a newfound sincerity of expression concomitant with Laura's sympathetic epiphany. But Laura's own subsequent reaction to this apparently felicitous serenity is its exact opposite, one of tearful confusion: 'But all the same you had to cry,' the narrator notes, and Laura walks out to the corner of the lane in tears, even as she denies their reality to her brother Laurie (who has gone to meet her). This sense of emotional aporia – of not knowing what to say about what she feels – finds its moment of crisis in her final exchange with her brother, when she fails to find words for her feelings but requests sympathetic assurance all the same:

> Laurie put his arm around her shoulder. 'Don't cry,' he said in his warm, loving voice. 'Was it awful?'
>
> 'No,' sobbed Laura. 'It was simply marvellous. But, Laurie –' She stopped, she looked at her brother. 'Isn't life,' she stammered, 'isn't life –' But what life was she couldn't explain. No matter. He quite understood.
>
> '*Isn't* it, darling?' said Laurie.[49]

There have been two strong critical tendencies in Mansfield scholarship regarding the interpretation of this ambiguous ending. Several scholars have taken the narrator's words here – 'No matter. He quite understood' – at face value, as if Laurie (as Laura's companion in 'prowl[ing]' the village lanes, and her male counterpart, as their similar names suggest) were her secret sharer here. For example, Antony Alpers writes of the story's conclusion, 'As she [that is, Laura] goes back to the house, only her brother understand her feelings,'[50] while Gerri Kimber also finds Laurie's final comment to his sister to be one of empathy: 'He understands; he does not condemn.'[51] We might extrapolate to say that according to this line of reading, since Laura cannot give a name to what life 'is', Laurie only echoes her words back to her sympathetically, creating in effect a verbal tautology: life 'is' what it 'is'. Only the elect and sensitive can know this ineffable truth, and know too that to name it by appending an adjective would only be to cheapen its mysteries, to *sentimentalise* it. But we do not know here which of its alternating possibilities for inflection the narrator uses for 'he quite understood': the voice coincident with the Sheridan sociolect, or that focalised through Laura's consciousness when she is in disagreement with her family. Laurie's very Sheridanian emphasis given to the first word in his response '*Isn't* it, darling?', and his appending of the 'darling' diminutive so favoured by his other family members, suggests it might be the former possibility. Like their sister Jose speaking coldly to Laura earlier in the day, then, Laurie might be affirming sympathy only hypocritically. Thus in recent years several Mansfield critics have often exactly *reversed* other readings of Laurie's final comment, arguing instead that it serves as proof of his emotional obtuseness. Christine Darrohn has termed Laurie's remark 'glib', for example, and posits, 'The truth is by the end of the story Laurie no longer understands Laura because she has been irrevocably changed by her encounter with [the dead workman].'[52] In a similar vein, Angela Smith has argued, 'Since he [that is, Laurie] sounds so much like Mrs. Sheridan he clearly has not quite understood.'[53]

Given these two contrasting but diametrically opposed trends in readings of Laurie's final comments, how can we finally decide whether Laurie truly understands his sister's dilemma or not? Even were we to hear his *tone* of delivery in actuality (something a written story cannot, of course, provide), we still could not know for certain. Earlier, Laurie speaks to his closest sister in extremely affected upper middle-class tones after she asks him if he loves garden parties as much as she does: '"Ra-ther!" said Laurie's warm boyish voice, and he squeezed his sister too, and gave her a gentle push. "Dash off to the telephone, old girl."'[54] But Laura apparently takes this as a sign of her brother's marked sympathy with her instead of a mark of his fatuousness. In the end, the question of whether Laurie 'quite understood' what Laura has gone through in viewing the workman's body cannot be truly verified by her any more truly than she can verify whether the corpse was smiling in sympathy with her, as she believed. Intense feeling, and intense co-feeling (or sympathy), defy and work against their very expression; to name them publicly is always to risk misinterpreting them or misnaming them.

This dilemma is where Mansfield's story positions both us and Laura by the conclusion of 'The Garden Party'. How will she – how *can* she – judge Laurie's claims of sympathy with her, given her own ultimate inability to speak of how she feels to him? How can we? What Mansfield points us to finally is the difficulty in judging expressions of emotion – that terrible and difficult experience of everyday life from which the modernists in Mansfield's cohort so often wished to look away.

Notes

I am grateful to Genevieve Brassard, Rishona Zimring, Gerri Kimber and Todd Martin for their suggestions in my revisions of this article.

1. Chris Mourant, 'Modernist Emotions: The Critical Writings of Katherine Mansfield and Virginia Woolf', in Todd Martin, ed., *Katherine Mansfield and the Bloomsbury Group* (London and New York: Bloomsbury, 2017), pp. 161–80 (p. 175).
2. T. S. Eliot, 'Tradition and the Individual Talent' [1919], in *Selected Prose of T. S. Eliot*, ed. Frank Kermode (San Diego, New York and London: Harcourt Brace & Co., 1975), pp. 37–44 (p. 43).
3. T. S. Eliot to Ezra Pound, 7 November 1922, in *The Letters of T. S. Eliot*, vol. 1, ed. Valerie Eliot (London: Faber & Faber, 1988), p. 592.
4. Leonard Woolf, *Beginning Again: An Autobiography of the Years 1911 to 1918* (New York: Harcourt Brace Jovanovich, 1964), p. 205.
5. Virginia Woolf to Vita Sackville-West, 8 August 1931, in *The Letters of Virginia Woolf*, 6 vols, ed. Nigel Nicolson and Joanne Trautmann (New York and London: Harcourt Brace Jovanovich, 1978), vol. IV, p. 366.
6. Elizabeth Bowen, 'A Living Writer: Katherine Mansfield' (1956), in *The Mulberry Tree: Writings of Elizabeth Bowen*, ed. Hermione Lee (San Diego, New York and London: Harcourt Brace Jovanovich, 1986), pp. 69–85 (p. 79).
7. Katherine Anne Porter, 'The Art of Katherine Mansfield', *Nation*, 145 (23 October 1937), pp. 435–6 (p. 435).
8. See Christopher Isherwood, 'Katherine Mansfield', in *Exhumations: Stories, Articles, Verses* (London: Methuen, 1966), pp. 64–72.

9. For example, Brigid Brophy in 1966 echoes Isherwood's depiction of the two sides to Mansfield's persona by terming her a 'polymorphous poseuse' in her ability to switch affects in her style. See Brigid Brophy, 'Katherine Mansfield's Self-Depiction', *Michigan Quarterly Review*, 5 (Spring 1966), pp. 89–93 (p. 89).
10. Pamela Dunbar, *Radical Mansfield: Double Discourse in Katherine Mansfield's Short Stories* (Basingstoke: Palgrave Macmillan, 1997), p. x. Lee Garver echoes Dunbar's distinction between the '"chocolate box" pieces' and the more serious 'political' fiction pieces: see Lee Garver, 'The Political Katherine Mansfield', *Modernism/modernity*, 8: 2 (2001), pp. 225–43 (pp. 225–6).
11. Virginia Woolf, 7 August 1918, in *The Diary of Virginia Woolf*, 5 vols, ed. Anne Oliver Bell (New York and London: Harcourt Brace Jovanovich, 1977), vol. IV, p. 179; Virginia Woolf to Janet Case, 20 March 1922, in Woolf, *Letters*, vol. II, p. 514.
12. See Aldous Huxley, *Vulgarity in Literature* (London: Chatto and Windus, 1930).
13. See T. S. Eliot, 'The Metaphysical Poets' [1921], in Kermode, pp. 59–67.
14. T. S. Eliot, 'Tradition and the Individual Talent', p. 43.
15. E. M. Forster, 'What I Believe' [1938], in *Two Cheers for Democracy* (1953; rpt New York and London: Harcourt Brace Jovanovich, 1977), p. 73.
16. Suzanne Clark, *Sentimental Modernism: Women Writers and the Revolution of the Word* (Bloomington: Indiana University Press, 1991), p. 2.
17. For more on Woolf's and Mansfield's expression of and regard of emotion in their writings, see Mourant, 'Modernist Emotions'.
18. Eve Kosofsky Sedgwick, *Epistemology of the Closet* (Berkeley: University of California Press, 1990), p. 150.
19. T. S. Eliot, 'Hamlet and His Problems' [1920], in Kermode, pp. 45–9 (p. 48).
20. For more on the history of modernist concerns with the stigma of sentimentality, see Jay Dickson, 'Defining the Sentimentalist in *Ulysses*', *James Joyce Quarterly*, 44: 1 (Fall 2006), pp. 19–38.
21. CW4, p. 282.
22. CW4, p. 139.
23. CW4, p. 375. For more on Mansfield's interest in expressing deep feeling in her private writings (later edited and published by her widower, John Middleton Murry), and how they intersected with the modernist distaste for sentimentality, see Jay Dickson, 'The Last of Katherine Mansfield: The Affective Life in the *Letters* and the *Journal*', in Maria DiBattista and Emily O. Wittman, eds, *Modernism and Autobiography* (Cambridge: Cambridge University Press, 2014), pp. 143–56.
24. See Virginia Woolf, 19 June 1923, in her *Diary*, vol. II, p. 248: 'She [i.e. Mansfield] said a good deal about feeling things deeply: also about being pure, which I won't criticise, though of course I very well could.'
25. See, for example, J. F. Holms, 'Review of *Mrs. Dalloway*', *The Calendar of Arts and Letters*, July 1925, p. 405: 'How [. . .] can such talent co-exist [in *Mrs. Dalloway*] with a sentimentality that would be remarkable in a stockbroker, and inconceivable among educated people?' See also W. H. Mellers, 'Mrs. Woolf and Life', *Scrutiny*, June 1937, p. 72: 'A rudimentary analysis of any characteristic passage [in *The Years*] suffices to prove [. . .] that, shorn of the "original" technique, what Mrs. Woolf has to say about the relationship between her characters, about the business of living, is both commonplace and sentimental.'
26. *Letters* 4, p. 181.
27. CW2, p. 209.
28. CW2, pp. 55–6.
29. CW2, p. 90.

30. CW2, pp. 355–6.
31. CW2, p. 142.
32. See, for example, Antonio Damasio, *The Feeling of What Happens: Body and Emotion in the Making of Consciousness* (New York and London: Harcourt, 1999).
33. See, for example, Antony Alpers, *The Life of Katherine Mansfield* (New York: Viking, 1980), p. 246.
34. CW2, p. 337.
35. CW2, p. 337.
36. CW2, p. 337.
37. CW2, p. 338.
38. Bowen, p. 83.
39. CW2, p. 401.
40. Angela Smith, '"Looking at the party *with* you": Pivotal Moments in Katherine Mansfield's Party Stories', in Kate McLoughlin, ed., *The Modernist Party* (Edinburgh: Edinburgh University Press, 2013), pp. 79–94 (p. 91).
41. CW2, p. 405.
42. CW2, p. 402.
43. CW2, p. 404.
44. CW2, p. 410.
45. CW2, p. 408.
46. CW2, p. 409.
47. CW2, p. 411.
48. CW2, p. 413.
49. CW2, p. 413.
50. Alpers, p. 46.
51. Gerri Kimber, *Katherine Mansfield and the Art of the Short Story* (Basingstoke: Palgrave Macmillan, 2015), p. 83.
52. Christine Darrohn, '"Blown to Bits!": Katherine Mansfield's "The Garden-Party" and the Great War', *Modern Fiction Studies*, 44: 3 (Fall 1998), pp. 513–39 (p. 525).
53. Smith, p. 92.
54. CW2, p. 403.

Dickens, Death and Mary Ann: Katherine Mansfield's 'Life of Ma Parker'

Martin Griffiths

> Our modern attraction to short stories is not an accident of form; it is the sign of a real sense of fleetingness and fragility; it means that existence is only an impression, and, perhaps, only an illusion. A short story of today has an air of a dream; it has the irrevocable beauty of a falsehood; we get a glimpse of grey streets of London or red plains of India, as in an opium vision; we see people, – arresting people, with fiery and appealing faces. But when the story is ended, the people are ended. We have no instinct of anything ultimate and enduring behind the episodes. The moderns, in a word, describe life in short stories because they are possessed with the sentiment that life itself is an uncommonly short story, and perhaps not a true one.
>
> – G. K. Chesterton, *Charles Dickens*[1]

Introduction

My discovery in 2019 of several forgotten stories almost certainly by Katherine Mansfield, including 'The Chorus Girl and the Tariff', drew me towards a reappraisal of *The Garden Party and Other Stories* in the context of theatre.[2] Theatrical, cinematic or performative tendencies in the writings of Mansfield have been examined by Gerri Kimber (2008), Delia da Sousa Correa (2011, 2013), Sarah Sandley (2011), Erika Baldt (2015) and Faye Harland (2020), and Claire Davison notes that, in Mansfield's stories, 'Cinema techniques are transposed back into writing, theatrical monologues and dialogues are re-mediatised as prose.'[3] To take one of many possible examples, the visual clarity of the story 'Millie' – published in the *Blue Review* in 1913 – is partially created by a cinematic cutting and splicing of short phrases: 'and the furniture seemed to bulge and breathe . . . and listen, too. The clock – the ashes – and the venetian – and then again – something else, like steps in the back yard.'[4] Yet with no creative prose by Mansfield pertaining directly to theatre – at least before 1909, when Mansfield was reading G. K. Chesterton's critical study, *Charles Dickens*, and when 'The Chorus Girl and the Tariff' was written – a reappraisal seems timely. To this end, I will examine 'Life of Ma Parker', the sixth story in *The Garden Party* collection, written in Menton, France, in February 1921. It is my thesis that stereotypes in 'Life of Ma Parker' – which is set in London – are consciously chosen aspects of popular theatre and literature, deliberately incorporated by the author from traceable sources.

'Life of Ma Parker'

A claim by Ida Baker (Mansfield's life-long friend) that housekeeper Mrs Bates was the inspiration for Ma Parker is almost impossible to verify.[5] Certainly, letters suggest that the character of Ma Parker was conceived while Mansfield lived in London, and scholars, including Ruth Mantz, name Bates as the model for Ma Parker.[6] After all, the same maid in Chelsea was referred to in a letter dated 13 December 1917: 'Ma Parker yesterday went to my heart. She said suddenly "Oh Miss, you do make the work go easy."'[7] However, John Middleton Murry refers to another Ma Parker at this time: 'As I feared, the Ma Parker arrangement ended in disaster. The next night Mrs Hardwick gave me notice [. . .] But I am really sorry to lose Ma.'[8] In her letters Mansfield uses the term 'Ma' to refer to several housekeepers and/or mother figures, and the name Parker connects with several real and fictitious characters including 'Mr Parky': 'Now I'm going in and I'm going to ask L.M. to make me a tiny fire in my room. Mr. Parky is certainly spending the day.'[9] 'Parky' is a British colloquialism for cold weather; thus, Ma Parker is 'parky' when left out in the cold at the end of the story. A real-life M. A. Parker – Millie Parker from Wellington – claims a different origin for the name:

> So realistic is [Israel Zangwill's] 'Merely Mary Ann' that one feels she must surely have been taken from life, just as K. Mansfield drew from life her pen sketch of 'Ma Parker'. Ma Parker was a well-known personage who lived in Wellington many years ago. I do not recollect ever having met her myself, but she was certainly a charlady of extraordinary qualities, who seems to have left behind her a decided record in her own sphere.[10]

Millie ensured an invitation was sent to Mansfield to accompany the touring party from Wellington to the Ureweras.[11] The journey is the subject of at least five of the Parker stories and articles, including one, titled 'Pickwick, the Premier, and Party', that parodies Dickens's *The Pickwick Papers*,[12] but Mansfield and Parker's shared passion for Dickens existed prior to this trip. Despite the connection, though, it is doubtful that the character of Ma Parker is either Millie Parker or any other Wellington 'personage'. Rather, I contend she is based on theatrical characters, including the main character of *Merely Mary Ann*, which the playwright Israel Zangwill, in turn, appropriated from Charles Dickens.[13] Mansfield, in a letter to Murry dated 12–13 December 1915, refers to a charwoman: 'I rang for Mary Anne to make me a fire but she is evidently gone a junketing for I can't find her.'[14] That Mansfield might have read or seen Zangwill's play, perhaps while living in New Zealand, is suggested by another review that Millie Parker wrote of *Merely Mary Ann*, the same year as Mansfield's letter to Murry. Here Parker refers to the reissue of *Merely Mary Ann* in a cheap paperback edition as 'an old friend come back'.[15]

Parker's direct comparison of *Merely Mary Ann* – which was originally published as a short story and then premiered as a stage play in New York in 1903 – with 'Life of Ma Parker' suggests that she has an ulterior motive: to draw attention discreetly to similarities in the details of the two stories.[16] The similarities are indeed striking. Both works begin and/or end on the threshold or doorstep of an urban house, with the main characters – Ma Parker (or Mary Ann, the housekeeper) and a 'literary gentleman' (or Lancelot, a composer) – in an awkward conversation accentuating their different social status. As the maid/housekeeper toils amongst the detritus of the respective artist's kitchen/bedsit, further exchanges take place. In Zangwill's theatrical version, Mrs Leadbatter tasks Mary Ann with cleaning boots:

MRS LEADBATTER. And who else is hout besides Mr Lancelot?
MARY ANN. The young man from the hospital.
MRS LEADBATTER. The 'Orspital! You country booby!
MARY ANN. The '*Or*spital.
MRS LEADBATTER. Well, you can wait to turn out the gas and lock up. Rosie and me is going to bed. *(takes candle from table.)*
MARY ANN. Yes'm. *(Gapes)*
MRS LEADBATTER. Don't stand opening your mouth like a pillar box. You needn't do the boots to-night.
MARY ANN. Please, mum, I don't mind, if I do them upstairs in my bedroom.
MRS LEADBATTER. What! Are you afraid of the black-beetles?
MARY ANN. No mum, but I can see the moon.
MRS LEADBATTER. The moon! So that's what you've been hup to hall this while – mooning the precious hours away.
MARY ANN. No, mum, the rain did hide the moon, but it's giving over now, and the stars are coming out.[17]

Black beetles, dirty boots, cockney dialogue and a Cinderella-like head-in-the-stars charwoman – 'sitting in the fire-place of a evening you could see the stars through the chimley' – are all transferred directly from Zangwill's story into 'Life of Ma Parker'.[18] Even the image of a gaping pillar-box appears in a Mansfield poem.[19] The character of Ma Parker, then, seems to be a distillation of an aged Mary Ann and Mrs Leadbatter, while the 'literary gentleman' – whom Mansfield does not name – appears to be a combination of Zangwill's Lancelot and Mr O'Gorman, a journalist. An exchange between Mrs Leadbatter and the journalist is typical:

> [O'Gorman] I dare say we lead you the divil of a life between us all. You must feel as if you had seven husbands to mother, each more unreasonable than the other six.
>
> [Mrs Leadbatter] Oh, no, no. Seven lodgers is child's play to one 'usband. And I've buried two.[20]

Ma Parker has only one dead husband and buries seven of her thirteen children: 'if it wasn't the 'ospital it was the infirmary'.[21] Thus 'Life of Ma Parker' is resolutely urban and squalid. Janet Wilson explains the situation: 'Mansfield's critique [in 'Life of Ma Parker'] draws on Edwardian stereotypes of the working class which emphasise its marginality and high mortality by associating their lives with death and mourning.'[22] That 'Mrs Leadbatter is, in *Merely Mary Ann,* referred to as 'Ma' twenty-one times in the script – in the short story of the same name the prefix is never used – shows an attempt, on behalf of Zangwill or his producer, to reinforce these class distinctions and stereotypes. Similarly, the ending of the theatrical version of *Merely Mary Ann,* in which the heroic Mary Ann marries her literary gentleman (she does not in the original story), suggests some concession to such populism.

The published version of the play *Merely Mary Ann* – which, unlike the short story, includes the exchange between Leadbatter and Mary Ann concerning 'black beetles' – may not have been known by Mansfield when she wrote 'Life of Ma Parker'. Rather, she had probably seen a live production of the play in 1904, one featuring Eleanor Robson – the actress also mentioned by Millie Parker in her 1915 review – as Mary, and Ada Dwyer as Mrs Leadbatter. Indeed, the single use of the name 'Mary Ann' for a servant (or a person) in a short story by Mansfield – 'Poor Mummy had to go and tell Mary Ann to say [baby] has suddenly become ill, and hopes that her little friends will be able to come again some other day' – is found only a few months after the September London production in 1904.[23]

Charles Dickens and Theatre

As early as 1892 Israel Zangwill was demonstrating an affinity with the comedic and theatrical potential of the author Charles Dickens's fiction: the former's *Old Maid's Club* presents female equivalents of the bachelors in the 'Pickwick Club' (Dickens's *Pickwick Papers* will be discussed later in this paper), to the extent that the characters even reference the same servant, Mary Ann.[24] Likewise, some of the inspiration for the character of Ma Parker stemmed from characters created by Dickens. During long periods spent in France from 1918 onwards, Mansfield's reading of the British author became fervent. Angela Smith – in her essay 'Mansfield and Dickens: "I am not Reading Dickens *Idly*"' – cites the reading of *Our Mutual Friend* at this time as an integral component in a 'shift [of Mansfield's] writing onto a different plane'.[25] Indeed, Mansfield's interest in Dickens is well documented: critical studies which note such a connection include Edward Wagenknecht (1965), Mary Burgan (1994), Angela Smith (2011), Holly Furneaux (2014), Michael Hollington (2015) and Gerri Kimber (2016). According to Furneaux, Dickens regularly adapted his own writings for public readings and 'saw his characters and narratives as part of a shared cultural imagination'.[26] Mansfield shared a desire to do likewise:

> I intend next Spring to go to London, take the Bechstein Hall and give readings of my stories – I've always wanted to do this [. . .] it would be a great advertisement. Dickens used to do it. He knew his people just as I know old Ma Parker's.[27]

Even from an early age, Mansfield's desire for the performative was tied to Dickens – 'I could make the girls cry when I read Dickens in the sewing class' – and her stage rendition of Mrs Jarley from *The Old Curiosity Shop* and the family recitation of Dickens's *A Christmas Carol*, as well as a debate of the author's relative merits at Queens' College in London, all contained more than an element of theatre.[28] Thus we may say that Mansfield was steeped in his fiction from an early age and absorbed his satirical style in both a written and a spoken, or theatrical, mode.

A recent study by Michael Hollington considers the extent to which both Mansfield and Dickens 'seek tragicomic effects from wholesale deliberate confusion of persons and things',[29] and Kimber's exposé on Mansfield's humour identifies both authors' use of the phonetic rendering of dialects.[30] As signalled by Kimber and Hollington, dialects and idiolects employed by Dickens and Mansfield 'reveal to the reader the type of character who is speaking' and circumvent manners and good taste to reveal the truth.[31] Mansfield's story 'His Little Friend' – written before 1900 but discovered only recently – confirms that the perspective of the child was a very early preoccupation for her. In the story, tearful little Bobbie – who ultimately dies – asks John for help: '"Oh, please sir", he said, "mother's ill and we hasent got nofing to eat."' John provides food and a toy boat, after which the boy replies, '"Oh, Mr Long [. . .] is it weally for me?" [. . .] "Fankshu" [. . .] "and next time you come, Mr Long, I'll have a pweasant for you."'[32] The idiolectic or baby-talk here demonstrates the influence of Dickens's *Oliver Twist,* his second novel and a book reread with fondness by Mansfield many years later.[33] A discussion of the theatrical traditions in *Oliver Twist* concerns tragicomic scene changes that

> appear absurd [but] are not so unnatural as they would seem at first sight. The transition in real life from well-spread boards to death-beds, and from mourning weeds to holiday garments, are not a whit less startling; only, there, we are busy actors, instead of passive on-lookers, which makes a vast difference.[34]

A further example of Dickens's influence – filtered through the lens of theatre – is seen in Mansfield's play *The Laurels,* in which Jane, the 'char-woman', cleans boots (symbolic of her illegitimate parentage) in the hall as she falls in love with the literary gentleman, Mr Tchek.[35] By focusing on the charwoman, Mansfield shows that she could identify with Dickens's 'most awkward' characters and appreciated their capacity to 'live beyond the texts'.[36] However, where Dickens uses conventional theatricality in his texts – with sudden shifts of scene – Mansfield presents a stage play, or, a narrator who *acts* out the story, rather than telling it to us. Thus, in 'Life of Ma Parker', unsignalled changes between first- and third-person narratives allow the narrator – in an experiential sense – to enter the story: 'And for five years Ma Parker had another baby [. . .] and young Jim went to India with the army, and Ethel, the youngest, married a good-for-nothing little waiter who died of ulcers the year little Lennie was born. And now little Lennie – my grandson . . .'.[37] The sense of breathlessness, created by the repetition of the conjunction 'and' – which Davide Manenti identifies as polysyndeton – creates a kind of 'stream of consciousness' in 'Life of Ma Parker'.[38] We can almost feel the urgent delivery of the narration – a free discourse defying grammatical conventions – and as readers, we follow, or at least are invited to follow, the example of the storyteller and *become* the character. This could explain the heightened sense of trauma at the end of 'Life of Ma Parker' – represented, according to Manenti, by the compounding of repetitive thoughts and images (including the frozen, icy wind) as signifiers of impending tragedy.[39] In terms of Dickens's influence on this ending, one might even relate the scissor-legged pedestrians (who ignore the broken Ma Parker upon the death of her grandson) to Mrs Wardle – whose legs are like 'a pair of compasses' – from *The Pickwick Papers.*[40] Interestingly, Smith identifies the influence of the character Alfred Jingle from the same story on Mansfield's 'Je ne parle pas français'.[41] Jingle's mannerism of placing adverbs, such as 'very' and 'warmly', after the verb at the end of a sentence is adopted by Mansfield, in several of her letters.[42] Further, her story 'Bliss', considered to be amongst her finest works, employs the Jingle-like broken style: 'Harry was enjoying his dinner. It was of his – well, not his nature exactly, and certainly not his pose – his – something or other – to talk about food and to glory in his "shameless passion".'[43] Similar passages, sometimes using ellipses instead of dashes, can be found in 'Prelude': 'But, my dear, if you could see Stanley's men from the club . . . rather fattish, the type who look frightfully indecent without waistcoats – always with toes that turn in rather – so conspicuous when you are walking about a court in white shoes.'[44]

'The Urewera Notebook' and The Pickwick Papers

As an adolescent, Mansfield had read Dickens biographies and novels multiple times. In her 'Urewera Notebook', for example, she refers to two books: G. K. Chesterton's *Charles Dickens: A Critical Study* (1906) and William Sharp's *Literary Geography* (1904), which contains a full chapter titled 'Dickens-Land'. Direct quotations from Chesterton are reproduced, in Mansfield's hand, with page numbers.[45] The same notebook contains details of Mansfield's trip to the central North Island of New Zealand, known as the Ureweras, in 1907: hence its title. Mansfield's use of the nicknames 'Fellow Traveller' [F.T.] and 'Mary' (possibly short for 'Mary Ann') in the 'Urewera Notebook' probably refer to Millie Parker.[46]

Parker's contemporaneous 'Pickwick, the Premier, and Party' fictionalises this journey. In the story, the Premier of New Zealand encounters the bumbling Pickwick with his associates – including Mrs Bardell, Mr Tupman, Winkle and Jingle – in the town of Rotorua. A case of mistaken identity creates the opportunity for a farce on an exotic Maori marae (meeting house). The text contains direct quotations from Dickens that would be considered plagiarism today. Though the parody is largely unsuccessful, the adoption of Jingle's broken-style monologue proves the exception: 'Present? Think I was – fired a musket – fired with an idea – rushed into an empty whare – wrote it down – back again – whiz! Bang! – another idea – whare again – pen and ink – back again – cut and slash – noble time, sir.'[47] Though the monologue is not attributed to any particular character, it is clearly in the voice of Jingle and, as such, reinforces the comic element that one would hope for, and expect, from a parody. Mansfield may have had a hand in this, and the new-found literary ambitions of Jingle at the marae seem to represent her compulsive note-taking during the trip. At the very least, she would have probably read Parker's publication and known *The Pickwick Papers*, and thus been familiar with Jingle.

The marriage of servant Mary Winkle and servant Sam Weller creates a prominent thread in Dickens's *The Pickwick Papers*. We know that Mansfield was familiar with the latter character: she imitates him several times when she describes 'cupboards full of wessels'; 'werry good omen' and 'having, like Sam Weller in the Divorce Court, "only a hordinary pair of eyes"'.[48] *The Pickwick Papers*' distinctly unlikeable and embittered Mary Ann Raddle, a sister of Mrs Cluppins and landlady to Bob Sawyer, is not a servant and possibly not even a woman: '"I beg your parding, young man," demanded Mrs. Raddle, in a louder and more imperative tone. "But who do you call a woman?"'[49] Mansfield's adoption of the same animism and cockney accent – '"Beg parding, sir?" said old Ma Parker huskily. Poor old bird! She did look dashed' – provides further evidence of Mansfield's familiarity with Dickens's first novel.[50]

As Melissa C. Reimer asserts, like Dickens, Mansfield 'uses both dashes and ellipses to reinforce the notion of a "slice of life", to suggest momentum, which in turn propels the narrative to subvert readers' expectations by leaving her characters' thoughts unfinished and their questions unanswered'.[51] And in this way the style, if not subject, of the 'Urewera Notebook' is reminiscent of Jingle's broken dialogue in *The Pickwick Papers*: 'This way – this way – capital fun – lots of beer – hogsheads; rounds of beef – bullocks; mustard – cartloads; glorious day – down with you – make yourself at home – glad to see you – very.'[52] Similarly, Mansfield, in the 'Urewera Notebook', uses the dash in lieu of virtually all punctuation: 'Next day walking and bush – clematis & orchids – meet Mary – by the ploughed field – & at last come to the Waipunga falls – the fierce wind – the flax and manuka – the bad roads – camp by the river.'[53] And Mansfield adapts a similar rhythm in 'Life of Ma Parker' in that – even though she does not use the dash – Ma Parker's reaction to Lennie's death is played out, internally as a monologue, in 'real' time:

> But to have a proper cry over all these things would take a long time. All the same, the time for it had come. She must do it. She couldn't put it off any longer; she couldn't wait any more . . . Where could she go? [. . .] But where? Where?[54]

The association of the name Marie with 'servant' is pervasive in Mansfield: Mary-Anne, Mary and Marie are employed as such in both letters and stories. In 'Epilogue I: Pension Seguin' (1913), the servant Marie's 'big red arms' recall the fiery rashes on the arms of Dickens's Mary Anne in *David Copperfield*.[55] Furthermore, her lack of class is noted in a letter: 'I think she [the bonne or maid-servant] is just the person – young, strong, pretty, with black, laughing eyes, a bit grubby, but only de la terre, a kind of Italian Marie of a lower class.'[56] The French servant Marie, in Mansfield's 1920 story 'Revelations', somehow avoids this undesirable earthiness. Servants were inspiration for other Mansfield stories, including the maid Mary in 'Bliss' and the posthumously titled 'Marie and the Cauliflower'. A notebook entry – 'Marie. She is little and grey with periwinkle – I feel inclined to write periwinkle' – reinforces the servile but sympathetic characters again.[57] Presumably, there were also likeable Mary Annes in Britain: Mansfield's idol and cousin, the famous author Elizabeth von Arnim, was, after all, christened Mary Annette Beauchamp.

Animalism in Dickens, Zangwill and Mansfield

The degradation and poverty of the East End of London – with which Zangwill, a descendant of Jewish immigrants, was familiar – anticipates Mansfield's own poverty, as an invalid in war-ravaged France during the First World War. In a sense, Zangwill contemporises the poverty depicted in the novels of Charles Dickens, whereas Mansfield personalises it. Either way, both writers' experiences inform the dialogue and the personalities of their characters, including Mrs Leadbatter, Mary Ann and Ma Parker. Mansfield appropriates the Dickens/Zangwill trope 'Black Beetles' – which is symbolic of that poverty – in her stories 'The Aloe' and 'Prelude': 'To dream of black-beetles drawing a hearse'.[58] Thus death, insects and isolation are linked in Mansfield's fiction. This is reinforced in correspondence of the same period: 'You can't imagine how I feel that I walk alone in a sort of black glittering case like a beetle.'[59]

If the beetle in 'Life of Ma Parker' represents the death of Ma Parker's grandson, the story, as a whole, represents the writer's own pressing mortality. Although Mansfield models her story on Chekhov's short story 'Misery',[58] details of character and symbolism are closer to Dickens's *Bleak House*, in which a beadle – a clergyman's assistant known today as a verger – is involved in the death and burial of Nemo. In 'Life of Ma Parker' Mansfield courts ambiguity by spelling 'beedle'– is it a beetle or a beadle? Dickens makes the association in reverse: though a benign cleric, Bung the beadle, from Dickens's *Sketches by Boz*, is decidedly insect-like by association and at times the beadle in *Nicholas Nickleby*, in his traditional black cassock, scares children.[61] Similarly, Bumble the beadle in *Oliver Twist*, who 'thrashed a boy or two, to keep up appearances', embodies animalistic behaviour.[62] Death and insects are closely associated with each other by Mansfield:

> There's such a sad widower here with four little boys, all in black – all the family in black – as though they were flies that had dropped into milk. There was a tiny girl, too, but she was not fished out again soon enough, and she died.[63]

These similes remind us that people, especially of the lower classes, were regarded as instinctively selfish and base, especially when treated as such.

At times, the animalism has a more explicit religious perspective: Dickens's Mr Smallweed conjures a biblical image when he complains to his wife, 'I am speaking of your brother, you brimstone black-beetle.'[64] Similarly Mansfield, in a letter to Richard Murry dated 9 August 1921, invokes a biblical image of the swarming insects in Egypt: 'There has been a battle of the Wasps. Three hosts with their citadels have been routed from my balcony blind.'[65] In *Barnaby Rudge* – in which Dickens fictionalises the still topical Catholic/Protestant conflict of 1780 – Mr Chester refers to Mr Haredale as 'a fly in the jug [of milk]'.[66] Mansfield had read *Barnaby Rudge* at least twice by 1922, when she wrote 'The Fly': a personal response to the carnage of a later conflict, the First World War.[67] Finally, the symbolism inherent in the death of Mary Ann's canary – namely, the loss of love, romance or marriage – is echoed in Mansfield's 'The Canary' (1922).

Some of the conditions of submission, servitude and unconditional love are tackled in the same way. Like Dickens – whose character Quilp has 'a very dog-like smile' – both Zangwill and Mansfield present people as dogs.[68] In Mansfield's 'After a Succession', Charlie Parker is animalised: 'as if 'e was a little dog [. . .] eager and merry and ready to play – someone who, if you did say a kind word, as good as jumped into the air for joy'.[69] Likewise, Zangwill's Mrs Leadbatter is a dog-like creature on all fours scrubbing the steps, with 'her faded print dress show[ing] like the quivering hide of some crouching animal'.[70] Thus the domesticated dog provides a further opportunity to represent the baseness of humanity, a humanity redeemed to some extent by its ability to serve and show affection.

Impressions, Illusions and Inequalities

The Jingle-like cadence, as presented in Dickens's *The Pickwick Papers* and translated into Mansfield's 'Urewera Notebook', contributed to Mansfield's lasting interest in an economic, experimental and imaginative prose. At the same time, it reinforces Chesterton's 1906 claim that short stories provide a 'real sense of fleetingness and fragility [such] that existence is only an impression, and, perhaps, only an illusion'.[71] Perhaps the New Zealand-born author took his words to heart and worked to fulfil his vision? More likely, both Chesterton and Mansfield recognised in Dickens the vital life-force that allowed characters, events and moments in time to take on a life beyond the limitations of plot. Certainly, Mansfield's debt to Dickens was shared by others, including Zangwill, author of *Merely Mary Ann*. However, where Zangwill's servant Mary Ann is romanticised, Dickens's hapless charwoman of the same name is mocked for her ineptitude. Although Dickens's Mary Anne is, within any single story, only a minor character, her presence in multiple stories, including *David Copperfield*, *Great Expectations* and *The Pickwick Papers*, establishes a significant thread – that of a widely imitated cockney caricature – influential enough to have an impact on Mansfield's 'Ma Parker'.

Unlike Dickens – whose chosen career, before the success of *The Pickwick Papers*, was acting – Mansfield initially wanted to be a musician. However, in England in 1909 she toured as a chorus singer, performed as an actress and entertainer at parties and aspired to read her stories on the stage. If the theatre was a 'den of iniquity' – as Charles Finney, a New York preacher considered it – it was not a spectre of *inequality*, or at least not consistently so.[72]

In 'Life of Ma Parker', inequality – only thinly disguised as satire – between the wealthy patron and the hard-up maid is thematically central. Similarly, Dickens uses the French Revolution as a backdrop to the manners of inequality and prejudice (for instance, in *A Tale of Two Cities*). At other times, theatre provides the ironic twist of inverted snobbery:

> 'I shouldn't care,' said the Daughter of the Father of the Marshalsea, 'if the others were not so *common* [my italics]. None of [. . . the dancers] have come down in the world as we have. They are all on their own level. Common.'[73]

For Mansfield – who herself had 'come down' in the world, both socially and financially since moving permanently to Europe, and who retained to some extent the romantic concept of the 'struggling artist' – the plight of William Dorrit probably resonated.

The characters of Samuel Pickwick, Mary Anne and Alfred Jingle gained international recognition in the popular culture of the nineteenth century, to the extent that one may consider them publicly recognisable characters. Further, in the role of the comic aside and without any impact on plot development, Jingle, the actor, and Mary Ann, the servant, are in essence populist creations: the latter appears as the subject in as many as eleven American songs, in 1868 alone.[74] By incorporating aspects of these characters in her short stories, Mansfield softens our aversion to the oppressed members of the class system in Britain. To this end, Dickens and Israel Zangwill – who was referred to as 'the Dickens of the Ghetto' – provided Mansfield with good 'copy'.[75] Familiar theatrical and literary figures in 'Life of Ma Parker' offer the reader an ugly sample of real life. However, the story of real life is – as the quotation from Chesterton at the start of this article suggests – perhaps 'not a true one'.

If scholars are correct in asserting that Chekhov's story 'Misery', involving the dead child and grieving (grand)parent, provided the scenario for 'Life of Ma Parker', then we must consider whether the inclusion of tropes and themes from 'Merely Mary Ann' compound the argument for the claim of plagiarism or – as is implied by Wilde's assertion that 'talent borrows, genius steals' – complement a narrative which is, in many ways, a unique one.[76] For a writer whose life was, like Chesterton's modernist story, 'uncommonly short', Mansfield was remarkably accomplished. Some credit must, of course, go to Dickens, whose fragmented and fast-moving prose – as presented, for instance, in the character Jingle – was a precursor to modernist traits emerging in the early 1900s. However, Mansfield's successful reframing of Dickens's various Mary Anne characters into that of Ma Parker, in a realistic rather than melodramatic or stereotypical way, clearly shows that her methods were justified. At the very least, the play *Merely Mary Ann* supports the case for the existence, and the seminal importance (for Mansfield's development as a writer), of connections between 'Life of Ma Parker' and the famous British author Charles Dickens.[77]

While Dickens's Mary Anne conforms to the then-current British practice of mocking French revolutionary tendencies, Mansfield's empathetic writing contains a more nuanced characterisation, in her fiction if not in her letters. Broadly speaking, Dickens was a source of inspiration for Mansfield's entire creative life (notwithstanding the specificity of Zangwill's brief influence as well), and her interest in the Victorian author – which began before she left New Zealand in 1903 – first peaked in 1907, during the Urewera trip, when she consciously connected his quest for egalitarianism with her own concern for truth and clarity.[78]

Notes

1. G. K. Chesterton, *Charles Dickens: A Critical Study* (London: Methuen, 1906), pp. 85–6.
2. Katherine Mansfield, *The Garden Party and Other Stories* (London: Constable, 1922). See Martin Griffiths, '"The Chorus Girl and the Tariff" by Katherine Mansfield', in Gerri Kimber and Todd Martin, eds, *Katherine Mansfield and Children* (Edinburgh: Edinburgh University Press, 2021), pp. 127–36.
3. Claire Davison, 'Foreword', in Gerri Kimber, *A Literary Modernist: Katherine Mansfield and the Art of the Short Story* (London: Palgrave Macmillan, 2015), pp. vi–xi (p. ix).
4. CW1, p. 328.
5. Ida Baker, *Katherine Mansfield: The Memories of L.M.* (New York: Taplinger, 1972), p. 105.
6. Ruth Elvish Mantz and John M. Murry, *The Life of Katherine Mansfield* (London: Constable, 1933), p. 331. An apparent connection between Mrs Bates and Ma Parker is also found in a letter from Mansfield to Anne Drey dated 22 December 1917 (*Letters* 1, p. 353).
7. *Letters* 1, pp. 343–5 (p. 344).
8. John Middleton Murry to Mansfield, 13 January 1918, *The Letters of John Middleton Murry to Katherine Mansfield*, ed. C. A. Hankin (London: Hutchinson, 1983), p. 98.
9. *Letters* 3, p. 38.
10. M. A. Parker, 'Old Books' *South Coast Bulletin* (Southport, Qld), 11 October 1929, p. 11.
11. Margaret Amelia 'Millie' Parker (c. 1882–1965) was a piano teacher and amateur writer. Her frequent contributions to Australasian newspapers – mainly essays, news and gossip – began while she was still in Wellington and continued until a year before her death.
12. M. A. Parker, 'Pickwick, the Premier, and Party', *Red Funnel* (Dunedin, New Zealand), 1 December 1907, pp. 337–44. As well as the Dickens parody of 1907, Parker published four further accounts of her journey: 'The Sphinx' and 'A Little Wild Horse', published in *New Zealand Herald Supplement* (Auckland), 12 May 1928, pp. 7, 11, and 11 October 1930, p. 4, respectively; 'No Water' and 'Close To History: A Summer Day in 1907' were published in *New Zealand Herald*, 21 March 1931, p. 4, and 4 April 1931, p. 6, respectively.
13. Israel Zangwill, *Merely Mary Ann: Comedy in Four Acts* (London: Samuel French, 1921).
14. *Letters* 1, p. 209.
15. M. A. Parker, 'Two Marys by M.A.P', *Daily Telegraph* (Sydney), 28 April 1915, p. 6.
16. The original short story, 'Merely Mary Ann', was published in Zangwill's *The Grey Wig: Stories and Novelettes* (New York: Macmillan, 1903).
17. Zangwill, *Merely Mary Ann*, p. 11.
18. CW2, p. 294.
19. CW3, p. 43.
20. Zangwill, *Merely Mary Ann*, p. 8.
21. CW2, p. 294.
22. Janet Wilson, 'Economic Women: Money and (Im)mobility in Selected Stories by Katherine Mansfield', in Aimee Gasston, Gerri Kimber and Janet Wilson, eds, *Katherine Mansfield: New Directions* (London: Bloomsbury, 2020), pp. 191–206 (p. 197).
23. 'Your Birthday', CW1, pp. 22–4. The London production at the Duke of York's Theatre ran from 8 September to 15 December 1904. See J. P. Wearing, *The London Stage 1900–1909: A Calendar of Productions, Performers, and Personnel* (Lanham, MD: Scarecrow, 2013), p. 199.
24. Israel Zangwill, *The Old Maid's Club* (New York: Tait, Sons & Co., 1892), p. 134.

25. Angela Smith, 'Mansfield and Dickens: "I am not Reading Dickens *Idly*"', in Gerri Kimber and Janet Wilson, eds *Celebrating Katherine Mansfield: A Centenary Volume of Essays* (London: Palgrave Macmillan, 2011), p. 194.
26. Holly Furneaux, '(Re)writing Dickens Queerly: The Correspondence of Katherine Mansfield', in Ewa Kujawska-Lis, ed., *Reflections on/of Dickens* (Cambridge: Cambridge Scholars Press, 2014), pp. 121–35 (p. 125).
27. Letter to Ida Baker, 30 April 1922, *Letters* 5, p. 160.
28. See Gerri Kimber, *Katherine Mansfield: The Early Years* (Edinburgh: Edinburgh University Press, 2016), pp. 74 and 138, respectively, and Redmer Yska, *A Strange Beautiful Excitement* (Dunedin: Otago University Press, 2017), p. 212.
29. Michael Hollington, 'Mansfield Eats Dickens', in Melinda Harvey and Sarah Ailwood, eds *Katherine Mansfield and Literary Influence* (Edinburgh: Edinburgh University Press, 2014), pp. 155–67.
30. Gerri Kimber, *A Literary Modernist: Katherine Mansfield and the Art of the Short Story* (London: Palgrave Macmillan, 2015).
31. Kimber, *Literary Modernist*, p. 53.
32. Yska, pp. 221–2.
33. See letter to John Middleton Murry, 19 December 1915, *Letters* 1, p. 218.
34. Charles Dickens, *Oliver Twist* (Oxford: Oxford University Press, 1966), p. 106.
35. CW2, pp. 5–9.
36. Furneaux, p. 125.
37. CW2, p. 295.
38. Davide Manenti, 'Unshed Tears: Meaning, Trauma and Translation', in Claire Davison, Gerri Kimber and Todd Martin, eds, *Katherine Mansfield and Translation* (Edinburgh: Edinburgh University Press, 2015), pp. 63–75 (pp. 66–8).
39. Manenti, p. 66. A change of weather in Mansfield's 'After a Succession' (CW2, pp. 297–300) is similarly symbolic: in this case, signalling the fall from grace of Ma Parker's son, Charlie (he is accused of stealing). Though no timeline can be established, one could confidently assert that 'After a Succession' was written before 'Life of Ma Parker'.
40. Charles Dickens, *The Pickwick Papers* (Oxford: Clarendon Press, 1986), p. 452.
41. Smith, p. 198.
42. 'very', *Letters* 5, p. 12 and p. 157; and 'warmly', *Letters* 5, pp. 295–6.
43. CW2, p. 148.
44. CW2, p. 89.
45. Alexander Turnbull Library, qMS-1244, p. 39a. See also Anna Plumridge, ed., *The Urewera Notebook by Katherine Mansfield* (Dunedin: Otago University Press, 2015), p. 91.
46. Millie Parker was not – despite reports to the contrary – a relation of Robert Parker, Katherine Mansfield's piano teacher. See Margaret Parker, 'The Apron Strings Were Snapping in All Directions', *Dominion*, 4 April 1964, p. 9.
47. M. A. Parker, 'Pickwick, the Premier, and Party', p. 538.
48. *Letters* 4, p. 36; Katherine Mansfield, 'The Nostalgia of Mr. D. H. Lawrence', CW3, p. 716, respectively.
49. Dickens, *Pickwick Papers*, p. 481.
50. CW2, p. 292.
51. Melissa C. Reimer, 'Katherine Mansfield: A Colonial Impressionist' (unpublished doctoral thesis, University of Canterbury, 2010), p. 57.
52. Dickens, *Pickwick Papers*, pp. 100–1.
53. Plumridge, p. 91.

54. CW2, p. 297.
55. Charles Dickens, *David Copperfield* (Oxford: Oxford University Press, 1948), p. 634.
56. *Letters* 3, p. 10.
57. CW4, p. 350.
58. CW2, p. 83. See also 'The Aloe', CW1, p. 504, and 'Poison', CW2, p. 257: 'There he is – look – like a blue beetle.'
59. *Letters* 2, p. 55.
60. See Joanna Woods, *Katerina* (London: Penguin, 2004), pp. 207–8, and Anton Chekhov, *The School Mistress and Other Stories*, ed. Constance Garnett (New York: MacMillan, 1921), pp. 55–66.
61. Bung the beadle appears in Chapter 4 of 'Our Parish' in Dickens's *Sketches by Boz* (Oxford: Oxford University Press, 1957), vol. 1, pp. 21–8. See also Dickens's *Nicholas Nickleby* (Oxford: Oxford University Press, 1981), pp. 645–6. Dickens's *David Copperfield* and *Our Mutual Friend* also refer to 'beadles'.
62. Dickens, *Oliver Twist*, p. 33.
63. *Letters* 2, p. 120.
64. Charles Dickens, *Bleak House* (New York: Norton, 1977), pp. 411–12.
65. *Letters* 4, p. 262.
66. Charles Dickens, 'Barnaby Rudge', in *Oxford Illustrated Dickens* (Oxford: Oxford University Press, 1954), p. 115. See also Katherine Mansfield, 'The Fly', CW2, pp. 476–80.
67. *Letters* 2, p. 16.
68. Charles Dickens, *The Old Curiosity Shop* (Oxford: Oxford University Press, 1951), p. 37.
69. CW2, pp. 297–300, p. 299.
70. Zangwill, *The Grey Wig*, pp. 314–445.
71. Chesterton, p. 85.
72. See Jeanne Halgren Kilde, *When Church Became Theatre* (Oxford: Oxford University Press, 2002), p. 29.
73. Charles Dickens, *Little Dorrit* (Oxford: Clarendon Press, 1979), p. 231.
74. Henry De Marsan, *Henry De Marsan's New Comic and Sentimental Singer's Journal* (New York: Henry De Marsan, 1868), pp. 7–8.
75. Emanuel Elzas, 'Israel Zangwill: A Sketch', *San Francisco Call*, 25 August 1895, p. 16.
76. See Saralyn R. Daly, *Katherine Mansfield* (New York: Twayne, 1965), p. 91, and Vincent O'Sullivan, 'What we mostly don't say about Katherine Mansfield', in Charles Ferrall and Jane Stafford, eds, *Katherine Mansfield's Men* (Wellington: Katherine Mansfield Birthplace Society, 2004), pp. 96–105 (p. 97).
77. See Antony Alpers, *The Life of Katherine Mansfield* (New York: Viking Press, 1980), p. 155.
78. In the 'Urewera Notebook', a definition of egalitarianism is quoted directly from Chesterton's *Charles Dickens: A Critical Study*. See CW4, p. 86.

'Passion in Movement': Katherine Mansfield – Gesture, Motion and Dance

Richard Cappuccio

In Katherine Mansfield's story 'At the Bay' (1921), Pip imagines finding an emerald while digging in the sand: 'The lovely green thing seemed to dance in [. . . his] fingers'; later in the story, Mansfield repeats the metaphor to describe Linda Burnell with 'tears [that] danced in her eyes' and a photo of Mr Kember that shows him to be 'a perfect dancer'.[1] Mansfield's writing records not just her interest in dance, but the meaning she finds through movement. Antony Alpers conjectures that some of her earliest, emotionally honest private writings occur after 'an incident following a ball [at which] Kathleen sat out a dance with one of her partners and an adventure followed'.[2] She reminds herself at the time to 'Be strong, be kind, be wise [. . .] Be more than woman.'[3] As will be shown here, Mansfield integrated dance that she saw performed and represented in visual arts as a trope to examine women's inner lives; her observations of movement and gesture culminate with two important stories which connect the body in motion and epiphany: 'Her First Ball' (1921) and 'Marriage à la Mode' (1921), both published in *The Garden Party and Other Stories* (1922). These stories stress the modern woman's need for strength and wisdom as they invite the reader to observe women through movement. Mansfield goes beyond a simple metaphor of dance; instead, she builds on her early writings and life-long influences to choreograph her stories and to vivify her letters. In the face of static, societal expectations, Mansfield affirms self-expression through dance, movement and gesture.

Mansfield expresses an expanded awareness of the interrelation of dance, music and writing after she returns to London in 1908: she links the nuances of artistic expression under the umbrella of the word 'tone'. In a letter to Garnet Trowell after a music recital she had heard, she writes, 'I am staggered by [. . . the pianist's] playing, by her tone, which is the last word in tonal beauty and intensity and vitality.'[4] Shortly afterwards, Mansfield saw Maud Allan dance in her *Vision of Salome* at the Palace Theatre of Varieties, and Mansfield links her goals as a writer with her understanding of tone because of Allan's intensity and vitality on stage: 'I have a strange ambition [. . .] It is to write – and recite what I write[.] *Tone* should be my secret – each word a variety of tone [. . .] I would like to be the Maud Allen [*sic*] of this Art.'[5] Mansfield knows that, for Trowell, 'tone' has a musical meaning, but she expands the word to include visual shading and colour: she explains, 'As [. . . Allan] dances, under the changing lights [. . .] she seems to sum up the appeal of everything that is passing, and coloured.'[6] Mansfield's inclusion of movement and iridescence to her use of the word tone sets the stage for incorporating the subtleties of dance in her writing.

Allan was, like Mansfield, a trained musician, but it was as a self-trained dancer that she became the talk of London in 1908; she performed as part of a music-hall programme of singers, comedians, a juggling act and even the horse Princess Trixie, 'The only animal in the world known to be possessed of responsive intelligence'.[7] Within a short time, however, Allan headlined the matinees at which she danced to Mendelssohn's spritely 'Spring Song' and Chopin's sombre 'Funeral March', selections that indicate the range of musical tone that inspired her. It was Allan's performance as Salome, however, to which her audience, critics and Mansfield responded. Contemporary reviews speak of Allan's innovations, which set the stage for women's free expression that would help define *Ausdruckstanz*, early twentieth-century expressionist dance. Many early reviewers pronounced this as a return to a classical tradition. The London *Observer* praises her as 'a reincarnation of the most graceful and rhythmic forms of classical Greece' whilst admitting one important difference: Allan adds 'exquisite movement [. . . rather than] the frozen forms in which they appear on Greek vases and reliefs'.[8] W. R. Titterton reviewed Allan in *The New Age*, which gave her a banner headline on page one: Titterton writes of Allan's 'free dancing [. . . with] its twin obsessions of sensual provocation and mechanical gymnastics'.[9] Titterton is confused by the contradiction of Allan's dance, an art that he thinks, like many of his contemporaries, harkens 'back to the grace, dignity and universality of the Greek' but at the same time 'past the limits of decency'.[10] Allan, today, is valued as a pioneer of self-expression for performing barefoot, bareheaded and bare-armed in the new style of Isadora Duncan. For her *Vision of Salome*, Allan discarded her 'classical' dress, adding instead a seductive costume that she designed, a shocking prop head of John the Baptist, and original music by Maurice Reny. The result was a 'Salomania' in Britain nearly two years before the London premiere of Richard Strauss's opera in December of 1910. For over a year, Allan dominated the London music-hall stage, catching the attention of both general audiences and sophisticated critics.[11]

Allan's effect on Mansfield is immediate; after the performance she writes of a new vision to 'revolutionise and revive the art of elocution'.[12] Mansfield describes 'the conventional reciter [as . . .] stiff – affected – awkward', words that would be a harsh condemnation not just for any performer but also for a writer.[13] Jeanne Beauchamp offers a relevant observation about her sister's creative process: 'Katherine was herself a performer. She would look on [. . .] as one pro would take tips from another [. . .] She was a natural entertainer.'[14] Mansfield articulates an important element of her craft that she had previously recognised only in music; her new desire 'to study *tone* effects' comes simultaneously with seeing Allan. Mansfield writes with confidence, 'I know I possess the power of holding people. [. . .] there's a big opening for something sensational and new in this direction – – – – – [.]'[15] Mansfield's deliberately elongated pause at the end of this sentence is a stylistic experiment in tone itself: it can be read as the musician slowly bowing the cello, the dancer holding a pose, or the moment of tense silence after any staged performance or reading.

Mansfield's Early Experiments Incorporating Dance

In a second letter to Garnet Trowell in which she discusses Allan, Mansfield includes 'The Winter Fire', a poem in blank verse which responds to the impact of seeing *Salome*:

> The firelight spins a web of shining gold
> Sears her pale mouth with kisses passionate
> Wraps her tired body in a hot embrace.
> [. . .]
>   And oh, the sun
> That kisses her to life and warmth again
> So she is young, and stretches out her arms.[16]

Mansfield's diction evokes Salome's passion and a dancer's movements: 'spins', 'stretches' and 'wraps her [. . .] body in a hot embrace'. The poem ends as a performance does: after the curtain drops, 'red ashes crumble into grey', and the reader moves from the theatre to 'the street, [and hears] a burst of sound / a Barrel organ [. . . in the] hiccoughing voice of London'.[17] The music and atmosphere of the theatre disperse quickly amid the urban noise; live music gives way to the harsh mechanical tones of a barrel organ.

Maud Allan appears through an imitator in 'The Luftbad', first published in *The New Age* in 1910, nine months before Strauss's opera premiered in London.[18] The story opens with women confined in a spa 'enclosure' but exposed and vulnerable, 'very nearly "in their nakeds"'.[19] While the setting probably reflects one Mansfield observed in Bad Wörishofen in 1909, the absence of green growth around the 'collection of plain, wooden cells' is an early mark of Mansfield's attention to tone in her writing, as she said she would incorporate it, after seeing the *Vision of Salome*: deprived of nature, these women are static and lack freedom in a colourless environment. The narrator is uncomfortable in her body and feels imprisoned: 'On the first day I was conscious of my legs, and went back into my cell three times to look at my watch'. Other women appear comfortable with restraints: a 'Hungarian lady' enjoys free time in her dead husband's vault that 'makes such a pleasant excursion for a fine Saturday afternoon'.[20] However, there is a 'young Russian' with a contemporary awareness:

> 'Can you do the "Salome" dance?' she asked. 'I can'.
>
> 'How delightful', I said.
>
> 'Shall I do it now? Would you like to see me?'
>
> She sprang to her feet, executed a series of amazing contortions for the next ten minutes, and then paused, panting, twisting her long hair.
>
> 'Isn't that nice?' she said.[21]

Having witnessed such freedom, the narrator takes to an unused swing against the warning of one woman: '"to swing is very upsetting for the stomach [. . .] A friend of mine could keep nothing down for three weeks after exciting herself so."'[22] Such an admonition cannot dissuade the narrator from feeling her body in motion: despite having said 'There are no trees in the "Luftbad",' she climbs on to a swing and, inspired by nature outside the walls, experiences a sensory freedom: 'From the pine forest streamed a wild perfume, the branches swayed together, rhythmically sonorously. I felt so light and free and happy – so childish!'[23] The cool and sweet air she experiences in motion matches her feelings as she embraces a new vision of herself. The title of the story focuses on this elemental and physically liberating act. Mansfield's narrator finds herself bathed in the air; rejecting the earth, unlike the man '"in the Luftbad next door [. . . who] buried himself up to the armpits in mud"', she allows herself the freedom of her body that she witnessed with the Salome dancer. The narrator moves freely to the rhythm of the natural world, 'not in the least ashamed' and newly empowered.[24]

Revisiting Personal Freedom through Dance in 'Her First Ball'

Mansfield revisits these ideas about freedom in movement in 'Her First Ball'. In the opening, Leila is constrained by her lack of worldliness: she naively imagines that 'her first real partner was the cab' and hears a staid triple metre in 'waltzing lamp-posts' that she passes.[25] Those two images are replaced by the poly-rhythmic world of the dance: Leila's card includes a measurable waltz and polka. However, Mansfield adds complexity with the spontaneous rhythms at the venue: 'A great quivering jet of gas lighted the ladies' room. It couldn't wait; it was dancing already. [. . . A] burst of tuning [. . .] leaped almost to the ceiling.'[26] Mansfield's diction – 'quivering', 'dancing', 'burst' and 'leaped' – contrasts not just with the mechanical rhythm of the cab and the imagined waltz of inanimate lamp-posts but highlights her expanded definition of tone that includes light and rhythm. The sounds and lights also contrast with the stillness to which Leila had retreated before leaving the house, when 'in the middle of dressing she had sat down on the bed [. . . and longed] to be sitting on the verandah'.[27] Claudia Tobin emphasises that 'Stillness is always the starting point for dance. [. . . Margaret Morris and Rudolph Steiner] draw on *Gesamtkunstwerk* [the totality of the art] and take sculpture, the static art form, as a reference point for dance.'[28] 'Quivering', a word Mansfield uses twice in a short interval, marks that moment of strained stillness before movement, which ushers in the new experiences that Leila must navigate.

Leila becomes transfixed by the intricate blend of rhythm and the power of movement after 'the fat man' writes his name on her dance card: 'He was tossed away on a great wave of music that came flying over the gleaming floor breaking the groups up into couples, scattering them, sending them spinning . . . .'[29] Lest there be any doubt that this image of the overwhelming force of the sea reflects Leila confronting personal control, note the distinct echo of a letter from Mansfield to Virginia Woolf, focusing on both her stillness and her desire for movement: 'the machine is a thoroughly unsound machine and wont stand a journey [. . .] And your letter promised such exciting things – a kind of sober walking by the sea with sudden immense waves of conversation scattering us, or flinging us together.'[30] Mansfield contrasts the 'unsound machine' of her body that restricts her to the forceful movements of the sea and the dramatic crescendos with which she defines her creative power.

Mansfield wrote 'Her First Ball' in July 1921, over a decade after Allan performed her *Vision of Salome*, but Allan was recently back in the news, having returned to London to perform in Oscar Wilde's *Salome*.

Although Wilde's play was still banned in theatres, it could be produced for private performances. Noel Pemberton-Billing, a Member of Parliament, attacked the production in his right-wing newspaper *Vigilante,* whose masthead proclaimed that it was 'in the interest of purity in public life'.[31] The fat man's role as a self-appointed policeman of Leila's sexuality suggests the newspaper headlines involving Maud Allan that Mansfield read the previous month.

In February 1918, Pemberton-Billing published a piece, 'The Cult of the Clitoris', which identified Allan as both a lesbian and a German conspirator, whose goal was to normalise and promote homosexuality in England. Pemberton-Billing claimed that Germany held the names of 47,000 British homosexuals, many of whom would have subscribed to Allan's two private performances of Wilde's *Salome.*[32] Allan sued Pemberton-Billing for criminal libel, and in June, Mansfield wrote to John Middleton Murry,

> What about this Billingsgate trial? Is it going to topsy-turvy England into the sea – What Ultimate Cinema is this. It is very nauseating – I feel a great sympathy for Maud Allen – but I have not seen much of the trial – only Daily News without tears.[33]

Pemberton-Billing's defence connected Allan's portrayal of Salome with the conviction of her brother, years earlier and a continent away, for the murder of two women in San Francisco and 'outraging them after death', as evidence of a heredity predisposition for sadism.[34] The defence further justified its position that Allan's performance of 'an obscene and indecent character' would promote 'unnatural practices among women'; when Allan admitted she knew the meaning of the word 'clitoris', Pemberton-Billing 'claimed that only those who were familiar with lesbianism or other "sadist" perversions knew the term'.[35] Mansfield again wrote to Murry when Alfred Douglas, Wilde's former lover, gave testimony as a witness for Pemberton-Billing: 'Nice lookout for Art when Billing is pelted with flowers and Lord A. D. our conquering Hero. I feel very sorry for poor Maud Allen.'[36] Mansfield's sympathy for Allan speaks to the injustice but also suggests Mansfield's continued awareness of and admiration for Allan, the artist. Much as had happened to Wilde two decades earlier, Allan became the target, and Pemberton-Billing emerged victorious, effectively ending Allan's career as a dancer on the British stage.

The spectre of the Pemberton-Billing affair haunts 'Her First Ball': empathy lies with Leila when the 'fat man' attempts to assert dominance over her with a bold and malicious prophecy summoning up the minor musical tones of Chopin's 'Funeral March', to which Allan performed in dark robes: '"Kind little lady [. . .] you'll be sitting up there on the stage looking on, in your nice, black velvet. And these pretty arms will have turned into little short fat ones, and you'll beat time with such a different kind of fan – a black bony one"'.[37] Leila considers retreat, but unlike Allan, who was brought down at trial, Leila returns to the dance floor and, much like the narrator in 'The Luftbad', experiences a triumphant epiphany, empowered with her body in motion. She forgets not only her antagonist's prophecy but the prophet himself; when she bumps into him, she does not recognise him. In the story's closing lines, Leila continues, comfortable in her body and free in her movement: her 'feet glided, glided'.[38] Mansfield elevates social dance from a couple's activity into an individual's transformation towards physical and personal freedom in line with the age's female solo champions of artistic expression – Allan, Duncan, Loie Fuller and Grete Wiesenthal.[39]

Mansfield's Reaction to an Effort by D. H. Lawrence and the Art of Raquel Meller

Murry recounts that Mansfield was sensitive to what she saw as a failed attempt by D. H. Lawrence to integrate dance in his novel *The Rainbow* (1915); Murry candidly admits, 'neither of us liked *The Rainbow* and Katherine quite definitely hated parts of it – in particular the scene where Anna, pregnant, danced naked before the mirror'.[40] In light of Mansfield's compressed style, that scene is wordy and simplistic in linking pregnancy to a heavenly event: Anna finds bliss first in the circular dancing of the saved in

> a cheap print from Fra Angelico's 'Entry of the Blessed into Paradise'. [. . .] The beautiful, innocent way in which the Blessed held each other by the hand as they moved towards the radiance, the real, real, angelic melody, made her weep with happiness.[41]

Lawrence connects this image to his own romanticised vision:

> Big with child as she was, she danced there in the bedroom by herself, lifting her hands and her body to the Unseen, to the unseen Creator who had chosen her, to Whom she belonged. [. . . S]he took off her clothes and danced in the pride of her bigness.[42]

Mansfield could only have been critical of this passage that culminates in a celebration of pain rather than freedom. When giving birth, Anna declares herself *victrix*:

> Even the fierce, tearing pain was exhilarating. She screamed and suffered, but was all the time curiously alive and vital. She felt so powerfully alive

> and in the hands of such a masterly force of life, that her bottom-most feeling was one of exhilaration. She knew she was winning, winning, she was always winning, with each onset of pain she was nearer to victory.[43]

By the time Mansfield read this, her experiences when pregnant did not match Lawrence's vision. She had also published 'Frau Brechenmacher Attends a Wedding' (1910), in which she, unlike Lawrence, explored dance's relationship to social constraints on women: the bride, already the mother of a 'free-born' child, has her final opportunity to dance under the solemn eyes of her own mother, who looks 'suspiciously at each man who danced with her'.[44] The other married women also watch but do not dance. Frau Brechenmacher, a mother of five, sits 'Wedged in between [. . .] two fat old women [. . . with] no hope of being asked to dance'.[45] The story stands witness to the power men claim in controlling women's movement and 'to heave and sway with laughter' at the thought of a woman's freedom.[46] Mansfield sums up women's status with the crude 'gift', a miniature 'baby's bottle and two little cradles holding china dolls', with which the male guests taunt the bride to remind her of the real reason for the marriage.[47] This early story, in contrast to Lawrence's vision, accentuates a rude awakening for women. In the final lines, Frau Brechenmacher 'lay down on the bed and put her arm across her face like a child who expected to be hurt'; anticipating the violence to follow, Frau Brechenmacher is static with fear.[48] Mansfield warns of the dark experiences that constrain women who do not have freedom of movement and control of their bodies, a constraint the young Leila challenges in 'Her First Ball' when she rejects the prediction of the story's male prophet.

When Mansfield, in a late letter, writes that she 'never really cared for dancing', she must have meant engaging in social events rather than attending dance performances.[49] Her brother-in-law, Richard Murry, recounts going with Mansfield 'to the ballet and the music hall'.[50] Mansfield's sensitivity to movement as a trope of personal insight and empowerment was not limited to seeing Maud Allan on the music-hall stage. In addition, Mansfield focused on the artistry with which others incorporated movement into their work. Richard Murry, in a radio interview, stressed that Mansfield 'was extraordinarily keen on Raquel Meller. Everything had to stop [. . .] when Raquel Meller came along' in 1920.[51] Today, Meller, like Allan, is largely forgotten, but contemporary reviews praise her for a combination of music, literary sensibility, and choreographed elements of her performance: in the *Athenaeum*, which John Middleton Murry edited, he had written glowingly about Meller, comparing her presence to Keats's poetry and mailed his essay to Mansfield, who was in Menton.[52] On returning to London the following month, she wrote to

Violet Schiff that 'When Murry *speaks* of [. . . Meller], she sounds wonderful.'[53] Aldous Huxley's review of Meller in the *Athenaeum* adds details that are important to the understanding of Mansfield's enthusiasm, more than listening to Meller's surviving recordings. Huxley stresses the importance of her movements: when 'Meller glided in like a swan', it changed the evening from one of 'post-prandial apathy' to an evening that 'was apocalyptic [. . .] watching her as she moved with gestures gradual or abrupt, gestures of an incomparable dignity and tragic grace, I understood, as I had never done before the whole beauty and enchantment of the romantic'.[54] Huxley's exuberant praise links Meller's movements to the stage, film, and the *Ballets Russes*:

> Like all good actors, Raquel Meller relies mostly on gesture. As all that she says and sings is in Spanish, her performance is, for most of us, virtually a dumb show. It is by miming that she makes her principal appeal. Excellence in miming is the supreme quality of good acting. Unless an actor can convey, by gesture and expression, as much as Charlie Chaplin [. . .] he is hardly worth going to see. I have good hopes that the cinema in general and Charlie Chaplin in particular, with the aid of the Russian ballet, may create a new school of Significant Gesture.[55]

Huxley sees a blend of the popular and the high arts as a new approach to movement; Mansfield would have probably known Huxley's views, either from reading or from conversations with him at Garsington, the country manor of Lady Ottoline Morrell. His capitalisation, which emphasises the final two words, aligns with Mansfield's thoughts that 'gesture is another art'.[56]

Mansfield's mastery of gesture plays significantly in 'At the Bay' in the scene when Pip shows off his 'nemeral':

> Pip took something out of his pocket, rubbed it a long time on the front of his jersey, then breathed on it and rubbed it again.
>
> "Now turn round!" he ordered.
>
> They turned round.
>
> "All look the same way! Keep still! Now!"
>
> And his hand opened; he held up to the light something that flashed, that winked, that was a most lovely green.[57]

Unseen by those near him, Pip's gesture of taking his find out of his pocket is elongated by polishing it, twice, before ordering Isabel, Kezia and Lottie to spin around to view it: the tone of the girls' amazement is amplified with the lighting effects that Mansfield adds. Pip's simple gestures are accompanied by his authoritarian position, the dance master ordering his group to spin and then hold a position. Mansfield stages the scene and holds her audience, as she predicted she could, in a scene that is both spontaneous and choreographed.

Degas's Modernism as Another Inspiration for Mansfield

Mansfield's genius for capturing movement can be traced to one last influence: Richard Murry recalls that, on 'visits to the galleries', Mansfield's 'great favourite, of course, was Degas', an artist who is synonymous with dance.[58] Mansfield confirms her ongoing interest in Degas in a letter to Richard from Montana-sur-Sierre in January 1922: 'I noted the Degas show was coming. I hope it's a good one. Tell us more about the pastels WHEN you are in the mood.'[59] Degas, like Mansfield, drew portraits of his characters with a seemingly fleeting glance, but Paul Valéry, a friend of both Mansfield and Murry, understood Degas's literary sensibility: 'he could have been, if he had given himself wholly to it, a most remarkable poet'.[60]

In both his art and his writings, Degas expresses a proto-modernist outlook about art and memory: 'you [should] reproduce only what has struck you, that is, the essential; in that way, your memories and your imagination are liberated from the tyranny that nature holds over them'.[61] In a notebook, Mansfield records a similar perspective from Prosper Mérimée:

> The artist becomes an artist by the intensification of Memory – extraneous. It is the clear sighted sensitiveness of a man who watches human things closely, bringing them home to himself with the deliberate essaying art of an actor who has to represent a particular passion in movement![62]

In recording this observation, Mansfield links the importance of memory to movement. Mansfield's poetic is in line with Degas's aesthetic that 'Nothing in art should resemble an accident, even movement.'[63] This shared idea is especially evident in her story 'Marriage à la Mode' (1921): the dissolution of William's and Isabel's marriage operates with an important integration of the characters' movements and gestures both in and outside the chronology of the story. The opening lines contrast William, dutifully walking on 'his way to the station' with the haunting memory of the disappointed reaction of his children after 'they ran to greet him'.[64] Readers might look for them later in the story, but while the children remain an important part of the composition, they are always off stage. Degas often demonstrates the same technique: for instance, in *The Ballet Scene from Meyerbeer's Opera 'Robert le Diable'* (1876), on display in the Victoria and Albert Museum in Mansfield's time, a figure in the left foreground twists his head and looks through his opera glasses out of the frame rather than at the dancers on stage.[65] That figure's action and private thoughts are as significant as every detail of movement in the painting, inviting the viewer to imagine events beyond the frame. Degas foreshadows the innovations of Mansfield and other modernist writers by radically breaking the standards of formal composition, employing a distinct asymmetry. Jennifer Gross explains that

> What should be the focal point of his image – the sitter, the orchestra, the performer, the race – slips from centre stage or becomes a decoy leading us to observe the subjects' (the artist's and our own) real sense of boredom, exhaustion, crass bestiality, or the painful silence of isolation.[66]

In 'Marriage à la Mode', Mansfield pushes the narrative out of the frame with a flashback to William in his younger days, when he displayed a freedom of movement he no longer enjoys: 'When he had been a little boy, it was his delight to run into the garden after a shower of rain and shake the rose-bush over him. Isabel was that rose-bush, petal-soft, sparkling and cool.'[67] Mansfield contrasts William's youthful abandon to his current conventionality: 'there was no running into the garden now, no laughing and shaking'. She stresses his immobility through his gestures: on the train, 'He drew up his legs [. . .] and shut his eyes.'[68] William's circular movement in trains and taxis travelling to and from London aligns with Rishona Zimring's analysis of Mark Gertler's painting *Merry-Go-Round* (1916) as an allegory of modernist life: 'The carousel literalised, in the form of an actual machine carrying human bodies [. . .] a passive capitulation to mechanical forms [.. . .] The painting represents an "oppressive cycle, seeming to obliterate freedom of action".'[69] William's acceptance of mechanical movement, in contrast to Isabel's fluidity, underscores their incompatibility and accents her need, like Leila's, to ignore those who would act to control her movement. Isabel embodies motion and Mansfield directs her, even in the earliest scenes, as if she were a dancer on stage: Isabel 'bent forward, and her fine light hair fell over her cheeks. [. . .] Isabel wheeled round quickly and faced him [. . . and she] tossed back her hair.'[70] Her actions, written as if stage directions, accentuate her potential outside the confines of her marriage.

William blames Moira for the change in the 'new Isabel', but Moira recognises Isabel's potential with a reference to the stage. She tells William, '"I'm going to rescue your wife, selfish man. She's like an exquisite little Titania"'; the analogy to *A Midsummer Night's Dream* casts William as either the jealous, controlling Oberon or the foolish Bottom.[71] 'Marriage à la Mode' adds further complexity in what

Jennifer Gross explains is the 'disruption, dysfunction, inconsistency, and vulnerability' found in the variety of reactions in Degas's paintings.[72] Mansfield stages her story with the reactions of Isabel's circle of friends, a painter, writer, dramaturge and dancer. The latter, Bobby Kane, sees everything in life as movement; even the selection of sweets he chooses for the table is '"a perfect little ballet"'.[73] Later in the story, he begins 'to leap and pirouette on the parched lawn', and when Moira jokes that their hosts' domestic drama might benefit from the score of a popular West End musical, he offers, instead, to think in terms of the *Ballets Russes* and to 'wear [. . . his] Nijinsky dress'.[74] Another guest, the artist Bill Hunt, drolly comments about the bag with the melon and the pineapple that William brings for his children, with a reminder of Allan's prop head of John the Baptist: 'De-cap-itated heads'.[75] The story is composed with theatrical characters, whose actions Mansfield has blocked for the stage.

When William, off stage, decides to end the marriage, Mansfield emphasises the strength of gesture. Isabel imagines herself as the 'shallow [. . . and] vain' lead in an ill-attended melodrama: 'She pressed her eyes with her knuckles and rocked to and fro.'[76] Her anxiety is quickly dispelled, however, when Moira calls to her, first by her stage name, 'Titania!', and then questioning, 'Isa-bel?', encouraging her to answer to her own identity.[77] Mansfield's final words depict the body in motion as Isabel 'laughing in the new way, [. . .] ran down the stairs' and transitions to that truer self.[78] William's worries about a 'new Isabel' were, after all, real, but she is, at the story's conclusion, truer to herself, and William is partnered to the censorious 'fat man' in 'Her First Ball' by harbouring criticism of Isabel's need to move freely.[79]

Mansfield's Empowerment Through Dance, Movement and Gesture

Isabel finding herself in movement foreshadows Mansfield's observations at Le Prieuré, where she writes, 'the dancing here [. . .] seems to be the key to the new world within one'.[80] In her final months, Mansfield had given up writing fiction but her letters are filled with images of dance and movement. She tells Murry that 'After dinner [. . .] there is music, [. . .] dancing & perhaps a display of all kinds of queer dance exercises.'[81] Mansfield's descriptions of life at the Gurdjieff Institute convey a passion for movement and gesture that describes the vibrancy of life there: Madame Ostrowska, the choreographer of the dances and Gurdjieff's wife, 'walks about like a queen'. Mansfield's verbs record her sensitivity to every movement:

> [Ostrowska's] chief helper [. . .] pounds things in mortars. The second Cook chops [. . .] bangs the saucepans, sings; another runs in and out with plates & pots, a man in the scullery cleans pots, the dog barks & lies on the floor worrying a hearth brush. A little girl comes in with a bouquet of leaves [. . . and] Mr. Gurdjieff strides in.[82]

Mansfield memorialises the movement and the musicality of the commonplace with the skill one recognises in Degas's technique connecting images that depict a variety of individual activities. Mansfield's understated tone in her letters is key: 'What I write seems so petty.'[83] Instead, one reads her depth of experience when she writes that 'I have never really cared for dancing before' as she goes on to reveal her profound understanding of the art: 'Its just the same all through – *ease* after *rigidity*,' the very tension transformed to fluidity that she builds into the awakenings of Leila and Isabel.[84]

Mansfield's late letters explain the essence of dance through rigidity and movement. When Mansfield tells Murry, 'I would like you to see the dancing here,' she tries to engage Murry to feel the dynamics of their relationship: 'Don't feel we are silently and swiftly moving away from each other.'[85] Shortly after, she again describes their relationship with a metaphor of the dancer's tension: 'it is so hard to write. We don't move in our letters.'[86] As her illness continues to limit her mobility, she writes to her father for his birthday: 'I could hardly move at all [. . .] I came to *concentrate* [. . .] on my heart for the next few months and then to see what I can do with my wings.'[87] In what might be one of her most considered sentences, Mansfield's comparison of her lungs to wings conveys the flow of her breath. In this moving recognition of her inability to 'fly', she adds that it has given her an opportunity to concentrate on the rhythm of her heart and feel more deeply. She continues to prod the immobile Murry to observe himself – 'Don't you *sicken* of shutting that door & sitting down to that table?' – adding, 'there are things I *long* to write' before again comparing herself to a dancer: 'Why do I strain to spin and spin?'[88] Forced into stillness by her illness, Mansfield shares her heightened awareness of movement:

> I must say the dancing here has given me quite a different approach to writing. I mean some of the very ancient Oriental dance. There is one which takes about 7 minutes & it contains the whole life of a woman – but everything! Nothing is left out. It taught me, it gave me more of woman's life than any book or poem.[89]

Readers today might see matters differently; Mansfield's stories about women, dance, movement and gesture offer a composite portrait of the life of women in which she conveys the range of experience, from those like Frau Brechenmacher, who feel trapped, to those like Leila and Isabel, who find 'the key to a new world within' by embracing freedom through a passion in every movement.[90]

Notes

1. CW2, pp. 350; 356; 352.
2. Antony Alpers, *Katherine Mansfield: A Biography* (London: Jonathan Cape, 1954), p. 99.
3. CW4, p. 56.
4. *Letters* 1, p. 64. To Garnet Trowell, 3 October 1908. Mansfield refers to the pianist Teresa Carreño.
5. *Letters* 1, p. 84. To Garnet Trowell, 2 November 1908. Mansfield consistently misspells Maud Allan's name, and that error is repeated in some Mansfield literature. The Palace Theatre, where Mansfield saw Allan dance, still stands on Shaftesbury Avenue and is a venue for popular live entertainment.
6. *Letters* 1, p. 61.
7. Felix Cherniavsky, *The Salome Dancer: The Life and Times of Maud Allan* (Toronto: McClelland & Stewart, 1991), pp. 161–3. The quotation about Princess Trixie is from the programme reproduced in an unnumbered section of photos between pages 128 and 129.
8. Qtd in Cherniavsky, p. 164.
9. W. R. Titterton, 'The Maud Allan Myth', *The New Age*, 27 June 1908, p. 171.
10. Titterton, p. 171.
11. An undated programme for Allan (in this author's collection) notes that she performed for King George V and Queen Mary, as well as King Edward VII and Queen Alexandra.
12. *Letters* 1, p. 84.
13. *Letters* 1, p. 84.
14. Moira Taylor, *Her Bright Image: Impressions of Katherine Mansfield* (Wellington: Replay Radio, 1995), audio CD.
15. *Letters* 1, p. 84.
16. *Letters* 1, p. 85. To Garnet Trowell. Punctuation, however, is that used in CW3, p. 65.
17. *Letters* 1, p. 86.
18. As Antony Alpers explains: 'K.M.'s title was *The Luft Bad*, but in German it is usual to write *Luftbad* as one word.' Antony Alpers, *The Stories of Katherine Mansfield: Definitive Edition* (Auckland: Oxford University Press, 1984), p. 548, n. 34. While Strauss's *Salome* premiered in Dresden on 9 December 1905 and in New York City on 22 January 1907 (with further performances cancelled and not revived until 1934), it was banned in London by the Lord Chamberlain until 1907 and was finally presented at Covent Garden on 8 December 1910. It was not performed in Vienna until 1918.
19. CW1, p. 175.
20. CW1, p. 176.
21. CW1, p. 176.
22. CW1, p. 177.
23. CW1, pp. 175; 177.
24. CW1, pp. 177–8. For *In a German Pension* (published December 1911) Mansfield either added or restored the final three words in the story: 'I was not ashamed *of my* legs'; see Alpers, *Definitive Edition*, p. 548, n. 34.
25. CW2, p. 324.
26. CW2, p. 325.

27. CW2, p. 326.
28 'Arts and Ideas: Queer Bloomsbury and Stillness in Art and Dance', Robyn Read, prod. BBC 3, 17 June 2020, available at <https://www.bbc.co.uk/sounds/play/p08gt7hb> (last accessed 29 October 2021).
29. CW2, p. 327.
30. *Letters* 2, p. 263.
31. The article was published under Pemberton-Billing's name but was written by Captain Harold Spencer. See Gay Wachman, *Lesbian Empire: Radical Crosswriting in the Twenties* (New Brunswick, NJ: Rutgers University Press, 2001), p. 16.
32. Robbie Ross, Wilde's literary executor, had organised the performances, which were produced by J. T. Grein.
33. *Letters* 2, p. 210. To JMM.
34. Wendy Buonaventura, *Dark Venus: Maud Allan and the Myth of the Femme Fatale* (Stroud: Amberley, 2018), p. 206.
35. Petra Dierkes-Thrun, *Salome's Modernity* (Ann Arbor: University of Michigan Press, 2011), p. 119.
36. *Letters* 2, p. 222. To JMM.
37. CW2, p. 326.
38. CW2, p. 328.
39. Fuller and Duncan are still widely remembered today. Wiesenthal transformed the staid waltz 'into a powerful form of solo movement'; see Meryl Cates, 'When the Viennese Waltz Went Solo', *New York Times*, 27 December 2020, p. AR6.
40. John Middleton Murry, *Between Two Worlds* (New York: Julien Messner, 1936), p. 351.
41. D. H. Lawrence, *The Rainbow* (New York: B. W. Huebsch, 1916), p. 168. Fra Angelico's painting is part of his *Last Judgement*, San Marco, Florence.
42. Lawrence, p. 171.
43. Lawrence, p. 180.
44. CW1, p. 187.
45. CW1, p. 187.
46. CW1, p. 188.
47. CW1, p. 188.
48. CW1, p. 189.
49. *Letters* 5, p. 310.
50. Taylor, *Her Bright Image.*
51. Taylor, *Her Bright Image.*
52. *Letters* 3, p. 289.
53. *Letters* 3, p. 6.
54. Autolycus [Aldous Huxley], 'Marginalia', *Athenaeum*, 26 March 1920, p. 417. The *Athenaeum* published a list of its contributors' initials, which identifies Autolycus as A. L. Huxley.
55. [Huxley], p. 417.
56. *Letters* 1, p. 84.
57. CW3, p. 350.
58. Taylor, *Her Bright Image.*
59. *Letters* 5, p. 4. To Richard Murry.
60. Qtd in Theodore Reff, *Degas: The Artist's Mind* (New York: Metropolitan Museum of Art, 1976), p. 9, available at Internet Archive, <https://archive.org/details/degasartistsmind0000reff/page/22/mode/2up> (last accessed 15 August 2020).
61. Reff, p. 21.
62. CW4, p. 110. Mérimée wrote *Carmen*, the basis for Bizet's opera.

63. Jennifer Gross, ed., *Edgar Degas: Defining the Modernist Edge* (New Haven, CT: Yale University Art Gallery, 2003), p. 10, n. 3.
64. CW2, p. 330.
65. Bequeathed in 1900, this was the first painting by Degas in a British public collection.
66. Gross, p. 9.
67. CW2, pp. 331–2.
68. CW2, pp. 331–2.
69. Rishona Zimring, *Social Dance and the Modernist Imagination in Interwar Britain* (Farnham: Ashgate, 2013), p. 60.
70. CW2, p. 332.
71. CW2, pp. 333–4.
72. Gross, p. 9.
73. CW2, p. 334.
74. CW2, p. 335.
75. CW2, p. 334. One can also see Mansfield's reimagining Allan's prop head of John the Baptist in 'Prelude' when Pat slaughters the duck, and the children, with the exception of Kezia, see the event as performance.
76. CW2, p. 338.
77. CW2, p. 338.
78. CW2, p. 338.
79. CW2, p. 330.
80. *Letters* 5, p. 310. To JMM.
81. *Letters* 5, p. 307. To JMM.
82. *Letters* 5, p. 310.
83. *Letters* 5, p. 310.
84. *Letters* 5, p. 310.
85. *Letters* 5, pp. 309–10.
86. *Letters* 5, p. 313.
87. *Letters* 5, p. 315. To Harold Beauchamp.
88. *Letters* 5, p. 322. To JMM.
89. *Letters* 5, p. 322. To JMM.
90. *Letters* 5, p. 311.

Acknowledgement

During the COVID lockdown, David Plunkett and Donna Howard at the Jefferson Madison Regional Library in Charlottesville, Virginia, made crucial arrangements for research for which the author is thankful.

Katherine Mansfield's 'Marriage à la Mode': 'far too facile'?

Anna Kwiatkowska

'Marriage à la Mode' (1921)[1] is one of six stories that Katherine Mansfield wrote for the *Sphere*, 'a fashionable illustrated newspaper targeted at British citizens living in the colonies'.[2] Due to the 'popular' rather than 'literary' character of the journal, 'Marriage à la Mode' tends to be regarded as one of her minor works, classed as one of 'the bill-paying magazine stories of 1921'.[3] However, on closer inspection, the story turns out to be technically complex and of literary merit. Indeed, Saralyn R. Daly argues that 'clearly Mansfield took the *Sphere* stories as seriously as her important "At the Bay"'.[4]

In this essay I would like to draw attention to the dialogic nature of the story, especially its connection with the realm of Mansfield's beloved 'old masters'[5] – about which she states, 'the more one *lives* with them the better it is for ones work'[6] – and to demonstrate how the artistic past influenced Mansfield's own contemporary criticism of modern English bourgeois life. I argue that the strength and complexity of the short story lies in its frequent allusions to the artistic and the literary realm of the Old Masters. They become the life and soul of the story and, as a result, enrich its reading.

The very first allusion to Old Masters is evident in the title, which seems to direct the reader to William Hogarth's series of paintings called 'Marriage à la Mode'. The connection introduced via the title suggests that the issues Mansfield addresses in the story reflect those depicted in Hogarth's works. Subsequently, his series may be understood in such a way as to reinforce Mansfield's satire and to complement the events of the story. For example, the reader expects a tragic end since Hogarth's narrative paintings tell the story of a fashionable marriage that ends in disaster. The series was targeted at the new merchant class of eighteenth-century England, which was gaining power because of its increasing wealth and, quite frequently, arranged marriages with members of aristocracy who offered their titles in exchange for money. The difficulties stemming from such marriages, which resembled business transactions and economic unions rather than relationships based on love and understanding, are vividly depicted and mocked in Hogarth's series.

The first of Hogarth's paintings presents the signing of a contract between two families, and neither of the future spouses seems to be interested in what is going on. On the contrary, they are both engrossed in their respective conversations with members of their own party. This apparently forced arrangement is emphasised by the two shackled dogs, recognisable as an English breed of foxhound,[7] equally bored and looking in two different directions. Of significance, the accumulation of wealth and the pursuit of pleasure are shown as central to the painting, which points to their importance later in the marriage: the room is extravagantly decorated with luxurious objects and a number of paintings, and the couple are wearing expensive clothes – the groom is dressed after the latest French fashion, and the bride wears a sumptuous, richly decorated dress. As for the father of the groom, the 'Earl of Squander', he proudly exposes his protruding belly – an obvious sign of overeating – and his bandaged foot reveals the mark of gout, which in the eighteenth century was easily read as an indication of an excessive preoccupation with sex as well as food.[8] The son, following in his father's footsteps, is already marked with a black spot – a sure sign of having contracted syphilis (which was also known as French gout).[9]

The second painting depicts the life of the newly-weds. Once more, it is obvious that they remain separated, despite living under one roof. We can see the wife smiling – she must have spent a delightful night partying with some lover, as suggested by the overturned chair, a musical instrument and a music book. In the eighteenth-century painting tradition, music and musical instruments were already firmly linked with eroticism, passion and love.[10] Additionally, two violins and an open music book with only one page filled clearly suggest a music teacher[11]; music masters 'were well-placed to provide fashionable and bored women with opportunities for intrigue'.[12] Thus, the overturned chair points to a hurried departure of the wife's music tutor, with whom she has probably had a flirtatious liaison. The position of the violins (one over the other) is also indicative of such conduct. The sexual connotation of the paintings regarding the music motif is further supported by the appearance of another instrument: namely, a flute, which appears in the fourth painting. As a wind instrument, the flute in visual arts often connotes lascivious behaviour or thoughts.[13] Therefore, the references to music in Hogarth's series are clear implications of lovemaking, pleasure and sensuality.[14]

As for the husband, he is sprawled on the chair, exhausted after a night out in some house of ill-repute, indicated by a maid's cap sticking out from his pocket. Reinforcing this scenario, the painting visible above the heads of the young couple tells a meta-story of lewdness and misbehaviour. Additionally, it is important to note the presence of the dog sniffing at the maid's cap, a fashionable little poodle associated with French culture and used here by Hogarth to critique the English upper class and its 'unquenchable and often mistaken thirst for French fashions and exotic goods'.[15] What is more, the young wife's reclining posture, her disregard for both the disorder in the house and the promiscuity of her husband, reveal not only her boredom but also her loneliness.[16] The only thing she seems to share with her husband is the pursuit of pleasure and careless spending of money. Such a lifestyle is suggested, on the one hand, by the messy interior – the result of the recent entertainment – and on the other, by the figure of an annoyed banker leaving the house with a handful of unpaid bills.

As in Hogarth's series, Mansfield's short story 'Marriage à la Mode' suggests that the marriage between William and Isabel is more of a business arrangement than an intimate relationship, despite the fact that at the beginning, according to William, the marriage was full of warmth and happiness. When the reader meets the couple, their marital life is clearly devoid of any signs of intimacy and closeness. They already lead two different lives – he is preoccupied with his work and she with entertaining her 'new' friends. Indeed, they appear to function better when apart; William feels more comfortable on the train and at work, rather than at home. During his weekend travelling, for example, he always goes for a 'first-class smoker',[17] where he can carry on working in a quiet environment:

> 'Our client moreover is positive . . . . We are inclined to reconsider . . . in the event of –' *Ah, that was better.* William pressed back his flattened hair and *stretched his legs across the carriage floor.* The familiar *dull gnawing in his breast quietened down.* 'With regard to our decision –' He took out a blue pencil and scored a paragraph *slowly.* (p. 157, my emphasis)

The emphasised phrases above conspicuously indicate that it is his work environment that makes him comfortable and at peace. A marked change befalls him once he bends over the business papers and immerses himself in all the familiar-sounding official phrases and questions. This is evidenced with his body language (stretching his legs), his attitude (feeling calm) and his unhurried disposition (the way he scores paragraphs). As a result, the space of the train carriage is transposed into a congenial study or drawing room. In other words, he is more at home when away from it.

Contrastingly, his comfort on the train clashes with Isabel's discomfort at home. William's weekend visits seem to resemble an inspection for which his wife prepares herself and her friends. They certainly impose a change on his wife's behaviour and mood; she becomes more apprehensive and expects her fun-loving companions to behave more seriously when William is around: '"Be nice to him, my children! He's only staying until tomorrow evening"' (p. 164). She is also anxious for William to go back to London. For example, during their parting at the gate, she feels uneasy, gives 'a little awkward laugh', looks 'anxiously along the sandy road' for a sign of a taxi which is to take William to the station, and when the taxi arrives, she shouts goodbye, gives her husband 'a little hurried kiss' and is gone (pp. 165–6).

Moreover, the potential love between husband and wife is mocked by Isabel's 'new friends' since they regard it as old-fashioned and quite sentimental, and therefore silly and pointless. And when William sends his wife a long love letter – 'Pages and pages' (p. 167) – they mock it, saying: 'He's sending you back your marriage lines as a gentle reminder. Does everybody have marriage lines? I thought they were only for servants' (p. 167). The words 'marriage lines' emphasise the business-like character of the union. Indeed, the mentioning of the official document confirming the marriage acts as a reminder that the pair are legally bound (or, metaphorically speaking, chained like the two dogs from Hogarth's painting) to each other, and, as a result, they are expected to fulfil their marital duties. The follow-up of this mock-serious comment – namely, 'I thought they were only for servants' – plainly not only diminishes the importance and legal power of the document but also serves as a critique of the institution of marriage, at least when it comes to the bourgeois. In other words, marriage is old-fashioned and thus both unsuitable and needless in modern times, certainly within the trendy circles in which they live. The business-like relationship and the separation of the husband and wife are additionally highlighted by the two different locations they occupy during the week: William stays in London, where he works, and comes back home only at weekends; Isabel spends her time in their new suburban house, where she entertains her new friends. Isabel's guests soon feel very much at home there while the husband starts to feel like an (unwelcome) guest.

As in Hogarth's series, the story also includes references to music, partying and playing, eating and careless money spending. The activities performed by Isabel and her friends are tinted with sexuality; for instance, Moira wonders aloud about the colour of legs under water, Dennis suggests smearing themselves with butter, and their acting noisily in the street or eating greedily contrasts with William's old-fashioned ways. He finds this 'new' life demoralising and blames it firstly on Moira and secondly on the French culture to which she has introduced his wife:

> If they hadn't gone to that studio party at Moira Morrison's – if Moira Morrison hadn't said as they were leaving, "I'm going to rescue your wife, selfish man. She's like an exquisite little Titania" – if Isabel hadn't gone with Moira to Paris – if – if . . . .' (p. 159)[18]

William, like Hogarth's series of paintings, seems to value traditional British ways of family life over the foreign, which he associates with moral vice and depravation.

Consequently, in Mansfield's narrative, this kind of fashionable and entertainment-oriented lifestyle characterises Isabel and her new friends, while William seems to be exempt from it. However, unlike Hogarth's paintings, it is only the wife who is associated with morally reprehensible behaviour, while the husband, from the very beginning, is to be looked upon as a loving husband (he cannot wait to see Isabel) and father (he buys presents for his little boys). Thus, Mansfield draws our attention to the position of a woman within the context of marriage. Despite changing attitudes towards unmarried, independent females like Moira, women are still discouraged from pursuing a life on their own, and those who dare to do it are frequently laughed at and mocked. The patriarchal element is shown as the most vital in a family, for it connotes financial security and caring; to satisfy the wishes of his wife, William buys a new, bigger house outside London, allows for furnishing it in a fashionable way, pays for the nanny and for the entertainment of Isabel and her new friends, and buys presents for his wife and children. Domestic life presented from such a perspective might be tempting since it implies luxury and independence. Yet, this bliss is illusionary. As in the case of Bertha Young in 'Bliss' or Linda Burnell in 'At the Bay', Isabel, in agreeing to such a life, has to sacrifice her personal freedom and focus on fulfilling the socially programmed, centuries-old obligations of a woman, such as looking after the house, and taking care of the children and the well-being of her husband. If she chooses not to comply with these expectations, she is classified as immoral and silly.

The next two paintings by Hogarth show the growing deterioration of the marriage. The husband keeps visiting prostitutes: a black spot on the woman's face, again a sign of syphilis, points to her promiscuity and a similar spot is now more evident on the neck of the man. Obviously, his health is ailing, for he appears to be visiting some dubious doctor. His approaching demise – both moral and physical – is indicated by the skull on the doctor's table, as well as by the skeletons, seen in an obscene embrace in the glass cabinet behind them. As for the wife, she is presented at home, seated at the table while having her hair done, surrounded by her new 'friends'. Curiously, the painting indicates that the woman is now a mother, for a coral rope is hanging over the chair, an item generally used by teething children.[19] However, the child is not in sight. The young mother, herself like a child, appears to care more for being with her fun-loving, money-loving friends than with her family.

In similar fashion, the motif of children being pushed aside, as if hidden from view, is even more pronounced in Mansfield's story. In Isabel's 'new' life, there is no longer a place for them. There are many references to them in the story, yet the two little boys never actually make an appearance. They are either away with their nanny or asleep. Even William, their father, does not manage to see them when he is at home. The *memento mori* present in the story, however, assumes a humorous form. The allusion to death is made through the scene when William brings home some fruit (a pineapple and a melon) for his boys as a present. The fruit makes 'two very awkward parcels' (p. 155) and is compared by Isabel's friends to severed human heads:

> The taxi started. 'What have you got in those mysterious parcels?'
>
> 'De-cap-it-ated heads!' said Bill Hunt, shuddering beneath his hat.
>
> 'Oh, fruit!' Isabel sounded very pleased. 'Wise William! A melon and a pineapple. How too nice!' (pp. 161–2)

This comic perception of fruit, on the one hand, and the usage of the word 'nice' in relation to 'decapitated heads', on the other, strips the situation of seriousness and at the same time displays a considerable lack of concern for both the giver and the would-be receivers of the gifts (that is, the children). As in Hogarth's painting, the characters seem to be unaware of the oppressive ambience and the consequences of their conduct: William's estrangement in his own house and his separation from his wife and children.

The last two pictures in Hogarth's series are dominated by obscenity, horror, greed, indifference and callousness. The young wife and her lover are found *in flagrante* by the husband. As a result, a fight ensues, and the husband is fatally wounded by the lover, who is seen trying to escape through the window. The wife has qualms of conscience and begs her dying husband to forgive her conduct. But it is too late now. Soon he dies and her lover is caught, declared guilty of murder and eventually hanged, evidence for which can be seen in the next, final, painting. On the floor, at the feet of the dying woman, there is a letter from which she learns her lover's fate and which draws the young wife to commit suicide. Subsequently, the painting shows how a lack of true feeling and greed in a marriage end in tragedy: the wife overdoses on laudanum (there is an empty bottle on the floor), killing herself. She leaves an orphan daughter, herself already marked with a black spot of syphilis, and a callously thrifty father, who hastily takes the rings off his daughter's fingers. Another symbol of greed is also expressed by the pig's head on the table being eaten by a dog. This time the dog – a greyhound, a favourite breed with the aristocracy[20] – is pictured as emaciated and neglected, evidenced by its ribs showing and the greed with which the dog falls on the food. The state of the animal reflects the state of the family, symbolising 'the pursuit of status at any cost',[21] and the failure of the marriage in general.

In Mansfield's story, the vices of greed, callousness, indifference and decadence are also present throughout the narrative. They are communicated through house guest Bobby Kane's shopping spree, Isabel's snatching of the presents William has bought for the children, and the masks and costumes that Isabel and her friends so eagerly put on during their sumptuous feasts. Dressing up, on the one hand, draws on the eighteenth-century English tradition of masquerade balls, which were synonymous with promiscuity, 'erotic conspiracy and licence',[22] and on the other hand harks back to the symbolism of masquerades present in the literature and art in the time of Hogarth, in which costumes were used to illustrate the concealment of questionable behaviour, falsity and lies. As Terry Castle notes, for Pope, Hogarth, Fielding and many others, the masquerade was 'the quintessential scene of Saturnalian excess and corruption, a Protean emblem of the decline in English morals'.[23] In a similar fashion, the fact that Isabel and her friends often wear costumes and Bobby refers to the stage and acting – '"would you like me to wear my Nijinsky dress to-night?"' (p. 164) – indicates the company's duplicitous nature. They merely pretend to be friends in order to achieve their own goals: Isabel's new friends to have an unlimited access to free food and a comfortable house, and Isabel to escape her otherwise boring domestic life with an entertaining, 'arty' crowd. Curiously, Isabel does not permit masquerades when William is at home but her conduct is still false: metaphorically speaking, she puts on another mask and pretends that nothing has changed between her and William.

Indifference and egoism are further illustrated by the behaviour of Isabel's friends towards William and the children. William is constantly and openly laughed at by them. His romantic approach to love and his old-fashioned way of speaking and thinking, as well as his music preferences, are mocked; for example, the friends suggest that they 'ought to have a gramophone for the weekends that played "The Maid of the Mountains"', a light-hearted Edwardian musical comedy full of romantic love songs. Their insensitivity towards the children is marked by the fact that they see nothing improper in helping themselves with great eagerness to the gifts that William brings especially for them. And William is quite helpless to do anything about it:

> And he saw the kiddies handing the boxes round – they were awfully generous little chaps – while Isabel's precious friends didn't hesitate to help themselves . . .
>
> What about fruit? William hovered before a stall just inside the station. What about a melon each? Would they have to share that, too? [. . .] Isabel's friends could hardly go sneaking up to the nursery at the children's mealtimes. All the same, as he bought the melon William had a horrible vision of one of Isabel's young poets lapping up a slice, for some reason, behind the nursery door. (p. 155)

Another vice – namely, the sin of debauchery – fills the place. Scenes featuring Isabel's friends greedily devouring food are frequent. For example,

> Bill and Dennis ate *enormously*. And Isabel filled glasses, and *changed plates*, and found matches, smiling blissfully. At one moment, she said, 'I do wish, Bill, you'd paint it.' 'Paint what?' said Bill loudly, *stuffing his mouth* with bread. 'Us,' said Isabel, 'round the table. It would be so fascinating in twenty years' time.' Bill screwed up his eyes and *chewed*. 'Light's wrong,' he said rudely, 'far too much yellow'; and *went on eating*. (p. 165, my emphasis)

Ironically, this kind of pleasure is also mentioned by William when he recalls the early days of his marriage:

> And the amount they ate, and the amount they slept in that immense feather bed with their feet locked together . . . William couldn't help a grim smile as he thought of Isabel's horror if she knew the full extent of his sentimentality. (p. 160)

What is more, in his recollection, the connection between eating and sex is vividly suggested ('the amount they ate, and the amount they slept', 'feet locked together', the ironic 'full extent of his sentimentality'). Indeed, this emphasis on the physicality of his sentimentality and the grim delight at Isabel's envisaged horror make him in some way similar to the group he despises and further indicate that he used to be quite fond of the pleasures Isabel now enjoys with her new friends.

As for the ending of Mansfield's story relative to Hogarth's series, it seems less horrifying. In the narrative, death is expressed metaphorically – the old Isabel dies along with her old life; likewise, the hopes and dreams William has of recapturing his old life die, too. And although William tries to do something about it, composing a long, passionate love letter to Isabel on the train back to London, the reader knows before he does that his action is futile. Isabel, upon receiving the letter, decides to read it aloud to her new friends, who find it hilarious. The content of the letter makes Isabel reflect briefly upon her treatment of William. However, after a momentary hesitation, Isabel resumes her new life:

> Now was the moment, now she must decide. Would she go with them or stay here and write to William. Which, which should it be? 'I must make up my mind.' Oh, but how could there be any question? Of course she would stay here and write.
>
> 'Titania!' piped Moira.
>
> 'Isa-bel?'
>
> No, it was too difficult. 'I'll – I'll go with them, and write to William later. Some other time. Later. Not now. But I shall certainly write,' thought Isabel hurriedly.
>
> And, laughing, in the new way, she ran down the stairs. (pp. 169–70)

The phrase 'Of course she would stay here and write' points to a conventional, socially expected, reaction. And if she were the old Isabel, 'she would stay'. However, the new Isabel has neither the will nor the time to engage in writing dutifully to her husband, and thus she merely makes a promise to deal with the letter later. Yet, she knows – and the reader does, too – that she is not going to keep her promise. Like all her other choices related to her marriage and to her husband, this promise is characterised by a lack of sincerity. She continues to pretend that her marital life is normal; however, the promise of writing is merely another sign that it is a sham, like seeing William off to the gate and carrying his suitcase for him as a sign of her love and devotion while giving him 'a little hurried kiss' (p. 166) and leaving him so quickly, as if running away, which suggest something entirely different. The unspecified timescale – 'some other time', 'later', 'not now' – vividly suggests that there is no place for either William or (long) letters within her ostensibly busy new life.

Such a reading is additionally reinforced by Mansfield's vivid allusion, pinpointed by Vincent O'Sullivan,[24] to Matthew Arnold's poem

'The Forsaken Merman'. The plot of the poem corresponds to the plot of Mansfield's story: in the poem, Margaret, a mortal woman married to a merman, decides to relinquish her home under the sea and go back to live on the shore. However, the day she leaves, she gives the impression that she is to come back, thus deluding her husband and her children: 'I must go, to my kinsfolk pray / In the little grey church on the shore to-day.'[25] And when the merman agrees to her leaving, saying: 'Go up, dear heart, through the waves; / Say thy prayer, and come back to the kind sea-caves!',[26] Margaret only smiles and goes 'up through the surf in the bay',[27] never to come back. As Todd Martin demonstrates in his article 'The Sense of an Ending in Katherine Mansfield's "Marriage à la Mode"', since Isabel resembles Margaret, the woman from Arnold's poem who 'left lonely for ever / The kings of the sea',[28] a similar decision may be expected from Isabel, who has made up her mind: she will desert her husband, whilst not necessarily informing him about the decision.

The allusions to Hogarth's series of paintings and the issues criticised in them are vivid throughout Mansfield's story. Yet, unlike in Hogarth's narrative, where the painter–narrator chooses and frames the scenes which offer a critique of the lifestyles of both the husband and the wife, in Mansfield's story the criticism seems to be directed merely at Isabel's conduct. In so doing, Mansfield simultaneously criticises the dubious behaviour of the protagonist and her decision to lead a life of carelessness and deserting her family, and draws the reader's attention to Isabel's restricted freedom (as a wife and mother, she is confined to the domestic realm; as a friend of seemingly emancipated Moira, she is limited to the stupefying company of pseudo-artists). What is more, through most of the story, Isabel and her new life are presented from the husband's perspective. Only towards the end of the narrative does one get some glimpse of Isabel's point of view on the situation. Her perspective is expressed via her reactions towards her friends, for example, when she finds out that the fish meant for lunch is gone – 'But Isabel couldn't help wondering what had happened to the salmon they had for supper last night. She had meant to have fish mayonnaise for lunch and now . . .' (p. 167) – or when she becomes quite vexed and annoyed with the behaviour of her friends while reading aloud William's letter to them:

> 'Let me hold it. Let me read it, mine own self,' said Bobby Kane. But, to their surprise, Isabel crushed the letter in her hand. She was laughing no longer. She glanced quickly at them all; she looked exhausted. 'No, not just now. Not just now,' she stammered. And before they could recover, she had run into the house, through the hall, up the stairs into her bedroom. Down she sat on the side of the bed. 'How vile, odious, abominable, vulgar,' muttered Isabel. (p. 169)

Mansfield's presentation of the individual, subjective perspectives of both William and Isabel serves to heighten the differences between them, whereas allowing more narrative time for William seems to underline the importance of the male voice in modern society. But this is the traditionally patriarchal domestic life that it extols. Within such a realm, there is no space for a woman's personal freedom. And although the old-fashioned and sentimental William is presented in such a way that the reader feels sorry for him, one should not be led into believing that the life he imagined for himself and Isabel is the one which makes space for an emancipated woman. Thus, recalling Hogarth, Mansfield reminds us of the traps of this ideal-looking world. She points to women's restriction of freedom within marriage and the ruthless control exercised by men over them. Unsurprisingly, then, the male voice is quite often hushed by Isabel's loud friends and their behaviour.

In order to make Isabel and her voice more audible, Mansfield alludes to yet another Old Master: namely, Johannes Vermeer. These allusions further expand the psychological dimension of her characters and add more depth to the story. Apart from that, they illuminate Isabel's 'new' conduct. Vermeer is especially known for his portrayals of women: 'In Vermeer's compositions, women appear in one guise or another about 46 times, while men make only 14 appearances, mostly in subordinate roles, three times with their backs to us.'[29] The women and their surroundings presented in Vermeer's paintings reflect the most important aspects of Dutch life in the seventeenth century and its new, thriving middle class, emphasising themes like 'family, privacy, intimacy, comfort and luxury, [and] encouraging the spectator to think about issues relevant to his or her daily life, sometimes with touches of humor'.[30] It comes as no surprise, then, that all these values link women with their socially assigned domestic space, especially when we consider that 'Vermeer was alert to the appearance of a new type of woman, better educated than her predecessors and more absorbed in her interior life.'[31] As Simon Schama emphasises, in seventeenth-century Holland, 'Dutch culture was overwhelmingly intimate, domestic and interior in character,'[32] and the view of women changed from one of fragile, almost unearthly, creatures to figures earthy in character, whose beauty stemmed from their surroundings rather than from their looks. Therefore, women started to be associated with the fulfilment of home duties and taking care of the family rather than with unreal muses.[33] Subsequently, as Gerard Koot points out, Dutch paintings with women were now painted in order to set an example of the domestic virtues that were to be followed.[34] We should also remember that these portrayals were executed by men. Therefore, Vermeer's blissful representations of women quietly engaged in sewing, looking after children, cooking or practising music and writing letters should be perceived to some extent as idealised.[35] As a consequence, Vermeer's women, as well as those presented on canvases by other seventeenth-century artists, should be viewed as epitomes of certain rules and values accepted by a male-dominated society.[36] Additionally, Vermeer's paintings often induce a feeling of curiosity, which in turn increases the charm of the female models presented. To achieve such a domestic atmosphere of mystery, to engage and intrigue the viewer, the artist mixed the real with the imagined.[37]

Mansfield filters the Vermeer female image through her own perception of the traditional role of women in her own 'modern' times. The painting titles that appear in the story allude to Vermeer but echo him in a distorted manner:

> 'Cruel Isabel! Do let me smell it!' said Moira. She flung her arms across William appealingly. 'Oh!' The strawberry bonnet fell forward: she sounded quite faint.
>
> 'A Lady in Love with a Pine-apple', said Dennis [. . .]. (p. 162)

> 'I've found the sardines', said Moira, and she ran into the hall, holding a box high in the air.
>
> 'A Lady with a Box of Sardines', said Dennis gravely (p. 164).

> 'Pages and pages! Look at her! A Lady reading a Letter', said Dennis (p. 167).

The structure of the titles, as well as their theme (a figure of a woman shown in connection with some domestic object or activity), recalls Vermeer's own paintings, such as *The Girl with a Wine Glass* (c. 1659–62), *Lady Writing a Letter with her Maid* (1670) and *Lady Drinking and a Gentleman* (c. 1658–60). Although the dialogue Mansfield enters into with the Old Master is in mock-seriousness, she nevertheless seriously considers the question of women and their place in society. The titles of the would-be paintings vividly connect the women with the domestic via the references to food and letter culture. Moira is presented as a food hunter, a less serious (female) version of a (male) breadwinner. Furthermore, in contrast to the models from Vermeer's paintings, Moira stands for the infantile and the silly – this is how modern society perceives the modern woman. On the one hand, the narrator communicates facts, such as her being single, leading a life of an artist, having her own studio or travelling on her own, which connote Moira to be a New Woman. On the other hand, the ironic narratorial voice is commenting unfavourably on Moira's way of living, presenting the woman as childish (jumping up and down, running through the house), lazy (sleeping is one of Moira's much-loved pastimes), egoistic (she seems to like Isabel very much and so she tries to keep her company for herself) and cruel (she entirely disregards the feelings of Isabel's husband). Mansfield also plays, quite amusingly, with the concept of defamiliarisation: the real – the fruit, the box of sardines and the letter – mixes with the unreal because the pictures are apparently never painted and are grossly exaggerated, as if acted out. Moira's overreaction at the sight of a pineapple – 'fl[inging] her arms across William appealingly', the exclamation 'Oh!', acting 'quite faint' – demonstrate counterfeit emotion. Curiously, only 'A Lady reading a Letter' seems to be less comical. Firstly, it seems to paraphrase rather than mock the title of one of Vermeer's works: for example, his *Woman in Blue Reading a Letter* (c. 1663–4) or *Girl Reading a Letter at an Open Window* (c. 1657–9). Secondly, the reading of the letter, in part, takes place in the solitude of Isabel's bedroom, which corresponds to the ambience of Dutch paintings. And thirdly, the letter itself becomes a source of quiet (domestic, intimate) mystery, for apart from a few opening sentences, the readers never learn the full content of the message. On top of that, the painterly associations are wrought by the very position of Isabel – she is poised on a chair with the letter, and those who listen to her reading compose a group of viewers. She becomes framed by their very gazes.

By referring to the tradition of the Dutch Old Masters, Mansfield clearly points to the domestic-oriented position of women in modern society, which is still, as in the past, largely ruled by men. On the one hand, she openly laughs at the fashionable and, in certain circles, socially accepted image of a woman, a figure which is silly, kitschy and childish: Moira seen with her huge strawberry bonnet, jumping up and down, being restless and overemotional about trifles like fruit or a box of sardines. It seems in Mansfield's portrayal that while trying to free themselves from the limitations of domestic life and male hegemony, these types of women end up becoming caricatures of themselves. On the other hand, Mansfield is quite serious about the domestic entrapment of women and the social limitations resulting from it.[38] That is why, when Isabel stops laughing, the reader follows her lead and becomes serious, too. Gaining Isabel's perspective for a while, accessing her mind and learning the fragments of her thoughts, results in holding back our criticism of her and in contemplating the cause(s) of the unhappiness in her marriage.

Thinking of Isabel and the reasons for her turn of heart forces us to look at the story still more closely. This eventually takes us back to the title. If we consider the fact that Hogarth borrowed it from John Dryden's play of 1672,[39] then it seems indispensable to consider Dryden as yet another 'Old Master' who influences the story. The play opens with a poem which ponders over a love that once was present in marriage but now is gone:

> Why should a foolish marriage vow,
> Which long ago was made,
> Oblige us to each other now
> When passion is decay'd?
> We lov'd, and we lov'd, as long as we could,
> Till our love was lov'd out in us both:
> But our marriage is dead, when the pleasure is fled:
> 'Twas pleasure first made it an oath.
> If I have pleasures for a friend,
> And farther love in store,
> What wrong has he whose joys did end,
> And who could give no more?
> 'Tis a madness that he should be jealous of me,
> Or that I should bar him of another:
> For all we can gain is to give our selves pain,
> When neither can hinder the other.[40]

The poem may serve as an extension for the half-expressed thoughts of Isabel. The emotionality and restlessness, as well as some irritability evident in the comments, along with the rhetorical questions in the poem, correspond with the spiritual and mental state of Isabel, especially at the close of the story. While reading William's letter, she experiences a whole range of emotions: 'astonishment', 'a stifled feeling' (p. 167), surprise – 'How extraordinary it was . . .' (p. 168) – confusion, excitement and fear simultaneously – 'She felt confused, more and more excited, even frightened' (p. 168) – and then anger with herself and William, in part due to the impossibility of explaining her rude conduct towards him. As Marvin Magalaner writes, as with 'Bliss', 'Marriage à la Mode' is 'a domestic tragedy [which] is played out against a background of broad social satire'.[41] The potential ties to Dryden, therefore, further emphasise that the story is more than a facile satire since underneath a simple plot there is a major personal conflict. Like Dryden's play, which is divided into two types of plot, one serious and one comic, Mansfield's story is concerned with the comic and the tragic, too, though in her case the two are tightly intertwined. The sentimental and the traditional perspective portrayed in the figure of William is both mocked and appreciated; the comic group of pretentious friends is amusing, but their influence in undermining Isabel's relationship – this 'marriage à la mode' – is tragic.

For her part, it seems Isabel realises that she does not love William any more but she has no courage to communicate this to him. Such a decision would certainly require divorcing her husband. But was life outside marriage possible for a woman? Moira seems to be proof that this is possible. Yet, Moira is single because she never married, and she is trying to pursue the career of an artist. In the case of a married woman who was financially dependent on her husband, becoming single through a divorce could mean a worsening of her living conditions. As a result, the decision to divorce, and so gain personal freedom, required a great deal of courage, especially on the part of an upper middle-class woman – after all, she was choosing between the comforts of a modern house and social esteem and economic impoverishment and social stigmatisation.

Moreover, Isabel's emotional situation is even more complicated because now she is attached to her friend 'à la mode' (Moira Morrison has more influence over Isabel than her husband does). Everything changed when the two women met and travelled to Paris together. Paris, itself, might be an indication of Isabel's sexual and emotional awakening since, as Ana Pérez notes, the cities in Mansfield's stories play a part in the creation of male and female identities. In some, the city is the space of male work, where men go every day ('Prelude', 'At the Bay', 'Marriage à la Mode', 'An Ideal Family'); it is where men shop with maximum freedom ('Prelude', 'At the Bay'); it is, for men, their refuge from the domestic space, which some find oppressive ('An Ideal Family', 'Marriage à la Mode'). As a result, since the city is associated with men in a traditional way, it is often a source of conflict for women and threatens their identity, especially when they try to occupy the same positions as men.[42] However, Paris is also the complex meeting-place for artists, intellectuals and *flâneurs* ('Je ne parle pas français', 'Feuille d'Album').

As the above discussion reveals, Mansfield's story 'Marriage à la Mode' is more than a facile satire. It includes deeper layers of meanings which, besides commenting on fashionable marriage, address the individual and the truly private within the relationship. Consequently, contrary to any open criticism of a fashionable marriage, in her short story Mansfield reflects upon the place of woman in a modern relationship and questions whether a woman can choose what type of relationship this is going to be. The freedom of choice and of emotional expression, as opposed to the loneliness and the estrangement within one's own house or room, is told through the subjective perceptions of both William's and Isabel's individual realities. However, because Mansfield lets William monopolise the narrative, limiting the time devoted to Isabel's thoughts and feelings, Isabel is left with much less narrative space to express herself, and thus Mansfield indicates the inferior and marginal position of women in both marriage and society. Nevertheless, Mansfield manages to foreground women's issues in her text by supplementing the fragmentary picture of Isabel's self, even though Isabel's voice is hardly audible, by including frequent allusions to the works of 'Old Masters'. She harks back to past centuries to highlight and criticise the vices of contemporary society. Moreover, the contrast of the old and the new, the old-fashioned and the modern, as well as the temporal juxtaposition of the past and the present, memories and the here-and-now, reveals the distance between William and Isabel. Following the Old Masters' perspective where women happily become wives and housewives, smilingly fulfilling their domestic duties, William longs for the time when things were more traditional; Isabel, his modern wife, however, is quite ready to break free from domestic entrapment and the conventionalities of marriage.

Thus, the correspondences between the figures of the past, both overt and veiled, allow us to look at the modern characters from some distance. As a result, William, Isabel and her new friends are presented in a wider cultural–social–temporal context. The mingling and overlapping of perspectives, in turn, introduce a certain anxiety and vibrancy to the otherwise very simple plot, making the story poignant, psychologically complex and emotionally charged.

Notes

1. Discussing 'Marriage à la Mode', Jeffrey Meyers notes, 'it is difficult to identify with – or even care about – either William or Isabel, and the satire is far too facile'. See Jeffrey Meyers, *Katherine Mansfield: A Biography* (New York: New Directions, 1980), p. 248.
2. Jenny McDonnell, '"The Famous New Zealand Mag.-Story Writer"': Katherine Mansfield, Periodical Publishing and the Short Story', in Janet Wilson, Gerri Kimber and Susan Reid, eds, *Katherine Mansfield and Literary Modernism* (London: Continuum, 2011), pp. 42–52 (p. 46).
3. Antony Alpers, ed., *The Stories of Katherine Mansfield: Definitive Edition* (Oxford: Oxford University Press, 1984), p. xxv.
4. Saralyn R. Daly, ed., *Katherine Mansfield* (New York: Twayne, 1994), p. 107.
5. The term 'Old Master' generally refers to 'an eminent European artist from the approximate period 1300 to 1800 and includes artists from the Early Renaissance through to the Romantic movement'. See <https://www.theartstory.org/definition/old-masters/> (last accessed 13 November 2021). In this essay, however, to suit Mansfield's understanding of it – 'About the old masters. What I feel about them (all of them writers too, of course)' – the meaning of 'Old Master' is extended to suggest 'a cultural icon, an emblem of present regard for past masteries'. See *Letters* 4, p. 247, and Dolora A. Wojciechowski, *Old Masters, New Subjects: Early Modern and Poststructuralist Theories of Will* (Stanford: Stanford University Press, 1995), p. 1.
6. *Letters* 4, p. 247.
7. Kaitlyn Farrell, 'A Dog's World: The Significance of Canine Companions in Hogarth's "Marriage A-la-Mode"', *British Art Journal*, 14: 2 (Autumn 2013), pp. 35–8 (p. 37).

8. C. D. O'Malley, qtd in Robert L. S. Cowley, *A Review of William Hogarth's 'Marriage a la Mode' – with Particular Reference to Character and Setting* (PhD thesis, University of Birmingham, 1977), p. 21.
9. Cowley, p. 21.
10. John Nash, *Vermeer*, trans. Halina Andrzejewska (Warsaw: Arkady, 1998), pp. 71–8.
11. Cowley, p. 64.
12. Cowley, p. 63.
13. Emanuel Winternitz, *Musical Instruments and Their Symbolism in Western Art* (New York: Norton, 1967), p. 48.
14. Nash, pp. 71–8.
15. Farrell, p. 37.
16. Cowley, p. 172.
17. Katherine Mansfield, *The Garden Party and Other Stories* (Harmondsworth: Penguin Books, 1983), p. 156. All references to the story are from this edition and subsequent references will be provided in parenthetical notation.
18. According to Lorna Sage, a trip to Paris is 'shorthand for avant-garde taste and sexual adventure'. See Lorna Sage, ed., *The Garden Party and Other Stories* (London: Penguin Classics, 2008), p. 157, n. 1.
19. *Hogarth: Modern Moral Series, Marriage A-la Mode*, available at: <https://www.tate.org.uk/whats-on/tate-britain/exhibition/hogarth/hogarth-hogarths-modern-moral-series/hogarth-hogarths-2> (last accessed 20 August 2021).
20. Farrell, p. 37.
21. Farrell, p. 35.
22. Terry Castle, 'Eros and Liberty at the English Masquerade, 1710–90', *Eighteenth-Century Studies*, 17: 2 (1983), pp. 156–76 (p. 156).
23. Castle, p. 157.
24. W. Todd Martin, 'The Sense of an Ending in Katherine Mansfield's "Marriage à la Mode"', *Explicator*, 69: 4 (2011), pp. 159–62 (p. 160).
25. Matthew Arnold, 'The Forsaken Merman', available at <https://www.poetryfoundation.org/poems/43589/the-forsaken-merman> (last accessed 9 November 2021).
26. Arnold, online.
27. Arnold, online.
28. Arnold, online.
29. Jonathan Janson, 'Vermeer's Women', *Essential Vermeer 3.0*, 2001–, available at <http://www.essentialvermeer.com/women%27s_faces/vermeer%27s_women.html> (last accessed 20 August 2021).
30. Alejandro Vergara, 'Vermeer: Context and Uniqueness: Dutch Paintings of Domestic Interiors, 1650–1675', *Vermeer and the Dutch Interior*, exhibition catalogue (Madrid, 2003), p. 204, available at: <http://www.essentialvermeer.com/books/books_vermeer.html> (last accessed 1 June 2020).
31. Vergara, p. 206.
32. Simon Schama, 'Wives and Wantons: Versions of Womanhood in 17th Century Dutch Art', *Oxford Art Journal*, 7 (1980), pp. 5–13 (p. 7).
33. Schama, p. 7.
34. Gerard Koot, 'The Portrayal of Women in Dutch Art of the Dutch Golden Age: Courtship, Marriage and Old Age', *Images and Illustrated Essays on the History of the Dutch Republic* (History Department, University of Massachusetts Dartmouth, 2015), pp. 29–30, available at: <http://www1.umassd.edu/euro/resources/imagesessays/theportrayalofwomenindutchartofthedutchgoldenage.pdf> (last accessed 28 February 2021).

35. Koot, p. 30.
36. Koot, p. 30.
37. Nash, p. 37.
38. For more on Mansfield's characters and Dutch art, see my 'Representations of Women in Selected Short Stories by Katherine Mansfield Viewed Through Seventeenth-century Genre Paintings', *Tekstualia*, 1: 4 (2018), pp. 35–52; 'Modern Mansfield and Old Masters. Hypotyposis in Selected Short Stories by Katherine Mansfield', *Modernism Re-visited*, 'Scripta Humana', XIV (2019), pp. 59–74.
39. Edith Appleton Standen, *William Hogarth, 1697–1764* (New York: Book-of-the-Month Club, 1955), p. 21.
40. John Dryden, 'Marriage à la Mode', available at: <https://www.poetryfoundation.org/poems/44182/marriage-a-la-mode> (last accessed 20 June 2020).
41. Marvin Magalaner, *The Fiction of Katherine Mansfield* (Carbondale: Southern Illinois University Press, 1971), p. 86.
42. Ana Belén López Pérez, '"A City of One's Own": Women, Social Class and London in Katherine Mansfield's Short Stories', in Wilson et al., *Katherine Mansfield and Literary Modernism*, pp. 128–38 (p. 130).

The Quest for Autonomy amid Shifting Gender Expectations and Relationships in Katherine Mansfield's Short Stories

Calvin Goh

Often overshadowed by contemporaries such as James Joyce and Virginia Woolf, who are widely acknowledged as two of the forerunners of literary modernism, Katherine Mansfield has, until the last couple of decades, been more or less overlooked, and her short stories remained under the radar as a topic for analysis. Yet recently, almost a century after her passing, there has been a renewed interest in her works, which are increasingly becoming the subject of discussion among modernist scholars, many of whom are returning to the conversation with a fresh arsenal of critical theories and newly published autobiographical material that potentially shed light on the author's œuvre. Recent scholarship is particularly concerned with recognising her contributions to the modernist tradition, as well as reassessing earlier criticism that may have been quick to jump to conclusions, especially with respect to narrative style and themes.

One such theme is Mansfield's attitude towards gender – her œuvre offers a telling reflection on the state of women during the early twentieth century and deals with issues ranging from public to private. In many of her stories, girls and women, often portrayed as innocent and vulnerable, are juxtaposed against men who are described as beasts. On the surface, therefore, it is easy to treat her works as feminist simply by virtue of her gender and subject matter.

Existing studies tend to examine the notion of gender in Mansfield's stories with respect to stereotypes, be it in conformity to or subversion of them. For instance, Pamela Dunbar notes that

> The 'coupling' stories were conceived according to the traditional notions that relations between the sexes are, and ought to be, ones of binary opposition [. . .] Yet while appearing to celebrate sharply defined gender differences many of these stories actually engage in subverting them. Characters who at first present as models of masculinity or femininity are

> shown to bear the qualities normally ascribed to their gender opposites: women turn out to be stronger than their partners, men are devoured by a terrible inner weakness.[1]

Dunbar's observation is certainly valid. There are various instances that offer a glimpse of this reversal: for example, in 'The Stranger' (1920),[2] where John Hammond is emasculated by his wife, his insecurities flaring when she intimates that she had spent a night alone with a male passenger who died in her arms:

> But at that he had to hide his face. He put his face into her bosom and his arms enfolded her.
>
> Spoilt their evening! Spoilt their being alone together! They would never be alone together again. (p. 203)

While there is no indication that Janey Hammond had performed any act of infidelity, the knowledge that she had held someone else, when 'she – who'd never – never once in all these years – never on one single solitary occasion –' (p. 203), is enough to cast doubt on the status of their relationship and what John means to her. His reaction, then, is an act of self-emasculation caused by an overactive imagination. Nevertheless, merely analysing the visible or superficial relationships between men and women established within the text is insufficient evidence to conclude that Mansfield was pushing a feminist agenda. On the contrary, alternative approaches backed by notebook entries and letters claim that Mansfield was not so much concerned with feminism as with the construction of the self. Indeed, Sydney Janet Kaplan comments that 'if anything, [Mansfield] strove to separate herself from any definition as a feminist theorist [. . .] she neither allied herself with the suffrage movement nor studied the ideology of feminism'.[3] It is important here to recognise Mansfield's self-imposed distance from feminism in order to consider new approaches for interpreting her texts. While feminist readings are no doubt still pertinent, there are other avenues worth exploring that could contribute to a deeper understanding of her attitude towards social relationships and gender roles. Specifically, the (de)construction of self is a consistent underlying theme that manifests, albeit in different capacities, across her stories. In this essay, I will focus primarily on women's search for selfhood and identity amid shifting gender expectations and relationships in the following stories from *The Garden Party and Other Stories,* Mansfield's last published collection before her death: 'The Young Girl' (1920), 'The Daughters of the Late Colonel' (1920), 'Life of Ma Parker' (1920), Marriage à la Mode' (1921) and 'At the Bay' (1921). That said, it is necessary first to provide some context prior to exploring her characters' search for identity and the circumstances that demand this shift in gender expectations.

The feminist movement of the twentieth century was an impetus that provided an opportunity for women to take a step forward towards gender equality. It is thus prudent to have a working definition of feminism and how Mansfield's stories toe the line. The contemporary waves of feminism notwithstanding, feminism is traditionally understood as a belief in and fight for women's rights, which generally involves a critique of male power and ideology. This is evident in Mansfield's work, where men are usually portrayed in a negative light as they oppress and exert dominance over women. Yet, beneath her recurrent feminist tone is a recognition that the quest for women to discover their autonomous selves is far more complex than overthrowing the patriarchy – there are sacrifices and adjustments that need to be addressed in any event of systemic change.

Hence, while acknowledging the undeniable feminist stance that permeates Mansfield's stories, one should be cautious about defaulting to the position that a female writer is necessarily feminist. It may be more illuminating to consider the representations of gender as a reflection of Mansfield's personal experience (conscious or otherwise) and observations of living in her society. In *Katherine Mansfield*, a book that offers a comprehensive biographical overview of Mansfield's life, authors Clare Hanson and Andrew Gurr note that

> there is what must be called a feminist awareness running through [Mansfield's] writing, in the sense that there is always a strong feeling of division and discontinuity between male and female experiences in life [. . .] male and female roles are polarized, and only rarely does the experience of the two sexes meet and become communicable.[4]

In response to Hanson and Gurr's observation, I would like to go one step further to propose that, in the context of Mansfield's stories, the experiences of both men and women cannot even be considered as two polarised ends on the same spectrum, as this assumes that gender equality is achievable or even within reach. On the contrary, I suggest that prior to the early twentieth century, the lines drawn between genders are distinct: men and women belong on their respective spectrums, where gender roles are arbitrarily assigned masculine/feminine qualities. Although the occasional overlap may occur, men and women generally conform to these expectations. This approach is in part supported by the existence of gendered spheres in society at the time: for instance, the private home as a site of domestication that holds different expectations for men and women – such as breadwinner versus homemaker – and the public space, where the expectations of men and women differ as well. For example, there is a clear distinction between masculine and feminine careers, with the latter being associated with positions such as caretaker duties or governesses that require a 'feminine' touch.

These gendered roles are exemplified in Mansfield's story 'Life of Ma Parker', in which a literary gentleman details his system as follows: 'You simply dirty everything you've got, get a hag in once a week to clean up, and the thing's done' (p. 231). Preoccupied with his professional commitments, the gentleman has a complete disregard for household chores, deeming them a woman's job. Subsequently, he questions Ma Parker about a missing teaspoonful of cocoa, reminding her of her duty to be honest with him, following which 'he walked off very well pleased with himself, convinced, in fact, he'd shown Mrs Parker that under his apparent carelessness he was as vigilant as a woman' (pp. 233–4). In this exchange, the simile ties the gentleman's vigilance specifically to the female gender and domestic space, where he expresses his pride in noticing a potential discrepancy in his household affairs, a noteworthy feat for a man who is not expected to pay attention to such trivial details. This brief example reveals how in this story roles and responsibilities are strictly gendered.

Beyond establishing the distinctly gendered expectations present in society, though, 'Life of Ma Parker' also reveals the additional difficulties faced by women, even within the private sphere. It is important here to highlight the difference between private and personal space – the former indicates a space closed off to outsiders or the public (that is, the home, which is reserved for family and close friends), while the latter refers to space designated for an individual. Such a personal space is absent for Ma Parker, as shown in the story's ending:

> She couldn't go home; Ethel was there. It would frighten Ethel out of her life. She couldn't sit on a bench anywhere; people would come asking her questions. She couldn't possibly go back to the gentleman's flat; she had no right to cry in strangers' houses. If she sat on some steps a policeman would speak to her.
>
> Oh, wasn't there anywhere where she could hide and keep herself to herself and stay as long as she liked, not disturbing anybody, and nobody worrying her? Wasn't there anywhere in the world where she could have her cry out – at last?
>
> Ma Parker stood, looking up and down. The icy wind blew out her apron into a balloon. And now it began to rain. There was nowhere. (p. 235)

H. E. Bates points out that 'Katherine Mansfield saw the possibilities of telling the story by what was left out as much as by what was left in, or alternately of describing one set of events and consequences while really indicating another',[5] an observation that draws attention to the form of Mansfield's stories: they tend to end inconclusively and abruptly, often leaving the female characters dangling in a compromised situation.[6] Naturally, such endings tend to invite a negative reading regarding those who are oppressed. Nonetheless, I posit that the ambivalence in her endings can be interpreted differently, so that the emphasis lies not in the success of the attempt to break free but rather in a reflection of the conditions that lead to such an ending. This particular ending highlights a couple of points which encourage the following retrospective: firstly, even within the 'private' sphere of the home, Ma Parker is not afforded privacy or personal space; secondly, Ma Parker is under constant surveillance and scrutiny by a public that expects her to behave a certain way, and any deviation from the norm would invite questions that she is neither ready nor equipped to handle. In other words, it is perceived that any attempt at self-expression would not invite empathy but would instead impose upon and inconvenience others. In essence, 'there was nowhere' for her to express herself truly. Ma Parker's experience is, for the most part, the average woman's experience of the time, where the expectation to behave in a way that is dictated by society quashes any effort at self-construction or autonomous expression.

Such a state of affairs is also exemplified in 'The Young Girl', where the unnamed titular character, referred to throughout the narrative as 'she' or 'her', struggles to reconcile society's expectations and her own desires. A girl of seventeen, she behaves in a manner befitting her privileged social status. She is clearly warned against the dangers of men: '"It's" – and she gave a faint shudder – "the stupidity I loathe, and being stared at by fat old men. Beasts!"' (p. 190). The pejorative adjectives attached highlight disgust against a specific group of men, which suggests that the girl's understanding of the opposite sex might be tied to generalisations of external appearances and behaviours. These visual, superficial indicators are problematic as they further categorise individuals according to socially defined stereotypes that reject any possibility of redemption. Ironically, she herself falls victim by conforming to a stereotype that clashes with what she desires. In other words, she is held to certain expectations imposed upon her by virtue of her social class, such as how she is to behave in the presence of others.

In the café, she at first appears indifferent when placing her order – 'Really she didn't mind. It was all the same to her. She didn't really want anything' – yet after her brother orders a chocolate, she 'cried out carelessly' (p. 191) for one as well. This occurs again when she is offered pastries and desserts, which she refuses until Hennie takes a couple; she asks for one and is given four, and her subsequent protests are betrayed when she 'nearly smiled' (p. 192). Her behaviour highlights how she is concerned with the way she is viewed by the speaker; her younger brother (whether because of his youth or gender, it is unclear) thus becomes the voice through which she echoes her own desires.

'The Young Girl' introduces another issue pertaining to the representation of women: the biased male narrative voice which reveals much of the young girl's characterisation. The narrative opens with a description of the young girl:

> In her blue dress, with her cheeks lightly flushed, her blue, blue eyes, and her gold curls pinned up as though for the first time – pinned up to be out of the way for her flight – Mrs Raddick's daughter might have just dropped from this radiant heaven. (p. 189)

The narrator also 'seized [his] courage' (p. 190) when inviting the girl to join him while her mother was occupied, an awkward turn of phrase that hints towards potentially lewd intentions. The story ends with the girl's request to wait on the steps:

> At that she threw back her coat; she turned and faced me; her lips parted. 'Good heavens – why! I – I don't mind it a bit. I – I like waiting.' And suddenly her cheeks crimsoned, her eyes grew dark – for a moment I thought she was going to cry. 'L – let me, please,' she stammered, in a warm, eager voice. 'I like it. I love waiting! Really – really I do! I'm always waiting – in all kinds of places . . . .'
>
> Her dark coat fell open, and her white throat – all her soft young body in the blue dress – was like a flower that is just emerging from its dark bud. (p. 194)

Paired with the overtly sexualised details, the girl's hesitant speech could be interpreted to some extent as an invitation of sorts – a combination of fear and desire. However, if read in a neutral tone sans visual description, it could simply indicate an innocent longing for independence, a decision to make choices instead of adhering to society's demands. The narrator's perspective is thus a literal male gaze that preys on the unsuspecting nature of the young girl, and her willingness to open up to him due to his appearance as a 'very good-looking elderly man' (p. 193) is perceived as a mistake. Overall, 'Life of Ma Parker' and 'The Young Girl' both reflect the flaws of separate, outdated gender spectrums that erroneously simplify how genders are expected to conform to a set behaviour as befitting their status or class in society, and any deviation is frowned upon. Such a mentality is dangerous, especially in the latter tale, for women whose ignorance could lead to unsolicited advances by men.

In an ideal world, both genders would make concessions for each other, but in reality, those in power fear losing that authority; as a result, men are often portrayed as rigid and incapable of change. Mansfield appears pragmatic in her depiction of men who are unwilling to compromise or accommodate the presence of women in their spaces. With this assumption that men are incapable of change, the onus falls on the women to protect themselves against unwanted advances, a request that may be unfair but is not unreasonable. Mansfield's portrayal of men as fixed and unchangeable thus demands action from the women who become responsible for their own change. Be that as it may, recognising the males' resistance to change may actually serve to empower females, who are spared the intricacies of navigating social niceties and are instead urged to treat with caution any and all interactions with males.[7]

However, this particular assessment underscores the limited extent to which females have agency: that is, the types of action women can take in response to men's anxiety and subsequent expression of dominance. Perhaps Mansfield's ambivalent endings are indicative of the lack of solutions that are available. This is further complicated when taking into consideration the aforementioned idea of the separate gendered spectrums merging, as women and men are no longer to be treated exclusively – their belonging on a combined spectrum highlights the need for women to renegotiate their original roles and responsibilities vis-à-vis the shift in expectations that the merger offers. Additionally, they are forced to contend with the men's unwillingness to be reassigned (as seen through their state of stasis) to perform what would have previously been deemed female or feminine roles; Mansfield characterises the males' response as overcompensation with an overt display of their masculinity that serves to plant the seeds of doubt in women who attempt to navigate the revised gender spectrum.

Insofar as it is convenient to blame men for women's subjugation and oppression, it is important to note that men, too, face difficulties in accepting the new expectations of sharing or accommodating women in a space that used to be exclusively theirs. Many of Mansfield's stories highlight how women's struggle for some semblance of equality and opportunity is thwarted by men who are portrayed as resolutely steadfast against any form of change. However, little attention has been given to the fact that underlying the men's resistance is an anxiety that threatens their masculine identity, should concessions be made. Such anxiety is prominent in two stories, 'Marriage à la Mode' and 'At the Bay'. In the former, William performs his duty as a husband, father and breadwinner admirably, but at the same time, he feels an inexplicable distance from his wife, Isabel. This distance is in part physical due to his work away in London and in part emotional – 'They walked together silently. William felt there was nothing to say now' (p. 247). Discomfited, William attempts to bridge the emotional gap between himself and his wife with an intimate love letter (re)declaring his love, a message intended for the recipient in private. However, Isabel shares it publicly with her visitors, a decision that she regrets subsequently – 'Oh, what a loathsome thing to have done. How could she have done it!' (p. 249) She faces a brief moment of self-doubt at the end of the narrative:

> Of course she would stay here and write.
>
> [. . .]
>
> 'I'll – I'll go with them, and write to William later. Some other time. Later. Not now. But I shall *certainly* write,' thought Isabel hurriedly.
>
> And, laughing in the new way, she ran down the stairs. (p. 249)

The 'new way' reflects a simple change: Isabel is bound by neither necessity nor expectation to reply immediately to her husband. While this detail is seemingly inconsequential, given that a response is required, as indicated by 'I shall certainly write', there has already occurred a shift in the balance of power. William's letter, while a commitment of his love, operates simultaneously as an imposition upon Isabel, presumably in accordance with duties or vows set during their marriage; however, her sharing of the letter among her friends plus her delayed response is an active choice she is able to make without any penalty. Ironically, it is the men who suffer, as they too are forced to behave or perform a certain way as a result of the lack of mutual or effective communication.

Such a state of affairs is similarly evident in 'At the Bay', where Stanley leaves for work, resentful, as evidenced by the following:

> The heartlessness of women! The way they took it for granted it was your job to slave away for them while they didn't even take the trouble to see that your walking-stick wasn't lost.
>
> [. . .]
>
> The worst of it was Stanley had to shout good-bye too, for the sake of appearances. Then he saw her turn, give a little skip and run back to the house. She was glad to be rid of him! (p. 255)

His departure is immediately followed by an account of the women, who are finally able to relax in the absence of the male figure:

> Oh, the relief, the difference it made to have the man out of the house. Their very voices were changed as they called to one another; they sounded warm and loving and as if they shared a secret. [. . .] [Beryl]

> wanted, somehow, to celebrate the fact that they could do what they liked now. There was no man to disturb them; the whole perfect day was theirs. (p. 255)

The scenario above serves to recontextualise the new relationship between men and women, in which the latter appear to be one step closer to achieving autonomy at the expense of the former. However, Mansfield complicates things by evoking further sympathy for Stanley, who apologises to Linda for not saying goodbye to her before leaving for work: '"I've been in tortures, Linda" [. . .] Stanley was very hurt [. . .] "I've suffered for it enough to-day"' (pp. 275–6).

Arguably, William and Stanley are themselves victims of expectations as dictated by the patriarchy – yet while theirs is a completely different experience from that of the ladies, it should not be discounted. For both, their suffering is inextricably tied to their fulfilling the societal expectations both of being male and in a committed relationship. Here Mansfield challenges the structures of patriarchy, highlighting how they are detrimental for both men and women in their respective search for identity and autonomous selfhood.

Another situation that Mansfield grapples with in 'At the Bay' is the expectations of childbirth and child-rearing that are synonymous with being a woman:

> Yes, that was [Linda's] real grudge against life; that was what she could not understand. That was the question she asked and asked, and listened in vain for the answer. It was all very well to say it was the common lot of women to bear children. It wasn't true. She, for one, could prove that wrong. She was broken, made weak, her courage was gone, through child-bearing. And what made it doubly hard to bear was, she did not love her children. It was useless pretending. (p. 262)

Even as Linda questions and rejects the biological demands that are forced upon women, she experiences a connection with her child that she tries but fails to deny, as seen below:

> There was something so quaint, so unexpected about that smile that Linda smiled herself. But she checked herself and said to the baby coldly, 'I don't like babies.'
>
> [. . .]
>
> Linda was so astonished at the confidence of this little creature . . . . Ah no, be sincere. That was not what she felt; it was something far different, it was something so new, so . . . . The tears danced in her eyes. (p. 263)

In the clamour for gender equality, Mansfield does acknowledge the biological differences between men and women, particularly in terms of childbirth and child-rearing. She distinguishes between a response to the imposed societal expectations and one's true or personal response to the condition or stimulus, in this case an inexplicable emotion made almost tangible through Linda's imaginary interaction with her baby. Insofar as Linda claims to be indifferent to her children, Mansfield underscores the invisible yet present bond between mother and child that ties them together, despite Linda's grudges. This episode draws attention to the fact that the quest for autonomy is not as simple as merely rejecting or challenging gendered notions and expectations, as there are perhaps biological inclinations that play a factor in the construction of one's self.

Finally, patriarchy as an institution is represented as both limitation and opportunity. It is important to acknowledge how Mansfield's fiction is interested in the spectre of patriarchy and how it oppresses women; at the same time, it is this structure that enables resistance. According to Marilyn Frye,

> The experience of oppressed people is that the living of one's life is confined and shaped by forces and barriers which are not accidental or occasional and hence avoidable, but are systematically related to each other in such a way as to catch one between and among them and restrict or penalize motion in any direction. It is the experience of being caged in: all avenues, in every direction, are blocked or booby trapped.[8]

Developed over centuries, the model of patriarchy has become the foundation of society that is often deemed responsible for the oppression of women. Even in the absence of men, there exists a set of unspoken expectations that continue to burden women. This is evident in the story 'The Daughters of the Late Colonel', in which the passing of an overbearing father figure does nothing to alleviate the fear and doubt that plague his daughters, who remain haunted by his spectral presence. Their decisions on any matter hinged on 'what would father say when he found out?' (p. 218), and his death poses yet another problem – the impossibility of seeking permission for the funeral procedures becomes an unforgivable transgression: '"One thing's certain" – and her tears sprang out again – "father will never forgive us for this – never!"' (p. 218). Josephine's only certainty in her father's absence is that any decision she makes henceforth will be incorrect. Ironically, the daughters, conditioned by the patriarchy running the household, thought themselves strong when their father was alive: '"Why shouldn't we be weak for once in our lives, Jug? It's quite inexcusable. Let's be weak – be weak, Jug. It's much nicer to be weak than to be strong"' (p. 220). The notion of strength and weakness is facilitated by patriarchy; it is within the state of subjugation that opportunity can arise when the figure of oppression is removed. The daughters' timidness stems from a lifetime of caring for their father, but in part it is this that allows them to consider, however briefly, alternatives that promised them autonomy. Jean Grimshaw notes that

> women are seen primarily as *victims*: the monolithic brutality and psychological pressures of male power have reduced women almost to the state of being 'non-persons'.
>
> [. . .]
>
> But behind this victimised female self, whose actions and desires are assumed to be not truly 'her own' since they derive from processes of force, conditioning or psychological manipulation, there is seen to be an authentic female self, whose recovery or discovery it is one of the aims of feminism to achieve.[9]

The removal of the patriarchal figure is therefore significant as it offers the daughters a chance of an existence without oppression. It is doubly ironic, then, that the weakness they speak of – that is, their position as subjugated females in a domestic environment – is, in fact, a strength, an opportunity for them to challenge the phantom of patriarchy that has haunted their lives thus far.

As the narrative progresses, the daughters are forced to confront the reality of their father's passing, along with the decisions they are suddenly fully responsible for, some of which include minor adjustments that require behavioural modifications, such as resisting the urge to stop the organ-grinder who plays in the street below: 'It didn't matter.' That dawning comprehension stirred something within both of them: '[Constantia] had such a strange smile; she looked different' and 'Josephine, too, forgot to be practical and sensible; she smiled faintly, strangely' (p. 227). Despite the spectre of patriarchy that lives on through the daughters, they slowly come to terms with the changing dynamics brought on by their father's passing, which present an unfamiliar, if not uncomfortable emotion. Constantia experiences a brief connection with her Buddha statue: 'The stone and gilt image, whose smile always gave her such a queer feeling, almost a pain and yet a pleasant pain, seemed to-day to be more than smiling. He knew something; he had a secret' (p. 228), but even before that, 'she had always felt there was . . . something' (p. 228). The secret is a recognition of the limits of language – traditionally, Buddhism and its 'practices, ideas, and institutions [. . .] have long been viewed as fundamental for dealing with existential distress, for responding to ethical questions of how ought one to live'.[10] Constantia's connection with the Buddha as a way of coping with her father's passing reveals the possibility of a spiritual transformation moving forward[11]: that is, a state of enlightenment and self-actualisation as achieved through the Buddhist practice of meditation. This invitation by the Buddha into a realm of experience beyond mortal understanding thus exposes the limits of language; yet it is precisely these limits that make thoughts of the indescribable possible, and the 'something' felt by Constantia is manifested and shrouded by the narrative's refusal to put them into words. All the caretaking duties she has had thus far 'seemed to have happened in a kind of tunnel. It wasn't real. It was only when she came out of the tunnel into the moonlight or by the sea or into a thunderstorm that she really felt herself' (p. 229). The epiphanic moment is ultimately quashed in the daughters' unwillingness or inability to impose on each other at the end of the story, '"I've forgotten what it was . . . that I was going to say"' (p. 229). Nevertheless, it realistically captures the flickering moment of transcendence that both daughters undergo but are unable to put into words.

The tunnel metaphor is apt; in exiting the tunnel of patriarchy, Constantia is granted the prospect of finding herself. Whether she does or not is moot; the ending reflects how women are complicit in the perpetuation of patriarchy, simply because they are unable to break free of the status quo. Yet, the hope or possibility for transcendence remains present, as Friedman claims: 'autonomy is always a matter of degree, of more or less. Reflective consideration still counts as a gain in autonomy even if done in the light of other standards and relationships not simultaneously subjected to the same scrutiny.'[12] As such, consideration is a step in the right direction, and the narrative's ending offers two points: firstly, the tantalising promise of freedom, as opposed to freedom itself, suggests that it is possible but comes at a cost; secondly, the attempt itself (that is, the moment of epiphany) indicates how Mansfield values the potential for change over the desired final outcome.

Across the stories I have chosen, I have explored the implications that the shift in gender expectations has, not only for women but for men as well. Granted, the search for autonomous expression comes at a cost, but Mansfield directs attention not to the battle between genders but to the institution of patriarchy as a whole. As Kaplan notes:

> Mansfield's practice – if not her theoretical explanation of it – is deconstructive, in that it insists on interpreting all *constructions* as finally arbitrary, not as representations of the real. Thus the presence of certain features in her writing which might be coded 'feminine' is not evidence of an underlying, essential female nature, but the result of a writing practice that is conscious, deliberate and 'artificial'.[13]

Mansfield's 'feminism' is unconventional in that instead of being a dichotomy in which one is right and the other is wrong, she reflects on how both genders are victims of patriarchy – even as men are responsible for oppressing women, they too are held to certain expectations where any suffering must be endured silently. Mansfield's portrayal of the male figure and perspective is also nuanced, ranging from men as despicable, lecherous beasts to those worrying about the state of their relationships and whether they are fulfilling their 'masculine' responsibility. Similarly, women too are complicit in their oppression, be it conscious or otherwise. Merging the originally distinct gender spectrums also serves to create an additional tension as women are given a glimpse of the freedom to express themselves; this freedom, however, is barred behind the gates of patriarchy, paradoxically within and beyond reach. It is only in recognising one's complicity in a patriarchal system that one can resist and effect systemic change which allows for the possibility of achieving an autonomous self.

Notes

1. Pamela Dunbar, *Radical Mansfield: Double Discourse in Katherine Mansfield's Short Stories* (London: Macmillan, 1997), p. 88.
2. Vincent O'Sullivan, ed., *Katherine Mansfield's Selected Stories* (New York: Norton & Co., 2006). Further references to Mansfield's stories are to this edition and page numbers are supplied in the text.
3. Sydney Janet Kaplan, *Katherine Mansfield and the Origins of Modernist Fiction* (Ithaca, NY: Cornell University Press, 1991), p. 10.
4. Clare Hanson and Andrew Gurr, *Katherine Mansfield* (London: Macmillan, 1989), pp. 13–14.
5. H. E. Bates, *The Modern Short Story: A Critical Survey* (London: Thomas Nelson and Sons, 1941), p. 129.
6. See Mansfield's stories 'The Little Governess' and 'At Lehmann's', among others.
7. This recalls a passage from 'The Little Governess': 'Well, I always tell my girls that it's better to mistrust people at first rather than to trust them, and it's safer to suspect people of evil intentions rather than good ones . . . . It sounds rather hard but we've got to be women of the world, haven't we?' (p. 51).
8. Marilyn Frye, 'Oppression', in Ann E. Cudd and Robin Andreasen, eds, *Feminist Theory: A Philosophical Anthology* (Oxford: Blackwell, 2005), pp. 84–90 (p. 85).
9. Jean Grimshaw, 'Autonomy and Identity in Feminist Thinking', in Cudd and Andreasen, pp. 329–38 (pp. 330–1).
10. Nalika Gajaweera and Darcie DeAngelo, 'Introduction: Buddhism and Resilience', *Journal of Global Buddhism*, 22: 1 (2021), pp. 77–82 (p. 77).
11. Damien Keown, 'Buddha', in *A Dictionary of Buddhism* (Oxford: Oxford University Press, 2004), p. 42.
12. Marilyn Friedman, 'Autonomy, Social Disruption, and Women', in Cudd and Andreasen, pp. 339–51 (p. 343).
13. See Kaplan, pp. 158–9.

‘Forgive my Hat’: Clothing as a Condition of Narratability in *The Garden Party and Other Stories*

Samantha Dewally

Whilst a woman’s hat was more likely to be linked to consumerism and fashion in the nineteenth and early twentieth centuries, as Diana Crane suggests, it was the man whose hat bore the marker of familial social standing. Being hatless in the street and removing one’s hat at work was not *de rigueur.*[1] Whilst Crane writes from a purely anthropological point of view, Charlotte Nicklas examines the role of the hat as an implicit indicator of social propriety in literature between 1890 and 1930:

> Authors assumed that readers knew the regions where hats should and should not be worn. Rather than explicitly describing female characters passing between public outdoor and more private indoor spaces, authors often indicated or emphasised their movement by referring to the taking off or putting on of hats.[2]

This cultural behaviour is exploited by Katherine Mansfield in a figurative sense to symbolise suppressed or subjugated behaviours, or the inverse, in the last collection of stories published before her death, *The Garden Party and Other Stories* (1922). Linda, in ‘At the Bay’ (1921), recalls meeting her husband, Stanley, as a young man, ‘a very broad young man with bright ginger hair’, his head ‘uncovered’. The Stanley without the hat is the one she loves: ‘Not the Stanley whom everyone saw, not the everyday one’.[3] In ‘The Stranger’ (1920), Mr Hammond’s emotions are quite clearly betrayed by his behaviour with his hat. He is excited to be seeing his wife after months apart. Mr Hammond takes off his hat when anticipating seeing his wife again as he prepares to board the ship – an outward signal of receptiveness and vulnerability (p. 129). He takes it off again in the cabin: ‘The strain was over. He felt he could have sat there for ever sighing his relief – the relief at being rid of that horrible tug, pull, grip on his heart’ (p. 132). In contrast to this, he 'seizes' his hat to reassert his authority when his wife goes to say farewell to the doctor, and he is suspicious. Janey, in contrast, has 'thrown back her veil', which suggests an openness towards the others on board (p. 132).

Hats – and, more widely, items of clothing and adornments – populate the pages of Mansfield's short stories. After mapping the intriguing recurrence of hats and clothing throughout *The Garden Party and Other Stories*, it becomes apparent that Mansfield's appropriation (or 'fetishistic overvaluation or misappropriation')[4] of the hat stretches beyond the standard hat-wearing conventions of the time – conventions that placed social and legal restrictions on women in terms of education, economic independence, occupational opportunities and sexual equality.[5] Like her contemporary, Virginia Woolf, Mansfield pushed back against these standard conventions, deliberately placing her hat alongside the men's to assert her equality within a traditionally male literary circle. As one friend recalled, she 'would flounce into a restaurant and sweep her wide black hat from her bobbed head and hang it among the men's hats on the rack'.[6] With questions of electoral reform and women's suffrage still being debated, this was a transitional period for women, and Mansfield found herself jostled between two worlds.

Mansfield arrived in London in 1908 into an 'adventurous and unorthodox society, open to new ideas, determinedly rejecting the values of its parents'.[7] She would go on to submit her writing to periodicals such as *The New Age*, which encouraged 'radical departures from established Edwardian ways of thought'[8] (represented by editor A. R. Orage's unconventional soft felt hat, which was, according to Antony Alpers, 'a slight expression of revolt'[9]), whilst facing familial pressure to conform to codes of dress and behaviour imposed by her middle-class, colonial background. For example, when Mrs Beauchamp arrived from New Zealand in May 1909, to be met by her daughter in a newly bought black straw hat, she disdainfully 'carried her off to her hotel in Manchester Street, and consigned the hat to the chambermaid'.[10]

As well as Mansfield using her hats to objectify a shift away from standard social etiquette, accounts by her friends highlight her personal use of clothing and objects for dramatic effect. Lawrence Mitchell suggests that:

> Mansfield's highly developed aesthetic sense was reflected in myriad ways: in her response to what Virginia Woolf called 'solid objects', in the colours in which she dressed, even in the way she organized her environment. At times she quite self-consciously worked for an aesthetic effect in which she became an integral part, indeed the centrepiece, of a sort of tableau vivant.[11]

Virginia Woolf and William Orton both recall visiting her in her rooms to find her centre-stage in her kimono, surrounded by carefully arranged objects.[12] Her style, influenced no doubt by her visit to the immense Japanese exhibition in Shepherd's Bush in 1910, was 'clearly many thousand miles from Thorndon and Edwardian hats'.[13] By adopting the trend for orientalism, Mansfield reveals that she was not immune to the trappings of consumerism, the same consumerism critiqued in 'The Garden Party' (1921). Nonetheless, her self-awareness of this conflicting position is discernible in the scene where Laura's sisters, Meg and Jose, are described as idly breakfasting in a turban, kimono and silk petticoat whilst the workmen busily prepare the party around them (p. 38). Indeed, she may well have been parodying herself.

This affiliation with inanimate objects, or 'sympathetic identification' as Mitchell puts it,[14] stretches beyond the personal into Mansfield's fictional world, where hats and clothing are 'recoded' to fulfil a narrative function. This idea of allowing a hat or an item of clothing as a 'condition of narratability'[15] is exemplified in the three short stories I draw upon for the purposes of this essay: 'Miss Brill' (1920), 'The Garden Party' and 'Bank Holiday' (1920). In these stories, hats are a symbol of social status and are employed to comment on the adherence (or non-adherence) to societal norms, so that 'cultural values become objectified in specific material forms',[16] or become, in Tomalin's words, the 'emblems and props of feeling'.[17] Francis Carco was also aware of Mansfield's 'hypersensitivity' towards everyday objects and commented on her capacity to fill them with life,[18] such as her 'entering into' or 'taking possession'[19] of the fox-fur in 'Miss Brill' (1920).

The 'vivification of the insensate', as Aimee Gasston puts it, allows the reader to enter the consciousness of Miss Brill,[20] and it is the concise form of the short story which, according to Gasston,[21] allows this emphasis to be placed on the objects in the external world of the character, affording agency and allowing the object to inhabit the human sphere: 'The box that the fur came out of was on the bed. She unclasped the necklet quickly; quickly, without looking, laid it inside. But when she put the lid on she thought she heard something crying' (p. 114). As Miss Brill's emotions are transferred on to the fur necklet, the fur plays its own part rather than just being a prop in the drama, demonstrating how Miss Brill disconnects from her human emotions and effectively locks them away inside a box. A truth Miss Brill has been refusing to acknowledge, but which is voiced by the fur at the beginning of the story – '"What has been happening to me?" said the sad little eyes' (p. 110) – is revealed by the comments directed at her at the end: '"Why does she come here at all – who wants her? Why doesn't she keep her silly old mug at home?" "It's her fu-fur which is so funny", giggled the girl. "It's exactly like a fried whiting"' (p. 113). This overheard comment makes Miss Brill realise that she is not in the centre of the action but rather is on the outside, looking in. Miss Brill does not engage with the other people in the park on a human level but eavesdrops on their lives as if watching a soap-opera; hence they are identified only by their costumes. Miriam Mandel notes that 'as Miss Brill catalogues what she sees, she reduces and dehumanizes it', concluding that 'whatever Miss Brill sees, she reduces to the parameters of her own constricted world'.[22] Those around her remain faceless and are instead described by what they are wearing, either individually – 'he wearing a dreadful Panama hat and she button boots' – or grouped according to common features: 'Little boys with big white silk bows under their chins, little girls like French dolls, dressed up in velvet and lace'. Some are even classified by a single colour: 'Two young girls in red came by and two young soldiers in blue' (p. 111). Mistakenly, Miss Brill believes that she plays a starring role alongside these bit players, whereas she is only play-acting and overplaying her own importance. She likes to listen to the lines the others are speaking, but never speaks any lines of her own. Miss Brill is under the illusion that she is a part of this community and has a false sense of belonging – 'no doubt somebody would have noticed if she hadn't been there; she was part of the performance after all' (p. 112).

There are two significant ironic moments in the story which hint at the real, lonely Miss Brill. Whereas her reduced description of those around her ignores human characteristics and focuses on clothes, there is one group where even this is absent, draining these people of any colour and life. She says that they are 'odd, silent, nearly all old, and from the way they stared they looked as though they'd just come from dark little rooms or even – even cupboards!' (p. 111). The poignancy of this one line is revealed at the very end when Miss Brill returns to her own cupboard of a room, mirroring the box where the fox-fur is stored. The second ironic moment, the arrival of a lady known only as 'an ermine toque' (p. 112), echoes the situation of Miss Brill and the fox-fur. The toque had been bought 'when her hair was yellow. Now everything, her hair, her face, even her eyes, was the same colour as the shabby ermine' (p. 112). The 'ermine toque' is rebuffed when she tries to engage in conversation, and Miss Brill hears the emotion of the moment played out by the band and sees the 'toque' move away to a more hopeful conclusion, smiling 'more brightly than ever' (p.112). The description of the woman parallels Miss Brill, as her fox-fur, with its age-related shabbiness, is representative of Miss Brill's appearance and her shift in social status towards the margins of society. The reader may interpret the woman's bright smile as a mask of her true feelings, but Miss Brill's interpretation of the soundtrack to her performance, with the band playing 'more gaily than ever' (p. 112), indicates that she does not look past the painted smile. Particularly poignant is the almost pleading repetition of 'than ever', hinting at Miss Brill's deliberate misinterpretation of the scene.

As Miss Brill transfers her sadness to her fur, Laura in 'The Garden Party' transfers her discomfort to her hat. Laura's hat is the most widely critiqued hat in Mansfield's writing. Karen Shaup suggests that Laura's hat is a symbol of bourgeois consumerism.[23] Indeed, 'The Garden Party' is laden with overconsumption – from a surfeit of lilies and roses, the extravagance of a cream puff right after breakfast and a basketful of leftovers. The leftovers, like Laura's mother's hat, can afford to be discarded, or given away in an act of false charity. Having originally bought the hat for herself, Laura's mother declaims it as 'much too young' for her and passes it to Laura (p. 46). Both acts, neither a sacrifice nor an act of generosity as their monetary worth is of little consequence, are tokens to distract Laura from an anxiety unbecoming of her class. Delivering the basket of leftovers to the family of the recently deceased young carter, Laura is ushered to where the dead man lies. In the room, she considers an appropriate response: 'But all the same you had to cry, and she couldn't go out of the room without saying something to him. Laura gave a loud, childish sob. "Forgive my hat," she said' (p. 51). Shaup interprets this apology as a rejection of her family's materialism. However, Laura does not take off the hat or discard it, even if she regrets its connotations. Putting on the hat temporarily masks her lack of self-confidence and subdues her developing social conscience, which is pulling her in a different direction to the rest of her family. It makes her believe she, too, can live happily in her environs, even if 'she seemed to be different to them all' (p. 49). Her fluctuating standpoint is seen in her behaviour through interactions with the hat, both by herself and by others at the party. Don W. Kleine views Laura's hat as a symbol of her move from child to adulthood.[24] Catching sight of herself in the mirror, she sees her other, adult self, playing the part assigned to her by her family. The hat allows her temporarily to satisfy her desire for experience, according to Kleine, and put aside her reservations. Whereas, when first presented with the hat, she 'couldn't look at herself; she turned aside' (p. 46) and continues to argue her point with her mother, she changes her mind when accidentally catching sight of herself in the mirror: 'Is mother right? She thought. And now she hoped her mother was right' (p. 47). At the party, she adopts the role of the hostess and whilst 'glowing' in the light of the comments from guests on her grown-up appearance, again shows slips in the illusion created by the hat by begging her father to take a drink to the band (p. 48). Although Laura's hat makes her seem more grown-up to both herself and others, her actions demonstrate that she is not ready to take on all that goes with the responsibility of adulthood, if adulthood means adopting certain behaviours or beliefs. By questioning the assumption that their charity would be well received by the deceased carter's family, she is thus questioning the role of someone of her class in society: 'to take scraps from their party. Would the poor woman really like that?' (p. 49). Her apology may also give voice to her developing awareness and personal moral code; she is questioning her own unformed judgement. She is conflicted and torn between how she is expected to think and behave and what she perceives to be morally responsible behaviour.

On arrival at the dead carter's house, Laura is self-aware enough to realise that she is out of place, but cannot engage emotionally with the experience; nor can she take up the stance of bourgeois philanthropist, as perhaps her mother would have done. Whether her apology is general or personal is open to interpretation. Andrew Martin argues that Laura's apology is on behalf of her social class, a general apology for what he terms a lack of 'sociomisery', a lack of sympathy and shared sorrow, of which the dress and hat are emblematic.[25] Laura is able to recognise grief only in physical, not emotional, terms, referring to the strange 'oily' voices of the women and their 'terrible', 'puffy', 'swollen' appearance (p. 50). The physical aspects of herself, such as her hat and her dress, therefore, are what she apologises for as she leaves the room.

Unlike 'The Garden Party', 'Bank Holiday' is not populated by characters in the traditional sense. As in 'Miss Brill', they are 'reduced' to what they are wearing; they are playing their part as extras in a film, with no central character or determined setting. The reader can make assumptions about certain aspects of personality or lifestyle within the confines of their described wardrobe. In 'Miss Brill' the reader encounters much the same challenges, but in 'Bank Holiday' we do not have the luxury of a Miss Brill character, whose inner discourse leads us to draw a conclusion of sorts about Miss Brill as a marginal figure. Although I agree with Lorna Sage's description of 'Bank Holiday' as a 'post-impressionist word painting',[26] it might also be seen as cinematographic: the camera pans across the view of a crowd, bringing a sense of movement to the opening tableau. Mansfield as narrator is sitting behind the camera and is thus able to describe the scene from many angles, allowing the viewer to overhear snippets of conversation as each of her characters in this montage is illuminated. If we are to believe the author, who has been quoted as writing 'there mustn't be one single word out of place, or one word that can be taken out',[27] then we need to delve deeper into the significance of the clothing used as the main character descriptor and its function in the narrative.

Written in 1920, 'Bank Holiday' could be read as a critique of the speed with which the tragedy of the First World War is forgotten in the frenzy of celebration following the armistice. In a letter to Ottoline Morrell, written on 13 July 1919, Mansfield wrote of her distaste at the 'preparations for Festivity':

> When I read of the preparations that are being made in all the work-houses throughout the land – when I think of all those toothless old jaws guzzling for the day – and then of all that beautiful youth feeding the fields of France – Life is almost too ignoble to be borne. Truly one must hate humankind in the mass – hate them as passionately as one loves the few – the very few.[28]

Amongst the crowd in the 'Bank Holiday' celebrations we find 'the Australian soldier' and 'men in khaki, sailors' and '"hospital boys" in blue' (p. 139), which suggest serving and injured soldiers. However, the 'beat' and 'force' of the musicians imply from the start that the music is not flowing naturally, that the jovial atmosphere is forced. The unsmiling, faceless musicians underscore the general lack of feeling, or denial of feeling, that Mansfield critiques, and the ease with which she feels their suffering is forgotten, trivialised and even commercialised by paper hats, ticklers and other frivolous items, as she explains in the same letter to Morrell: 'Ticklers, squirts, portraits eight times as large as life of Lloyd George & Beatty blazing against the sky – and drunkenness and brawling & destruction'.[29] By creating a crowd of contemporary social stereotypes through the wardrobe of her characters, each with a negative or critical slant, Mansfield is asking her readers to pick out the hat which belongs to them.[30]

The submissive Victorian 'old fat women in velvet bodices' are compared to 'dusty pincushions'. The women are rounded like pincushions, both in physical appearance and in reference to Victorian dress styles. Mansfield implies by this that these types are undynamic, as they gather dust, and subservient, as they let themselves be used to stick pins in. The thinner women with a more contemporary silhouette are described as 'worn umbrellas with a quivering bonnet on top'. 'Worn' again signals an older woman, who is perhaps worn out through 'do-gooding' or 'busy-bodying', described here by the bonnet which quivers as she talks animatedly – behaviour which is unfavourably coloured through the use of 'hags' (p. 139). The hats of the younger women 'might have grown on hedges' (p. 139), which suggests they are from the lower classes, who, unable to afford the services of a milliner, would trim their own hats in the latest fashion, and their exuberance indicates a slightly overdone vulgarity. This contrasts to the static, colourless description of the 'ragged' children (p. 139), which makes a statement about the poverty of the working classes. They are 'the only ones who are quiet' (p. 139). Perhaps they do not understand the significance of the moment, cannot find anything to celebrate, or are demonstrating an empathy or collective sadness lacking in the adults, whose emotions are kept firmly wrapped under their three-cornered paper hats – 'the only way of saving yourself' (p. 140), as with Miss Brill's fox-fur being confined to its box, or Laura masking her misgivings with her hat.

The choice of the simple present tense consigns the opening tableau of musicians to replay this scene over and over, permanently fixed to the painted canvas (p. 139), just as Mansfield keeps 'seeing all these horrors, bathing in them again & again (God knows I don't want to)', and asks herself: 'What is the meaning of it all?'[31] The musicians are 'stout', 'little' and 'thin' (p. 139), but apart from that we know them only by their clothing. Mr 'Stout' wears 'dingy white flannel trousers, a blue coat with a pink handkerchief showing and a straw hat much too small for him, perched at the back of his head' (p. 139). Even the music is described in terms of clothing, the fiddler drawing 'long, twisted, streaming ribbons' out of his instrument (p. 139). The flute player, or piper, wears a 'felt hat like a broken wing' (p. 139). The mysterious, unknown destination to which the parade is led at the end of the story, alongside the description of the piper's hat, creates a Hamelin-esque atmosphere: 'Up, up they thrust into the light and heat, shouting, laughing, squealing, as though they were being pushed by something far below, and by the sun, far ahead of them – drawn up into the full, bright, dazzling radiance to . . . what?' (p. 142).

Many versions of the legend of the Pied Piper of Hamelin exist, in both European and Oriental folklore. The destination of the children in the legend remains a mystery, one that Mansfield asks us to ponder at the ending of 'Bank Holiday: 'to . . . what?' (p. 142). The truth, if any, behind the legend of the Pied Piper and what happened to the children is not known. However, the tale holds a certain fascination, having been translated into many languages and reworked by Browning, Brecht and Goethe, amongst many others. There is much theorising on its origins. One suggestion is that the children were recruited into the crusades, another that they were led into migration to colonise Eastern Europe. Whatever the theory, the tale is one of deception and tragedy.[32] Traditionally, the piper is dressed in colourful garments. In Browning's poem the piper wears a long coat 'half of yellow and half of red' and 'a scarf of red and yellow stripe', and the frontispiece illustration in the published version referenced shows the piper's hat to contain a feather.[33] The Brothers Grimm tale is of a man wearing a coat of multi-coloured fabrics.[34] But the piper in 'Bank Holiday' has most in common with the version titled 'The Ratcatcher', included in Andrew Lang's *The Red Fairy Book*, published in 1890, itself a translation from Charles Marelle's French adaptation of the Grimm legend.[35] Lang's piper, like Mansfield's, hides his eyes under his hat. On being refused payment for ridding Hamelin of rats, and plotting his revenge, he 'pulled his hat down over his eyes, went hastily out of the hall, and left the town without speaking to a soul'.[36] The hat acts as signifier in Mansfield's allusion to this tale. Lang's description of the piper, with his 'two great yellow piercing and mocking eyes, under a large felt hat set off by a scarlet cock's feather',[37] can be compared to Mansfield's character, whose face is 'hidden under a felt hat like a broken wing' (p. 139). The 'broken wing' not only mirrors the adornment of the piper's hat but subverts it. Removing any trace of colour from the feather and replacing it with a broken, disfigured limb is our first indicator of an underlying darkness. In the legend, the piper returns with more sinister motives: namely, to draw the children away into the mountain. This parallels the possible motivation of Mansfield's 'faceless', 'unsmiling' musicians (p. 139) – to draw mothers' sons into war.

The musicians in 'Bank Holiday' whip up the crowd and add to the almost frenzied atmosphere as the people are drawn (or pushed) up the hill. Just as music created a spirit of community in the post-war celebrations, it played its role equally well in the establishment of a sense of duty. Men from all corners of society were drawn into recruiting offices by bands, were fêted by them on station platforms and departed in lines or parades accompanied by them. Military bands played an important role out in the field, often leading men into battle:

> A war correspondent reporting from the Battle of the Somme described the powerful impact of the pipes as Highland regimental pipers went into battle 'screaming out the Charge', and how afterwards the pipers played a Scottish 'love song' as a lament to fallen comrades.[38]

Mansfield's musicians, as the piper is not alone in this tale, 'beat' and 'force' the music out of their instruments, and 'the fiddler's arm tries to saw the fiddle in two' (p. 139). Behind her camera lens, Mansfield zooms in on the piper's ring with its turquoise gemstone, which links to the violent or aggressive playing through its mythical associations. One legend is that turquoise was worn by Persian warriors in ancient times as protection when going into battle, and that it predicts impending doom by changing colour.[39] Turquoise, it is said, bridges the physical and spiritual world and can help the wearer reveal the truth, a truth which Mansfield seeks to expose through the allusion to the Pied Piper story. Idiomatically, a 'Pied Piper' is someone who others follow blindly,[40] so as well as criticising the 'bawdy' celebrations at the end of a war, Mansfield calls into question the jingoism which encouraged young men into recruitment offices, with little idea of what they were about to face. Lang's piper calls the children into the market square, and they follow him: 'If you do not pay me I will be paid by your heirs,' he had warned.[41] Mansfield's parade follows the band up the hill to an unknown destination, following a faceless piper wearing the ring of a warrior, who is intent on taking their heirs as payment. Mansfield's imagery is multi-stranded, as the same idea is personified in the swindler Professor Leonard (p. 141), arriving fresh from Paris, Brussels and London, a reference to the seats of governments controlling the conflict, and is continued in the allusion to Lang's version, where the piper delivers his promise of ridding the town of rats. He calls upon an old white rat, 'the king of the band',[42] to help him achieve this. The white rat is present in the clothing of the musicians, in their 'dingy white flannel trousers' and the 'white canvas shoes' (p. 139). By creating the analogy to rats, the lowliest and most disliked of all creatures, Mansfield critiques the apparent disposability of the thousands of young men who were sent to war and critiques those who sent them. It is the piper who leads, but it is the King who gives the shout and is followed blindly to death, into the 'light and heat' (p. 142), here with the darker connotation of flashes of light and the heat of the battle.

The crowd reaches the top of the hill, 'as though they were being pushed by something' (p.142). I have argued that Mansfield feels that men were pushed to do their duty and were deceived into a false sense of what lay ahead, represented by government propaganda. At the close of 'Bank Holiday', it is not mountain doors that swing shut at the top of the hill, as in the Pied Piper, but those of a public house. The doors swing shut behind the men who disappear inside: 'The mother sits on the pavement edge with her baby, and the father brings her out a glass of dark, brownish stuff, and then savagely elbows his way in again' (p. 141). The female figure features heavily in this story, and it is interesting that the mother remains outside the public house, just as the women were left behind with their children when their husbands left for war. If we link this to one of the items on sale at the fair, it becomes clear that Mansfield lays the blame for so many lost lives on the behaviour of women as part of the propaganda machine, for encouraging their menfolk through the doors of the metaphorical public house: 'Fevvers! Fevvers! They are hard to resist' (p. 140). Even the babies in bonnets are wearing a feather (at the time a popular adornment, after Queen Mary was photographed wearing a feather and pearl headdress),[43] which underscores the level of emotional blackmail critiqued in this short story.[44] Mansfield's feathers are not white, but bright and vibrant, providing a contrast between the light and dark themes which feature throughout the story. The innocent, ale-coloured liquid the man brings his wife out of the pub becomes something altogether more sinister in this light, identifiable as the mud of the battlefield, or even the blood of the dead and wounded.

The presence of flowers and happy, laughing people in the closing lines is reminiscent of the Wilfred Owen poem 'The Send-off'. The poem shares similar contrasts between light and darkness and juxtaposes the idea of darkness and death with the gaiety of the flowers women presented to soldiers on their departure, alongside the singing and music that accompanied their leaving from station platforms:

> Down the close darkening lanes they sang their way
> To the siding-shed,
> And lined the train with faces grimly gay.
> Their breasts were stuck all white with wreath and spray
> As men's are, dead.

Owen's poem continues:

> So secretly, like wrongs hushed-up, they went.
> They were not ours:
> We never heard to which front these were sent;
> Nor there if they yet mock what women meant
> Who gave them flowers.[45]

Whilst Owen's critique quietly bobs near the surface, buoyed by oxymoron and juxtaposition, readers of 'Bank Holiday' may simply be blinded by the dazzling brightness and deafened by the shouts and squeals which envelop them at the close of the story, in so much as they choose to view 'Bank Holiday' simply as a short, curious but relatable snapshot of a bank holiday fair. However, as Mansfield's characters are dehumanised and impersonalised through the use of clothing as character descriptors, a sense of emotional distance is created which allows the reader to take a step back and reflect; the faceless characters in 'Bank Holiday' expose and critique common attitudes, and readers must potentially face up to seeing their own face in the crowd.

By using clothing figuratively, Mansfield exploits the interaction between it and the wearer to reveal underlying behaviours or to signal changes to their state of mind or in their perception of the world, as exemplified in Laura in 'The Garden Party'. Clearly, however, Mansfield goes beyond the use of the hat simply as a signifier of cultural value. Hats and clothing are exploited to fulfil a narrative function in the absence of an external, omniscient narrator. A hat can work as a link between two worlds, as in the allusion to the folktale of the Pied Piper. The most telling hat, however, is the three-cornered paper kind in 'Bank Holiday'. The seller reminds us that 'the only way of saving yourself' (p. 140) is to keep it all under your hat, which demonstrates the power of the hat in maintaining social order, but also one's personal emotional stability.

Notes

1. Diana Crane, 'The Social Meanings of Hats and T-Shirts, Excerpted from Fashion and Its Social Agendas: Class, Gender, and Identity in Clothing', in *Fashion and Its Social Agendas: Class, Gender, and Identity in Clothing* (Chicago: University of Chicago Press, 2000), available at: <https://press.uchicago.edu/Misc/Chicago/117987.html> (last accessed 5 March 2021).
2. Charlotte Nicklas, '"It is the Hat that Matters the Most": Hats, Propriety and Fashion in British Fiction, 1890–1930', *Costume*, 51: 1 (2017), pp. 78–102 (p. 80).
3. Katherine Mansfield, *The Garden Party and Other Stories* (London: Penguin, 1997), pp. 18–19. All subsequent quotations from this edition are placed parenthetically in the text.
4. Bill Brown, 'The Secret Life of Things (Virginia Woolf and the Matter of Modernism)', *Modernism/modernity*, 6: 2 (1999), pp. 1–28 (p. 1).
5. Juliet Gardiner, *The New Woman* (London: Collins & Brown, 1993), pp. 6–7.
6. Claire Tomalin, *Katherine Mansfield: A Secret Life* (London: Penguin, 1988), p. 113. As retold by Mansfield's friend, Beatrice Campbell.
7. Tomalin, p. 48.
8. Antony Alpers, *The Life of Katherine Mansfield* (London: Jonathan Cape, 1980), pp. 107–8.
9. Alpers, p. 147.
10. Tomalin, p. 67.
11. J. Lawrence Mitchell, 'Katherine Mansfield and the Aesthetic Object', *Journal of New Zealand Literature*, 22 (2004), p. 50.
12. Mitchell, pp. 50–1.
13. Alpers, p. 118.
14. Mitchell, p. 32.
15. Brown, p. 12.
16. Brown, p. 1.
17. Tomalin, p. 201.
18. Qtd in Mitchell, p. 31.
19. Mitchell, p. 31.
20. Aimee Gasston, 'Phenomenology Begins at Home: The Presence of Things in the Short Fiction of Katherine Mansfield and Virginia Woolf', *Journal of New Zealand Literature*, 32: 2 (2014), pp. 31–51 (p. 37).
21. Gasston, p. 32.
22. Miriam B. Mandel, 'Reductive Imagery in "Miss Brill"', *Studies in Short Fiction*, 26: 4 (1989), pp. 473–7 (p. 475).

23. Karen L. Shaup, 'Consuming Beauty: Aesthetic Experience in Katherine Mansfield's "The Garden Party"', *Papers on Language & Literature*, 51: 3 (2015), pp. 221–43 (pp. 240–2).
24. Don W. Kleine, '"The Garden Party": A Portrait of the Artist', *Criticism*, 5: 4 (1963), pp. 360–71 (p. 369).
25. Andrew Martin, 'Putting on a Hat for "The Garden Party": Sympathy and Societal Roles in this Short Story', *Those Passions Read* (2015), available at: <https://thosepassionsread.wordpress.com/2015/04/27/putting-on-a-hat-for-the-garden-party-sympathy-and-societal-roles-in-this-short-story> (last accessed 4 March 2021).
26. Lorna Sage, 'Notes', in Mansfield, *The Garden Party*, pp. 154–9 (p. 159).
27. Stephanie Forward, 'An Introduction to Katherine Mansfield's Short Stories', *Discovering Literature: 20th Century* (2016), available at: <https://www.bl.uk/20th-century-literature/articles/an-introduction-to-katherine-mansfields-short-stories> (last accessed 25 February 2021).
28. *Letters* 2, p. 339.
29. *Letters* 2, p. 339.
30. Here, I use the term 'wardrobe' to include millinery, clothing, footwear and accessories such as jewellery and adornments.
31. *Letters* 2, p. 339.
32. Stadt Hameln, *The Pied Piper of Hamelin* (2017), available at <https://www.hameln.de/en/> (last accessed 19 August 2021).
33. Robert Browning, 'The Pied Piper of Hamelin: A Child's Story', in *The Pied Piper of Hamelin and Other Poems: Every Boy's Library* (Project Gutenberg, 2013), available at: <https://www.gutenberg.org/files/42850/42850-h/42850-h.htm> (last accessed 9 August 2021).
34. 'He was wearing a coat of many colored, bright cloth, for which reason he was called the Pied Piper'. See Jacob and Wilhelm Grimm, 'The Children of Hameln', in *The Pied Piper of Hamelin and Related Legends from Other Towns*, ed. D. L. Ashliman (1999–2021), available at: <https://sites.pitt.edu/~dash/hameln.html#grimm245> (last accessed 9 August 2021).
35. Andrew Lang, 'The Ratcatcher', in *The Red Fairy Book* (London and New York: Longmans, Green and Company, 1890), pp. 208–14. For alternative versions of the Pied Piper story see Ashliman. For the original German version by the Brothers Grimm, see Brüder Grimm, 'Die Kinder zu Hameln', in *Deutsche Sagen* (Munich: Winkler, 1981). The notes alongside this version signal the presence of a similar tale published in French, which is a translation of a Chinese folktale: *Cabinet des fées; ou, Collection choisie des contes des fées, et autres contes merveilleux: Volume 19* (Paris: Barde, Manget et Compagnie, 1786), pp. 340–6.
36. Lang, p. 212.
37. Lang, p. 208.
38. 'How Pipers Called the Shots at the Somme', *The Scotsman*, 21 January 2017, available at: <https://www.scotsman.com/heritage-and-retro/retro/how-pipers-called-shots-somme-1457833> (last accessed 26 July 2021).
39. American Gem Society, *Legends and Folklore of Turquoise* (2020), available at: <https://www.americangemsociety.org/legends-and-folklore-of-turquoise/> (last accessed 29 March 2021).
40. Andrew Delahunty and Sheila Dignen, 'Pied Piper', in *A Dictionary of Reference and Allusion* (Oxford: Oxford University Press, 2010), available at: <https://www-oxfordreference-com.ezproxy.uwtsd.ac.uk/view/10.1093/acref/9780199567454.001.0001/acref-9780199567454-e-1452> (last accessed 9 August 2021). Elizabeth Knowles,

'Pied Piper', in *The Oxford Dictionary of Phrase and Fable* (Oxford: Oxford University Press, 2005), available at: <https://www-oxfordreference-com.ezproxy.uwtsd.ac.uk/view/10.1093/acref/9780198609810.001.0001/acref-9780198609810-e-5435> (last accessed 9 August 2021).

41. Lang, p. 212.
42. Lang, p. 211.
43. Nicklas, p. 91.
44. See Nicoletta F. Gullace, 'White Feathers and Wounded Men: Female Patriotism and the Memory of the Great War', *Journal of British Studies*, 36: 2 (1997), pp. 178–206 (p. 182).
45. Wilfred Owen, 'The Send-off', in *The Poems of Wilfred Owen*, ed. Jon Stallworthy (London: Hogarth Press, 1985), p. 149.

Katherine Mansfield's Desperate Housewives and Metonymic Desire

Sovay Hansen

'[M]ake me your mistress.'

– Katherine Mansfield[1]

Despite her parents' early efforts to shape her into a respectable Edwardian lady, Katherine Mansfield had a multiplicity of unconventional desires, many of which she unapologetically pursued throughout her short, secretive and provocative life.[2] Still, in a 1906 teenage letter to her favourite cousin, Sylvia Payne, we see that Mansfield's desire to determine her own destiny – and the futility of that desire – is potent:

> I am so keen upon all women having a *definite* future – are not you? The idea of sitting and waiting for a husband is absolutely revolting – and it really is the attitude of a great many girls [. . .] It rather made me smile to read of your wishing you could create your fate – O how many times I have [. . .] felt just the same. I just long for power over circumstances.[3]

Clearly, Mansfield saw traditional marriage and gender roles as obstacles to women creating their own fates and defining their futures. What is also evident in this letter is that Mansfield does not see an avenue for such 'power over circumstances' available to women, but she longs for it all the same.

Indeed, Mansfield's constant condition in life was one of longing for more than the social expectations that were impressed upon women – such as heteronormative marriage and its generic domestic trappings. Her fervently desirous self is further evidenced in a 1915 letter that Mansfield wrote to her then lover, John Middleton Murry, whom she married in 1918:[4]

> I *want* things. Shall I ever have them? To write all the morning and then to get lunch over quickly and to write again in the afternoon & have supper

> and *one* cigarette together and then to be alone again until bed-time – and all this love and joy that fights for outlet – and all this life drying up, like milk, in an old breast. Oh, I want life – I want friends and people and a house. I want to give and to spend.[5]

The first sentence is direct and audacious. Mansfield's own emphasis on the word 'want' makes it the focus of her letter, forcefully proclaiming that what follows in her note will be more about what she desires and, indeed, she does go on to list several items: to write, to have friends, to have a house. How to convey that desire accurately became a dominant preoccupation in both Mansfield's personal writing and her fiction.

Mansfield was unrivalled in her capacity to perceive sharply – and then to convey in her fiction – impressions of daily life. So claims Virginia Woolf in her essay 'A Terribly Sensitive Mind' (1927), in which she analyses passages of Mansfield's diary. We witness, writes Woolf, 'the spectacle of a mind [. . .] receiving one after another the haphazard impressions of eight years of life'.[6] Woolf saw Mansfield precisely capturing 'the moment itself', which 'suddenly puts on significance, and she traces the outline as if to preserve it'.[7] This attempt to solidify and present the moment itself is, of course, reminiscent of Woolf's aim in her own writing to create 'moments of being', in which scenes are rendered into still, solid objects, crystallised in order to see them clearly and conserve them. What is evident from Woolf's essay is that Mansfield's writing had, for Woolf, an almost mystical quality, the ability to articulate that which lies behind the 'cotton wool' of the quotidian visible realm, that which flickers just out of sight, just out of reach.[8]

Mansfield's fiction attempts to make these 'flickers' visible, particularly with regard to her female characters' unspeakable desires. Mansfield's female characters consistently grapple with the irksome impression that they not only want something else for their lives, but also do not have the language to articulate that desire to themselves. I argue that Mansfield's fiction creates a literary ecosystem in which such desire is articulated through physical objects. Mansfield relies on metonyms to make this designation, which allow her maximum flexibility in creating a new vocabulary of female aspiration and longing. Here metonymy is able to signify something entirely new, without depending on any existing resemblances or associations as successful metaphors and symbols must. Mansfield's metonyms allow for the elaboration of novel, unexpected associations between an object and an abstract or unwieldy idea, which then results in the creation of a new language of objects with the new meanings that they accrue.

In Mansfield's short stories 'Prelude' (1917), 'Miss Brill' (1920) and 'At the Bay' (1921), the protagonists are women with desires they cannot articulate with the language at hand, so they rely on metonymy to create new ways of describing what they want which do not fit within a traditional middle-class home and class structure. The stories take place, predominantly, within the confines of the bourgeois homes these women inhabit with their families (with the exception of Miss Brill, who lives alone in very modest, even shabby, conditions). For example, Linda Burnell, in 'Prelude' and its sequel 'At the Bay', desires to escape her roles of wife and mother, and she finds refuge and 'anchor' in natural objects in the external world and outside the home space: her consciousness uses these external objects as earthly manifestations, as distillations, of her desires for other realities – as metonymy for a desire that cannot be put into language.

'Distilling' is a productive way to think about this type of metonymy, in that it likens the representational system to a substance that is transformed into its purest form, free from other matter or meaning, untainted by existing symbolism. This distillation of language in Mansfield's fiction creates an aesthetic of the enchanted, unnameable, utopic space that exists for women exterior to the patriarchal home, in an imaginary state where women were not chained to domestic and therefore heteronormative positionalities and relationalities. These moments of enchantment by way of metonymy in Mansfield's short stories occur within the minds of her female characters, but they are lent a level of permanence by the fact that the objects through which the desires are metonymised – an aloe plant, flowers, a fur coat – exist and can actually be seen in the world, rendering the taboo desires tangible (albeit encoded) rather than merely imagined. The desire gets to be real to the women without having to be directly named.

The stories on which I focus are populated with women of the early twentieth century who are precariously 'teetering between domination by their menfolk and the first tentative steps towards independence', as Linda Grant notes in her 2003 Foreword to Mansfield's first collection of stories, *In a German Pension* (1911).[9] Mansfield's female characters, to be sure, seem to teeter between patriarchal domination and future possibilities for what it means to be a woman. Mansfield's fiction is representative of its New Woman milieu,[10] as it is full of modern women tiptoeing toward – but decidedly not achieving – enfranchisement in any sense of the word. The ambience of Mansfield's stories, though often exploratory and imaginative, feels ultimately tragic – the female characters remain trapped within their domestic contexts. This tension between these disparate aesthetics of exploration and confinement is consonant with the stories' content, which often portray female characters who are suspended between the effervescent escape of their own minds and the cemented tether of their social condition(ing).

In his 1922 review of Mansfield's story 'Bliss', Conrad Aiken said of her writing: 'It is the song of a sensibility ecstatically aware of the surfaces of life.'[11] These 'surfaces' on which Aiken sees Mansfield focusing are evident in her use of metonymy. Rather predictable of a male writer reviewing a female contemporary, Aiken claims that Mansfield 'has little skill at characterization – substituting for "character" a combination of vivid externalities and vivid mood – one must even observe that even in 'mood' her range is very small'.[12] Aiken's observation of what he deems a weakness, that Mansfield substitutes 'vivid externalities' for character, is ironic, as she *does* create a vivid external world, but does so in service to articulating characters' interiorities more effectively.

Clothing serves precisely such a function in 'Miss Brill'. The titular character is a woman who, we glean, is no longer young and who is also unmarried, as indicated by 'Miss'. In fact, her first name is never used, emphasising how contingent her position in society is on her marital status. The short story begins in a way that is common in – almost characteristic of – Mansfield's later stories, many of which open with the word 'Although', which casts a quiet pall over the scene: 'Although it was so brilliantly fine – the blue sky powdered with gold and great spots of light like white wine splashed over the Jardins Publiques – Miss Brill was glad she had decided on her fur.'[13] The immediate grammatical function of 'although' is to suggest that Miss Brill's fur is an unnecessary choice for such fine weather. Beyond this, however, 'although' sets the mood for the entire story: it is a warning. Whatever momentary loveliness is about to be given, it is coupled with a precarity, an obstacle, a loneliness, a limitation. Beginning the story with this particular subordinating conjunction has the unsettling effect of establishing a conflict before explaining what the trouble is.

Miss Brill's fur is the controlling object, the controlling metonym, of the story and is something important to her; yet its full significance is unnameable:

> Miss Brill was glad that she had decided on her fur [. . .]. Miss Brill put up her hand and touched her fur. Dear little thing! It was nice to feel it again. She had taken it out of its box that afternoon, shaken out the moth-powder, given it a good brush, and rubbed the life back into the dim little eyes. 'What has been happening to me?' said the sad little eyes. Oh how sweet it was to see them snap at her again from the red eiderdown! . . . But the nose, which was of some black composition, wasn't at all firm. It must have had a knock, somehow. Never mind – a little dab of black sealing-wax

> when the time came – when it was absolutely necessary . . . . Little rogue! Yes, she really felt like that about it. Little rogue biting its tail just by her left ear. She could have taken it off and laid it on her lap and stroked it. She felt a tingling in her hands and arms, but that came from walking, she supposed. And when she breathed, something light and sad – no, not sad, exactly – something gentle seemed to move in her bosom. (p. 204)

Miss Brill has an intense tenderness for her fur that is peculiarly directed toward mere clothing. This tender bond is amplified by Miss Brill's particular fur – evidently a fox-head stole – which has a face that Miss Brill fusses over, as one would a pet's or child's. Miss Brill has an oddly affectionate relationship with her fur that is at once sensual ('She felt a tingling in her hands and arms') and playful ('Little rogue!'). It is plain to see that the fur, for Miss Brill, is something more than a mere garment and signifies something beyond itself. The fur functions as a metonymic placeholder, as an object that holds space for something crucial for which Miss Brill has no sufficient language – her desire to gain social acceptance as an independent woman. That she hopes to circulate freely and without public censure, as an unmarried woman of little means, is evident in her self-conscious and tender relationship with the fur. That the stole is her sole companion on her outing, a fact that renders her 'glad', emphasises her contentment with her single state. Her decision to wear the fur signals her intention to be read as upwardly mobile and aesthetically pleasing, all on her own, in this public setting.

After she recasts such desire to the fur, we witness Miss Brill grasping at the words 'light and sad' in an attempt to match language to her feelings. These two words are such a curious pairing, however. They are not opposites and yet they are disparate. The coupling of these two words renders each less certain and unsettles the meaning of each. 'Lightness' is associated with happiness, with ease, with freedom, with warmth, with health, with the dawn of a new day. 'Sadness' conjures images of darkness, heaviness, wetness, death, cold, loneliness. The idea of a feeling at once light and sad forces one to consider how these sentiments commingle. Such a strange pairing suggests a word not thought of, a word that does not, perhaps, exist.

Mansfield's harnessing of disparate words in an attempt to find an ideal description for a feeling is a common preoccupation of modernist poets such as T. S. Eliot. Take, for example, his 1921 essay 'The Metaphysical Poets', in which he argues that modern poetry pays homage to the metaphysical poets of the Elizabethan era. Eliot sees both as 'engaged in the task of trying to find the verbal equivalent for states of mind and feeling. And this means both that they are more mature, and that they wear better, than later poets of certainly not less literary ability'.[14] Eliot goes on to diagnose what modern poets grapple with and what their poetry must comprehend:

> We can only say that it appears likely that poets in our civilization, as it exists at present, must be *difficult*. Our civilization comprehends great variety and complexity, and this variety and complexity, playing upon a refined sensibility, must produce various and complex results. The poet must become more and more comprehensive, more allusive, more indirect, in order to force, to dislocate if necessary, language into his meaning.[15]

Eliot mentions that Samuel Johnson criticised the Metaphysical Poets' work because, within it, 'the most heterogeneous ideas are yoked by violence together'.[16] However, Eliot emphasises that such violent yoking is sometimes needed. Modern poets, too, must have recourse to the violent yoking of disparate concepts in order to convey the verbal equivalent of a feeling adequately. This conjoining of terms is Mansfield's tack also, but hers is more delicately dexterous than violent. And even more than verbal conjunctions, Mansfield appoints objects to house and index women's contumacious feelings.

Miss Brill attaches just such disparate and multiple meanings to items of clothing, both hers and those of other people, whom she observes from her perch on a park bench: 'And now an ermine toque and a gentleman in grey met just in front of her' (p. 205). Here Miss Brill is so focused on the fur toque (a small brimless hat) that the woman wearing it all but disappears for her. The hat serves as a metonym for the entire woman, since the item of clothing *is* the expression of the woman's character. Thus Miss Brill *objectifies* the woman in order to conceive of her.

Miss Brill interprets the ermine toque and close-reads it for information about who the woman is:

> And now an ermine toque and a gentleman in grey met just in front of her. He was tall, stiff, and dignified, and she was wearing the ermine toque she'd bought when her hair was yellow. Now everything, her hair, her face, even her eyes, was the same colour as the shabby ermine, and her hand, in its glove, lifted to dab her lips, was a tiny yellowish paw. Oh, she was pleased to see him – delighted! She rather thought they were going to meet that afternoon. She described where she'd been – everywhere, here, there, along by the sea. The day was so charming – didn't he agree? And wouldn't he, perhaps? . . . But he shook his head, lighted a cigarette, slowly breathed a great deep puff into her face, and, even while she was still talking and laughing, flicked the match away and walked on. The ermine toque was alone; she smiled more brightly than ever. But even the band seemed to know what she was feeling and played more softly, played more tenderly. (pp. 205–6)

Here, the shabby toque is metonymy for the woman's grey, aged and smoke-shrouded invisibility, for her thwarted desire to be seen, valued and loved. Her gloved hand is, in Miss Brill's eyes, a small, yellowish, faded paw. The shabby hat and glove signify this woman's dehumanisation. Indeed, the man impatiently blows smoke, grey as his attire, into her face, before leaving her standing alone. This poor single woman's shabby clothes reflect who she is, as far as he is concerned. Her clothing denotes her disposability, her disappointment, her deterioration.

When an elderly couple sharing Miss Brill's bench leave, replaced by a young and well-to-do couple – who Miss Brill notices are 'beautifully dressed' (p. 207) – it is now Miss Brill who experiences a very painful sense of discrimination and objectification, solely on the basis her appearance. She hears the couple whispering:

> 'No, not now,' said the girl. 'Not here, I can't.'
>
> 'But why? Because of that stupid old thing at the end there?' asked the boy. 'Why does she come here at all – who wants her? Why doesn't she keep her silly old mug at home?'
>
> 'It's her fu-fur which is so funny,' giggled the girl. 'It's exactly like a fried whiting.'
>
> 'Ah, be off with you!' said the boy in an angry whisper. (p. 207)

This humiliation to which Miss Brill is subject operates under a logic of appearance as giveaway of class. The 'beautifully dressed' young couple feel entitled to sneer at Miss Brill – indeed, to shoo her angrily away from a public bench like a ragged stray dog that is ruining the romantic aesthetic. Like the shabby ermine toque, Miss Brill's 'funny' fur is what attracts the girl's disgusted giggles. The girl compares Miss Brill's beloved, prized garment to a fried fish, conjuring images of greasy, stiff, dead flesh. Miss Brill, dressed in her Sunday best, is nothing but a 'stupid old thing', with a 'silly old mug', who should never go out in public, whom no one 'wants'. In the boy's eyes, Miss Brill's ratty attire renders her a stupid, old, silly thing that no one could possibly desire, even as the fur manifested, for Miss Brill, her pride and aspiration toward social mobility, desirability and respectability.

After the couple's merciless ridicule, there is a large break in the page and then a jump in the narrative that finds Miss Brill hurrying home. This blank space on the page, with no reaction from Miss Brill, is poignant, as it suggests that she cannot process, emotionally or intellectually, such mortification – her mind is blank and she flees for the shelter of home. The narrative then explains that Miss Brill skips her usual Sunday bakery treat of honey-cake and

> climbed the stairs, went into the little dark room – her room like a cupboard – and sat down on the red eiderdown. She sat there for a long time. The box that the fur came out of was on the bed. She unclasped the necklet quickly; quickly, without looking, laid it inside. But when she put the lid on she thought she heard something crying. (p. 208)

The derision Miss Brill faced regarding her poor appearance, regarding – specifically, her treasured fur – has done damage to her. Once back inside her dark cupboard of a room, she places her fur, *herself*, her desire for more, back in its box, replaces its lid and is so traumatised that she does not know that it is she who is the 'something' that she hears weeping. She has been disciplined, reminded of her place, which is out of the public's view, preferably in a box with a lid. In the end, rather than attempting to articulate the depth of Miss Brill's unspeakable mortification and grief, the story leaves us with a metonym for her shattered hopes and ensuing shame: a tattered and tired fur being once again stowed away until it is wanted. Putting Miss Brill's feelings or thoughts into words is either too painful or too difficult. The fur, which began the story as Miss Brill's prized garment and that articulated the kind of special day she wished to have – indeed, the kind of desiring self she wished to be! – ends the story being stowed away and out of sight.

Like 'Miss Brill', 'Prelude' (1917) and its sequel, 'At the Bay' (1921), utilise metonymy to articulate that which eludes language. But unlike 'Miss Brill', here the dominant metonyms are objects in the natural world. In 'Prelude' we witness this metonymic association between Linda's yearnings and fears and an aloe plant, evident in a scene in which Linda and her mother are out in the yard. Up until this point, our experience of Linda has been of her apathy toward her children and husband and what seems to be her depressive state of mind. When Linda wakes up the morning after the move to the new house, she wishes that she could escape from her family: 'Looking at them she wished that she was going away from this house, too. And she saw herself driving away from them all in a little buggy, driving away from everybody and not even waving' (p. 89). This desire to escape to somewhere beyond her home is Linda's consistent wish that she does not speak, but thinks, although what exactly lies beyond such an exodus is never articulated.

Linda's unmarried (and, probably, younger) sister, Beryl, who lives with them, also thinks about that which she cannot articulate: 'but there was something at the back of Beryl's mind, something she did not even put into words for herself' (p. 94). Language allows their thoughts to go only so far. A few lines later, when Beryl is alone in the dining-room, she mutters to herself: '"One may as well rot here as anywhere else"' (p. 94). Beryl is able to articulate to herself in the harshest terms that she hates her circumstances, just as Linda is able to register that she despises her family. But what lies beyond their situations? This is where their words and minds are not quite able to go, and the prose becomes mystical. Take, for example, the scene in which Linda regards the aloe plant, which has a distinct air of an enchanted otherworld. Here, Linda gazes at the yard alongside her mother:

> As they stood on the steps, the high grassy bank on which the aloe rested rose up like a wave, and the aloe seemed to ride upon it like a ship with the oars lifted. Bright moonlight hung upon the lifted oars like water, and on the green wave glittered the dew.
>
> 'Do you feel it, too,' said Linda, and she spoke to her mother with the special voice that women use at night to each other as though they spoke in their sleep or from some hollow cave – 'Don't you feel that it is coming towards us?'
>
> She dreamed that she was caught up out of the cold water into the ship with the lifted oars and the budding mast. Now the oars fell striking quickly, quickly. They rowed far away over the top of the garden trees, the paddocks and the dark bush beyond. Ah, she heard herself cry: 'Faster! Faster!' to those who were rowing. (pp. 110–11)

This is the most important scene in the story for Mansfield's use of metonymy as a tool to sidestep a lack of language for inchoate female desires. Linda never goes so far as to say that she will escape – it will only ever be a fantasy. She gets only as far as the 'bush beyond', which one imagines is dark, shapeless and unknown. Nonetheless, Linda contrasts her thoughts of escaping on a ship with her actual life and determines the former to be the more 'real' of the two:

> How much more real this dream was than that they should go back to the house where the sleeping children lay and where Stanley and Beryl played cribbage.
>
> 'I believe those are buds,' said she. 'Let us go down into the garden, mother. I like that aloe. I like it more than anything here. And I am sure I shall remember it long after I've forgotten all the other things.'
>
> Looking at it from below she could see the long sharp thorns that edged the aloe leaves, and at the sight of them her heart grew hard . . . . She particularly liked the long sharp thorns . . . . Nobody would dare come near the ship and follow after. (pp. 110–11)

Linda will, she suggests, forget her family before she will forget this aloe. Unlike her family and its domestic context, the aloe provides her with the means to imagine her own escape – to imagine a life outside of the confines of her social roles as mother and wife. It is fitting that Linda affixes her desire to escape to this thorny, intimidating plant, that would seem to thwart manhandling. Yet, Linda's thoughts become darker:

> She hugged her folded arms and began to laugh silently. How absurd life was – it was laughable, simply laughable. And why this mania of hers to keep alive at all? For it really was a mania, she thought, mocking and laughing.
>
> 'What am I guarding myself for so preciously? I shall go on having children and Stanley will go on making money and the children and the gardens will grow bigger and bigger with whole fleets of aloes in them for me to choose from.' (p. 112)

Her thoughts suggest some level of helplessness and suicidal ideation ('And why this mania of hers to keep alive at all?') and helplessness in the face of her foretold future as a body that produces without agency ('I shall go on having children'). Even still, she notes that the aloe will remain for her to use as a vehicle for imagining new articulations for her desire to escape.

William Kupinse makes the argument that what Linda Burnell calls an 'aloe' in the story could actually be *Agave americana* and this confusion of species was, Kupinse explains, a very common error in New Zealand at the time. White settlers attributed Native American 'mystique' to these plants.[17] Kupinse does, as I do, see the aloe/agave functioning metonymically in his reading 'to register the simultaneous exoticization and erasure of the indigenous cultures of the United States, a settler nation like New Zealand'.[18] But Linda fears having children, an act that furthers colonialism's logic of unrelenting coloniser repopulation, not unlike an aggressive weed. Indeed, Kupinse sees the agave insinuating 'maternal mortality' as well in the story, as it 'reproduces once in its lifetime, then dies'.[19] Linda, too, associates reproduction with her own death. Kupinse further explains that aloe has a long history as a 'birth control agent and abortifacient'.[20] In this way, then, the aloe does indeed represent a means of escape from unwanted pregnancy and helps to articulate for Linda a reality beyond her lack of reproductive agency. What is clear from Kupinse's reading is that the aloe operates as a multivalent metonym that distils and concretises Linda's desires. What Linda uses to attempt to imagine life outside of her Victorian coloniser womanhood is a relationship with the natural world, one in which nature is consulted for new ways of knowing, a practice in which native peoples have always already been engaging. In Kupinse's view, this homage to Indigenous ways of knowing, which colonisers have attempted to snuff out, is latent in Mansfield's fiction.

Linda's vital relationship to objects in the natural world continues in 'At the Bay' (1921), although whatever magic she had attributed to them has waned. Linda's dismayed and passive prediction in 'Prelude', that her family would continue to grow, as if totally without her consent, comes to pass. She has a baby boy, toward whom she feels nothing. In this story, Linda's previous imaginative plunges with the aloe plant seem almost entirely of the past, and she is even more depressed and apathetic. However, during a scene in which Linda is by herself in the yard with her baby lying next to her, we do glimpse Linda once again attempting to articulate something beyond her current life, by way of the natural world:

> Dazzling white the picotees shone; the golden-eyed marigolds glittered; the nasturtiums wreathed the veranda poles in green and gold flame. If only one had time to look at these flowers long enough, time to get over the sense of novelty and strangeness, time to know them! But as soon as one paused to part the petals, to discover the underside of the leaf, along came Life and one was swept away. And lying in her cane chair, Linda felt so light; she felt like a leaf. Along came Life like a wind and she was seized and shaken; she had to go. Oh dear, would it always be so? Was there no escape? (p. 262)

Again, Linda fantasises about escaping, and again a natural object is her vehicle for this explorative thinking. Here, the flowers that she examines and attempts to know begin to blur into a metonym for herself, the self that 'Life' does not afford her the time or space to examine. Her fleeting experience of being a leaf that could escape ends as quickly as it began. She cannot imagine anything past the need to flee – what lies beyond an escape is barred to her.

Mansfield herself made proximate objects repositories of keenly felt desires that she could not bring to fruition. She herself was an amalgam of disparate terms; she 'was pale and dark, innocent and decadent, first too fat and then too thin'.[21] She was sexually ambiguous, with a husband and a 'wife', and lovers of both sexes.[22] Her sexuality did not fit into a definable category and could not, therefore, be precisely labelled with the language available to her. Mansfield's interest in the multiplicity of desire and how to name it adequately is evident in her diary, too. In one of the final entries, which was written a few months before she died of tuberculosis at the young age of thirty-four,[23] Mansfield wrote a striking list of desires that begins with her wishing for the return of her good health:

> By health I mean the power to lead a full, adult, living, breathing, life in close contact [with] what I love – the earth and the wonders thereof, the sea, the sun. [. . .] Then I want to work. At what? I want so to live that I work with my hands and my feeling and my brain. I want a garden, a small house, grass, animals, books, pictures, music. And out of this – the expression of this – I want to be writing.[24]

It matters to understanding Mansfield's relationship to language to notice that rather than discussing what her emotions *feel* like, she instead names objects in the external world such as 'the sea – the sun', an attempt to articulate her feelings via nameable external objects. The en-dash between the two words matters, too, since she is not providing a list, but rather is trying to find the right metonym to present accurately what she most loves about the earth. In the above excerpt, Mansfield repeats the word 'want' four times in six sentences, emphasising that her desire is the focus. Her initial attempt at articulating her desires begins fairly abstractedly and questioningly. She states that she wants to work and then asks herself what she wants to work 'at'. Then, she attempts to answer her question: her language, although by no means nonsensical, is still far from pellucid. She wants 'so to live that [she] work[s] with [her] hands and [her] feeling and [her] brain'. What does it mean to work with one's 'feeling'? Abruptly, as if knowing her language has become too untethered, Mansfield names her desires in concrete and material terms: garden, small house, grass, animals, books, pictures, music. After the first few sentences, in which baggy language is used to describe what she desires, the list of banal objects is extremely concrete by comparison, emphasising the way one's pursuit of health brings one down to earth – narrows the scope of one's needs and aspirations. And out of this narrowed scope Mansfield proclaims that she wants 'to be writing'. Mansfield's final distilled desire is to write: to continue to create new articulations for the desperate and desirous women in her fiction and in the world beyond.

Notes

1. Quoted in Claire Tomalin, *Katherine Mansfield: A Secret Life* (London: Viking, 1987), p. 104. This bold request was an invitation Mansfield made to John Middleton Murry, which he initially rejected but ultimately acquiesced to.
2. According to Tomalin's biography, Mansfield 'transformed into multiple alternative versions to suit different moods, different friends, different facets of her personality: Kass, Katie, K.M., Mansfield, Katherine, Julian Mark, Katherine Schönfeld, Matilda Berry, Katharina, Katiushka, Kissienka, Elizabeth Stanley, Tig' (p. 5). This etymology of her name is worth noting and contemplating here, as it speaks to Mansfield's personal interest in language's simultaneous mutability and insufficiency. For Mansfield, even her own name did not always seem to describe her adequately.
3. *Letters* 1, p. 18.

4. Tomalin, p. 40.
5. *Letters* 1, p. 177.
6. Virginia Woolf, 'A Terribly Sensitive Mind' (1927), in *Granite and Rainbow: Essays by Virginia Woolf*, ed. Leonard Woolf (London: Harcourt Brace Jovanovich, 1958), pp. 73–5 (p. 73).
7. Woolf, p. 74.
8. Virginia Woolf, 'A Sketch of the Past', in *Moments of Being*, ed. Jeanne Schulkin (London: Harcourt Brace Jovanovich, 1976), pp. 64–159 (p. 72).
9. Linda Grant, 'Foreword', in Katherine Mansfield, *In a German Pension* (London: Hesperus, 2003), pp. vii–x (p. viii).
10. This was a late nineteenth-century nomenclature that was used to describe women whose lives became more public and economically independent in contrast to the previous domestic ideal of Victorianism. The New Woman became especially conspicuous at the beginning of the First World War when women entered the workforce in droves in order to replace deployed men. Mansfield's female characters discussed here, although not necessarily working women, are nevertheless restless regarding their social positionalities in a way that is consonant with the way gender roles were being troubled and challenged during this period.
11. Conrad Aiken, 'A Short Story as Colour', in *Katherine Mansfield's Selected Stories*, ed. Vincent O'Sullivan (London: W. W. Norton, 2006), pp. 339–42 (p. 341).
12. Aiken, p. 342.
13. O'Sullivan, p. 204. All references to Mansfield's stories are to this edition; subsequent references will be placed parenthetically in the text.
14. T. S. Eliot, 'The Metaphysical Poets', *Selected Essays*, ed. Valerie Eliot (London: Faber and Faber, 1932), pp. 281–91 (p. 289).
15. Eliot, p. 289.
16. Eliot, p. 283.
17. William Kupinse, 'What Plant's in "Prelude"? Colonialism, Gender, and Speculative Botany', in Aimée Gasston, Gerri Kimber and Janet Wilson, eds, *Katherine Mansfield: New Directions* (London: Bloomsbury, 2020), pp. 77–91 (p. 79).
18. Kupinse, p. 80.
19. Kupinse, p. 80.
20. Kupinse, p. 83.
21. Tomalin, pp. 5–6. Mansfield's mother had a habit of cruelly criticising her about her weight, and Tomalin recounts a moment when, returning from a long trip abroad, the first words Mansfield's mother spoke to her were: 'I see that you are as fat as ever' (p. 13). Then, when Mansfield became pregnant out of wedlock in 1909 – yet another visible manifestation of her fulfilled desire – her mother swiftly cut her out of her will. Mansfield certainly experienced punishments for making her desire visible.
22. Tomalin, p. 6.
23. According to Tomalin, although Mansfield did, indeed, die of tuberculosis, what is less discussed is the fact that her system was weakened and made hospitable to the illness when she was infected with gonorrhoea in 1909 while in Germany. At the time, a gonorrhoeal infection in women was essentially impossible to cure and would sometimes become systemic; this is what occurred in Mansfield's case. Due to this, Mansfield's body was plagued with arthritis, heart issues and lung problems. She suffered from these symptoms until her death (pp. 77–8). Mansfield's early death was thus connected to her licentious behaviour: her untimely death can be readily traced to her desire.
24. CW4, pp. 434–5.

'If only one had time to look at these flowers long enough, time to get over the sense of novelty and strangeness': The Political Language of Flowers in Katherine Mansfield's *The Garden Party and Other Stories*

Sharon Gordon

Katherine Mansfield's life-long love of flowers and her passion for them feature strongly in much of her writing. In early childhood, as Ruth Elvish Mantz notes, her 'great-uncle Craddock' had told her 'about some flowers' and 'had written some verses with a little moral – something about flowers having personalities; they never should be burned, never thrown into the fire'.[1] Mantz also indicates that all of the Beauchamp family shared a passionate love for flowers. These sentiments became embedded in Mansfield's imagination and remained with her throughout her life. In a letter to her friend Dorothy Brett, Mansfield writes: 'I had so many flowers when I was little, I got to know them so well that they are simply the breath of life for me. Its no ordinary love; its a passion.'[2] In another letter to Brett, written a month earlier on 22 December 1921, she writes 'what wouldn't I give for some flowers [. . .] this longing for flowers. I *crave* them', declaring that 'I could kiss the earth that bears flowers. Alas, I love them TOO much!'[3] The urgency of the language, expressed in quasi-erotic terms, reveals the sensuous pleasure Mansfield derived from flowers. Writing to her sister, Vera Beauchamp, in late March 1908, Mansfield declares, 'flowers like Tom's music seem to create in me a divine unrest – They revive strangely – dream memories' and 'show me strange mystic paths – where perhaps I shall one day walk – To lean over a flower [is] to commune with the soul.'[4] There are echoes in these lines of the writings of the Swiss philosopher, Henri Frédéric Amiel (1821–81), whom Mansfield admired. In his *Journal Intime* he writes:

> Each bud flowers but once and each flower has but its minute of perfect beauty, so in the garden of the soul each feeling has [. . .] its flowering instant, its one and only moment of expansive grace and radiant kingship [. . .] in the heaven of the mind each thought touches its zenith but once, and in that moment all its brilliancy and all its greatness culminate.[5]

Flowers overpowered Mansfield's imagination, and her deeply felt passion for them is transmuted into her last collection, *The Garden Party and Other Stories.*

In the nineteenth century, 'language of flowers' books, as Beverly Seaton explains, 'belong[ed] to a larger class of sentimental flower books [. . .] which d[id] not treat flowers in botanical or horticultural terms, but rather in terms of sentiment, feeling and association'. The 'most popular type of sentimental flower book was the prose work with religious and moral themes'.[6] Other types were anthologies of nature poetry, literature and folklore. The plethora of the language of flowers books in the nineteenth and early twentieth centuries were targeted at a female readership. Charlotte de Latour's *Le Langage des fleurs* (1819) was the beginning of the proliferation of language of flower books in Europe, and much of today's flower symbolism and many interpretations owe much to de Latour's work. The impact of her book was such that its ninth edition appeared in English in 1843. Jack Goody explains that de Latour 'sees flowers primarily as a means of communication between the sexes [. . .]. As with any other language, one can manipulate the flowers in order to elaborate one's meanings!'[7] Popular English flower books were Frederic Shoberl's *The Language of Flowers: With Illustrative Poetry* (1834), Jane Loudon's four-volume *The Ladies Companion to the Flower Garden* (1840–8) and Kate Greenaway's *The Language of Flowers* (1884). Mansfield's deployment of a coded flower symbolism in her stories indicates that she was perhaps familiar with some of these publications, though it could be argued that she had no botanical interest in flowers. She was, however, familiar with the upmarket illustrated magazine *Country Life.* In a letter to John Middleton Murry, written on 28 March 1920, she informs him that 'Country Life has come. It has some flower pictures in it. Do you know [. . .] flower pictures affect me so much that I feel an instant tremendous excitement and delight,' adding that 'I REALLY nearly fainted. I had to lie down.'[8] These words capture Mansfield's aptitude for hyperbole, a characteristic of the unrestrained emotional aspects of her life and writing.

The physical attributes of women have a strong association with flowers and femininity. As Sam George suggests, the 'sentimental analogies between women and flowers perpetuate the notions of the feminine in which women are not only defined by, but are assumed to identify with, the beautiful, innocent and delicate'.[9] George further states that 'Linguistic conventions were already in place whereby flowers were emblems of purity, beauty and frailty – the so-called female virtues – and their ephemeral beauty was associated with the female body.'[10] By the eighteenth century, floral imagery proliferated in contemporary literature and in philosophical and scientific writing, and it was the prevailing opinions of men such as the philosophers Jean-Jacques Rousseau (1712–78) and Edmund Burke (1729–97), and the Swedish botanist Carl Linnaeus (1707–78), who perceived women, like flowers, as delicate and fragile creations. In this way, women's beauty, like the flower, is fleeting, transient and impermanent. Karina Jakubowicz suggests that Mansfield

> often invokes the impermanence of flowers in order to show that [. . .] relationships are fragile and fleeting. As her perspectives on romantic relationships changed throughout the course of her life, and as she matured in her writing style, it is possible to see flowers occupying a subtler and more sophisticated place in her work.[11]

In Mansfield's collection *The Garden Party and Other Stories*, most of which was written in 1920 and 1921 and published in 1922, her more sophisticated and mature writing style was, as I argue, a response to, and a reflection of, her modernist sensibilities. In order to evoke 'the sense of novelty and strangeness' in her floral narratives, Mansfield subverts the sentimental metaphoric association of women and flowers in order to indicate something darker, more subversive, even transgressive. Mansfield's political language of flowers, closely associated with the wider cultural issues in terms of female sexuality, class and gender, is explored through her deployment of floral motifs in 'At the Bay' (1921), 'The Garden Party' (1921), 'Her First Ball'(1921), 'The Young Girl'(1920), 'The Singing Lesson' (1920) and 'The Lady's Maid' (1920).[12]

Flowers, Femininity, and the Feminine

A fictionalised account of Mansfield's mother, Annie Beauchamp, who, for most of her life, was weighed down with the burden of motherhood, finds expression in the portrayal of Linda Burnell in 'At the Bay'. In *The Life of Katherine Mansfield,* Mantz wrote that 'the mother [Annie Beauchamp] seems to have lived in the condition of aloofness in which she appears [as Linda Burnell] in *Prelude,* "The Aloe" and "At the Bay"'. Annie 'would go out among the flowers for which she had a passion:

arum lilies and pincushions [*scabiosa*] in the front garden; and to the wild gully at the back – filled with green and tree ferns; beyond that the world appeared unreal'.[13] Like that of Annie Beauchamp, Linda Burnell's aloofness is captured while sitting under a manuka tree in her garden. She

> looked up at the dark, close, dry leaves of the manuka [when] now and again a tiny yellowish flower dropped on her. Pretty – yes if you held one of those flowers on the palm of your hand and looked at it closely, it was an exquisite small thing. Each pale-yellow flower shone as if each was the careful work of a loving hand [of a benevolent God] the tiny tongue [of a baby] in the centre gave it the shape of a bell [. . .] But as soon as they flowered they fell and were scattered. (pp. 353–4)

The metaphorical suggestiveness of the image connotes that a flower is the sexual and reproductive part of the plant, manuka flowers having an open centre. Initially providing aesthetic pleasure for Linda, the beauty and the heavily scented manuka flowers are transmogrified into 'horrid little things [which] got caught in one's own hair' (p. 354). Thus, the manuka flowers become the metaphor for her little children, who entrap her. As Shelley Saguaro explains, the manuka tree 'takes on a private significance in the eye and consciousness of the beholder', and the notion of this is foregrounded when Linda is 'languorously musing on the futility of fertility'.[14] In her quest for answers, Linda asks, 'Why, then, flower at all? Who takes the trouble – or the joy – to make all these things that are wasted, wasted . . . It was uncanny' (p. 354). Consequently, notions of the 'unreal' and the 'uncanny' align with Linda's fears and anxieties and her feelings of estrangement and alienation from the world, which are expressed through the exquisiteness of the manuka flower.

Having 'the garden to herself', Linda's memories, dreams and desires are encapsulated in the garden's flowers:

> the dazzling white picotees shone; the golden-eyes marigolds glittered; the nasturtiums wreathed the veranda poles in green and gold flame. If only one had time to look at these flowers long enough, time to get over the sense of novelty and strangeness, time to know them! (p. 354)

The sensory experience of gazing expresses an intimacy between Linda and the flowers. The striking individuality of the flowers, communicated by the adjectives 'dazzling', 'shone' and 'glittered', is expressed in a language of heightened sensuousness which capture the flowers' vitality – a condition which is lacking in Linda's life. The suggestive imagery of the white picotees, also known as day lilies because they open in the morning and die at the end of the day, serve as an expression of the transience of life. Symbolic of love and innocence, the picotees, arguably, encapsulate memories of Linda's happy childhood, which she describes in the story.[15] Her emotional engagement with the marigolds, embodying energy and warmth, joy and happiness, convey her wished-for desires, which are unattainable. However, in keeping with Linda's mental state, the marigolds also symbolise the darker emotions of grief and despair. The coded significance of the nasturtium flowers, which have shield-like leaves, function as symbols of protection in times of adversity and the yellow-gold variety, which Linda engages with, epitomise creativity and growth; in terms of her personal development, these qualities are denied her. The transitory nature of flowers, like life itself, is revealed when Linda's introspective self muses: 'As soon as one paused to part the petals, to discover the under-side of the leaf, along came Life and one was swept away [. . .]. Linda felt so light; she felt like a leaf. Along came Life like a wind she was seized and shaken', forcing her to question, 'Was there no escape?' (p. 354). Her sense of entrapment and the futility of her life as a wife and mother are expressed in forthright terms when the reader is informed that 'Linda was broken, made weak, her courage was gone, through child-bearing' (p. 355). In keeping with the evolution of New Woman politics in the early twentieth century, Mansfield's unambiguous political statement addresses the reality of many women's lives during a period of cultural and social flux in the aftermath of the First World War.[16] At this time, marriage and motherhood were no longer considered (mostly by women) to be a woman's only fulfilment.

Class and Cultural Politics

Family life is depicted in another of the collection's stories with a New Zealand setting: namely, 'The Garden Party'. As the title suggests, 'The Garden Party' evokes a quintessentially English colonial event. In a 1915 notebook entry, Mansfield recalls that 'Our house in Tinakori Road stood back from the road'; its position 'was high, it was healthy'. At the front, 'the garden sloped away in terraces [. . .] until you reached the stone wall covered with nasturtiums'. Opposite the Beauchamp's house 'in a hollow [. . .] was Saunders Lane'.[17] In terms of height and class hierarchy, the Beauchamp's house, positioned above, literally looked down on to the cottages of their social inferiors, which is fictionalised in 'The Garden Party' as 'the hollow' in which 'the little cottages were in deep shade' (p. 411).

Set on the lawn of the fictional Sheridan family's garden, the young protagonist, Laura, anguishes over where the garden party marquee might be erected, a workman suggesting that it be placed 'Against the karakas?'. But Laura's concern is that 'the karaka-trees would be hidden' because 'they were so lovely, with their broad, gleaming leaves and their clusters of yellow fruit' (p. 403). Karaka trees are a native New Zealand species and were often planted around Maori villages; in the story they are placed in a marginalised position, behind and beyond the marquee. In this way, the garden and the karaka trees are a reflection of two cultural and social positions, and thus function as a demarcation line between the colonised and the coloniser. Whilst the marquee is being erected, Laura saw 'a tall fellow' who 'bent down, pinched a sprig of lavender. Put his thumb and forefinger to his nose and snuffed up the smell.' Astonished at seeing a social inferior caring 'for things like that', this is a moment of awakening for Laura, who rapidly becomes aware of 'these absurd class distinctions' (p. 403).

The roses in the garden are also socially and culturally positioned, functioning as the embodiment of a nostalgic association with Britain and Empire. Personified in terms of class, they are a hallmark of social status:

> As for the roses, you could not help feeling that they understood that roses are the only flowers that impress people at garden parties; the only flowers that everybody is certain of knowing [. . .] literally hundreds, had come out in a single night. (p. 401)

As cultural icons and symbols of patriotism, roses were desirable acquisitions for the upper and middle classes and prolific in the gardens of large country houses, thus representing a nostalgic sense of old-world charm.

The social pretensions of the guests at the garden party, articulated as an expression of their false existence, are a popular theme in Mansfield' s stories. For example, in 'The Garden Party', 'wherever you looked there were couples strolling, bending to the flowers, greeting, moving over the lawn. They were like bright birds that had alighted in the Sheridans' garden for this one afternoon, on their way to – where?' (p. 410). Corresponding images of people strolling in gardens and observing the flowers are described in one of Mansfield's earlier stories, 'In the Botanical Gardens' (1907), where the strollers name the flowers in Latin, thus displaying their intellectual prowess. Similarly, in 'Miss Brill' (1920), the titular character observes the 'to and fro, in front of the flower-beds', as 'the couples and groups paraded, stopped to talk, to greet, to buy handful of flowers from the old beggar' (p. 252). The commodification of the flowers as a means of economic exchange in this instance takes on a more politically overt interpretation.

Class politics are further played out when the guests at the Sheridans' garden party hear the news that a local labouring man has been killed in an accident, Mrs Sheridan's only concern being that it was '*Not* in the garden?' But Laura, sensing the sadness of the news, offers to visit the man's family and is ordered by her mother to 'take the arum lilies' because 'people of that class are so impressed by arum lilies' (p. 411). In this way, the arum lilies serve as the embodiment of class. Known as 'the lilies of sadness' due to their association with death and mourning, the lilies constitute a motif that has a dual role in the story. Gerri Kimber makes an interesting point regarding the type of lily Mrs Sheridan prefers, contending that

> Mansfield deliberately chooses to mistake the name of the lilies, clearly identified as 'canna' lilies earlier in the story. Mrs Sheridan's love of 'canna lilies' is seen as nothing more than artifice and whim – by the end of the story she cannot remember which sort of lilies she had ordered. The fact that the word 'arum' is mentioned twice in two consecutive sentences indicates, firstly, that this is no species oversight on the part of the author and secondly, that the change in name is significant.[18]

Flowers and Female Sexuality

The canna lily in the story, as Kimber notes, is pink, when in fact they are bright red or yellow, while the arum lily is white and often used in bridal bouquets or funeral wreaths.[19] This reinforces the role of the lily in the narrative as one symbolic of class, death and the virginal. According to Catherine Maxwell, lily flowers 'fuse connotations of purity and eroticism'; in this way, their metaphorical suggestiveness is subversive, even transgressive.[20] The lily motif in the story is therefore complex.

Unlike Linda in 'At the Bay', who paused to part the petals' in her contemplation of the meaning of life, the suggestive imagery associated with Laura's 'big pink flowers' in 'The Garden Party' have an erotic dimension, and as such are seductively described in terms of their enticing and alluring qualities. The erotically charged symbolism of the 'canna lilies' standing inside the Sheridan's house serves as an expression of Laura's emerging sexuality in terms of the 'big pink flowers, wide open, radiant, almost frighteningly alive on bright crimson stems' (p. 404). Their sensuousness is intensified when Laura 'crouched down as if to warm herself at that blaze of lilies; she felt they were in her fingers, on her lips, growing in her breast'. Possessing all the characteristics of a hoped-for sexual encounter, Laura's *jouissance* reaches a climax, intimated by an orgasmic 'little moan' (p. 404), thus embodying her being in a 'blaze' of heightened sensuousness. As the embodiment of desire, these images evoke the Wildean cult of the lily and the heady culture of the *fin de siècle*, which had a major influence on Mansfield's work.

Floral metaphors deployed in the context of blossoming youth and burgeoning female sexuality find expression in two other *Garden Party* stories: namely, 'Her First Ball' and 'The Young Girl'. In a notebook jotting, Mansfield speaks of Walter Pater's 'voluptuous pleasure in garden scents',[21] and, like Laura's lily epiphany, the notion of perfume and seduction is conveyed by the intoxicating scent of 'Meg's tuberoses' in 'Her First Ball', although the allure of their perfume is never explicitly stated (p. 324). The Sheridan girls, Meg and Laura, and their brother Laurie, who also feature in 'The Garden Party', are on their way to their cousin Leila's first ball. The story is told from Leila's point of view, and it is her observations, and her emerging sexual awareness, that the reader is privy to. Although Leila's observations of the young men at the ball are in keeping with her romantic notion of boy/girl first love, it is the coded significance of 'Meg's tuberoses' that imply either that she is a seductive *femme fatale* who attracts the leering old men at the ball, or that there is a shadowy homoeroticism lurking in the narrative. Although the tuberose is white and has associations with purity and innocence, its perfume has erotic connotations, releasing a strong and lingering musky smell at night, and signalling what Maxwell describes as being 'bound up with dangerous or voluptuous pleasures'.[22]

It is conceivable that Mansfield was familiar with the popular writings of Elinor Glyn and Mark André Raffalovich, which are imbued with the tuberose trope. The powerfully evocative tuberose perfume and its association with eroticism and carnality find expression in Glyn's popular novel *Three Weeks* (1907). The potent scent of tuberose and its connotations pervade Glyn's novel and it is the signature scent of the seductive *femme fatale* in its depiction of female sexuality.[23] The highly popular *fin-de-siècle* poem 'Tuberose and Meadowsweet' (1885), by Raffalovich, is imbued with tuberose imagery, as the title suggests. In the poem, Raffalovich seductively alludes to the tuberose as one 'Whose scent in living pulses seems to beat / Magnetic ardour, drowsy scent of love' (ll. 3–4); it continues – 'Of tuberose, desirous tuberose' (l. 116) and later 'Too much has my desire been heard to moan' (l. 119).[24] The coded significance of the word 'tuberose' in Mansfield's story is withheld, but in keeping with her modernist innovations, its indeterminate meaning hints at a larger reality. The tuberose is similar in appearance to the arum lily: it is white and also known as the Madonna lily. Because of its association with purity and the Virgin Mary, its symbolism foregrounds the notion of the virginal. Nonetheless, Laura's emerging sexuality is expressed in eroticised terms when Leila observed her 'little head' pushed 'above her white fur like a flower through snow' (p. 324). In this way, the white flower symbolism in the story conflates the notion of purity and eroticism.

Unlike the exotic and seductive tuberose, the pink carnation used as a motif in 'The Young Girl' demonstrates hatred and resentment. The story's setting is Monte Carlo, eleven kilometres from Menton, where Mansfield was then living at the Villa Isola Bella. 'The Young Girl' was in fact the first story Mansfield wrote after renting the villa. The young girl in question, who is not named, is referred to only as 'Mrs Raddick's daughter' (p. 230). She is a resentful and truculent young woman, who finds herself with her mother at the casino in Monte Carlo. Intent on visiting the casino, she is barred because of her age (she is only seventeen years old). Her mother, however, determines to go and leaves the young girl and her younger brother in the care of an assumed male, shadowy first-person narrator, who recounts events from his point of view. When the young girl and her brother are chauffeured to a hotel for afternoon tea, she takes exception to a display of pink carnations on the table, demanding 'take those flowers away'. As she pointed to the carnations, the narrator recalls, 'I heard her murmur "I can't bear flowers on a table". They had evidently been giving her intense pain, for she positively closed her eyes as I moved them away' (p. 232). Pink carnations symbolise a mother's undying love, but in the story, Mansfield subverts any sentimental association with the carnations in order to express the girl's hatred of her mother. Arguably, Mrs Raddick's daughter is a fictionalised account of Ottoline Morrell's fourteen-year-old daughter, Julian. Morrell and her daughter were in Monte Carlo in November 1920 and Julian was fascinated by the notorious casino. As Miranda Seymour explains:

> Discovering the pleasures of gambling had not been part of Ottoline's grand design; her dreams of turning her daughter into the mirror-image of herself as a young girl were doomed to failure. Julian was no sighing maiden and this was 1920; who would expect a lively fourteen-year-old not to prefer seeing the casino to going to tea with Katherine Mansfield in Menton. Julian 'refused to go and Ottoline was obliged to make the visit alone. There was an angry scene afterwards [. . .] in which Ottoline's accusations of selfish ingratitude were met with justifiable indignation by Julian![25]

Seymour's comments, therefore, substantiate my argument that the young girl in Mansfield's story may be a fictionalised account of Morrell's daughter.

By the end of the story, the voyeuristic narrator is emboldened to murmur to the young girl,

> 'I scarcely like to leave you [at the hotel . . .] I'd very much rather not leave you here.' In a gesture of defiance she threw back her coat; she turned and faced me; her lips parted. 'Good heavens – why! I – don't mind a bit. I – I like waiting.' (p. 234)

Her hesitation, illustrated by the broken syntax, serves to bring the young girl's eagerness to a slowly building climax, as 'suddenly her cheeks crimsoned, her eyes grew dark' and 'her dark coat fell open, and her white throat – all her young body in a blue dress – was like a flower that is just emerging from its dark bud' (p. 234). The clitoral symbolism connotes the floral metaphors of blooming and ripening, thus implying an erotic interplay between the narrator and the young girl, the object of his desire.

Jennifer Cooke argues that 'sex and flowers, sex and blossoms, petals and orgasms, are coupled in Mansfield's work; coupled deliberately', adding that Mansfield 'puts them to work as symbols of erotic longing and ecstasy – whether characters identify this feeling or not – in ways which highlight [. . .] the types of representations of sexuality and sexual desire that women have at their disposal in language and imagery'.[26] The binaries of love and hate, fantasy and desire, are 'coupled', as Cooke would describe it, in the representations of sexuality and homoerotic desire which find expression in the language and imagery ascribed to the yellow chrysanthemum in 'The Singing Lesson', in which the singing teacher, a Miss Meadows, has been spurned in love by her perfidious male suitor, Basil, who now wishes her back. However, in the intervening period she has come to terms with her own sexuality, expressed through a yellow chrysanthemum. Symbolically, the yellow chrysanthemum sends a message of scorned love or sorrow, although in the story the flower also functions as a symbol of homoerotic desire. When one of Miss Meadows's students, Mary Beazley, 'handed her mistress a beautiful yellow chrysanthemum' on this particular morning – a ritual which 'had been gone through for ages and ages' – 'instead of taking it up, instead of tucking it into her belt while she leaned over Mary, and said "Thank you, Mary. How very nice!", to 'Mary's horror [. . .] Miss Meadows totally ignored the chrysanthemum' and spoke to her 'in a voice of ice' (p. 236). Her coldness towards Mary becomes clear when the reader is informed that she had received a letter from Basil implying that their 'marriage would be a mistake' (p. 237), followed by a telegram suggesting that she 'pay no attention to letter' (p. 239). This is a revelatory moment for Miss Meadows when it dawns on her that Basil is fickle. Rushing back to her class 'on the wings of hope, of love, of joy', and looking at Mary, she picked up 'the yellow chrysanthemum' and flirtatiously 'held it to her lips to hide her smile' (p. 239). At this point her voice became 'full, deep, and glowing with expression' (p. 239).

Similarly, the suggestive power of the imagery in these lines finds expression in an earlier Mansfield story, 'The Yellow Chrysanthemum' (1908). In this story the voluptuous and alluring yellow chrysanthemum intimates an erotic interplay between the character Radiana and the chrysanthemum, when 'shaking the petals of a yellow chrysanthemum over her hair' she became 'wrapt in the perfume of the chrysanthemum'.[27] Chrysanthemums have a strong, musky scent and as such serve as an evocative emblem of sexual desire. In a letter to her sister Vera, written in late March 1908, Mansfield expresses her infatuation with her young friend 'Trix' in Wellington. Rhapsodising that she put 'flowers in my soul', she adds that 'I do verily think that a woman is one of the most delightful creations possible [. . .] The voice of the chrysanthemum is heard in the land. Two blossoms – so full of colour.'[28] The emotional intensity expressed in these lines is seductively subversive, thus revealing Mansfield's sexual desires and fantasies.

The notion of sapphic love also finds expression in Mansfield's story 'The Lady's Maid'. Sappho's poetic fragments are imbued with images of flowers, in particular purple ones. In this way, purple flowers became synonymous with lesbian love. Purple pansies have an association with ardent love, remembrance and loss. However, the purple pansies which feature in 'The Lady's Maid' arguably metamorphose into something sinister and grotesque. The one-sided conversation which takes place in the story is expressed through the focalised thoughts of Ellen, the lady's maid, who relates events to a nameless character known as 'madam'. When she had 'laid out' madam's mother, Ellen had placed 'just to the side of her neck' the 'most beautiful purple pansies' (p. 262). At this point in the narrative, there is a sense of heightened homoerotic tension between the purple pansies and the dead woman. As the story unfolds, the vampiric image of the pansies being placed at the neck arguably hints at the more transgressive notion of sexual depravity. This is underpinned when Ellen recalls, 'Those pansies made a picture of her [. . .]. I shall never forget them. I thought to-night when I looked at my lady, "Now, if only the pansies was there, no-one could tell the difference."' Ellen, projecting her fantasies on to 'madam', the dead woman's daughter, implies that 'madam' looked just like her 'dear mother when I laid her out!' (p. 262). However, the complexities are compounded by the sense of uncertainty in the narrative. For example, there is a slippage between the past and present, the present and the past, and there are more questions than answers regarding any clear interpretation of the coded significance of the purple pansy. Arguably, the story is transgressive and the gothicised imagery hints at the notion of sexual gratification. This raises the notion of what Barbara Creed describes as 'the monstrous feminine', and, arguably, Ellen emerges in the story as the monstrous woman archetype, in vampiric and necrophilic terms.[29] The pansies have a dual role in the narrative. In keeping with Ellen's loyalty to 'madam' and her 'lady', the pansy is symbolic of faithfulness and loyalty, but these emotions are transformed into abhorrent, fetishised images associated with death.

Mansfield's emotional affinity for flowers was both passionate and illuminating, and has powerful resonance in her *Garden Party* stories. Flowers are not just flowers per se in the stories; her genius lies in her ability to subvert their suggestive imagery and to expose a shared and meaningful intimacy between the flowers and her protagonists. In her deployment of floral metaphors, therefore, Mansfield successfully explores the various aspects of the political language of flowers in terms of female sexuality, class and gender, whilst negating the overly sentimental associations with flowers which were frequently ascribed to women. Her originality and influence are reflected in these more mature stories and reflect her commitment to modernist literary innovations and the evolution of a new literary style, of which she was so much a part.

Notes

1. Ruth Elvish Mantz and John Middleton Murry, *The Life of Katherine Mansfield* (London: Constable and Company, 1933), p. 85.
2. *Letters* 5, p. 23.
3. *Letters* 4, p. 347.
4. *Letters* 1, p. 43. 'Tom' referred to here is Tom Trowell, a musician and New Zealand friend for whom Mansfield had a youthful attraction.
5. Henri Frédéric Amiel, *Amiel's Journal: The Journal Intime of Henri-Frédéric Amiel* (London: Macmillan, 1921), p. 5.
6. Beverly Seaton, *The Language of Flowers: A History* (Charlottesville and London: University of Virginia, 1995), p. 2.
7. Jack Goody, *The Culture of Flowers* (Cambridge: Cambridge University Press, 1994), p. 238.
8. *Letters* 3, p. 263.
9. Sam George, *Botany, Sexuality & Women's Writing 1760–1830: From Modest Shoot to Forward Plant* (Manchester: Manchester University Press, 2012), p. 29.
10. George, pp. 28–9.
11. Karina Jakubowicz, '"Ces femmes avec ces fleurs!": Flowers, Gender and Relationships in the Work of Elizabeth von Arnim and Katherine Mansfield', in Gerri Kimber, Isobel Maddison and Todd Martin, eds, *Katherine Mansfield and Elizabeth von Arnim* (Edinburgh: Edinburgh University Press, 2019), pp. 70–85 (p. 80).

12. All references to Mansfield's stories are to CW2 and indicated in parentheses.
13. Mantz, p. 76.
14. Shelley Saguaro, *Garden Plots: The Politics and Poetics of Gardens* (London and New York: Routledge, 2017), p. 27.
15. There are numerous books on the subject of flower symbolism. For the purposes of this essay, I have referred to Samantha Gray, *The Secret Language of Flowers* (London and New York: Cico Books, 2015); S. Teresa Dietz, *The Complete Language of Flowers* (New York: Wellfleet Press, 2020); and <https://www.petalrepublic.com> (last accessed 8 October 2021).
16. Three years before the publication of 'At the Bay', Marie Stopes had published her pioneering book *Married Love* (1919), which offered birth control advice to women.
17. CW4, pp. 176–7.
18. Gerri Kimber, *Katherine Mansfield and the Art of the Short Story* (Basingstoke: Palgrave Macmillan, 2015), p. 36.
19. Kimber, p. 36.
20. Catherine Maxwell, *Scents and Sensibility: Perfume in Victorian Culture* (Oxford: Oxford University Press, 2017), p. 212.
21. CW4, p. 109.
22. Maxwell, p. 13.
23. Maxwell, p. 324.
24. Mark André Raffalovich, *Tuberose and Meadowsweet* (London: David Bogue, 1885), pp. 37–43 (p. 37).
25. Miranda Seymour, *Ottoline Morrell: Life on a Grand Scale* (London: Faber and Faber, 2008), p. 431.
26. Jennifer Cooke, 'Katherine Mansfield's Ventriloquism and the Faux-Ecstasy of All Manner of Flora', *Literature Interpretation Theory*, 19: 1 (2008), pp. 79–94 (p. 79.)
27. CW1, pp. 116, 117.
28. *Letters* 1, p. 43.
29. Barbara Creed coined the phrase in her radical book, *The Monstrous Feminine: Film, Feminism, Psychoanalysis* (Abingdon: Routledge, 1993).

CREATIVE WRITING

SHORT STORIES

'How Loud the Birds'

Ailsa Cox

'"How loud the birds are," said Linda in her dream.'

– Katherine Mansfield, 'Prelude'

First thing in the morning. Sea fades into a dove-coloured sky, wind turbines churn half-visible on the horizon. Oyster shells, fathoms deep, discarded a hundred years ago, two hundred – broken crocks and house bricks, rounded into egg-shapes by the tide. On the shoreline, crushed shells and polished sea glass, the greenish shade of jellyfish. A rope filthy with weeds, driftwood the size of a human torso. A yellow jeep makes its way towards a pale boulder that turns out to be the massive corpse of a seal, half-buried in a sand pit of its own making.

Inland, the roads are deserted, the pavements free of rubbish. McDonald's closed, the nail bars and the hairdressers shuttered – and the carpet shop and the dentist on the corner. The gulls have moved on, the only sound the songbirds now, or if you come in closer, you can hear Lindsay breathing as she runs down the middle of the road, running, running, running in sweatpants, elbows scissoring, ponytail bobbing, zipping along with a spring in her step. It's happening, she can feel it, something changing deep inside.

At Number 23, the kitchen's fragrant with the scent of new-baked bread, and not the fake smell either, like they pump out in supermarkets. This is real, an achievement. Steve takes a picture of his first successful loaf looking splendid on the breadboard – *splendid*, that's a word you don't hear often, one he stashes in his mind for later.

'Ten more minutes!'

Sweeping Max's stuff to one side – felt pens, scribbled paper, railway timetables, Mario figures, Steve lays the table for three. Knives lined up by the side of matching plates – cereal for Max. He searches the top cupboard for a milk jug, and the glass butter dish. Butter. Good for you, no matter what they say. Forgot to write his dream down this morning. Cows in a field. Covered in flies. And some one said, look, just look, who was it that said just look, see *there* . . . . ?

Lindsay zig-zags back and forth across the road as she comes closer to her street, negotiating lines of parked cars, keeping to the pavements now, dodging the dog walkers – yapping shitzu on long leads, a stately Alsatian – along the rows of terraces, their windows whited out with blinds – past clematis scrambling over alley walls, roses coming into bud while the magnolia's still out, springtime accelerating into summer faster than a heartbeat, and if she could just keep on running forever, but here she is at her own gate, up the stairs and in the shower, *don't forget to remind Steve, don't forget.*

The boy in the Super Mario pyjamas is curled in a corner of the sofa, watching coloured stick men fall from a great height.

Steve hovers in the background. 'Five more minutes.'

'The athlete who has the lowest score will be eliminated.'

'Great.'

'Which colour do you want to be?'

'Cyan.'

'You be Navy.'

They're weirdly hypnotic, those faceless bodies, their seamless limbs rolling and cascading, electronic soundtrack pounding away like they're at some kind of mad rave.

'Last game, right?'

'This is nice! I didn't know it was my birthday . . .'

Max does a double take. 'It's not your *birthday.*'

'No, but it's special like a birthday,' Lindsay says, twisting her damp hair back inside its band. 'What do you think of the bread that Daddy made?'

It's important to have a routine. The whole family together, Lindsay in her uniform, her work face on. In normal times, Max would've been in his uniform too, and then Steve would have dropped them both off, Max at the school, Lindsay at the shop, before getting on with his day.

There's something different about Lindsay this morning. She seems happy, smiling to herself as she checks her phone.

'What is it?'

'Nothing.'

'Give us a look.'

'No it's nothing . . . .' She lays her phone down resolutely, reaches for the butter. 'This bread is amazing.'

'Is it all right?'

She nods, mouth full.

Max is pulling his slice to bits, digging out the soft inside, discarding the crusts, a far-away look in his eyes.

Outside, the blue tits are swooping round the bird table, one of them disappearing inside the stack of bricks that's meant to be a barbecue.

'Can I get down now?' says Max.

The bird pops out, and then dashes back again, a thread of something in its mouth.

'They're nesting.' Steve realises so suddenly he has to speak out loud. 'I think there's a nest. Hey Max . . . .'

This too will be educational. Making bread is educational. Observing nature. Building a barbecue. Everything they do together.

The chair scrapes back. Lindsay's off to work.

'Make sure he draws the rainbow today. Okay? Bye Max, don't forget I want to see it in the window. Love you both.'

A kiss on the cheek.

'What time are you finishing?'

But she's gone already.

There's something different about Lindsay. She never used to kiss goodbye, never used to do that 'love you' thing. And she never used to hide what's on her phone.

Max isn't a difficult child. He's happy inside his own world, staging races with scraps of paper – Cyan, Gold, Navy – or playing another obscure game, involving Merseyrail timetables. The school's sent out a list of goals for his year group, but since Max has been reading since he was in nursery, and can multiply any numbers you give him, there doesn't seem much point.

Max used to pretend he couldn't read. Poor little bugger.

When the teachers ask him questions, he doesn't want to answer.

Are they those sort of parents? Pushy. Think their child's a genius?

Just want him to be happy. And he is. Especially if you let him have five minutes on his Nintendo.

If Steve wanted to, he could get on with his novel in the mornings, just like before. This was supposed to be his year, his time to give himself a chance, or he'd always regret it, that's what Lindsay said; she was the one who pushed for it, *we can manage.* But he might as well have stayed in that crappy office. He wouldn't be in the office anyway; he'd be working from home like everyone else.

He writes down what's left of the dream in the black notebook he keeps by the bed. This is supposed to free up his unconscious mind. Then he loads the dishwasher, puts Max's crusts on the bird table, chases away the pigeons lumbering towards them. The yard is Lindsay's territory – the bulbs in pots, the climbers running along the trellis her dad put up. The half-built barbecue. Frank'd be back like a shot to finish it off for them if he had half a chance. Thinks all this business is just a load of rubbish, everyone falling into line like bleeding robots.

Steve could always have another go.

But then the birds.

If there really is a nest.

Lindsay's phone's lying on the hall table, a mute black slab amongst the bills and the flyers.

That's not like Lindsay, to leave her phone behind . . .

As if she wanted him to find out whatever it is she's been hiding.

Unconsciously.

Her code's probably the same as his. The date of Max's birthday.

23 is a prime number.

So are 5 and 7. Not 6. Max will be 7 in September. September is named after 7 but you write number nine.

23 × 7 = 161

23 × 37 = 851

23 × 41= 943.

1955 ÷ 23 = 85

The remaining athletes will compete in equestrian dressage. The score is determined by . . .

'Hey, Mad Max. Time for exercise.'

'I don't need exercise.'

'Yes you do. Find your shoes.'

'Why do adults make all the decisions?'

'Do you want to go out in five minutes or do you want to go out in three minutes?'

'Three minutes.'

'Okay.'

Max lines up his remaining athletes. The members of the winning team will receive . . .

'One minute.'

'Time to go.'

'I don't need my coat.'

Max puts on his angry face

but

then . . .

. . . Cyan whooshes his scooter round the corner, stopping promptly at the kerb while Navy catches up, dashes over and then round the corner, waiting by the crossing, and he waves to Gold who is standing with her scooter on the opposite side.

Well done Cyan! You are doing great!

Sometimes Mummy or Daddy ask Max if he misses school. If he misses all his friends.

He doesn't know. He thinks so.

Misses.

Miss the train.

He misses the trains.

Services are running on the Northern Line, the Wirral Line and City Line, with connecting services to Manchester, Wigan and Wales, but Max isn't on them any more. His favourite stations are Bromborough Rake, West Kirby and Brunswick. There is no East Kirby. Or North Kirby or South Kirby. He has never been to Eastham Rake but he has been to Bromborough. One day he will go on an adventure to Eastham Rake. Eastham is not East Ham. West Kirby is not Kirk-bee.

Change at Sandhills for stations to Southport.

Bad luck Navy! Try again.

Back at 23 they have a snack. Custard creams.

Navy says to Cyan, you know the colours of the rainbow, don't you Max?

Navy is Daddy. Daddy with the beard, a different daddy to the one who used to go to his office but still the same sometimes. Like when he lifts Max high on his shoulders, and Mummy says you're going to do your back in, but Daddy's strong, and he puts his two hands on the top of Daddy's head while Daddy holds on tight to his two legs, and Max can see the whole world. Now he's the one in charge.

'Max can you hear me? I need you to do this.'

Max drags first a red crayon over the paper, then a green and a purple.

'Can I play on Mummy's phone?'

'Don't worry,' Lindsay says. 'I messed up loads of times. I fainted on my first day.'

'You fainted?' The Future Business Leader has such a look of shocked innocence, he reminds her of Max, and she does want to mother Jon sometimes, can't help herself, poor lad, blushing scarlet when the girls take the piss – *You and me Jonathan, how about it?* – laughing along with them when all the time he must be curling up inside – *I bet your girlfriend won't do what I'd do to you, Jonathan . . . .* But one day Jon will be in his own office at headquarters, while another Graduate Trainee is being tormented in his place.

It would have to be Jonathan who was on the till when Irene went through. And it would have to be the work experience girl on the next till. And Lindsay would have to be on her break when Irene did her I-can't-find-my-purse routine. All for a tin of corned beef, some salad cream and three cherry tomatoes. This is the kind of shop Lindsay runs, not like the bigger supermarkets, not even like the bigger branches of her own company, and because they're smaller they were the last to sell out of toilet rolls and pasta.

She isn't sure it actually was her very first day when she fainted, but it makes Jonathan feel better. She sticks a note in the cash-register for when Irene's daughter pops by, takes over Jon's till, and sends him out on deliveries, twenty-five items per customer, in the boot of the car.

Stay at home, save lives.

But the regulars keep coming in, no matter what – the elderly and bewildered, shuffling along the aisles on their daily expedition, and the lads, not lads any more but they think they are, dashing in for their ciggies and a pint of skimmed milk, their concession to healthy eating, and go on, let's have a lucky dip for Saturday. How many of them wash their hands for two whole minutes, how many of them wash their hands ever?

Lindsay isn't scared. She'll be all right. They'll pull through this, they all will. Because Lindsay has been touched by a miracle. She can't wait to tell Steve the news, but she knows what he's like, it's too soon to tell him, it's impossible he'll say. We were lucky to have Max.

He wanted to chuck those two envelopes straight in the bin, but Lindsay couldn't bring herself to throw money away, even two old fivers that went out of circulation years ago.

'One for Max,' said Lindsay's nan, 'and keep the other for the baby.'

Her nan had always been sharp as a pin – she and Max watched *Countdown* together – but she was ninety-three, and sometimes she did get confused. Lindsay couldn't bear to remind her how much they'd gone through just to have the one child. It breaks her heart to think of it, just as it breaks her heart when she remembers the look in Nanna's eyes, the pressure of her hand: 'You'll have to keep the baby's card till *next* Christmas.'

Part of Lindsay feels glad that her Nan's not around anymore. How could she have coped without the family calling by? Lindsay's seen the doctor parked outside the care home, unpacking the PPE from the boot of his car. That could have been her Nan he was on his way to visit, suited up like an invader from Mars.

Max's fiver is pinned up in his bedroom, next to his Merseyrail leaflets and his map of the world. The other envelope's in the cupboard where they keep the old photos. She'd nearly forgotten about it till she was having an argument with Steve about whether he'd had a beard before – and there it was, amongst the baby pictures and the ribbons from the wedding cake, and a box of shells Max collected from the beach – a faded blue note tucked inside a card showing a robin chirping on a log.

Someone up there's thinking about us, Lindsay thought, suddenly and clearly, like it was the answer to something.

And then the miracle, a new life budding invisibly inside – curled up like a tiny seahorse, deep below the surface of her everyday existence. Lindsay knew even before she missed her period – a surprise thought she quickly dismissed, but then it drifted back and forth across her mind almost continuously – a light-headedness, a heightened sense of smell and taste, those were the signs, she was sure without even looking them up, and it was just as well she left her phone at home because she kept checking the facts, she couldn't stop herself . . . .

Absentmindedness. Another sign.

Wait, just wait one more week, and then she'll take the test, and she can show him, without any room for doubt; she can tell him for sure what she already knows. Two become three, become four, a tiny miracle unfurling day by day.

Album Challenge – Day 6

I've been given a task to choose ten albums that greatly influenced my taste in music. One album per day for ten consecutive days. No explanations, no reviews, just album covers.

Every day I will ask someone else to do the same. Today I nominate Steve Burnell.

Ten of them? Ten?

Back in Steve's novel, a solar storm has turned night into day. People have gathered on the streets, mesmerised by waves of luminous colour sweeping through the skies, colours far beyond the normal spectrum, colours that are indescribable. Those who aren't afraid wake their children, so they too can share in what they still imagine is a unique event. Steve's hero is one of the few not reaching for their phone. He senses this is something you can't save or copy, though he's as yet unaware that he could never get a signal anyway. Nothing's working any more. Satellites are dead, phone masts useless skeletons. You can't switch the telly on to find out what's happening. Not even the battery works in your laptop. Even the light's gone off inside the fridge.

A few months ago, when Steve first started drafting out this passage, coming back to the real world felt like a shock. He never expected to hear his own fridge humming, or the sound of the traffic going by. Now it's his fictional world that seems remote – outdated and irrelevant, a flimsy confection, outdone by the bizarre events unfolding in real life. He still has moments when he has complete faith in this novel, convinces himself that one day he'll be a published author. But he can't settle down to anything much any more, except for the practical things he never used to be much good at. Cooking, cleaning, baking bread. He tries not to check on the news too often. Tries not to get distracted.

Nirvana, *Nevermind.* If he did post an album cover. Or the *Star Wars* LP, still somewhere at his mum's house with all the old figures. Could Max get into *Star Wars*? That's what he thought having a son would be like. Watching films, playing footie. Being best mates.

Sometimes he wakes up in the night feeling sweaty, thinking *this is how it starts, the ambulance, intensive care* . . . Or there's an irritation in his throat, or a crushing headache. He used to be a good sleeper. Never felt a thing when Max crept into bed on Sunday mornings. Now Lindsay's the one snoring softly, never troubled, not afraid of anything.

What kind of man sends his wife into danger while he stays at home trying to write science fiction?

The answer's to keep moving. Stick to the routine. Each day the same – Lindsay off and back again, a bit of schoolwork, exercise, mealtimes – what is there to show? Max's drawing of a red stripe, a green stripe, a purple. A page or two of handwriting. 'I'm rubbish at writing,' says Max. 'Just do your best,' says Steve, like that ever made any difference.

In the next chapter of Steve's novel, a single streetlamp turns on of its own accord. Somewhere, in a deserted operating theatre, the machines whir and bleep, as if in conversation. The hero's laptop suddenly comes back to life, but what is it he sees when he looks at the screen?

Lindsay's phone vibrates softly from the hallway, but the sound registers too late for Steve to answer. He tries unlocking with a different combination – 1234, the numbers most people choose, the stupid gets. Then 0123, then 4321. He's done all the birthdays. Wedding anniversary – but he'd have to check that one with Lindsay.

Steve knows how this works. Some one new at work, you're showing them the ropes, and then you start sharing in-jokes, and there's a flirty edge to the texts.

Are you imagining . . . . ?

Something different about her.

Like she doesn't care any more.

Like there's a different person inside her, pretending to be Lindsay.

Wow, this is amazing, must be my birthday . . .

Like there's nothing to worry about. Smiling to herself, like she knows a secret.

That Jon, the Future Business Leader.

Bet it's him.

The divvy.

Taking the rubbish to the bins, he sneaks a peek at the hollow inside the brick barbecue, glimpses pale coils of something in the half-second before a bird rises up to snap at him, fierce as a snake.

'Was I there?' says Max.

'No, you weren't born yet.'

This is a difficult thought for Max to process.

They've been talking about when she and Steve got married. Steve was asking at teatime what date was it was, and she said, 'Don't you remember, it was that year when it never stopped raining? We thought it was going to be a washout and then just for that one day . . .'

She wonders if Steve's trying to plan a surprise for their anniversary. Maybe this will all be over by August; they could splash out for a meal or something.

Max says, 'Don't go. I don't want to be on my own.'

'You're not on your own,' she says, tucking the teddy under the duvet, 'look here's Eddie.'

'Eddie's not alive.'

'Yes he is. Everything's alive.'

She can tell he's not convinced.

Bedtimes have been taking longer and longer, Max calling her back when she's already said goodnight, and always his mother he wants, never Steve. But it's also kind of nice – that special time, just the two of them, Max listening quietly to what he calls a story, though it isn't really. The story of a time when he did not exist, and then the story of the night-time beyond his bedroom window, where all the other children are falling fast asleep.

'. . . and all the animals and all the birds – except the nocturnal ones.'

Max laughs. He likes the word *nocturnal.*

'And the moon and the stars are watching . . .' She keeps her voice low, trying to make the words soothing and hypnotic.

'The moon turns round the earth . . .'

'And the earth turns round the sun . . . and the universe keeps turning, and the Milky Way . . .'

She's not sure if the Milky Way is part of the universe, or the other way round, but Max doesn't contradict her. He's stopped wriggling at last, lying still, if not quite sleeping. She strokes his silky head, half-asleep herself, drifting for a moment, thinking it's morning.

She can't imagine loving a second child as much as she loves Max. But she knows that she will.

Two become three become four. By Christmas, there'll be a new life at Number 23. Steve will be going back to work, and Max at school. By Christmas, these times will be over, and everything back to how it was, only even better. And by this time next year they'll look back and it will all seem like a dream.

She can hear Steve moving round in the bedroom. Maybe she should say something now; he seems so down all of a sudden.

Or just leave well alone.

The look he sends towards her when she walks into the room. The bedding all heaped up in a pile, the drawers pulled open, the washing basket upturned.

'Have you seen my notebook?'

'What notebook?'

'The one by the bed. You've moved it.'

His face is dark with anger.

'Why would I touch your notebook?'

'Well I haven't moved it.'

'It'll turn up, just sleep on it. You don't need it right this minute.'

She remembers now, it's that dream diary. Supposed to help him be creative.

The sooner he goes back to work, the better.

There's a place where lost things go, and then they turn up again.

Or they don't.

She tries to touch him but he pulls away. That dark, angry face.

Sooner things get back to normal for everybody's sake.

The boy in the Super Mario pyjamas is lying awake, the door left open a sliver, to let the stair light in, the ebb and flow of voices, quiet, then loud, then quiet at the edges of his mind. His thoughts run along the lines of the Merseyrail network – red, black, blue and green – counting off the stops, Kirkdale, Sandhills, *change here for the Southport line* – Moorfields, Liverpool Central – until he's chanted himself to sleep. 'Mummy,' he mutters, 'Mummy . . . . ?' as he tips into unconsciousness, the voices raised again across the landing.

Inside the half-built barbecue, the blue tit shifts on her nest, the eggs warm beneath her body. Further down the alley, a black-and-white cat is slinking over walls, listening for movement, its narrow pupils sharp as moonlight. It drops down at Number 23, relieves itself and scents the air. The lights go off inside the house, except for the stair light. All is still.

'The Marquee'

Paula McGrath

Early morning. Laura crunched across the gravel at the front of the house. To her left lay the orchard, to her right the avenue, curving away through the trees towards the road. Purple mist lingered on the grass and droplets hung from shrubs whose names she could not seem to learn. From every tree some bird sang. May Day. In four hours, her sister would be married.

Soon, she would be expected inside to fuss with hats and flowers but for now the day was hers. Wash your face in the dew, she remembered from school, it's good for the complexion. After another sleepless night, she could use all the help she could get. With a glance over her shoulder, she stooped and ran her palms over the wetness. She trembled a little. Should have worn a fleece. She patted her face more vigorously than necessary. If it were not for damn Florian, she would be radiant.

The marquee nestled among the apple trees, its awning tinged pink with fallen blossoms. She had watched while the crew erected it the day before from her vantage point behind the rose bushes where she was pretending to read; it was a well-rehearsed choreography of poles and ropes which filled the orchard with unfamiliar clanks and bangs and agreeable bursts of a language she did not recognise. They were almost finished by the time her mother was able to get away from a last-minute seating crisis to supervise. There followed generous gesticulations and the frequent rising trill of her mother's laughter before she bustled back indoors and the crew began to disassemble and reassemble the entire structure a foot closer to the house.

As soon as Laura stepped inside the marquee, the texture of her breath changed. One moment she was in the orchard, the next she was in this great white womb, a hushed universe of infinite possibility. That it had been created by the mere separation of so many cubic metres of air from the everyday world with fabric as flimsy as the lining of an egg seemed close to miraculous. It filled her with an overwhelming urge to dance. Fifth position, fourth, second, the muscle memory trained into her body when she was small was still there. She caught herself humming as she pointed and stepped: Offenbach's *Barcarolle*. She never should have quit. She used to dream of being a ballerina princess, chiffon and lace frothing round her shins as she *jetéd* and *fouettéd*, her feet barely touching the ground. For the first time, she had a glimmer of insight into Julie's passive, dreamy state of these past few months. A mere five minutes before, Laura would have attributed it to a year of bridal Insta and airbrushed photos and rolled her eyes at Julie for being such a cliché. Her sister, who in the past would have annihilated her with a comeback, these days would look hurt, maybe even cry. Which was why she had not been able to tell her about Florian. Laura came to a standstill, her arms falling to her sides like clipped wings, her quickened breath amplified in the empty marquee. Her mouth tasted of metal and PVC and dread. It was time to go back.

'Tell me the truth,' Julie said when Laura entered her bedroom. Her eyes in the mirror were challenging, a flash of her sister of old. She was referring to her Roman tiara updo. 'Mum says it's fine.'

Laura picked experimentally at the foliage. 'Lose it unless you want to risk birds nesting on your head.'

Julie's eyes widened. 'That bad?'

'Worse. But fear not, help is at hand. That's what bridesmaids are for, right?'

'That's what sisters are for,' Julie said, taking Laura's hand. Her eyes had filled with tears.

Laura tried to concentrate on removing the laurel leaves without disturbing the intricate plaiting. 'It will be great,' she said, avoiding Julie's gaze. Ever since Megan dropped her bombshell, Laura did not know how to be a sister. Megan had got work experience in the doctor's office, where her mother was the nurse. It was a cinch, she told the friend group. All she had to do was sit there looking pretty, tell patients to take a seat and the doctor would be with them shortly. She spent her days filing her nails, got told off for stinking up the surgery with nail polish, apparently. But there was only so much Candy Crush a girl could play, so when this finer came in, gave her a big sexy smile, told her his name was Florian Kenny, Laura's sister's –

Despite Laura's best efforts, the leaves snagged and strands of hair pulled loose.

'Damn.'

They surveyed the damage.

'A couple of grips. I have some,' Laura said quickly, in case Julie started to cry.

But when she returned from her room, the brown pins stuck out a mile on Julie's flaxen head.

'They have the right ones in the Maxol. I'll be there and back before you've had your breakfast.' She held out her hand, which Julie took and squeezed before she understood that Laura wanted her car keys. 'They're on the hall table.' Her eyes had filled again; it was impossible; Laura would never be able to tell her sister what she learned from Megan.

She was half-way out the front door when she heard Julie calling her to wait, she was not supposed to drive without a qualified driver in the car.

Julie's ice-blue Mini Cooper was waxed and gleaming. Florian cleaned it for her every week. Bloody Florian. Laura accelerated hard, gouging skid marks in the gravel as she took off.

'What else could I do?' Megan had asked, all innocence. She had read his patient file when he left. They delighted in shocking one another and Megan had hit the jackpot. Laura waited with trepidation while Megan dragged out the tension as long as she could. 'Gonococcal infection,' she enunciated gleefully. A pause. 'Gonorrhoea, you thicks. Julie's fella has the clap!'

Laura was certain Julie did not know. Why else would Florian, new to the area, have gone to the clinic at the far end of the town instead of their family doctor? The next time they came over, she made a point of asking him as meaningfully as she could if everything was ok *now*. He gave her a strange look, glanced in Julie's direction before saying everything was great, couldn't be better, mate, with his New Zealand accent and his insufferable smile.

That was when it hit her. She might not be able to tell Julie, but there was nothing stopping her from telling Florian. He should be the one to tell Julie. Why hadn't she thought of it before? She had better get a move on. She floored the Mini, praying she would not meet another car on the lane. She reached the main road safely. Look left, look right, look left again. She sped out towards the town.

Up ahead, a lone figure was shuffling along, clad in black from her headscarf to her wellington boots. If you hadn't known who it was, you'd think she was an extra from *Game of Thrones*, but it was just Juju on her way out to the old graveyard, where she went every day to talk to her long-dead mother. Everyone laughed about it, but Laura liked the idea that the membrane between this life and the next should be so thin and permeable that you could hold a conversation across it. As she overtook the old woman, she was prodded with guilt; she should give her a lift.

But she was rushing. Hairpins! Besides, there was no nice way to say it, Juju stank. She had debated aloud whether it was because she had so many cats or because she was incontinent and Julie said Laura was cruel. Whatever, her sister would not want her car reeking of cat pee.

She nipped into the remaining parking space.

Magda nodded at the hairclips. 'Bride all set?'

'Bag of nerves.'

'Her fella is only gorgeous.'

Laura forced a smile.

'You're next,' Magda said. 'Wonder who the lucky man will be?'

Laura rolled her eyes. As if. 'See ya, Magda.'

She slipped into first gear and pulled out on to the main road. There was some commotion up ahead on the straight stretch. Shit, she didn't want to get delayed. Double-shit, the Garda car was there, lights flashing. What emergency explained why she was alone in the car with only a provisional licence. Hairpins? They seemed so urgent before. As she got closer she saw that there had been an accident, a Honda Civic wrapped around a tree. That must be the driver, pacing around, pushing his hand through his hair. About her age. She peered. Didn't recognise him. At least no one was hurt. She slowed, prepared to stop. The underarms of her top were wet, mortifying if they questioned her. But the Garda waved her on. Relief flooded through her and she made to comply but something on the road made her hesitate. Her eye followed a dark trickle to its source behind the parked Garda car, a pool, spreading out beneath a black scarf.

The Garda was getting impatient. In her hurry to oblige, she ground the gears and felt herself blush, which only deepened the shame: embarrassed, when Juju was dead. At last she turned into the lane. She pulled over in a gateway, scrolled her news apps. Nothing. Maybe she was just injured. She'd be taken to the hospital. Laura would visit. She would bring the biggest bunch of wedding flowers. Shame surged through her again. But it would be a waste not to. No, she would not have to agonise; there was blood coming from Juju's head and she was not moving. Laura was certain: Juju was dead. She raced home, bursting with the news.

To her surprise, Florian's car was parked outside. What was he doing? Julie would go mad if she saw him. Unlucky to see the bride and all that. She was crossing the gravel when he emerged. This was it, her chance to tell him. But something stopped her. He did not look his usual no-worries self; instead he seemed distracted, as if he would have avoided her if he could.

'Hi Laura.'

'All right?'

'Pre-wedding jitters, I guess.' He ran his hand through his spiky blond hair, reminding her of the boy at the accident. She nearly felt sorry for him. But he must be told. Julie had to know.

In a breathless rush, she told him about the blood, the Garda, the hairpins; she waved them at him. She should have given Juju a lift.

Florian was looking at her as if she was raving. 'Okay, well I better get cleaned up,' he said.

'Don't tell Julie,' Laura warned. 'It would spoil her day.'

Soon after that, the cars began to arrive: first the florist, followed by the caterers, the photographer, the band. Then it was time: Julie like a princess, floating up the aisle; photographs on the striped lawn; guests in brightly coloured outfits sipping coupes of pink champagne, voices slowed to a drawl in the afternoon heat, their discarded jackets and shawls draped over every hired chair. Trays of stuffed mushrooms and sausages wrapped in bacon and miniature tacos and hamburgers held together with a toothpick waving tiny Julie & Florian flags appeared at elbows, and pizza slices, each in its own tiny box. Evening and the marquee, transformed with the palest pink roses, all the plastic windows rolled to let a welcome breeze caress bare legs. Soft jazz swelled then retreated. Couples wandered into the orchard. Smokers found the boiler house to dodge behind and Laura joined them to be a part of it. She was a stunner in the silk sheath Julie selected, everyone said. She danced with all the men, even Florian, and most of the women too. The newly-weds left first, in the Mini, Julie looking so happy; then the guests with babysitters, then those without. The caterers were next, then the band. Laura's friends and Julie's were last.

'That went well,' her mother said, 'but I am falling asleep on my feet. Good night, all.'

Laura pulled the lights down on the marquee, then the hall downstairs, then her bedroom.

In the morning, Laura pulled on her cosy grey sweatpants and made her way to the marquee. A cool mizzle was falling, polishing the gravel and making the grass slippery. A plastic chair had been abandoned by the rose bed, a pint glass with its yellow dregs beside it. Somebody's jacket was over there; and there, somebody's shoe; she wondered how they got home. When she drew the door aside, she half-expected to disturb some last, forgotten guests, but there was no one, just an empty tent. But no, not that, exactly. It was not empty; merely without an observer.

She could almost have believed, if she were to stay very still, that the confidences and gossip, the purposeful walk to the bar, the joke over the shoulder, the laughing and arguing and dancing would carry on around her in ghost form. She breathed in, half-expecting to inhale perfume and sweat and brandy.

A second sniff dispelled the fantasy. Ugh. Why did yesterday's alcohol always smell so unpleasant? She wandered among the tables, with their stained and crumpled paper cloths, their wilting centrepieces. How different everything looked in the aftermath. It was strange to think that a few hours from now the crew would dismantle it all and real life would begin again. It all seemed so sad somehow, so final.

The sweet scent of dying flowers drifted up from one of the arrangements, a reminder of something she had forgotten. She pulled a rose out by its long stem. It was holding up well, considering. She extracted another, then another, moving from table to table to select the best specimens. By the time she reached the head table, where hours before she sat with Julie and Florian and his sister and brother and their parents, groaning through speeches, forgetting to eat, remembering too often to drink, she was surprised to find her arms quite full. That was it: yesterday's promise to visit Juju in the hospital. Then she remembered Juju's face where she lay on the road, saint-like, eyes turned to heaven as if she couldn't wait to be with her mammy. She pictured the grave that no one would visit. Weeds would claim it and the weather would wear the inscription away until Juju and her mother were forever erased from memory.

Then it came to her. *She* would visit the grave! Every day. She would bring the very best of the roses, the marigolds, the zinnias. Starting right now. If she walked quickly, she could be there and back before her mother was awake. She must find a suitable vase, something she could leave there and refill with water. Flushed with her plan, she skipped back to the house, rehearsing in her head the news she would bring to Juju's mother.

'Endless Sea'

Bronwyn Calder

The ice-strengthened ship *Endless Sea* powers south of Tierra del Fuego into the Antarctic Ocean.

Phyllis leans on the guard rail and watches the seabirds dip and soar above the waves, her heart pounding with excitement more and more as the temperature plummets. The rail is now rimed with frost, and the deck covered in grit to prevent the passengers sliding on the ice.

An albatross glides over the ship's wake – a wandering silhouette against the sun that doesn't quite set – gliding over gigantic wave tops also silhouetted, like a range of mountain peaks.

Phyllis pulls herself off the rail, her gloves leaving a deposit of suede fibres and a few tufts of lambswool from the wrist bands.

She flew out the day of Melissa's wedding. It had been coming for five years. The five years since Melissa left home.

She had started putting more time into her painting and had exhibited every year for the five years. She had sold quite well – developing a line in abstracted doors and gates, arches and porticos which spoke of possibilities, journeys, fresh revelations. But after five years she realised they weren't going anywhere. When Melissa announced she was getting married, Phyllis sat down and made a list of things she wanted to achieve. The top one was 'adventure' and, after much thought, she decided on a trip to the Antarctic. She wanted to see a new landscape – to be inspired by a different light, to find meaning in the beauty of the place, in nature itself, in humanity's place in it. The second thing on the list was leaving Henry. There was no way forward with him. The doors and gates and all the other portals kept beckoning, but he kept her from moving through them. She told Henry as Melissa drove away with her new husband. She flew to South America that same evening. She had no intention of returning to him. Her real life was beginning now.

The first ice they see is a white crag, like a slice of glass fractured and split, sharp against the featureless grey sky. The next day they see the underside of a whale's tail flip high out of the water before disappearing beneath the iron-grey swell. The others gasp, but Phyllis wonders how the creature can live in that ghastly cold darkness. The guidebook tells her icebergs are fresh water, split off from glaciers that terminate at the Antarctic coast. Sea ice, which they haven't seen yet, is the frozen ocean breaking up. Antarctica is 14 million square kilometres, double that in winter.

Helmut, the German adventurer, is standing next to her. 'Do you ever feel', she says, 'when you're on a high place, a compulsion to jump? That's how I feel about the water.'

'If you jumped in, you would quickly die,' he says.

Phyllis goes below. Her bid for freedom has come down to a nauseated huddling in her bunk against the cold.

The windows of the cabin have iced up; as the sun shines through them the frost, settled in long white feathers, glows gold like a strange midnight forest alight with wildfires.

She tries to make something of the events of the day. Blue and white is all that comes up, and the way she really wanted to hurl herself into the sea, and yet feared it. She understands the ship's name, the sea that has no end as it swirls around and around the last wilderness (as the guidebook says). She writes a quick description of the whale's tail. It was white on the underside, although nobody could tell her what species it was. Helmut took photos; perhaps he would identify it. She tries to sketch it from memory, but that doesn't capture the complete silence, until the ridiculous oohs and aaahs shattered the peace.

More icebergs every day. And then the mosaic of the sea ice – the sun riding low and metallic in the sky, burning across the sheet of ocean broken in paving stones of ice. It looks like solid paving, except for the subtle heaving of the water beneath. The light merges towards a point above the horizon. Everything is cold, from the soft snow frosting on wind-hollowed icebergs to the ghostly translucent fragments of ice just below the ocean surface. Here, though the sky is still light grey, the sea is deep radiant blue, as if from somewhere sunlight has got in and stained it. Penguins gather together, riding on an ice floe. They are so tiny the scale of the landscape becomes real. It looks as if you could cross the sea ice, as on stepping-stones, in 30 seconds. But the penguins look half a mile away.

The ice floes are eroded just under the sea surface, their submarine ledges are aqua blue in the low sun. An iceberg rolls. Its flat top reaches to the sky and suddenly the swell tips it and it rolls, its massive hidden self lurching into view as it settles with a crash and a huge surge on to another side. Spumes of sea water mount the air.

The Southern Ocean greets the ship head on – smashing across her bows like a giant waterfall spilling itself directly on to the deck. The sea lashes the window in Phyllis's cabin as she lies on her side, all her organs sloshing around in her body. She heaves the contents of her stomach into the bucket again. The cabin pitches around her and her head explodes again as a cleaver enters her skull and slashes down, as far as her eyes. The shadows of the waves cast on the wall, black against the endless and relentless bronze sun. The sun watches her all the time. It is unblinking, barely moving in the sky, and it knows it has defeated her. 'Even I', it says, 'have no purpose but to make sure your skull explodes behind your eyes and you wish yourself in hell for relief'.

Helmut and the American woman slap their arms happily against their sides. 'That was a good blow,' the American woman says cheerfully.

The other passengers squeal in delight with each sighting of life. A seal sunning itself on the low outlier of an enormous glacier shaped like a sandy beach. An orca fin two metres tall.

Helmut stops slapping his arms and takes a picture of the American woman. Phyllis imagines the woman tipping over the rail, her bright white hair that whips in the wind as a fringe around her furred hood, slipping beneath the iron-grey surge.

'Nice morning!' the woman calls to her. Phyllis smiles in return.

Close to the ice the air is even colder. Ice falls away under the sea, endlessly falling. The ship moves closer and closer. The sea is dead calm. Icebergs perfectly reflected. But beneath they spread their arms – monstrous tentacles to trap and ensnare – Leviathan, monsters of the deep.

The floes and the bergs and the monstrous mountains of snow and ice. The sea breaks through and pitilessly sculpts the ice into a wild architecture of hills and valleys and arches and holes and cones and sound shells. There is one, not far off like a breaking wave – if she could just get out and touch and see and taste and feel and disappear into the freezing water. This alone is real. The ice blue, the deep, the frost the endless moving ocean endless ending.

The glacier terminus is hundreds of feet high. The splinters the size of houses, the falling ice the impact of a demolition ball. The deep cold fissures of dark blue. Worn fissures that look like organic forms – the whorls of trees – or perhaps she just longs for signs of warmth. Dripping daggers of ice.

The others cheer as they see their first glimpse of the Antarctic mainland. The indifference of the black mountains. A perpetual wilderness of ice and snow. There are places where no one has ever stepped. The mountains hunch their ice-covered backs, completely oblivious to anything of man. Mountaintops, too steep for snow and ice, rise black to the sky, great skirts of ice at their bases, veils of ripped cloud trailing from their peaks.

We have no place here, she thinks. We have no place anywhere. I have no place anywhere. There is nothing. This all means nothing but cold and darkness and pitiless sea. She feels the ache in her throat of tears, but she does not let them fall. If she started she would not stop.

She skypes Henry.

'Henry', she says, 'Henry, I want to come home.'

There is a delay on the line. She hears his words before his face jerks into movement. 'Come home, Phyllis. I want you to come home.'

It feels like defeat. Outside the wind is whistling through the ship's rig. A normal night on the Southern Ocean. The great dark beneath, Leviathan awaits.

Note: 'Endless Sea' won the 2014 Graeme Lay Short Story Competition, run by the NZ Society of Authors. It was previously published in Landfall 229.

POEMS

Twenty Immortal Minutes: A Poem by Xu Zhimo

Stuart Lyons

On the death of Katherine Mansfield

Last night I dreamed I did a valley seek
  And heard a cuckoo in blood-red lilies cry;
Last night I dreamed I climbed an Alpine peak
  And saw a teardrop falling from the sky.

A graveyard tombstone on Rome's western bound
  Marks Shelley's death a hundred years ago;
A hundred years on, Hell's grim wheels resound
  Over the green forest of Fontainebleau.

They say the world is a ruthless instrument,
  Yet our ideals, like beacons, guide our tread;
If beauty, truth, virtue are fortune's friend
  Why do five rainbows not gleam overhead?

Was it just once or for infinity,
  Those twenty immortal minutes spent with you?
Who can believe that your divinity
  Has faded from the earth like morning dew?

No! Life is but material delusion;
  The beauteous soul rests in the love of God;
A thirty-year sojourn, a mere illusion;
  I weep, but see you smile in heaven's abode.

In London, Mansfield, we'd a summer date
  To meet on Lake Geneva, as you recall,

Where Mont Blanc's snows refract upon the lake;
  Now stare I at the clouds and sad tears fall.

When I was young, my life embraced new things;
  I sensed as in a dream the worth of love;
Mature love comes from life's awakenings;
  Now to death's brink my love and life I move.

True love is crystal that will never shatter;
  Love is the road to completeness of being:
Death is a cauldron of material matter,
  The gods' condensed conflux of everything.

Would my thoughts flew like electricity
  And I could touch your distant soul in heaven!
I shed my tears on the wind: 'When, when,' I cry,
  'Can the dread gate 'twixt life and death be riven?'

XU ZHIMO
[*Translation by Stuart Lyons, 2021*]

[Written on 11 March 1923, first published in *Effort Weekly* (Shanghai), 44 (18 March 1923), and reprinted in *Complete Works,* 1, pp. 398–9. English verse translation by Stuart Lyons, 2021.]

Xu Zhimo was an emerging Chinese poet who had just gone down from a year's study at King's College, Cambridge, when he met Katherine Mansfield. At the invitation of John Middleton Murry, he went to her temporary lodgings in Dorothy Brett's house at 6 Pond Street in Hampstead on the evening of 24 August 1922. It was raining heavily, but eventually Xu found the terraced dwelling and rang the bell. Leaving his coat and umbrella in the hallway, he followed his host into a narrow drawing-room. Xu was a practised observer with an acute visual sense. He registered the fireplace opposite the door, the mantelpiece decked with coloured ornaments, and the low chairs with patterned covers that were ranged about. A hanging lamp cast a subdued yellow light. There were paintings on the walls, most of them Brett's work.[1]

For the next two hours, Xu Zhimo conversed politely with a sequence of visitors and showed them a scroll of Chinese calligraphy. They included Mansfield's cousin, Sydney Waterlow, and J. W. N. Sullivan, a science journalist and colleague of Murry, each of whom was invited by Murry to go upstairs and visit her. It was not until 10.30 pm that Xu was finally led up the narrow staircase to Mansfield's room.

When Xu Zhimo entered, he found a small space with a large bed. The walls were papered and on them hung more of Brett's oils. There were two lamps with, as Xu recalled, red lampshades. There was a sofa against the wall, upholstered in blue velvet, where Mansfield sat upright and he leaned back. She was wearing a pale-yellow silk blouse with sleeves down to the elbow, a burgundy velvet skirt, bright green stockings and patent leather shoes. Her jet-black hair was well combed, cropped Chinese-style with a neat fringe at the front. She wore a string of pearls around her neck. He later described her features as crystalline, like an Alpine lake bathed in autumn moonlight. Her beauty was like the purest Indian jade, her gaze alive with spiritual revelation, her manner gentle as a spring breeze: 'I stared into her mystical eyes, letting her sword-like gaze penetrate my being, while the music of her voice washed over me and flooded into the depths of my soul.'[2] When she spoke, her windpipe vibrated like a reed; when she paused, her chest heaved and her cheeks were flushed.

They talked about the English novelists, Chinese poetry and the plays of Chekhov. 'That's not the thing,' she said, more than once, when she was not in tune with certain writers and translators.[3] She shared his admiration for the novels of Joseph Conrad and Thomas Hardy. She despised politics. They talked about her own writings and she seemed pleased when Xu said he might translate some of her stories into Chinese. She invited him to visit her in Switzerland. 'Listening to her', he wrote later, 'I thought I could feel the waves softly lapping against our boat and see the mountains across the lake.'[4] Xu's 'twenty immortal minutes' were over.[5] She saw him to the door and shook his hand in farewell.

They would never meet again. The following spring Xu received news that she had died in France. He composed an elegy in Chinese rhyming verse, of which this is a translation.

Notes

1. The descriptions in this and the following paragraphs are taken from Xu Zhimo, 'Mansfield', *Short Story Monthly* (Shanghai), 14: 5 (10 May 1923), reprinted in Xu Zhimo, *Complete Works* (Nanning: Guangxi National Publishing House, 1991), 5 vols, vol. 2, pp. 197–209.
2. Translation by Shifen Gong in *The Turnbull Library Record*, 22: 2 (1 October 1989), pp. 85–97 (p. 93).
3. Xu Zhimo, *Complete Works*, 2, p. 208. Although writing in Chinese, Xu noted her comments verbatim in the original English.
4. Shifen Gong, p. 95.
5. Xu Zhimo, *Complete Works*, 2, p. 199.

A Poem by Philippe Chabaneix

Gerri Kimber

K. M. 1932

Au souvenir de Katherine Mansfield

Sur les vieux quais de l'île
Si chère aux amoureux,
Le soir tombe tranquille
Et je suis presque heureux.

Nulle brise marine,
Mais le ciel doux et gris,
Et vous, ô Katherine,
Souriant à Paris,

Dans votre manteau sombre
D'il y a dix-sept ans,
Qui passez comme une ombre
Où danse le printemps.

K. M. 1932

In memory of Katherine Mansfield

On the old quays of the island
So dear to lovers,
Evening falls quietly
And I am almost happy.

No sea breeze,
But the sky soft and grey,
And you, O Katherine,
Smiling in Paris,

In your dark coat
Of seventeen years ago,

You pass like a shadow
Where Spring dances.

PHILIPPE CHABANEIX
[*Translation by Gerri Kimber, 2021*]

This hitherto unknown poem about Katherine Mansfield, by French poet Philippe Chabaneix (1898–1982), was published in the French journal *Mercure de France* on 1 January 1955, on page 47. It was brought to my attention by Professor James Sexton, of the University of British Columbia in Canada, to whom I extend my grateful thanks. The poem offers a tantalising, ephemeral portrait of Mansfield in the spring of 1915, when she was residing at Francis Carco's little apartment on the quai aux Fleurs, situated on the Ile de la Cité in the heart of Paris, and offers a hitherto unknown connection to yet another French writer.

The story of Mansfield's visit to Francis Carco at the Front in early 1915 is well known. In February 1915, Mansfield had become increasingly disillusioned by her relationship with John Middleton Murry and believed herself to be in love with Carco (whom she had first met in 1912 in the early days of her relationship with Murry), and with whom she was sharing an increasingly amorous correspondence. Thus she travelled to Paris, and from there made the difficult journey to see Carco, who was now stationed in the war zone, working as a military postman in Gray (Haute-Saône), in north-east France. After four nights with her new lover, she suddenly returned to London and Murry on 25 February, disillusioned but with plenty of 'copy', which she would make full use of in her fiction. Though Mansfield soon became cynical about her affair with Carco, nevertheless she clung on to the relationship for a few more months – long enough to make use of his apartment in Paris on the quai aux Fleurs, overlooking the Seine. There, in May 1915, she wrote the story 'An Indiscreet Journey', an account of her visit to Gray and her affair with Carco, as well as 'Spring Pictures' and 'The Little Governess', and she also started the first draft of her long story 'The Aloe', which in 1917 she would later refine into 'Prelude'.

At this point in her life, as Jeffrey Meyers observes, she was both disillusioned by the selfishness of Carco and wounded by the indifference of Murry.[1] The trip to Gray having somehow not come up to her expectations, she had returned to Murry, only to leave him again a few days later to return to Paris and Carco's flat. Two weeks later, she was back in England, and a month later back at Carco's flat again. And all the while she was writing cheery, loving letters to Murry and breezy, vaguely flirtatious ones to Carco (having told Murry she was no longer in contact with him), perhaps, cynically, because she wanted the use of his flat, perhaps because she still held a candle for their relationship.

The ramifications of the Mansfield/Carco relationship are to be felt in the annals of French as well as English literature, for in Carco's novel of 1916, entitled *Les Innocents*, he portrays Mansfield unsympathetically as Winnie Campbell, a predatory and exploitative character.[2] Thus, whilst she was alive, the none too flattering portrait of herself as Winnie, which she undoubtedly read, had already entered the domain of French literature via Carco's novel, published seven years before her death. Later on, as the hagiography of her personality developed in France following her early death in Fontainebleau-Avon in 1923, Carco could not alter his novel, but he certainly could and did change his attitude towards Mansfield, and in particular his published recollections of her. With the passage of time, Mansfield's reputation in its ascendancy, and not wishing to rock any critical boats, his biographical portrait of Mansfield was considerably softened and romanticised in order to accommodate the sentimental French legend which had developed after her death.

What of the connection to Philippe Chabaneix? Ten years younger than Mansfield and twelve years younger than Carco, he was a French poet who spent his early childhood in Nouméa, New Caledonia, coincidentally the same Pacific island where Carco grew up. Little known today, he was nevertheless one of the foremost representatives of the group of French poets known as the *fantaisistes* (which included Carco). A 1966 volume on Chabaneix mentions a connection with Katherine Mansfield:

> It was during these last months of the war that the sympathy that united gunner Chabaneix to his elders Francis Carco, then an aviator pilot, Tristan Derème, Jean Pellerin, Pierre Como and Vincent Muselli was strengthened through an exchange of letters and poems. A leave of absence allowed him to meet the author of *La Bohème et mon Coeur* in the small apartment on the quai aux Fleurs where Katherine Mansfield stayed for a little while. [my translation][3]

It is clear from the above quotation that Chabaneix did not meet Carco or visit the quai aux Fleurs apartment until a few months before the end of the war, and thus never met Mansfield in 1915 (when he would have been a youthful seventeen years old). Further evidence to support this is supplied by Chabaneix himself in a volume on Carco that he wrote in 1949, where he states:

> [It was] in December 1917, during a period of leave, [that] I met the author of *Jésus-la-Caille*. [. . .] I remember, as if it were yesterday, Carco welcoming me with his usual kindness in this apartment on the quai aux

> Fleurs, whose windows looked out over the Seine, criss-crossed by tugs and barges [. . . and] in this study [. . .] where the memory of Katherine Mansfield was still present.[4]

Despite Chabaneix having never met Mansfield, it is clear that the influence of Carco's later sycophantic memoirs of Mansfield, who by then was well known in France, together with his visit to the quai aux Fleurs apartment and the ensuing conversations and recollections, engendered his poetic response to Carco's erstwhile – and now much celebrated – female friend. In the same volume, Chabaneix also noted that Carco's volume of memoirs, *Montmartre à vingt ans,* published in 1938, 'contains an enchanting chapter on Katherine Mansfield, with a dream-like innocence' (my translation),[5] thus promulgating the same reverential nonsense that continues to beleaguer Mansfield's reputation in France to this day.

Notes

I would like to record my thanks to Professor James Sexton, Professor Todd Martin and Brigitte Martin for their feedback during the preparation of this article.

1. See Jeffrey Meyers, *Katherine Mansfield: A Darker View* (New York: Cooper Square Press, 2002), p. 85.
2. Francis Carco, *Les Innocents* (Paris: Albin Michel, 1916). Antony Alpers describes the character of Winnie as 'a predatory huntress out for "copy"'. Antony Alpers, *The Life of Katherine Mansfield* (New York: Viking, 1980), p. 178.
3. Robert Houdelot and André Blanchard, *Philippe Chabaneix* (Paris: Seghers, 1966):

   > C'est au cours de ces derniers mois de la guerre que se resserra, grâce à un échange de lettres et de poèmes, la sympathie qui unissait l'artilleur Chabaneix à ses grands ainés Francis Carco, alors pilote aviateur, Tristan Derème, Jean Pellerin, Pierre Como et Vincent Muselli. Une permission lui permet de rencontrer l'auteur de la *Bohème et mon Coeur* dans le petit appartement du quai aux Fleurs où Katherine Mansfield séjourna quelque temps. (p. 40)

4. Philippe Chabaneix, *Francis Carco* (Paris: Pierre Seghers, 1949), pp. 35–6.

   > [C'était] en décembre 1917, au cours d'une permission, [que] je liai connaissance avec l'auteur de *Jésus-la-Caille.* [. . .] Je revois, comme si c'était hier, Carco m'accueillant avec sa gentillesse habituelle dans cet appartement du quai aux Fleurs, dont les fenêtres donnaient sur la Seine sillonnée de remorqueurs et de chalands [. . . et] dans ce cabinet de travail [. . .] où restait présent le souvenir de Katherine Mansfield.

5. '*Montmartre à vingt ans* contient un attirant chapitre sur Katherine Mansfield, d'une fraîcheur de rêve.' Chabaneix, p. 61.

CRITICAL MISCELLANY

Returning to 'Kathy': Christopher Isherwood's Katherine Mansfield Fascination

Sydney Janet Kaplan

There has been considerable discussion about the use of the nickname 'Kathy' by Christopher Isherwood's long-time close friend, W. H. Auden. In Auden's poem 'Here on the cropped grass of the narrow ridge I stand', he includes the lines: 'And Kathy in her journal, "To be rooted in life / That's what I want."' Gerri Kimber brought the poem to our attention when she arranged to have it reprinted in 2012 in the fourth volume of *Katherine Mansfield Studies*. Susan Reid's 'A Note on Auden's "Kathy"' appears in the same volume and beautifully draws out interesting parallels between Mansfield and Auden in both their writing and their lives.[1]

Yet it was actually Isherwood who introduced Auden to that nickname, many years before Auden's poem appeared in 1936. Auden had been collaborating with Isherwood in writing and producing several verse plays, most recently *The Dog Beneath the Skin*, which was first performed on 30 January 1936 at the Westminster Theatre. It is conceivable that their current close association might have reawakened Auden's memory of Isherwood's adolescent literary game-playing: Brian Finney, Isherwood's biographer, mentions that Isherwood and Edward Upward, his closest friend at Repton Public School, enjoyed dividing literary figures into enemies and allies and referring to them with nicknames.[2] They had been influenced by Robert Nichols, a well-known poet of the Great War, who liked to refer to writers that way, such as using 'Wordy' for Wordsworth.[3]

Later, when Isherwood and Upward were students at Cambridge in 1923, they added to their 'allies' (which had included Wilfred Owen and Baudelaire) both Katherine Mansfield and Emily Brontë, whom they now called 'Kathy' and 'Emmy'. Finney calls it 'a strange amalgam, united possibly by their cult of strangeness and their early deaths'.[4]

Without delving too deeply into Freudian territory, I might mention that there could also be an oedipal element in Isherwood's attraction to the name 'Kathy'. His mother's name was Kathleen and he had a very complicated relationship with her, especially after his father died in battle in 1915 (the same year that Mansfield lost her brother).

* * *

Ironically, in writing about Isherwood's responses to Mansfield, I am also making a personal return. I find myself reminiscing about the very beginning of my academic career and how I once spent a day with Christopher Isherwood. It was in the autumn of 1964 and I was in my first semester as a graduate student at UCLA (the University of California, Los Angeles), bewildered and unnerved by the sophistication and the knowledge – possibly pseudo-knowledge – of many of the other students who had been undergraduates at Ivy League colleges. In our required class on bibliography, I decided to do my term project on Isherwood, because I had been greatly affected by his novel, *Goodbye to Berlin* (1939), and especially by its movie version, *I Am a Camera* (1955), based on John Van Druten's play.[5] I was completely unaware then that the play's title had a link to Mansfield. Isherwood's well-known opening to *Goodbye to Berlin*, 'I am a camera with its shutter open, quite passive, recording, not thinking,' echoes Mansfield's remarks to A. R. Orage in his 'Talks with Katherine Mansfield', 'I've been a camera [. . .] I've been a selective camera,' as she tells him that her new plan is 'To widen first the scope of my camera'.[6] It would not be until 1978, when I read Jeffrey Meyers's biography of Mansfield, that I learned of that linkage.[7]

In order to compile our bibliography of a living writer (in hopes of publishing it), we were told by our professor that we needed to seek permission from that author. I wrote a letter to Isherwood, and to my great surprise, he telephoned me a couple of days later. I was overwhelmed when he extended an invitation to come to his home and agreed to allow me to peruse all the reviews and clippings he had amassed and to include them in my bibliography of Isherwood criticism.

A few days later, I drove to his house in Santa Monica, where he introduced me to his life partner, the artist Don Bachardy, who graciously showed me his paintings and drawings in his studio overlooking the ocean. I spent several hours poring through Isherwood's scrapbooks, which were filled with the reviews of his many books. He made my work easier by bringing out tea and biscuits, which I felt was very British! While sitting beside me, in his charming manner he regaled me with stories about his encounters with Bloomsbury, especially Virginia Woolf, as well as fascinating accounts of his experiences during the Second World War with the German emigrés who had taken up residence in the Santa Monica canyon, such as Thomas Mann, Arnold Schoenberg and, most intriguing for me, Greta Garbo.

Looking back on that day now, I deeply regret that I did not write down immediately afterward some of the details of our discussions. I keep hoping that out of the morass of disconnected images that one's brain accumulates, there might have been a reference to Katherine Mansfield! However, at that time, the last thing I would have thought important was the very woman who would dominate the trajectory of my scholarship two decades later. In 1964, I only knew her name, and perhaps remembered that I had read 'The Doll's House' in high school.

Nevertheless, Isherwood might well have referred to Mansfield during our afternoon together because he had already written so much about her. Not only had he published an important review of Sylvia Berkman's *Katherine Mansfield: A Critical Study* in 1950, but even more significantly, he had created a major character patterned after Mansfield in his 1954 novel, *The World in the Evening*.[8]

* * *

It might not be coincidental that Isherwood chose to review Berkman's book. He was already writing the first section of *The World in the Evening* and would have had Mansfield on his mind.[9] (I should mention that Isherwood was not happy with his review of Berkman's critical study. In his diary on 6 May 1950 he remarked that he wrote 'a rather stupid review of a book on Katherine Mansfield'[10]).

It is not surprising to discover that in Isherwood's review he returns once more to 'Kathy'. This time there is a hint of ambivalence about Mansfield in his tone:

> There are some writers you revere; others you fall in love with. The loved ones are seldom the greatest; indeed their very faults are a part of their charm. For several years I was violently in love with 'Kathy', as my friends and I (who never knew her personally) used to call her. Then the love affair turned sour and ended in unfair belittlement. I am truly grateful to Miss Berkman for bringing us together again. From now on, I am sure my affection will be more constant, more intelligent and much less sentimental.[11]

He seems to appreciate Berkman's objectivity, and remarks that she 'is admirably determined to weigh and measure accurately what others have overpraised or undervalued. Where so many have lavishly emoted, Miss Berkman tidies up the mess with grave commonsense.'[12] He also admits here that he realised in reading her book that

> I loved Mansfield ('Kathy' sounds mawkish now, and 'Miss Mansfield' absurdly formal) for her life rather than her work. I identified myself romantically with her sufferings and her struggle. And today I still find it impossible to think of Mansfield simply as the author of her stories, without relating her to the Journal and the Letters. For she is among the most personal and subjective of all modern writers; and, in her case, fiction and autobiography form a single, indivisible opus.[13]

What Isherwood already knew about Mansfield's life must have been considerably enhanced by the biographical information – much of it newly discovered – that Berkman revealed in her book. (Alpers's first biography of Mansfield was not published until 1953, just as Isherwood was completing his novel.) Berkman's references to Mansfield's letters and journals were from Murry's edition of *The Letters of Katherine Mansfield*, which had been published in Britain by Constable in 1927 and in the US by Knopf in 1929, together with his *Journal of Katherine Mansfield*, which appeared in both Britain and the US in 1927. Isherwood probably was already familiar with those books, and they undoubtedly helped him in creating Elizabeth Rydal, a character patterned after Mansfield in *The World in the Evening*.

* * *

Only four years before my visit with Isherwood, Stanley Poss, who published their conversation in the *London Magazine* in June 1961, had interviewed him. Poss asked him whether 'there was anything [. . .] of Katherine Mansfield or Virginia Woolf in your mind?' Although Poss did not distinguish between Mansfield and Woolf in his question, and Isherwood did not make a distinction in his response, the details of Elizabeth's illness and death in the novel clearly evoked Mansfield more than Woolf. Isherwood answered:

> Yes, there undoubtedly was. That's another thing which I think is wrong with that book. She somehow or another doesn't have any real roots for me in life. That is, she seems to me a sort of literary character, and I wish I had desanctified her more. The funny thing was that everybody said it must have been very difficult to write her letters. But actually those letters were much the easiest part of the book to write. And perhaps that shows something suspicious. They just flew off the pen. I could write you a whole volume of the letters of Elizabeth Rydal.[14]

I realise now, as I look back on my acquaintance with Isherwood, that I had actually heard him directly link Elizabeth with Mansfield when he gave a lecture at UCLA on 11 May 1965. In his lecture, he described how he wrote *The World in the Evening* and again admitted some of his later dissatisfaction with how he had created Elizabeth:

> The character of Elizabeth Rydal [. . .] is very ambiguous. I was much complimented on the letters that I wrote for this woman, but there was something extremely sinister in the fact that I could write them so easily. I realized that they were a sort of pastiche of the letters of Katherine Mansfield and that they don't consist of any real emotion or artistic insights but only a kind of clever little monkey-like sensibility. (I'm not saying that this characterizes Katherine Mansfield's letters, because she was a woman who was suffering deeply and in many ways had a very rich, powerful, emotional nature underneath a great deal of surface artificiality, I'm told by people who knew her.)[15]

* * *

The World in the Evening begins in April 1941, eight months before the United States entered the Second World War. The title of the novel duplicates the title of Elizabeth Rydal's most famous book. Its central character, Stephen Monk, who had been Elizabeth's husband, narrates Isherwood's novel. Stephen and his glamorous second wife, Jane, had just recently moved to Hollywood from New York. It was six years since Elizabeth died and during those years he spent much of his time in managing her legacy, writing the introduction to her *Collected Stories* and responding to readers and critics about her life and work, and is still in the process of gathering and compiling her letters for eventual publication. His collecting, editing and managing clearly resemble Murry's handling of Mansfield's work and reputation.

What Isherwood might have known about Murry is unclear. He refers to him only briefly in his review of Berkman:

> In 1911 Katherine Mansfield met John Middleton Murry, who was later to become her second husband. Their relationship was beset with many difficulties, both financial and temperamental, but it survived them all and remained, until the end, a central, steadying emotional factor in Katherine's life.[16]

He probably heard gossip about Murry, however, even years earlier when he still lived in England, especially from Virginia Woolf, who disliked his maudlin promotion of Mansfield after her death. Moreover, as a close friend of Aldous Huxley's in Los Angeles, Isherwood probably heard anecdotes from him about his experiences when working as Murry's assistant editor at the *Athenaeum* in 1919. He had read Huxley's 1928 novel, *Point Counter Point,* and it was well known that Huxley had used Murry as the model for the character Denis Burlap, the editor of a literary paper and a smarmy mourner of his dead wife, Susan (based on Mansfield).

Despite the similarities between Murry's and Stephen's managing of their deceased wives' literary legacies, their life experiences and personalities are completely different (with the exception that they both were unfaithful husbands). Isherwood struggled with the character of Stephen. Soon after he started work on the novel, he wrote in his diary on 17 August 1949: 'Stephen Monkhouse has got to be me – not some synthetic Anglo-American. The few circumstances can so easily be imagined – his ex-wife, his Quaker background, etc. But it must be written out of the middle of *my* consciousness.'[17]

The first scene in the novel takes place at a Hollywood party, where Stephen, surrounded by actors, screenwriters and directors, is approached by a film producer who hopes to convince him to write the screenplay for a movie version of Rydal's novel. The producer emotionally declares: 'Every word Elizabeth Rydal wrote is sacred to me. Sacred. I'm not kidding. I'd want to make this picture just as she'd have wished it – catch that wonderful delicate style and preserve it in celluloid.'[18] Those words seem to echo Murry's statement in his introduction to Mansfield's *Journal*: 'I can only say that her work seems to me to be of a finer and purer kind than that of her contemporaries. It is more spontaneous, more vivid, more delicate and more beautiful.'[19]

The contrast between the crassness of movie-business talk and Elizabeth's 'delicate style' becomes one of a number of satirical moments in Isherwood's novel. Mansfield herself might have enjoyed such satire; those moments have a similarity to her characterisations of Bertha's guests at the dinner party in 'Bliss' and the parasitic artistes in 'Marriage à la Mode'. There is also a resemblance to 'The Garden Party', in which a party must go on, despite the death of someone right outside the house. Mansfield's use of that situation could reflect her awareness of all the deaths during the First World War, happening at the same time as, at home, people went on with their usual lives, parties and all. Isherwood also suggests an implicit dichotomy between the Hollywood party's hilarity, gossiping and flirting, and the underlying realisation that the country would soon be at war: 'There was talk about the London blitz [. . .] but you could tell that none of them cared very much.'[20]

An odd image, that also obliquely evokes Mansfield's writing, is a 'doll's house', a children's playhouse situated outside the house where the party is taking place. Its owners 'thought it was cute' to have their children show it off to their visitors because it was decorated 'like the witch's candy cottage in Hansel & Gretel'. It is the doll's house that serves to reveal the novel's initial turning point for Stephen because it is there that he discovers his wife having sex with a young, handsome actor: 'two mating giants filling the dwarf world of the doll's house, and nearly bursting it apart with their heavings and writhings'.[21]

Stephen's shock and anger send him running quickly away from the scene, and then from Jane and Hollywood altogether. The very next day he takes a plane from Los Angeles to Philadelphia to seek solace from his aunt, and throughout the flight he carries on internal dialogues with both Jane and Elizabeth. At first, he expresses an outburst of fury towards Jane: 'I hate you for what you made me do to Elizabeth.'[22] He now must face his longstanding guilt over having an affair with Jane while Elizabeth was in the last stages of her illness. Yet he also begins to feel resentful against Elizabeth, and then guilty about so doing:

> Yes, I admit it, you invented me. Until you'd told me who I was, I didn't begin to exist. I was the most lifelike of all your characters. People admired me, and that pleased you. But I don't believe you ever cared for me at all.
>
> No Elizabeth. No forgive me; I didn't mean that. It wasn't your fault; it was my own selfishness. It was I who used you. I clung to your strength. I insisted on your being perfect, and got scared and angry when you weren't. I never considered how you must be feeling. I never helped you through your bad times. But you didn't complain, not even at the end. Even then, you were helping me. You were the bravest person I'll ever know.[23]

In trying to justify his relationship with Jane, he implies that his sexual relationship with Elizabeth was inadequate:

> Naturally, you hate Jane. I don't blame you for that. You couldn't help it. She gave me the one thing you never could give me; the thing you talked all around and were so brilliant and wonderful and funny about, and didn't have. I realize now how you must have hated the others, too. Only you were much too clever to show it. [. . .] What do you expect me to do? Go into a monastery? Or spend the rest of my life keeping up your precious cult – editing and annotating and explaining you, until people get sick of the sound of your name?[24]

Stephen is depicted as a promiscuous man, with a history of many relationships with both women and men. Isherwood included two homosexual characters in his novel and referred to Stephen's earlier experiences with other men. Katherine Bucknell states that *The World in the Evening* 'was more explicit and more sympathetic about its homosexual and bisexual characters than any of Isherwood's previous books'.

She noted that he 'had to manipulate his publishers in order to achieve this degree of artistic candour'.[25]

Stephen's reference to 'a monastery' is an early hint that this very duplicitous character will eventually be headed towards a spiritual awakening. The novel then takes us through his long journey towards enlightenment. Isherwood himself was in the process of seeking for a deeper truth. He wrote the first part of the novel while he was living at the Vedanta monastery in Los Angeles. He had discovered Vedanta after moving to the United States and was introduced to that Hindu spiritual practice by Aldous Huxley, who had become a close friend. His review of Berkman's book reveals that, unlike so many of Mansfield's followers and critics, Isherwood was much more amenable towards her search for 'someone who could heal her divided psyche. Once the spirit had been made whole, she felt the body would imitate its wholeness and grow well.' He states that 'much has been said against Gurdjieff, and there is no doubt that he was something of a charlatan. But his basic ideas were perfectly sound, and he certainly helped many of his pupils toward self-integration.'[26]

* * *

Other associations with Mansfield, including images and phrases in her stories that Isherwood seemed to imitate in the novel, are not as outrageous as the doll's house, however. For example, in one of Elizabeth's letters to her sister, she writes: 'Do forgive me, darling, for this long silence. It's weeks, now, since I wrote to anyone. This wretched novel – I'm so *heavy* with it, I feel sometimes as if I could scarcely drag myself upstairs.'[27] The last phrase evoked, at least for me, Mansfield's description of Bertha Young in 'Bliss', who, after exulting over her perfect life and her 'modern, thrilling friends, writers and painters and poets', is suddenly 'so tired she could not drag herself upstairs to dress'.[28]

Isherwood also has Stephen say that 'Elizabeth was an extraordinary mimic' who was able to imitate people 'to the life'.[29] Mansfield was renowned for that same ability, and even earned money to perform imitations at parties.[30] Also, as with Mansfield and Murry, Elizabeth and Stephen enjoyed childlike role-playing. Stephen remarks: 'While we were having fun like this we might just as well have been children in a nursery. Our age didn't have any significance at all.'[31] Although Isherwood would not have had access to Murry's letters, I can imagine that he would have enjoyed seeing the similarity of Stephen's remark and the following words from Murry, where he says that he and Mansfield

> belong to our own kingdom, which truly is when we stand hand in hand, even when we are cross together like two little boys. Somehow we were born again in each other, tiny children, pure and shining, with large sad eyes and shocked hair, each to be the other's doll.[32]

Isherwood had praised Sylvia Berkman for calling 'attention to Mansfield's preoccupation with littleness. In the stories "tiny" is used over and over again as a synonym for "beautiful" or "exquisite"'.[33] In *Prelude*, Mansfield describes how five-year-old Kezia Burnell is fascinated by 'a square of coloured glass' in the window of the house the family is leaving and delighted to see the objects of the world outside take on its varied colours.[34] Similarly, Stephen Monk has a recollection of his aunt's 'small stained-glass window' and how, as a child, he loved 'peering out at the garden through the different colors of the glass; changing the scene, at will, from color-mood to color-mood and experiencing the pure pleasure of sensations which need no analysis'. He recalls how when he had told Elizabeth about his aunt's window, she exclaimed 'That's my idea of heaven [. . .] a place where you don't have to describe *anything*.' Stephen now questions his memory: 'How had red felt, at the age of four? What had blue meant? Why was yellow?' But he realises that, for him, 'the whole organ of cognition had changed' and if he 'looked through that window now, I should see nothing but a lot of adjectives'.[35]

As he wrote in his review of Berkman, Isherwood appreciated Mansfield's 'clairvoyant flashes of perception which one associates particularly with the New Zealand stories. Some creature or object – a flower, a painted teapot, a flying bird – is seen, for an instant, in its own right as a marvel, a microcosm of all creation, and the reader gasps with wonder'.[36] In his novel, Stephen emphasises Elizabeth's brilliance in creating startling imagery and how it transferred to his own consciousness so deeply that he had difficulty distinguishing such images from reality:

> Now and then, these sense impressions were so vivid that I wondered if this wasn't something more than memory; if I wasn't, in some way, actually reliving the original event. That day we had lunch with Rose Macaulay in Carcassonne – did I merely remember a bright green snail crawling up the table leg, or was I noticing it right now for the first time?[37]

That reference to the snail is undoubtedly related to Mansfield's well-known comment to Murry in her letter on 19 October 1919: 'this vileness – this snail on the underside of the leaf – always there!'[38]

The use of the minuscule in both Elizabeth and Mansfield's fiction also provided opportunities for larger social and political critiques. For example, when Gerda, a German refugee, tells Stephen that she disliked Elizabeth's writing because it did not take into account the terrible events taking place in Nazi Germany, Stephen tries to explain to her that

> 'Elizabeth transposed everything she wrote about into her own kind of microcosm. She never dealt directly with world situations or big-scale tragedies. That wasn't her way. But she tried to reproduce them in miniature, the essence of them. For instance, her reaction to the news that a million people had been massacred might be to tell a story about two children stoning a cat to death for fun. And she'd put into it all the pain and disgust and horror she felt about the things then Nazis do [. . .] I think, instinctively, she was always protesting against the importance the newspapers give to numbers and size. She knew what most of us won't admit to ourselves, that numbers and size actually make tragedy less real to us.'[39]

The most clearly relevant example of Mansfield's use of the miniature to evoke the enormous reality of the First World War is 'The Fly' (which has been the subject of uncountable interpretations by readers and critics). Another famous example of her use of the miniature is the little lamp in 'The Doll's House'. It, too, has political implications in its implicit criticism of the injustices of class inequities.

Mentioning Rose Macaulay is one of the ways that Isherwood situates Elizabeth amongst other British writers and her sophisticated literary and artistic environment, which included friendships with the Woolfs, E. M. Forster, Hugh Walpole and D. H. Lawrence. Stephen remembers how he used to see her sitting at her writing table, which held 'the inkwell and the dictionary and the flowers in the jam jar, the lump of fool's gold from Utah, the sharp-nosed Aztec idol which Lawrence had given her'.[40]

When Stephen's aunt had introduced him to Elizabeth Rydal, he was only twenty-two, just out of Cambridge, and was in awe of that famous writer, who was twelve years his senior. He also was unnerved when his aunt referred to 'Those grand intellectual friends of hers':

> I was acutely conscious of their presence, around you, all the time; even though you seldom referred to them, and then only in the most casual way. Occasionally, you'd suggest taking me to see Virginia Woolf or Ethel Mayne, or ask me to come up to the flat when you were having them to tea. But I always refused. I regarded these people as my natural enemies. I imagined them looking through and through me, judging me, dismissing me; and them, when I'd gone, making some clever, sneering remark about me to you which would work in your mind like slow poison until

> you began to agree with them, to see me as they did, and stopped having anything to do with me.[41]

* * *

The last time I spoke with Christopher Isherwood was on 27 December 1974 at the Modern Language Association convention in New York, where he was the major speaker for its new 'Homosexuality and Literature Forum'. The auditorium was packed, and everyone was excited to hear Isherwood actually say for the first time in public that he was gay. (At least they assumed that it was. Isherwood, in an interview three years later with Tony Russo, said that the MLA was not 'by any means the first place where I had spoken in that way. It was more that the MLA "came out".'[42] Finney also said of that event: 'Regarded as a daring innovation by the organizers, it actually turned out to be a case of preaching to the converted.'[43]

What I remember of that occasion is that Isherwood received a standing ovation from the crowd, some of whom were even crying. Of course, it was not really a surprise to most of the audience. Those who chose to attend that particular session probably had assumed he was gay from reading his novels. I certainly was one of them! (I was also excited that the Forum was chaired by Katherine Stimpson, the founder and editor of the feminist academic journal, *Signs*.) I stood in line to thank Isherwood for his talk, and I was shocked when he remembered me by name. I was delighted to have the opportunity to tell him how much he had influenced me, both through his writing and through his kindness to me a decade earlier.

When I had first met Isherwood I expected to centre my research on him and eventually to write my dissertation on his work. But something very important intervened while I was in graduate school: the Women's Movement. I put Isherwood aside and turned my attention to women writers. My dissertation and the book based on it, *Feminine Consciousness in the Modern British Novel*, did not include short-story writers, but I soon discovered Katherine Mansfield and she has been with me ever since. For Isherwood, too, Mansfield had an enduring presence, as is noticeable in his diary entry of 18 December 1955:

> The day before yesterday, we rented a car and drove to Avignon. Yesterday we returned by way of Marseille and all along the corniche, through the little seaside towns that are shrines to the great names of the twenties – Picasso painting, Kathy writing her journal and looking out of the window at the cruel mistral vexing the sea, [D. H.] Lawrence dying.[44]

Notes

1. W. H. Auden, 'Here on the cropped grass of the narrow ridge I stand', *Katherine Mansfield Studies*, 4 (2012), pp. 79–82. Susan Reid, 'A Note on Auden's "'Kathy"', *Katherine Mansfield Studies*, 4 (2012), pp. 122–5.
2. Brian Finney, *Christopher Isherwood: A Critical Biography* (New York: Oxford University Press, 1979), p. 48.
3. When, in 1958, Isherwood reissued his first novel, *All the Conspirators*, written in 1926, he dedicated it to Edward Upward. But he also included a note in his Foreword that he would 'now extend my dedication to include Edward's wife Hilda, their daughter Kathy and their son Christopher'. See Christopher Isherwood, *All the Conspirators* (New York: New Directions, 1958), p. 10.
4. Finney, p. 48.
5. Kenneth Ligda asserts that Isherwood's Berlin Stories are 'our most influential document of the Nazification of Germany'. See Kenneth Ligda, *Serious Comedy: British Modernist Humor and Political Crisis* (Dissertation, Stanford University, Palo Alto, 2011), p. 218.
6. A. R. Orage, 'Talks with Katherine Mansfield', in Herbert Read and Denis Saurat, eds, *Selected Essays and Critical Writings* (London: Stanley Nott, 1935), pp. 125–32 (p. 129).
7. Jeffrey Meyers, *Katherine Mansfield: A Biography* (New York: New Directions, 1978), p. 261.
8. Sylvia Berkman, *Katherine Mansfield: A Critical Study* (New Haven, CT: Yale University Press, 1951). Christopher Isherwood, 'Katherine Mansfield', in *Exhumations* (New York: Simon and Schuster, 1966). This review of Sylvia Berkman's book first appeared in *Tomorrow* in 1950.
9. Christopher Isherwood, *The World in the Evening* (New York: Farrar, Straus and Giroux, [1954] 2013).
10. Katherine Bucknell, ed., *Christopher Isherwood Diaries, Volume One: 1939–1960* (London: Methuen, 1996), p. 435.
11. Isherwood, 'Katherine Mansfield', p. 64.
12. Isherwood, 'Katherine Mansfield', p. 64.
13. Isherwood, 'Katherine Mansfield', p. 65.
14. Stanley Poss, 'A Conversation on Tape', in James J. Berg and Chris Freeman, eds, *Conversations with Christopher Isherwood* (Jackson: University of Mississippi, 2001), p. 14.
15. Christopher Isherwood, 'The World in the Evening. Los Angeles, May 11, 1965', in *Isherwood on Writing*, ed. James J. Berg (Minneapolis: University of Minnesota Press, 2007), pp. 199–212 (pp. 206–7).
16. Isherwood, 'Katherine Mansfield', p. 66.
17. Bucknell, *Isherwood Diaries*, p. 414.
18. Isherwood, *The World in the Evening*, pp. 6–7.
19. John Middleton Murry, 'Introduction', in *Journal of Katherine Mansfield*, ed. John Middleton Murry (New York: Alfred A. Knopf, 1927), pp. xiii–xiv.
20. Isherwood, *The World in the Evening*, p. 5.
21. Isherwood, *The World in the Evening*, p. 15. Isherwood wrote in his diary on 5 July 1960, six years after the novel was written: 'The party at the Selznick's' was quite fun [. . .] Norma Shearer [. . .] introduced herself and told me how honored she was because I'd used her pool doll's house for a model in *The World in the Evening*,' *Isherwood Diaries*, pp. 876–7.
22. Isherwood, *The World in the Evening*, p. 16.
23. Isherwood, *The World in the Evening*, p. 19.
24. Isherwood, *The World in the Evening*, p. 19.

25. Katherine Bucknell, 'Why Isherwood Stopped Writing Fiction', in Zachary Leader, ed., *On Modern British Fiction* (Oxford: Oxford University Press, 2002), pp. 126–48 (p. 132).
26. Isherwood, 'Katherine Mansfield', p. 68.
27. Isherwood, *The World in the Evening*, p. 65.
28. CW2, p. 145.
29. Isherwood, *The World in the Evening*, p. 165.
30. A fine description of Mansfield's performing is in Kathleen Jones, *Katherine Mansfield: The Story-Teller* (Edinburgh: Edinburgh University Press, 2010), p. 97.
31. Isherwood, *The World in the Evening*, p. 165.
32. C. A. Hankin, ed., *The Letters of John Middleton Murry to Katherine Mansfield* (London: Constable, 1983), p. 71. See also Sydney Janet Kaplan, *Circulating Genius: John Middleton Murry, Katherine Mansfield and D. H. Lawrence* (Edinburgh: Edinburgh University Press, 2010), p. 67.
33. Isherwood, 'Katherine Mansfield', p. 70.
34. CW2, p. 59.
35. Isherwood, *The World in the Evening*, p. 26.
36. Isherwood, 'Katherine Mansfield', p. 70.
37. Isherwood, *The World in the Evening*, p. 101.
38. *Letters* 2, p. 54. See also Toby Silverman Zinman, 'The Snail under the Leaf: Katherine Mansfield's Imagery', *Modern Fiction Studies*, 14: 3 (Autumn 1978), pp. 457–64 (p. 457).
39. Isherwood, *The World in the Evening*, p. 119.
40. Isherwood, *The World in the Evening*, p. 42.
41. Isherwood, *The World in the Evening*, p. 86.
42. Tony Russo, 'Interview with Christopher Isherwood', in *Conversations with Christopher Isherwood*, p. 162.
43. Finney, p. 280.
44. Bucknell, *Isherwood Diaries*, p. 558.

Katherine Mansfield's *Daily Herald* Review of Joseph Conrad's *The Rescue*

John G. Peters

Katherine Mansfield wrote two reviews of Joseph Conrad's *The Rescue*. Her review in the *Athenaeum* (originally signed merely as 'K. M.') is well known to Mansfield scholars, but her review in the *Daily Herald* has not been previously collected. It was not unknown for a reviewer to review the same work in multiple venues but it was somewhat uncommon. Such instances typically occurred when the reviews were unsigned, or one was either unsigned or signed only with the reviewer's initials. Although both of Mansfield's reviews are very favourable, they are also quite different. Her *Athenaeum* review devotes much more space to plot summary, and her evaluation focuses primarily on Conrad's 'delightful airy perch among the mountains' above even the 'front rank' of authors, along with his 'romantic vision' in the novel.[1] In contrast, Mansfield's *Daily Herald* review includes far less plot summary and far more commentary, and although she does evaluate Conrad's novel, she also takes the opportunity in this review to broaden her commentary, contrasting the 'psychological novel' with the adventure novel, arguing that the psychological novel should be as thrilling as adventure fiction but that more often 'we are presented instead with something drab,[2] something dull that neither feeds us nor thrills us'.[3]

Overall, this review is in keeping with the enthusiastic tenor of other reviews of *The Rescue*. After the publication of *Chance* (1914), it seemed that Conrad could do no wrong with the reviewers. It was the rare individual who dissented from the approbation of what Franklin P. Adams would term the ubiquitous 'Conradicals' of the day.[4] By the time of *The Rescue*'s publication, Conrad's literary stature was such that every new book was greeted as a literary masterpiece. Such was certainly true of *The Rescue*. Interestingly, the most prominent exception to this drift was Virginia Woolf's unsigned review in the *Times Literary Supplement*, where she admitted to the book's merits but also to her reservations concerning it:

'It is as if Mr. Conrad's belief in romance had suddenly flagged and he had tried to revive it by artificial stimulants.'[5] In expressing reservations regarding the novel, Woolf would anticipate later Conrad commentators who would similarly question the quality of his writings after *Under Western Eyes* (1911).

Book Review by Katherine Mansfield

Mr. Conrad's Masterpiece

In spite of the flood of evidence to the contrary, in spite of psychoanalysis which has granted to our young writers the freedom of that delectable land of secret paths, no thoroughfares, and private ways, we do not think that the popularity of the psychological novel over the novel of adventure is, as yet, firmly established. After all, novel reading, except for those unfortunates who desire to kill Time rather than bid him live for ever, will always be regarded as an escape from familiar surroundings, a running away to sea. How otherwise shall we fulfil our childish, persistent longing to travel in unknown countries, on unknown seas – to be an explorer? Little creatures of 70 summers, we fain would possess the freedom of this small world we inhabit. Can we do better than creep between the covers of a book and dream that it is ours?

There is, of course, every reason why the psychological novel should be as thrilling as the novel of adventure. Has not the mind its own tropical seas, desert islands, icebergs, and shadowy shores? But, for some strange reason, they are seldom revealed to us, and we are presented instead with something drab, something dull that neither feeds us nor thrills us. Who, we find ourselves wondering as we bump through the choppy grey pages, would dream of reading this if it were translated into terms of ships or oceans or jungles?

No writer of our time has so abundantly satisfied our sense of adventure as Mr. Conrad; and in none of his earlier books has he found such perfect expression as in this new novel, *The Rescue*. Here we have combined as never before his vision of the universe as a spectacle of which man is but a part and his belief that the part man plays can only be worthy if it is governed by a few very simple ideas, of which Fidelity is perhaps the greatest.[6] It is of the very essence of adventure that none shall know at what moment man may be put to the test and called upon to engage with the sea, the sky, a treacherous shore, or a savage horde, and we are made to feel in these opening chapters that Captain Tom Lingard, of the brig *Lightning*, is doubly prepared to meet it. He is prepared by virtue of the noble love he feels for his boat ('To him she was always precious – like old love; always desirable – like a strange woman; always tender – like a mother; always faithful – like a favourite daughter of a man's heart') and because of the passionate loyalty with which he serves the cause of the Rajah Hassim and the Lady Immada, who are trying to regain their kingdom. Our first glimpse of Lingard is on the deck of the brig, becalmed among the islands of the Malay Sea. While he is waiting for a wind so that he may land his cargo of ammunition for Hassim, an English boat comes out of the blue and asks him to go to the help of a pleasure yacht that is stranded on a mud bank. There, in the presence of the owner, an autocratic, puffed-up English gentleman, his wife and a chill courtier-diplomatist friend, Lingard meets his real enemies. They are creatures of the other world, of a corrupt, unworthy, hollow society, far removed from such a man and his purpose. The two men show for what they are; but in Edith Travers, beautiful as a goddess, with her paleness and fairness, he sees the embodiment of that spirit of romance by which his life is guided. From that first moment he dedicates himself to her, and she, whom civilised society has scorned to make use of, finds in him the man who possesses all that she has lost – ardour, passion, loyalty. So she binds him, absorbs him, until the long-awaited hour comes when at the crisis of their lives she must act alone. Then she fails, and leaves Lingard staring at a wasted, desolate life.

The story advances by slow stages, each of which is composed of rich beauty, of strange circumstance, of a kind of delicate suspense which omits nothing, yet leaves nothing untouched by the intense emotional atmosphere. Figures of sailors, ships, savage chiefs, and the sea – the bright purple banner of romantic adventure floats over them all.

Notes

1. K[atherine] M[ansfield], 'Mr. Conrad's New Novel', *Athenaeum*, 2 July 1920, p. 15 (CW3, pp. 622, 623).
2. One wonders whether Mansfield has Dorothy Richardson in mind. In her unsigned review of Richardson's *The Tunnel*, Mansfield complained of the indiscriminate nature of the 'bits, fragments, flashing glimpses, half scenes and whole scenes' in the novel, concluding, 'Only we feel that until these things are judged and given each its appointed place in the whole scheme, they have no meaning in the world of art.' See 'Three Women Novelists', *Athenaeum*, 4 April 1919, p. 141 (CW3, pp. 446, 447). Similarly, in her review of Richardson's *Interim*, Mansfield remarks that Richardson 'leaves us feeling, as before, that everything being of equal importance to her [Miriam Henderson], it is impossible that everything should not be of equal unimportance'. See K[atherine] M[ansfield], 'Dragonflies', *Athenaeum*, 9 January 1920, p. 48 (CW3, p. 558).
3. Katherine Mansfield, 'Mr. Conrad's Masterpiece', *Daily Herald*, 21 July 1920, p. 7.

4. F[ranklin] P. A[dams], 'The Conning Tower', *New-York Tribune*, 2 April 1914, p. 8.
5. [Virginia Woolf], 'A Disillusioned Romantic', *Times Literary Supplement*, 1 July 1920, p. 419.
6. This phrase echoes a comment by Conrad: 'Those who read me know my conviction that the world, the temporal world, rests on a few very simple ideas, so simple that they must be as old as the hills. It rests notably, among others, on the idea of Fidelity.' See *A Personal Record*, eds Zdzisław Najder and J. H. Stape (Cambridge: Cambridge University Press, 2008), p. 17.

REVIEW ESSAY

Redrawing Katherine Mansfield's Critical Horizons

Elyse Blankley

Kevin Boon, *From the Colonies to Katherine Mansfield: The Life and Times of Sir Harold Beauchamp* (London: Olympia Publishers, 2021), 181 pp., £8.99. ISBN 9781788306249

Aimée Gasston, Gerri Kimber and Janet Wilson, eds, *Katherine Mansfield: New Directions* (London: Bloomsbury Academic Press, 2020), 266 pp., £85. ISBN 9781350135505

Aimée Gasston, Gerri Kimber and Janet M. Wilson, eds, Special Issue on Katherine Mansfield, *Journal of New Zealand Literature*, 38: 2 (2020), 157 pp.

Alice Kelly, *Commemorative Modernisms: Women Writers, Death and the First World War* (Edinburgh: Edinburgh University Press, 2020), 297 pp., £85. ISBN 9781474459907

Todd Martin, ed., *The Bloomsbury Handbook to Katherine Mansfield* (London: Bloomsbury, 2021), 534 pp., £130. ISBN 9781350111448

Anna Neima, *The Utopians: Six Attempts to Build the Perfect Society* (London: Picador, 2021), 320 pp., £25. ISBN 9781529023077

Beverley Randell, ed., and Jenni Shoesmith, artist, *Heart of Flame: Katherine Mansfield's Flowers and Trees* (Wellington: Steele Roberts, 2020), 116 pp., $30 NZD. ISBN 9781990007163

In 1906 Katherine Mansfield wrote to a friend, 'Would you not like to try *all* sorts of lives – one is so very small – but that is the satisfaction of writing – one can impersonate so many people.'[1] Less than fifteen years later, her confidence in the multifaceted self appears to falter: one might be 'True to oneself!' but 'Which self?'[2] This plurality and instability of 'real' and fictional selves challenges us; how can we fix the object of our readerly gaze when the object is in flux, like the fluid dynamism of a celestial body whose speed and location disorient us continually? The pleasures and problems of reading Katherine Mansfield's writing are the changing horizon of her fiction. If the works under review here are any indication, recent scholarship has made significant inroads in charting Mansfield's remarkable, multidirectional work.

The largest and perhaps most ambitious recent project is *The Bloomsbury Handbook to Katherine Mansfield*, edited by Todd Martin. At 534 pages, with twenty-six chapters and a selected annotated bibliography, this anthology offers a superb introduction to Katherine Mansfield that will be useful to students and scholars alike. Its broad compendium of critical approaches to, histories of and trends within Mansfield studies suggests further avenues for scholarly work. The topics addressed are many and varied: genre, the First World War, colonialism, art, cinema, music, childhood in New Zealand, Bloomsbury, continental and Eastern influences, magazine culture, mysticism and literary antecedents, all contextualised by Mansfield's place as one of modernism's premier innovators. The challenge of so many individual pieces is how to introduce these key subject areas without superficiality: that is, how to show the history and structure of critical thinking while also providing plenty of analytical substance. The contributors balance these difficulties with enviable erudition and clear prose, largely unencumbered by critical vagaries. Most of the essays focus on a cluster of stories, such as 'The Garden Party', 'The Doll's House', 'Prelude' or 'Bliss', which have the benefit of being widely read and accessible to readers. Drawing on reception theory and the work of Hans Robert Jauss, Todd Martin's Introduction argues that the 'horizon' of a reader's expectations is continually shifting and being transformed by Mansfield herself (p. 2). By 'altering perception' (p. 3), she reshapes her audience and thus moves the fixed boundaries of 'high' modernism; not surprisingly, Enda Duffy in the first chapter calls Mansfield the 'consummate modernist' (p. 24), who worked in what we now recognise may be the consummate modernist genre – the short story – through which Mansfield was freed from literary history's dead weight. Viewed in this way, Mansfield's stories are not preludes or overtures but the composition itself: magnificent modernist artefacts, bustling with what Duffy identifies as 'excess' and recording a character's 'fluctuation of sensation and energy', always in tandem with an 'implied social commentary' (p. 34).

The book's six different sections display Mansfield in context. How she developed as a story writer is highlighted in the first section's essays addressing Mansfield at work. These chapters describe not just her beginnings but her strategies for moving beyond the stasis of nineteenth-century literary traditions. To this end, Gerri Kimber and Alex Moffett engage with Mansfield's early works. Kimber's essay illustrates how Mansfield's novel fragments, *Juliet* and *Maata*, reveal Mansfield as a 'proto-modernist' at the vanguard of 'modernist autobiografiction' (pp. 52, 38). Moffett argues how 'Prelude', which evolved from the much longer 'The Aloe', reimagines the classic *Bildungsroman* by representing several women at one moment in time and in their lives; in this way, serial narrative sequencing of the nineteenth-century novel is replaced by a 'parallel' structure (p. 73). Jane Stafford's tight readings of Mansfield's early New Zealand stories invite us to consider how the complex fissures and faults of Mansfield's colonial experience evade the totalising order of the nineteenth-century narrative. Jenny McDonnell extends our sense of Mansfield's development within the late nineteenth- and early twentieth-century culture of popular magazine fiction and the emergence of avant-garde 'little' magazines. Probing the rich possibilities of magazine publication, McDonnell shows how the short story became a transnational, easily circulated commodity as well as a new cultural artefact dialogically engaged with other magazines. Within magazine culture, Mansfield could hone her craft, playing with identities, voices and audience expectations.

Mansfield's interactions with her contemporaries are another crucial subject matter, and the second section details the celebrated circles within which her personal and professional life took shape. This is an area of Mansfield scholarship that has received a good deal of attention, most recently in Todd Martin's edited collection *Katherine Mansfield and the Bloomsbury Group* (2017). In the *Handbook*, both Jay Dickson and Ruchi Mundeja revisit the Bloomsbury connections with intriguing observations for Mansfield's work. Dickson sees the chatty, gossipy performative space of Bloomsbury as directly implicated in the evolution of her 'dialogic' stories wherein the emphasis is placed on the *unsaid*, thereby moving away from nineteenth-century realism toward modernist innovation (p. 118). Mundeja shows how the fictions of Woolf and Mansfield represent the differing subjectivities of travelling women and domestic women, although each writer approaches this polarity from opposite ends. Woolf tends toward the 'domestic sublime', whereas Mansfield's home dwellers erupt in transgressive laughter (p. 130). Likewise, voyages for Woolf are 'select forays into the unknown' (p. 137), epistemically saturated, whereas Mansfield's female traveller is frequently imperilled and alone. Two other peers of Mansfield receive attention in the *Handbook*: Mansfield's frequently volatile acquaintance with D. H. Lawrence is reviewed by Andrew Harrison, and Isobel Madison highlights how Mansfield and her cousin, Elizabeth von Arnim, were both burdened by overbearing fathers, leading to sometimes fraught father–daughter relationships that played out in both writers' fictions.

All Mansfield's modes of writing – short stories, letters, poetry and critical reviews – have contributed to the increasingly complex portrait of Mansfield's genre work, examined in the *Handbook*'s third part. To be sure, the scope of these enquiries is directly linked to the publication within the last decade of Mansfield's collected stories, notebooks and book reviews, and the updated collected letters. Taking advantage of these source materials, Alisa Cox reinforces the fact that Mansfield welcomed the short story's 'spaciousness' as a place where an unstable, elliptical point of view could provide her with a 'linguistic playground' (p. 196). Chris Mourant finds another source of literary innovation within the pages of Mansfield's many book reviews of middlebrow novels, where she shunned the easy scorn of Bloomsbury and instead engaged with these works critically, thereby helping to articulate her own artistic vision. Anna Jackson likewise sees Mansfield's copious letters and journals as adding to her aesthetic development, especially in recent years, since the legacy of these materials has finally been wrested from John Middleton Murry's sentimental bowdlerising. And finally, Erika Baldt argues for a full-scale 'reappraisal' of Mansfield's poetical works (p. 244). Those published pseudonymously as 'Russian translations' became opportunities, Baldt proposes, for stylistic experimentation under cover of an imagined author. With wellsprings of inspiration from Wordsworth to Whitman to Swinburne, the poems, says Baldt, await a fresh scholarly approach.

Part four of the *Handbook* addresses Mansfield's relationship to the arts, including three fascinating investigations of music, Post-Impressionism and the cinema. These pieces remind us of Mansfield's well-known non-literary influences in her own creative life. It may well have been, as Angela Smith argues, that Mansfield's glimpse of Van Gogh's *Sunflowers* in 1910 at the first Post-Impressionist exhibition in London encouraged her to privilege form over mimesis, thereby feeding her interest in interiority. We know, too, that Mansfield was an accomplished cellist who used the pause, the motif and the metrical rhythmic measure in her own writing; but as Claire Davison reminds us, Mansfield was also living in a modern soundscape that was transformed by technology. Faye Harland adds that the concept of the 'dissolve' in cinematic form resonated with

Mansfield's sense that reality could be fundamentally unstable, as when Linda Burnell's furniture fancifully comes alive, a technique of Surrealist cinema that Harland argues helped Mansfield challenge prevailing notions of representation.

Part five's six essays give us the world of Katherine Mansfield, and the term is quite literal in its transnational scope. Not only did Mansfield lead an exilic life, as Kathleen Jones describes in her essay about Mansfield's expatriation, but she was also keenly aware of both the privilege and the curse that such marginalisation might confer, as Janet Wilson makes clear. Wilson shows how the changing parameters of postcolonial theory have had a marked impact on how we read Mansfield as the 'little colonial'; we now recognise how much her own sense of Empire was never unclouded by an alternative vision of counter-narratives, and the 'multi-locatedness' of her stories speaks to her sense of fungible national and imperial limits (p. 327). Further afield, Galya Diment addresses Mansfield's interest in popular forms of Russian mysticism in the early twentieth century, particularly her much-debated connection to the occult philosophies of George Gurdjieff and his famed institute in France. It is often difficult to reconcile the sardonic and worldly Mansfield with this spiritual environment, and yet as her illness increased, she felt pulled toward the non-intellectual and 'viscerally emotional' worldview espoused at Gurdjieff's Fontainebleau-Avon priory (p. 393). It was in France, too, that John Middleton Murry worked hard to establish the saintly Mansfield posthumous myth, where it took root, as Gerri Kimber tells us in her probing account of Murry's reconstruction and marketing, an effort that had failed in London but gained traction in Paris. Mansfield's 'world' also extended to her interest in the Orient. Tracy Miao argues how Mansfield, with her Chinese robes or kimonos and cropped hair, was fashioning a new and decidedly 'modern' version of self and femininity, part of her aesthetic journey to an 'imagined East' (p. 379). Finally, Mansfield was part of the century's most globalising event, the First World War, and Christine Darrohn contends that, as Mansfield's attitude toward the war matured, especially after her brother's death at the Front, she began writing from a war-conscious state of mind, even if war as a subject matter is largely absent from her fiction. Nevertheless, traces of it linger, Darrohn says, in Mansfield's use of repetitive style, revealing dialogue, and characters who grieve and see their own boundaries drawn tight with emotional estrangement or dissolved within emotional excess.

The last section of the *Handbook* offers three extended essays from multiple critical perspectives. These illustrate contemporary criticism as sustained praxis, and all three speak to the vitality and intellectual rigour of our current moment in the development of Mansfield studies.

Rishona Zimring analyses what she calls the 'generative entanglement of reading and writing' that sustained Mansfield's life straight through her illness (p. 422). Giving us a history of Mansfield's eclectic reading habits, Zimring uses theories of surface reading to help us see how Mansfield's own habit of surface reading – enjoying words – could give her sensual and 'life-affirming pleasures' (p. 429). Claire Drewery draws on gender and queer theory as well as cultural materialism to investigate Mansfield's fascination with the costumes, gestures and speech of the Wildean dandy, a performative figure whose deceptive, blurred surface that hides and reveals also works aesthetically to represent interiority. William Kupinse offers a spirited ecocritical reading of Mansfield's nature imagery, more specifically the contexts where anthropomorphised bushes speak and flowers whisper. Locating these talking plants within the traditions of negative capability and pathetic fallacy, Kupinse also details how plant sentience was taken seriously by early twentieth-century researchers in the emergent field of plant neurobiology. Each of these essays speaks eloquently to the goals of *The Bloomsbury Handbook to Katherine Mansfield*, which moves us beyond questions of Mansfield's centrality to modernism and asks us to survey the rich currents already carrying scholars to critical shores unimaginable just a few decades ago.

Mansfield also figures in an important new monograph by Alice Kelly, *Commemorative Modernisms*, which explores how modernist women writers sought aesthetic answers for the profoundly changed landscape of modern military mourning post-First World War, characterised by mass cemeteries in foreign lands, missing bodies, and civilian war memorials erected to provide focal points for profound absence. As Christine Darrohn observes above, war rarely appears in Mansfield's fiction, but Kelly emphasises how it resonates very personally in her letters. In an illuminating chapter titled 'Mansfield Mobilised: Katherine Mansfield, the Great War and Military Discourse', Kelly shows how Mansfield's war letters evolve from exhilarating, surreal descriptions of a zeppelin floating over Paris, to a jaunty account of 'going over the top' to the railway station (p. 121), to sober reflections on what, by 1915, had become, with her brother's death, her 'tragic knowledge' (p. 145). By appropriating military discourse in her personal writing, Mansfield was tempering her own war anxieties, which eventually became intertwined with and supplanted by the reality of her own declining health. Kelly describes the figurative language deployed in these letters as 'hybridized' precisely *because* Mansfield was a civilian, moving through syntactical levels from playful and parodic to serious (p. 135). 'Fight' becomes a loaded word as Mansfield's tubercular decline accelerates and she transforms into a combatant in her own private struggle (p. 142). Kelly argues that the war provoked in Mansfield a new aesthetics of civilian modernism, informed by the 'tragic knowledge' that soon was every survivor's obligation in the war's wake. It made Mansfield the 'theorist of modernism which she might not otherwise have become' (p. 147).

Kelly continues to refocus Mansfield as a 'war' writer in her chapter 'Modernist Memorials: Virginia Woolf and Katherine Mansfield in the Postwar World'. Woolf and Mansfield arrived at disparate answers to the problem of obsolescent forms of Victorian mourning. In a shrewd reading of *Jacob's Room*, Kelly details how Woolf parodies forms of memorialising (the tomb, the cenotaph, the pageant) and substitutions, for example, Jacob Flanders's boots. In contrast, Mansfield's 'The Garden Party' offers a 'consolatory narrative' (p. 222) accompanied by the whole, unblemished body, whereas in 'The Fly', the war cemetery fails to relieve the protagonist's buried grief. If Jacob's empty room is the tomb of the unknown/unknowable soldier/character, then, Kelly avers, 'The Garden Party' is a *Bildungsroman* for a generation that came of age through the recognition of death (p. 222). In this sense, Mansfield substitutes a good Victorian death for the terrible modern one. These lucid arguments give depth to Kelly's welcome addition to the subject of women and war.

One of the utopias addressed in Anna Neima's amiable *The Utopians: Six Attempts to Build the Perfect Society* is the aforementioned project of Russian spiritualist George Gurdjieff in Fontainebleau, France. In a chapter entitled 'The Forest Philosophers of Fontainebleau: G. I. Gurdjieff's Institute for the Harmonious Development of Man', Neima uses the correspondence of the Institute's best-known guest, Katherine Mansfield, to give voice to the community's most aspirational qualities. Mansfield's missives to her husband, John Middleton Murry, and other friends form a persuasive (if tragic) counterpoint to the more public campaign by P. D. Ouspensky in Britain to rally followers for Gurdjieff's mystical social system that blended Russian orthodoxy, Buddhism, the teachings of Eastern fakirs and the cult of personality to create a community that Mansfield, deathly ill, felt offered comfort and a clear vision of the self. Mansfield 'put the [Fontainebleau] priory on the cultural map' (p. 145), and the sincerity of her letters shows those months leading up to her death as permeated with real belief, a counter to subsequent cynics who claimed that Gurdjieff's system hastened her death. Hers is the voice of clarity in an otherwise obscurely mystic system wrapped in the demands of a capricious and authoritarian leader. She plays a small but intriguing role in this drama, which would likely have found audiences less interested in reading this now, were it not for her letters and tragic personal story illuminating it.

Another book aimed at a popular audience is Kevin Boon's *From the Colonies to Katherine Mansfield: The Life and Times of Sir Harold Beauchamp*, a slender biography of Mansfield's father. This is the work of an enthusiast, not a scholar, who was inspired to find the 'real' person behind Mansfield's Stanley Burnell. Boon discovered a scrappy, self-made man whose rise from childhood financial uncertainty was eclipsed by colonial success and a knighthood. The story is promising, but what we get here is a tame and sometimes turgid portrait of the man who, among other accomplishments, steered the Bank of New Zealand as Chairman of its Board for many years. Beauchamp was a member of many other boards and commercial enterprises, a canny investor and steady economic hand, as well as a patron of the arts and, after Mansfield's death, a booster of his daughter's legacy in her home country. Nonetheless, the Harold/Stanley who emerges in this book is scarcely less dull than the father in Mansfield's oft-quoted description from *Juliet*: 'thoroughly commonplace and commercial' (p. 71). There is nothing 'commonplace' about Harold's record, as Boon reminds us, but the book produces the opposite effect. This is partly due to its style: earnest snippets of narrative interrupted by swathes of italicised quoted materials and chronological information, all relying heavily (albeit not exclusively) on Beauchamp's own *Reminiscences and Recollections*, published in 1937.

The prose comes alive when Boon quotes from Mansfield, yet he uses her work chiefly as fiction *à clef*. He concludes that 'Prelude' and 'At the Bay' are among the stories 'that portray a happy and supportive family in which Harold played a vital part' (p. 52). One can reach this anodyne conclusion only by ignoring, for instance, the rage simmering inside the fictional wife, Linda Burnell. Boon considers Harold's ongoing financial support of Mansfield, which began in 1909 at £100 per annum (approximately $17,000 in 2021 US dollars, or £12,340) and increased over the years, as more than ample proof of his generosity and concern – a not-so-subtle implication that Mansfield was far from impoverished.[3] This pleading on Harold Beauchamp's behalf is clearly necessary if Boon's purpose is to rescue Stanley/Harold from the long shadow of his daughter and render him more central and sympathetic than he is allowed to be in most of Mansfield's fiction. Beauchamp may have had a 'domineering' personality, as Boon admits (p. 64), but we see very little of it or of anything negative that might interrupt the placid surface of this largely uncritical book.

Scholars continue to push the boundaries of Mansfield studies with another excellent, recently published collection of fourteen essays, this one titled *Katherine Mansfield: New Directions*, edited by Aimée Gasston, Gerri Kimber and Janet Wilson. Gasston's Introduction gives clear shape to the collection, which at first glance seems amorphous, unfocused: these essays emphasise that '[m]any-sidedness – multidirectionality – is intrinsic to [Mansfield's] aesthetic newness' (p. 2). In this way, the plenitude of readings here reflects the very nature of Mansfield's own uneasily classified themes and stories that take her readers in so many different directions. Drawing on a range of critical approaches including ecocriticism, gender theory, postcolonial studies, narrative theory, relevance theory and new discoveries in primary sources, the collection shows how vital Mansfield continues to be. This point is at stake in Ali Smith's account of her obsession with Mansfield's correspondence. In a lively talk originally delivered at Birkbeck College, Smith ruminates on temporality, mistranscription, permeability and risk-taking, all evidenced in Mansfield's correspondence but especially in what may have been her last, unsent letter (to Ida Baker) from Fontainebleau. Other entries in this first section of the collection, 'Form and Force', include Elleke Boehmer's use of relevance theory to reread Mansfield's ellipses and gaps in 'The Wind Blows', which she argues changes our 'horizon of expectations' (p. 30, quoting from Jauss). It is a story whose dashes and repetitions force us to pause, reassess and reconsider, thereby rupturing the conventional pattern of reading a story. In this way, Mansfield defies our cognitive expectations, denying us the ability to impose a design and forcing us to re-evaluate meaning as a continuing series of temporal revisitations. Enda Duffy also rereads Mansfield's form in a compelling comparative interpretation of 'Je ne parle pas français' and Joyce's 'The Dead', two tales that signal a 'crisis point in modernist aesthetics' (p. 45) with the image of snow suggesting an aporia beyond which modernist knowledge cannot go. Situating his reading within modern culture (the monochrome of early films, the kitsch of the newly invented snow dome), Duffy reads these as stories of people who cannot live genuine lives, caught in modern 'anomie' (p. 55), suggested by the black and white palette of swirling snow. Ruchi Mundeja explores another dimension of Mansfield's form in the silences of women characters that may signal oppression or resistance. The danger for the storyteller is presuming to speak for that silence, a kind of trespass of which Mansfield is acutely aware. In close readings of several stories, including 'Life of Ma Parker', Mansfield illustrates the tension between the temptation of giving oppressed women a voice and the peril of daring to do so.

The book also offers a cluster of readings on Mansfield's modernisms, the first of these a brilliant ecocritical reading by William Kupinse that teases out conflicting messages about the aloe in 'Prelude', which may be read as either a once-blooming agave (a different plant) or a true aloe, known for healing and as an abortifacient. Both messages 'illuminate how gender roles and colonial power structure intertwine' (p. 88), given how each flower also resonates with cultural meanings embedded in historical/geopolitical realities. This 'irreducible duality' – the agave as reproductive and/or the aloe as protective against fertility (p. 88) – gives us a story that is 'botanically realist *and* formally modernist'. What some readers find textually confusing (aloe or agave?), Kupinse sees as productive 'species duality' (p. 88). Chris Mourant speculates on another dimension of Mansfield's complex modernism when he asks what might have been the next direction of her writing, based on her lending library card from Shakespeare and Company, from which, toward the end of her life, she borrowed Sherwood Anderson, Dorothy Canfield and Gertrude Stein. Theosophy would influence Mansfield's work in other ways, as Erika Baldt argues through her reading of Orphic mysteries in 'An Indiscreet Journey' and 'Bliss'. These mythic connections place Mansfield among writers like Eliot and Joyce, who also plundered the Greeks in search of modernist meanings. Nick Hocking explores the ways in which Mansfield's stories 'enact a war between two incompatible aesthetic approaches, which might retrospectively be termed "high modernist" and "late modernist"' but which found their earliest expression in Henri Bergson's influential theories of comedy (p. 132). Bergson sees comedy as tragedy's opposite because it deals with the benign and commonplace, which is incompatible with the high art of the singular tragic figure. But Mansfield, Hocking argues, creates stories with strands of both, which becomes her aesthetic of 'contrariety' that sends comedy and tragedy flowing in multiple directions simultaneously (p. 128). All these readings in this section secure Mansfield not simply as the 'consummate modernist', as Duffy claims in the *Bloomsbury Handbook to Katherine Mansfield*, but also at the vanguard of modernist experimentation whose inventiveness continues to surprise us.

In the book's section on 'Literary Influence and Life Writing', Katie L. Jones invites us to consider Mansfield's serious literary ambitions as pre-dating the London years at *The New Age* with A. R. Orage and to review how her early letters, short poems and dramatic performances reveal her professional aspirations. A very different picture of George Bowden, Mansfield's first husband, emerges from Gerri Kimber's reassessment, which draws on letters in the Harry Ransom Collection at the University of Texas, Austin. Kimber argues for a compassionate Bowden who was genuinely friends with Mansfield and not simply the hapless figure that emerged from the Murry-orchestrated portrait of him. Kathleen Jones unearths some unlikely influences Mansfield has had on writers as disparate as Philip Larkin and the Chinese expatriate writer Yiyun Li, an essay that may inspire further investigations into the Mansfield legacy.

Finally, the section on 'Social and Domestic Transactions' offers rewarding readings of Mansfield's awareness of social politics, a somewhat underdeveloped thread of her work. Janet M. Wilson's sophisticated essay explores how economic issues – debt, consumer capitalism, domestic contract labour, and sexuality – permeate some of her stories, such as 'Life of Ma Parker' and 'The Tiredness of Rosabel'. They illustrate how, in Frederic Jameson's terms, the market generates profit at the expense of the human, an issue further complicated by gender's place in the changing economies of the early twentieth century. Mansfield was sensitive to a range of familiar masculinist portraiture of women, as Ann Herndon Marshall shows in her discussion of Miss Moss in 'Pictures', a woman with a complex relationship to economics and sexuality and paralleled by Marshall with Jean Rhys's *Voyage in the Dark.* Mansfield is not, Marshall argues, advocating for a particular politics; she 'avoids both the reformist agenda and the sensationalism that had served feminist politics since the Victorian era' (p. 222). But her Miss Moss is at odds with the ideology-driven portraits of prostitutes as victims that we find in the sentimentalised writing of Mansfield's lover, Francis Carco. Alex Moffett gives another perspective on women and labour in an essay that highlights how characters whose lives are spent engaged in hard labour 'exist in a tension with the short story form in which Mansfield inscribes it' (p. 209). Moffett shows how protagonists in 'Life of Ma Parker', 'The Lady's Maid' and 'An Ideal Family', for example, deviate from those of the conventional *Bildungsroman,* and the short story may ironically be the best genre for illustrating lives of tedium and repetition. Not surprisingly, two of these stories were adapted by BBC radio during the Depression, an interesting historical connection that shapes Moffett's discussion. All three of these essays round out this provocative collection of writings in *Katherine Mansfield: New Directions,* offering us once again sustained and bracing evidence of the muscularity of Mansfield studies.

Heart of Flame: Katherine Mansfield's Flowers and Trees is a charming book aimed at the general audience and Mansfield enthusiast. It offers coloured illustrations by artist Jenni Shoesmith of nearly every flower or tree mentioned in Mansfield's fiction, diaries, letters and notes. The book organises Mansfield's floral observations by people and by place: family and friends, Wellington, the New Zealand bush, Europe, England, the Mediterranean. Each drawing is keyed to relevant quotations selected by Beverley Randell from the full range of Mansfield's works. While not an exhaustive inventory, the cumulative effect of reading one excerpt after another is kaleidoscopic, and the book is more properly a place for casual thumbing and dipping, such is the saturated atmosphere of Mansfield's writing on flora. Indeed, her love of flowers is arguably exceptional, always capable of producing raptures, whether Mansfield smells roses that make her feel 'faint' (p. 23), violets that 'one longed [. . .] almost to eat' (p. 10), 'sinister, seductive but poisonous' anemones (p. 19), 'divine' heliotrope (p. 106), or flowers that enchant, bewitch or fill her brain with 'a delicate flower melody' (p. 47).

What this slim volume does not do – nor should it necessarily, for a non-academic audience – is question the gap between fact and fiction, that space where we know a flower is never simply an 'illustration' for Mansfield. To put aside theories of 'surface' reading, Mansfield's wide-ranging knowledge of plants, as this book richly makes evident, is occasionally and tellingly wrong or, more properly, ambiguous. Consider, for instance, William Kupinse's analysis above of Mansfield's alleged confusion between an aloe and an agave. Or consider the meaningful lilies of 'The Garden Party'. The house has a 'lily-lawn',[4] and Mrs Sheridan indulges her love of flowers by ordering pots and pots of pink 'canna lilies' on 'bright crimson stems'.[5] These are presumably the same stems that, later in the story, might conceivably 'ruin' Laura's frock, were she to carry them to the dead workman's family.[6] But the flowers that Mrs Sheridan suggests Laura take are different altogether; they are 'arum lilies'[7] and, we might infer, flowers from the lily garden. This sleight of hand is considerably muddied when Mrs Sheridan, sending Laura off to the workmen's cottages, changes her mind about the flowers and cautions Laura, 'don't on any account –'.[8] What appears vague to Laura is clearer to the reader – don't go off-piste into potential personal/sexual danger – but the classed/sexed meanings of that message are cross-pollinated in the ambiguity of the flowers. If the flowers Laura leaves behind are indeed arums, which 'people of that class are so impressed by',[9] as Mrs Sheridan alleges, then they are probably from the garden, not from Mrs. Sheridan's canna lily display of conspicuous consumption. But the arum lily can stain a white frock with the pollen from its long phallic spadix, surrounded by a folded bract, the spathe: this is an altogether clearer sexual initiation than even the canna lily suggests. Are these points mere critical byways? Hardly. This is the kind of productive meandering *Heart of Flame* can encourage in the critic's imagination, without deterring the enjoyment of the non-scholarly audience.

This review essay would be remiss not to mention another important recent publication in Mansfield scholarship, which is the 2020 *Journal of New Zealand Literature* special issue devoted to Katherine Mansfield. These seven essays were first presented at an international Mansfield conference held at Birkbeck, University of London, in 2018, and the special edition represents the second time since 2014 that the journal has devoted an entire issue to Mansfield. Once again, editors Aimée Gasston,

Gerri Kimber and Janet M. Wilson have assembled a strong collection of writings that reflect the increasingly global reach of Mansfield's academic stature. Kym Brindle examines how letters function as 'epistolary betrayals' of the mundane realities they tear apart; Julie Neveux uses neuro-cognitive theory to show how Mansfield renders strong emotion without resorting to sentimentality; and Karen D'Souza uncovers how Mansfield's influence on contemporary Indian writer Anita Desai reveals the permeability of modernist influence across time and culture. Gaurav Majumdar argues that Mansfield pushes back against patriarchal Lockean liberalism to resist order, even when female characters must ultimately conform to that order, while Richard Cappuccio explores Wordsworth's influence on Mansfield's rhythmic prose and her privileging of memory and loss. Anna Jackson deconstructs contemporary verse and graphic novel biographies of Mansfield that offer vibrant approaches to the concept of subjectivity, and Qiang Huang details how Katherine Mansfield has been one of China's most popular Western writers since Mansfield was first translated in the early 1920s.

All the articles and chapters reviewed here suggest that critical studies on Mansfield continue to develop in deep and sometimes unpredictable veins. Her work now resonates globally, across disciplines. Interestingly, almost all the pieces are also brief (essay-length), which tempts one to ask whether Mansfield's preference for the more economical form — the short story – has any relationship to the shorter forms of critical exegesis under review here. The *Handbook* lends itself to this kind of treatment, and edited collections are frequently the fruits of conferences. The connection may be nothing more than a correlation this year, but it also suggests larger ways in which Mansfield scholarship answers the challenge of reading a consummate shape-shifting modernist in the short-story genre, as bright and as brief, as Ali Smith observes above, as the dozens of lives sketched therein.

Notes

1. *Letters* 1, p. 19.
2. CW4, p. 349.
3. As Alpers points out, all Beauchamp's daughters received the same 'allowance', which by 1921 was £300 per year. Antony Alpers, *The Life of Katherine Mansfield* (New York: Viking Press), 1980, p. 335.
4. CW2, p. 402.
5. CW2, p. 404.
6. CW2, p. 411.
7. CW2, p. 411.
8. CW2, p. 411.
9. CW2, p. 411.

Notes on Contributors

Daisy Birch is a recent graduate from the University of Oxford in English Literature and Language. Her essay is adapted from her undergraduate dissertation, 'Redefining "Photographic Realism" in the Short Fiction of Katherine Mansfield and Virginia Woolf'. She now works at the publishing company Pearson, and will begin an MPhil in English Studies at the University of Cambridge in October 2022.

Elyse Blankley is Professor Emerita of English at California State University, Long Beach. She has published reviews and critical articles on contemporary novelists, novel/film adaptation, modernism, literary Bloomsbury, and expatriate writers in Paris. Her most recent essay, 'Gendered Violence and Narrative Complicity in Katherine Mansfield and Leonard Woolf', appears in *Katherine Mansfield: International Approaches* (2022).

Bronwyn Calder is a New Zealand writer. She has worked in publishing for forty years and is now on the executive board of Cloud Ink Press, a boutique publishing press founded out of the Masters of Creative Writing programme at the Auckland University of Technology. She has a Masters in Creative Writing from AUT and has had stories published in anthologies and journals, including *Takahe, Landfall* and *Fresh Ink 2021.* At present she is a research student at AUT, researching her Māori ancestry in preparation for writing a creative memoir. She lives in Auckland with her husband and two adult daughters, and has self-published fantasy titles *Askar* (2007) and *The Master Weaver* (2021).

Richard Cappuccio has written several essays on Katherine Mansfield for the yearbook of the Katherine Mansfield Society, the *Journal of New Zealand Literature,* the *Journal of the Friends of the Dymock Poets, Modernism Re-Visited* and *Katherine Mansfield and the Bloomsbury Group.* He lives in central Virginia.

Ailsa Cox is Professor Emerita of Short Fiction at Edge Hill University, UK. Her books include *Alice Munro* (2003), *Writing Short Stories* (2005), *The Real Louise and Other Stories* (2009) and the limited-edition short-story chapbook, *Cocky Watchman* (2021). She has also published essays and book chapters on Katherine Mansfield and other short-story writers, including Helen Simpson, Daisy Johnson, Malcolm Lowry and Jon McGregor. 'Katherine Mansfield and the Short Story' appears in *The Bloomsbury Handbook to Katherine Mansfield*, edited by Todd Martin (2021). She is the editor of the journal *Short Fiction in Theory and Practice* (Intellect Press) and Deputy Chair of the European Network for Short Fiction Research (ENSFR).

Samantha Jayne Dewally is a postgraduate student of Modern Literature at the University of Wales Trinity St David, having previously studied Modern Foreign Languages and Literatures at the University of Leeds. She worked in education in the fields of language and literacy before returning to further study; she has interests in poetry (as both reader and writer) and children's literature.

Jay Dickson is Professor of English and Humanities at Reed College in Portland, Oregon. He is the author of many essays on British and Irish modernist fiction and culture, including most recently 'Katherine Mansfield, Garsington, and Bloomsbury' in *The Bloomsbury Handbook to Katherine Mansfield*, edited by Todd Martin (2021).

Calvin Goh graduated with an MSc in English Literature from the University of Edinburgh in 2020. He is currently enrolled in the Post-Graduate Diploma in Education course at the National Institute of Education, Singapore. His areas of interest include adaptation studies as well as contemporary and children's literature.

Sharon Gordon is an independent scholar who lives in Edinburgh. Her research interests focus on garden narratives in the work of Katherine Mansfield and Dorothy Richardson. She has previously published essays on Katherine Mansfield. Sharon holds an MA on Katherine Mansfield's and Virginia Woolf's short stories, and a PhD on the Victorian poet Isabella Blagden.

Martin Griffiths is a cello teacher and examiner for the New Zealand Music Education Board and principal cellist of Opus Orchestra (NZ), as well as guest member of NZ Barok and founding member of Vox Baroque ensemble. He performed 'Katherine Mansfield, Cellist' at the 2019 Katherine Mansfield Society (KMS) conference in Krakow, Poland. Martin is the former editor of the KMS Newsletter and has published in Katherine Mansfield Studies (vols 12 and 13) and in *Tinakori.*

Sovay Hansen is a PhD Candidate in English Literature with a minor in German Studies at the University of Arizona. Her dissertation focuses on how female desire is articulated in interwar fiction and personal papers by Mansfield, Woolf, Sinclair and German writer Irmgard Keun.

Sydney Janet Kaplan is Professor of English and Adjunct Professor of Gender, Women and Sexuality Studies at the University of Washington in Seattle. She is the author of *Circulating Genius: John Middleton Murry, Katherine Mansfield and D. H. Lawrence* (2010), *Katherine Mansfield and the Origins of Modernist Fiction* (1991) and *Feminine Consciousness in the Modern British Novel* (1975), as well as numerous reviews and articles on modernist literature. She serves on the International Advisory Board of Katherine Mansfield Studies.

Gerri Kimber, Visiting Professor at the University of Northampton, is co-editor of *Katherine Mansfield Studies* and was Chair of the Katherine Mansfield Society for ten years (2010–20). She is the author of *Katherine Mansfield: The Early Years* (2016), *Katherine Mansfield and the Art of the Short Story* (2015) and *Katherine Mansfield: The View from France* (2008). She is the deviser and Series Editor of the four-volume *Edinburgh Edition of the Collected Works of Katherine Mansfield* (2012–16), and together with Claire Davison is currently preparing a new four-volume edition of Mansfield's letters, also for Edinburgh University Press.

Anna Kwiatkowska is an Assistant Professor at the Institute of Literary Studies in the Department of Humanities at the University of Warmia-and-Mazury in Olsztyn, Poland. Her academic interests centre on literature and its links with broadly understood art. She specialises in the works of Katherine Mansfield and E. M. Forster. She is the Secretary of the International E. M. Forster Society, a member of the Katherine Mansfield Society and a member of the International Society for the Study of Narrative.

Stuart Lyons, CBE, was a major scholar in Classics at King's College, Cambridge, where, after a career in industry, he is now a Fellow Commoner and helps lead the College's entrepreneurship programme. His writings include three books on Horace and articles on the classics, art history and government. Stuart's verse translations of the *Odes* of Horace were a *Financial Times* book choice in 1996 and he was awarded the Stephen Spender Prize 2020 for his translation of Xu Zhimo's *Wild West Cambridge at Dusk*. His most recent book, *Xu Zhimo in Cambridge – Life* *and Poetry* (2021), features translations of twenty-four of Xu's poems and is available from the shop at King's College, Cambridge.

Paula McGrath is the author of two novels, *Generation* (2015) and *A History of Running Away* (2017). She is an Assistant Professor of Creative Writing at University College Dublin.

Todd Martin is Professor of English at Huntington University and President of the Katherine Mansfield Society. He has published articles on John Barth, E. E. Cummings, Clyde Edgerton, Julia Alvarez, Edwidge Danticat, Sherwood Anderson and Katherine Mansfield. He is the co-editor of *Katherine Mansfield Studies*, and editor of *Katherine Mansfield and the Bloomsbury Group* (2017) and *The Bloomsbury Handbook to Katherine Mansfield* (2021). He is currently editing manuscripts of several Mansfield stories for publication with Bloomsbury.

John G. Peters, University Distinguished Research Professor at the University of North Texas, is current General Editor of *Conradiana* and past President of the Joseph Conrad Society of America. He is author of *Joseph Conrad's Critical Reception* (2013), *The Cambridge Introduction to Joseph Conrad* (2002) and *Conrad and Impressionism* (2001). He is also editor of the Norton Critical Edition of Conrad's *The Secret Sharer and Other Stories* (2015) and translator of the Japanese poet Takamura Kōtarō's book, *The Chieko Poems* (2007).

Index

Also available in the series:

Katherine Mansfield and Continental Europe
Edited by Delia da Sousa Correa and Gerri Kimber
Katherine Mansfield Studies, Volume 1

Katherine Mansfield and Modernism
Edited by Delia da Sousa Correa, Gerri Kimber and Susan Reid
Katherine Mansfield Studies, Volume 2

Katherine Mansfield and the Arts
Edited by Delia da Sousa Correa, Gerri Kimber and Susan Reid
Katherine Mansfield Studies, Volume 3

Katherine Mansfield and the Fantastic
Edited by Delia da Sousa Correa, Gerri Kimber, Susan Reid and Gina Wisker
Katherine Mansfield Studies, Volume 4

Katherine Mansfield and the (Post)colonial
Edited by Janet Wilson, Gerri Kimber and Delia da Sousa Correa
Katherine Mansfield Studies, Volume 5

Katherine Mansfield and World War One
Edited by Gerri Kimber, Todd Martin, Delia da Sousa Correa,
Isobel Maddison and Alice Kelly
Katherine Mansfield Studies, Volume 6

Katherine Mansfield and Translation
Edited by Claire Davison, Gerri Kimber and Todd Martin
Katherine Mansfield Studies, Volume 7

Katherine Mansfield and Psychology
Edited by Clare Hanson, Gerri Kimber and Todd Martin
Katherine Mansfield Studies, Volume 8

Katherine Mansfield and Russia
Edited by Galya Diment, Gerri Kimber and Todd Martin
Katherine Mansfield Studies, Volume 9

Katherine Mansfield and Virginia Woolf
Edited by Christine Froula, Gerri Kimber and Todd Martin
Katherine Mansfield Studies, Volume 10

Katherine Mansfield and Elizabeth von Arnim
Edited by Gerri Kimber, Isobel Maddison and Todd Martin
Katherine Mansfield Studies, Volume 11

Katherine Mansfield and Bliss and Other Stories
Edited by Enda Duffy, Gerri Kimber and Todd Martin
Katherine Mansfield Studies, Volume 12

Katherine Mansfield and Children
Edited by Gerri Kimber and Todd Martin
Katherine Mansfield Studies, Volume 13

Katherine Mansfield and The Garden Party and Other Stories
Edited by Gerri Kimber and Todd Martin
Katherine Mansfield Studies, Volume 14

www.edinburghuniversitypress.com/series/KMSJ

Katherine
Mansfield
Society
New Zealand